Sugar, Spice, and Can't Play Nice

Annika Sharma

sourcebooks
casablanca

Copyright © 2023 by Annika Sharma
Cover and internal design © 2023 by Sourcebooks
Cover illustration by Sanno Singh

Sourcebooks and the colophon are registered trademarks of Sourcebooks.

The characters and events portrayed in this book are fictitious or
are used fictitiously. Any similarity to real persons, living or dead,
is purely coincidental and not intended by the author.

All brand names and product names used in this book are trademarks,
registered trademarks, or trade names of their respective holders. Sourcebooks
is not associated with any product or vendor in this book.

Published by Sourcebooks Casablanca, an imprint of Sourcebooks
P.O. Box 4410, Naperville, Illinois 60567-4410
(630) 961-3900
sourcebooks.com

Cataloging-in-Publication Data is on file with the Library of Congress.

Printed and bound in the United States of America.
WOZ 10 9 8 7 6 5 4 3 2 1

To every woman who armored up and steeled weary spines so we could stand on your shoulders—now, more than ever, you have my thanks and a promise to do the same.

Chapter One

AYAAN

Despite a late night at a club opening and an even later night in the bedroom, Ayaan Malhotra woke up miraculously energized and lacking the hangover he'd anticipated.

It was a sign, he'd decided. Of what, he wasn't sure, but it was going to be a good day.

The city hadn't woken up yet. It was still dark out. The sky was navy blue and the streetlights were on, lazily twinkling in the early hours.

He glanced at his phone absentmindedly, and an email from his manager appeared on his notifications.

Ayaan,

The marketing campaign you designed for Divinity's wellness brand is outstanding. They've seen a monster rise in sales since using your social strategy. Great work.

He couldn't stop the goofy grin that crawled across his face. Ayaan shifted his weight, burrowing his head into the pillow, and glanced to his left where Neha slept, still spent from last night's antics.

Neha Dev was a model—she'd recently landed a campaign with an up-and-coming South Asian fashion house. Her star was on the rise, and he liked feeling the warmth of its glow.

And they had shared a bed at her place, around the corner from his best friend Kai's, for what felt like the millionth time in the last year.

He'd say she was his—they'd been dating for some time, after all—but that felt too committed...as though they'd never get a chance to be anyone else's. He wasn't ready for that.

Not to mention they broke up every few weeks for a myriad of reasons: he'd eyed the waitress in front of her, she'd gotten too close to an old flame on the dance floor, he'd forgotten to call her back, and therefore, she "wasn't a priority," and a couple of times he barely remembered why because they'd both been too drunk.

But as he watched her sleep, her long black hair with chestnut-brown highlights splayed out on the pillow after a passionate night of not resting, the jolt inside his chest told him he certainly felt *something*. Perhaps even something strong.

He appreciated her confidence, her drive, and her focus. It was sexy as hell being with a woman who had no problem saying she was busy but that she'd make time for him later. Selfishly, it allowed him his freedom, which he'd moved from London for, and it made their reunions that much more fun when they'd been apart for a few days, hustling at their respective endeavors.

Yeah. Neha was a catch. And she gave him something to look forward to. God knows he didn't have much of that in London. To Ayaan, Neha was synonymous with the hope New York offered him, away from his family, obligation, and the weight that dragged him down when he spent too much time around them.

He rolled over, ready to sleep again, when his phone vibrated loudly on the bedside table.

Scrambling so he wouldn't wake her, he grabbed it and jumped out of bed, glancing down at the screen as he made his way to the bathroom for a private space where he could speak.

Arun.

Ayaan wondered if Arun sensed his passing thoughts about the family. His older brother consistently forgot—or, Ayaan knew, likely didn't care—that there was a five-hour difference between them, and calling at noon in London still meant Ayaan had to answer at the ass crack of dawn in New York.

"Do you ever consider that I could still be sleeping?" he furiously whispered as a form of greeting when he'd shut himself into the white-tiled space.

"I do," Arun said in an infuriatingly smug way. "But if I depended on your ability to get out of bed and be productive, then I'd be waiting forever, wouldn't I?"

Ayaan bristled but refused to take the bait. "What's up? Did I miss a birthday or something?"

"While that wouldn't be surprising, no, I was calling to see how you're doing."

"Sorry, you'll have to pick me up off the floor. I've died of surprise."

"You're hilarious," Arun replied, sounding bored. "We had dinner with Mum and Dad last night. Mum said she missed you. I thought I'd give you a call to see how you're holding up across the pond."

"I'm doing well. I've been seeing someone."

He blurted it out before he knew what he was saying, and he had no idea why. Perhaps he was prompted by the way Neha had elicited tenderness out of him just moments before, or perhaps he was ready to settle down after all. Or—even he wasn't dense enough to deny it—perhaps he wanted a moment to bond with his older brother...a moment where Arun was proud that his wayward younger sibling had landed a steady girl, and a beautiful one at that, and he'd give Ayaan a virtual pat on the back for finally doing something right for a change.

Maybe he'd tell Ayaan how he'd pined for Sarika, his wife—and, Ayaan would admit to anyone who would listen, the best thing to ever happen to the Malhotra family—since they were preteens, feigning surprise each time that she was at dinner parties their families attended when in truth, he'd asked his parents for days who would be attending, hoping her name would come up. Maybe he'd say he was happy Ayaan had found anything that bordered on a similar thrill.

"Well, it's about time," Arun said instead. There was no warmth, just the tone of an impending lecture ahead.

Ayaan pushed away the stab of disappointment. "I have no idea what that means, but she's great. She's smart and funny—"

"What does she do?"

"She's a model. She graduated from—"

"A model, Ayaan? Seriously?" Arun's exasperation was impossible to miss.

"What? What's wrong about that?"

"You know Mum and Dad are worried about you settling down, don't you? You're over thirty. At some point, you're going to have to buckle down, go for a nice girl with some prospects for the family, and quit being such a noncommittal flake."

"I just told you I was in a relationship."

"Did you now?" Arun sounded amused. "I thought you said you were 'seeing someone,' like how you would describe seeing a therapist...which, by the way, you should probably do."

"Oh, fuck off, Arun," Ayaan grumbled.

"Anyway…aside from your dating life, I kind of lied about why I called."

"Is everyone okay? Is Sarika all right?"

"Everything's great—for me, especially. Dad is going to name me CEO of Veer."

The words hung in the air, and Ayaan, who had been running his fingers through his hair, grasped onto it in shock instead.

"CEO? You?"

"Why are you surprised? I've been running the show behind the scenes for years."

"I–I thought they were still deciding. Besides, Dad isn't retiring yet, is he?"

"If you were around more often, you'd know that Dad's thinking about stepping down early and staying on the board instead."

"And so you're getting the job?"

Arun seemed to grow exasperated. "Yes. How many times do I have to repeat myself?"

"I'm just surprised. I thought there was more time. I could—"

"What? You could take over instead?"

"No," Ayaan said slowly. "I thought I could be included in the new direction."

"If you have any CMO candidates, send them our way. Vincent is leaving for nonprofit life and I'm leading the search."

His brother had turned the knife painfully. Had they not considered Ayaan as the rightful fit for the chief marketing officer job?

His silence wasn't taken well.

"Well, I'll take that silence as congratulation," Arun said. "But as a note of advice—"

"You mean as a directive?"

Arun continued as though he hadn't heard Ayaan. Come to

think of it, he probably hadn't. "You need to grow up, Ayaan. Get it together. That's probably why Dad didn't consider you for the advancement of the company." Then he dug the knife in a little more. "Given your history, I'd think you'd try twice as hard to prove yourself, but you keep demonstrating you don't deserve a second chance."

Then he hung up.

Ayaan stared at the phone, tempted to hurl it against the wall before deciding that it wasn't worth paying more money to Apple to compensate for a moment's frustration.

He set the phone on the counter, leaning against the sink and staring at his face in the mirror.

Traces of dark bags under his eyes were visible, souvenirs from late nights out. A five-o'clock shadow gave his face a ragged appearance, though he was nearly always clean-cut and took pride in his good looks.

"You're not lazy and you're not worthless," he whispered to himself.

He'd just gotten an email from his boss telling him so, for God's sake. This wasn't the time to feel sorry for himself or doubt his abilities. He was a rock star at marketing. Arun wouldn't have known what the hell to do with a fizzling company. He didn't even know how to use Instagram properly. Ayaan was the whiz in that department. He'd jumped on the platform early and now regularly had brand sponsorships. He talked about personal branding on TikTok and knew his good looks had won him more than a few hundred followers there. Arun had no instincts with connecting with people in comparison to Ayaan's public persona.

But he still had a hard time believing he was worth anything at all.

He hated, *hated*, how Arun could get under his skin so quickly.

Their parents had given them both names starting with A, in a common but bemusing tradition of Indian parents naming their children with similarly sounding monikers, but that was exactly where the commonalities ended. For the two men couldn't have been more different: Arun was logical, deliberate, even cruel, and shrewd. And Ayaan, for as much as he secretly wished he was more like his brother, was creative, spontaneous, a bit spoiled, and rebellious...which was exactly what Arun had used as a verbal grenade—his younger brother's history of fucking up.

Ayaan splashed water on his face, allowing the piercing chill to permeate his pores and remind him of the energy he'd felt when he'd woken up.

It seemed as though hours had passed, not minutes.

"Ayaan?" Neha's sleepy voice called out to him.

"Yeah. I'll be out in a second." He took a stabilizing breath, exhaling the irritation he felt.

Returning to the bedroom, he found Neha with her eyes closed. Her lashes fluttered as she opened them again, smiling at his appearance in her room.

"Good morning!"

"What're you doing awake?" he asked, trying to smile back, though Arun's voice was now ingrained in his mind.

"I heard voices."

"Ugh, I'm sorry," he said, shaking his head. "I didn't mean to wake you up."

"That's okay! Who called you so early?" She turned to her side, propping her head upon her hand.

"Arun."

"Uh-oh. You have a face."

"I do not have a face." Then he paused. "Okay, well, obviously I have a face. But I'm not making one."

"If you say so. Everything okay?"

He wanted to open up and tell someone about the inadequacy he was feeling—but Neha was coming off a successful night. What would she know about failure?

Instead, he shook his head.

"I'm fine, but thanks. I'll probably head home actually. I've got some work to do."

He returned to the bathroom to collect his phone and gather his wallet and keys from the dresser on the other side of the bedroom.

"Any plans next weekend?" he asked, attempting to use small talk as a distraction. "Kai and I were thinking about hiking in the Poconos."

He glanced at Neha, who was still lying in bed, her long legs creating mountain ranges underneath the sheets, and froze at her expression. A deep sense of foreboding drowned him as he registered her disbelieving eyes and pursed lips.

She sat up, covering herself with her bedsheet. "Ayaan! You're supposed to meet my parents next weekend."

Shit. "Well—" He tried to think fast but with the inopportune timing, he was left with the equivalent of erectile dysfunction of the mind. *This isn't the time for performance anxiety, Ayaan.* "You'd mentioned grabbing brunch because they were in town. I didn't think it was a scheduled event or a big deal—"

"A big deal?" she shouted as she whipped the sheets off herself and climbed to her feet.

"Okay, it's a big deal," he corrected. "Just...not a remarkable request. Something said in passing, not plans that were cemented."

"Are you fucking kidding me?" she snapped. "We've been dating for almost a year, Ayaan. What exactly did 'meeting my parents' sound like if it wasn't a big deal?"

"I... Can I ask when we discussed this?"

Neha's eyes widened and her mouth dropped open. "The night you told me you loved me! We were at that rooftop in Midtown, and we talked about how you would meet my parents and you were excited because you didn't get along with yours. You wanted to meet my sister because you said you and Arun didn't get along."

"Oh..." Ayaan cringed. It was as though Arun's admonishment rang out in the bedroom. *You need to grow up, Ayaan. Get it together.*

The truth was that he couldn't recall that night very well. It was vague at best, flashes of twelve drinks too many, drunken laughter with Kai, and Neha getting more and more attractive with each drink, prompting what had apparently become a declaration of love. Which, to be fair, he'd thought about, but he wasn't going to confess that so early. And opening up about his family... Well, that was definitely the influence of alcohol because he didn't do that often either.

Now, it was clear he did disclose his thoughts before he was ready to explore them in earnest. Forget erectile dysfunction of the mind. He had early explosions of the mouth as well.

"You don't remember any of it, do you?" she asked now, after a few seconds of watching the faces he must have been making.

Her full lips quivered a little, but her brown eyes, lined with trace remnants of kohl from last night, were nothing but fire and brimstone.

"Of course I remember," Ayaan lied.

"You're full of shit."

"Okay, I may have had too many drinks that night. I didn't *not* mean the words I said, but maybe they came too soon."

"Too soon? How much longer do you need? Another year? Four? Ten?"

"I don't know!" he snapped.

She stood, and he wished she didn't look so good naked.

"Ayaan, you have always been a legendary player, and I over-looked that when we got together. You were such a gentleman—flowers, date nights, meeting friends—that I went against my better judgment to give you a chance because, God, you couldn't possibly have been an asshole if you treated me that well. But are you so goddamn dense that you can't even muster up some adult-ing skills and act your age? Grow up. You're so fucked up, you can't commit to anything!"

He didn't even have the chance to reflect on the fact that two people had told him to act his age in the last ten minutes, because Neha stomped around the room, swiped his boxers, Armani blazer, dress shirt, and jeans off the floor, pushed open the window, and threw them out onto the Chelsea street below.

"What the fuck?" he yelled, dropping the phone and wallet in his hands. "*I'm* supposed to grow up? You just threw my bloody clothes out the window! Are you crazy?"

Neha's eyes narrowed, and the anger that flashed through them reminded Ayaan of the National Geographic specials he was obsessed with as a child. The cobras he was fascinated by had the same unique proclivity for striking before their prey could escape.

And escape, Ayaan could not.

He would die a painful death here, naked, with his dignity strewn across the sidewalk alongside his clothes.

"Crazy?" she repeated, with deadly venom in her voice.

"No, not crazy—unhinged perhaps, but not crazy. You were just talking about acting like an adult, Neha. For fuck's sake, you're supposed to be the better of us."

There it was.

The truth had exploded out: that Ayaan hadn't believed it would get serious because *he* wasn't serious. He wasn't cut out for relationships, commitment, and any kind of tie that bound him to anyone else because he wasn't good enough for it.

The more alone he remained, the less damage he caused.

He thought she knew that.

Neha, however, seemed to be realizing only now that she was, in fact, leagues ahead of him, and the recognition dawning upon her face was unexpectedly jarring for Ayaan.

He watched as her eyes fell, and the future she'd imagined with him vaporized from a colossally inflated balloon to nothingness. Worse still, and somewhat surprising, was the disappointment he felt in himself for bringing that look—the utterly letdown expression on her face—to someone who had hoped for so much in him.

"You're right," she said finally. "I am better than you. Now get out."

"What?"

"I said, get out!" she screamed, hurling a pillow—soft but aimed remarkably well—at his head.

"You just threw my clothes out into the street!"

"Well, maybe that's where you belong. Go."

Naked, vulnerable, and cursing himself for feeling any optimism about the day, Ayaan stuck his head out the door to make sure no one was coming, snuck into a side stairwell, and with an angry huff, called for help.

· · · · · · · · · · ·

PAYAL

The smell of perfume and ambition filled the air.

It was six in the morning and Payal Mehra's body clock was regimented, waking her before her alarm rang.

She rolled over, the glorious ache of a good night's sleep in her joints, and pulled herself to a sitting position, raising her arms above her head and stretching out all the nooks and crannies that had tightened over the workweek.

Group texts had blown up between her three best friends. Sonam had read an article in a medical journal about women's health inequities, and she was ranting about sexism in medicine, to which Payal rolled her eyes in amusement and continued onward. Kiran was calmly allowing Sonam to vent. Akash, Payal imagined, was reading this in the company of a pretty girl, unresponsive now but logging it all in his mind for later.

They were all going to meet for dinner today—a rare day they were all free. And it was already a perfect day, made even more spectacular by the email in her inbox.

Dear Payal,

Congratulations! You've been selected to show your designs at Asian EnPointe, a fashion show for budding Asian designers to showcase their work during Fashion Week in New York...

She could hear her father's voice in her mind. *Hard work never sleeps.* It was the single thing she was happy to inherit from him—the ability to allow passion to fuel her.

And these days, Payal hustled like a boss. She no longer relished the late mornings and the lie-ins, the lackadaisical participation in an 11:00 a.m. hot yoga class at the studio down the street, with a stop at the coffee stand on the corner on the way home, and a lazy afternoon of sketching in her favorite cream-colored armchair in the living room.

Now, she was building a clothing line. It was no longer a pipe dream.

Quietly, she'd been working on this vision for her life over the last three years, sketching fusion Indian and American fashion in a sketchbook she kept in her bedside table drawer. She'd built a reputation styling clients under the label Besharmi by Payal Mehra.

Then last year, after watching her best friend, Kiran, risk everything for love, Payal decided to take a leap of her own by selling her designs...and word of mouth from her styling clients, PR work, and social media had done the rest, establishing a steady income.

Her family was loaded—they ran a business, Luxuriant, in London with multiple locations across the UK—but she didn't want to rely on them for this. This was her project. Her baby.

She sat up and made her bed—a routine to establish her entire day with—carefully folding the gray-and-cream-designed duvet over the corners of her mattress and fluffing her four pillows just so before throwing accent pillows on top. She adjusted her phone, added water to the vase of flowers she always had filled with lilies, and put her clothing in a hamper before setting off for a quick shower.

By seven thirty, she was in her comfortable chair. A vast array of colored pencils and watercolor pens were spread out on the coffee table next to her for when she finished sketching the two outfits she was designing today—a lilac lehenga of ball-gown proportions with a crisscrossing blouse to match, both set with paisley sequins, and a gown inspired by the royal wedding from a few years ago with a long, trailing skirt.

After a full day of focus and a stop to pick out materials, she headed to meet her best friends, affectionately called the Chai Masala Club, for dinner.

And as usual, she was ten minutes late.

Tardiness was one of her biggest flaws. It was something she actively made sure not to do with business meetings, setting three alarms to ensure she'd be out of her apartment in plenty of time to walk in the door a few minutes early. But the CMC knew her soul was that of a person perpetually five minutes behind schedule. She had stopped apologizing for it long ago, and they had taken it the way they took everything in life: together and with love.

"We ordered a chai for you," Kiran said in a manner of greeting as Payal set her bag on the floor and settled onto her chair, crossing her legs immediately.

"Thank you, love."

"Where were you, Guatemala? That took forever," Akash said.

"Garment District...choosing some new fabrics with Niyathi and cross-checking with Saachi about whether she can lead the tailors on how it's supposed to look."

"How goes the designing? When do you think your first show will be?" Sonam asked.

"Actually...I got an email this morning inviting me to show at Fashion Week."

"What?" they all yelped in response.

"That's huge!" Akash said with his eyes wide.

"I also turned in my resignation letter this week. I'm doing this full-time."

All three cheered.

"My parents have funded my existence by helping with rent and allowing me a little nest egg—but I've been saving money on my own to start the line, a couple of connections decided to invest some money, and it's finally time. We've made enough that I can do this, as long as I have their financial support...and your moral backing, of course."

"Have you told them you don't want their company?" Sonam asked.

"I've conveniently left that out until I absolutely have to confess. By then, the line will be established enough that they'll have to understand. Besides, Papa isn't retiring for another ten years, at least."

Kiran laughed. "You know, I have to admit, even after all this time, I'm in awe of your ability to breeze ahead and not worry too much about the details."

"Actually, having my parents around rather than their money would have been nice, but the money's been working for me! Besides, I have you three and the line. I have nothing to worry about."

Chapter Two

PAYAL

Just as her thrill at seeing her friends was the height of the day, Payal's joy plummeted afterward, like a hangover she couldn't kick. Energy pulsed through her, but the way it contained itself was akin to a pressure cooker that needed a release.

Her tiny vibrator awaited in her bedside drawer. But she wasn't craving a self-created surrender. She wanted lip-biting kisses, the sensation of physically being filled to match her emotional contentment, and skin underneath hers...reckless abandon with someone else.

Thank God for hookup apps.

Love was far too much work. But sex...sex was easier. *And hard and fast, if you get the right person with the right proportions,* she thought wryly.

She loved this time of her life, when she could enjoy someone for a night for her own purposes and on her own terms, going about her life without any concern about a commitment to someone else.

She opened the app on her phone, gazing at the photo of a brown-haired man who stared back, intensity in his blue eyes, shirtless, six-pack exposed, leaning against a brick wall. His jeans clung seductively around his hips. There were snowflakes in the foreground.

What, you decided to go for a Christmas stroll with no clothes on? Trying too hard.

She gave the first three profiles a longer-than-usual examination. She'd made it a habit to peruse profiles carefully, to examine each photo and description. She imagined UX engineers touting statistics about how each user gazed at a photo for one second on average—but Payal spent a hell of a lot more time seeing what she could figure out about each prospect.

She also didn't want to swipe without being careful. Once, she'd accidentally swiped right on Akash, so surprised by his face staring back at her that she'd jolted her finger in the wrong direction. While she swore up and down it was a reflexive action from shock and excitement—and not the horny kind—Akash never let her live it down.

"You still want me, don't you?" he'd teased countless times over coffee. "Still harboring that college insta-lust toward me?"

Yeah. Better to be careful.

But just when she thought she was wasting time and should call it a night, a familiar face gazed back at her and she startled, not expecting anyone else she knew to appear on the screen.

Ayaan Malhotra, the son of Payal's parents' friends in London and a notorious player. She hadn't spoken to him much, but she'd heard about him plenty. She'd forgotten he lived in New York City too.

She willed her fingers not to move, recalling the last time she'd seen him, months ago when she was at a coffee shop with the CMC, and his lips had been conspicuously attached to another girl's...a model of some sort, goddess-like in her proportions, who

Payal had heard rumblings about in her fashion circles. *What had she heard?*

They were dating, she remembered.

What happened?

It was inevitable. The aunty-like quality that Payal and all her friends swore up and down they would never carry into their lives reared its head again: there was gossip nearby, and she wanted to know what it was.

She made a move to swipe away, attempting to be a better person than she was, but curiosity flooded her senses again. Instead, she clicked through his photos.

She had to admit that his photos were classy, laidback, and fun.

The first was on King's Road. New Yorkers might not know that location, but a keen-eyed native Londoner would recognize it in an instant. Ayaan was leaning against a white wall, with a crowd behind him—aviator sunglasses on, laughing at a joke Payal couldn't hear but could tell was genuinely great. His black hair was slicked back in clean chunks that reminded her of a painter's brushstrokes. She'd never seen him in anything but suits, but he was casual here—a black crewneck tee (that Payal couldn't help noticing accentuated his chiseled arms) over a pair of jeans that sat neatly at his waist, belted by brown leather.

He had a thick fringe of black eyelashes that nearly looked like eyeliner and big, round brown eyes that were expressive and mysterious at the same time.

He appeared friendly, even warm. Inviting, certainly.

The second photo was an action shot. Rock climbing at an unknown indoor location, Ayaan had scaled to the top of a wall and his face was hidden from view. Taken from below but zoomed in on his body, the shot showed the muscles of his back rippling underneath a white tank top. His gloved hands gripped the top of a ledge and his legs were bent, one making a move to climb a few feet higher. His butt was round, firm, and looked damn good in red shorts, and Payal wondered what it'd be like to squeeze it.

And the third image, a well-put-together professional photo, displayed him in a pale-blue sherwani, ornately decorated with beadwork, and a bottle-green turban at an Indian wedding and standing next to a man who looked like an older version of him—a brother or cousin, perhaps.

Nothing got Payal like a man who knew where he was from.

Well, he knows his marketing matters—a casual shot, an action one, and a formal one are more likely to get a date...and look, he added a bio. She remembered reading an article about women placing more importance in bios on dating apps and men being attracted to photos. *This guy knows what he's doing.*

A London transplant in the Big Apple with a penchant for sarcasm, whiskey, and adventure.

Simple and to the point.

She didn't know what the pull was. Perhaps it was loneliness in the apartment after a full night with friends. Maybe it was the minuscule taste of home and London she'd get if she matched with Ayaan.

She swiped right.

You've matched with Ayaan! Animated ribbons and heart-shaped confetti sprinkled themselves across her screen.

Payal typically didn't have to be the one to make the first move, but she had no inhibition about taking the first step to getting what she wanted.

She opened up the message box and began typing. Hey, Ayaan. Fancy seeing you here. It's been a while—how are you?

The answer returned less than a minute later. What's up, Payal?

Long time, no talk. I'm doing well, thanks. How are things on your end? New York is treating you well, I hope?

Being talkative was a good start.

Payal: It is—it's been amazing. Good friends. A fashion line. Life is good. Missing London some days, though. Then, in a second message, Weren't you seeing someone? Did I make that up?

She knew very well she hadn't made it up.

Ayaan: I miss London, though home is probably better without me causing trouble! And nah...I'm single now.

Payal paused. She thought about carrying the conversation forward—to jobs, their families, more of London, and anything else...but the night was ticking by, and conversation wasn't exactly the reason she'd opened the app.

Emboldened by the night, she typed. Then come over.

Ayaan: You're bold.

Payal didn't bat an eyelash. And you like it.

Ayaan: It is incredibly sexy. Send me your address and I'll be on my way.

They exchanged numbers.

In minutes, Payal had touched up her makeup—a thin line of the darkest black eyeliner around her russet eyes, powder brushed over her face, and lip pencil from NARS that made her lips look like the fluffed-up pillows she loved laying her head on at luxury hotels.

She thought about changing her clothes, but she was confident and sexy in her cream dolman sweater and black leggings, her hair curled to her waist, and she didn't want to try too hard. It would only lead him to think this was a date or that she craved connection.

She only wanted the physical kind, and even that was for just a night.

When the knock sounded, Payal felt an uncharacteristic, funny little flutter in her rib cage.

She opened the door.

Ayaan stood with one arm crooked against the doorframe, leaning against his elbow. He had loosened his tie so the knot hung at his collarbone, but his white shirt was tucked into blue dress pants under a matching blue suit jacket.

"Hi, Payal," he said with a grin.

She hadn't heard him talk often, and she'd forgotten the sound of his voice in the years between their minimal interactions. It was smooth and had a low tenor.

"Hello, Ayaan," she said.

They gazed at each other for a moment, and Ayaan's smile grew at his appraisal of her. He didn't have to take his eyes off her face to know that his judgment of her was yielding good results. He was impressed.

And she'd be lying if she said she wasn't. Ayaan's confidence was undeniable, a force she could sense as he stood at her door.

"Come on in," she said after a beat and moved aside so he'd enter.

He placed his shoes by the door, on the white shoe rack, without asking. Payal couldn't help but attribute that to his Indian upbringing, and the custom that they had in common seemed to break up any lingering awkwardness, as Ayaan met her gaze and seemed to register her expression.

"Old habits, right?" he said.

"You too, huh? You'd think we'd have forgotten these traditions or ignored them now that we're on our own!"

"Do you touch your heart and apologize if you accidentally step on a book?" Ayaan asked with a laugh.

"One hundred percent. And you didn't leave your shoes upside down on that rack, did you?" Payal jokingly peered around him to check.

"I'll try not to sneeze on the way out later too."

"Oh, thank you, my mind is at ease that you haven't jinxed my life." Payal laughed.

"Never," he said. "Unrelated to superstitions but fully related to being brown, do English words come out with an Indian accent when you're speaking in Hindi to your parents?"

"Every time. I speak to my nani, mostly, and an Indian accent creeps in midsentence. Born and bred in London and suddenly, my brain thinks I was raised in Mumbai. Worse is that I don't sound as graceful as my cousins in India do. My friend Kiran has the most beautiful singsong voice, and here I am, sounding like a yak."

He burst out laughing and the sound was delightful.

"You have a lovely place," he commented about the large (by New York standards) one-bedroom she was lucky enough to live alone in as they walked down the foyer hallway and passed her small galley kitchen on the left, followed by the bathroom.

The hallway opened up to the living room. A gray love seat and cream armchair were positioned around a gray wooden industrial-style coffee table. The place had high ceilings, which added to the vibe that it was a larger apartment than it really was. Payal's small bedroom opened to the right with sliding barn doors and continued the neutral color scheme.

"It's like my own little oasis—my corner of the world," she replied.

"Working on some designs?" He pointed at the corner of the living room. "Fashion, right?"

"Indeed. I spend so much time designing these days. But I styled a couple of Bollywood actresses for Cannes, and that still gives me clients."

"Oh, so you're a big deal."

She shrugged. "I will be." Perhaps it sounded cocky, but men had bragged for far less and Payal wasn't willing to dim her light when the world would try to douse it anyway.

"You keep your colored pencils in chromatic order," he said.

She was startled at the observation. The sudden gesture of intimacy, of observing someone's habits when you hadn't met them before, caught her breath.

"I do."

"I do the same with my underwear."

Payal burst out laughing. "Yes, the color pencils on which my budding career depends are definitely on the same level of importance as your boxers."

"Boxer briefs, actually," he corrected with a twinkle in his eye.

"What color do you have on today?"

He gazed at her. "Maybe you'll find out."

Warmth crept up her cheeks. "Do you want some wine?"

"I'd love some."

"Red or white?"

"Red. I don't have much of a sweet tooth."

"Me either! I'm also glad you said red because it's all I have."

Ayaan chuckled. "What would you have done if I'd said white?"

"I'd tell you to leave." She grinned.

"Well, we can't have that."

Their eyes locked for a split second longer than Payal would have noticed otherwise, and she felt an electric charge, a jolt that spread from her heart to between her legs.

She cleared her throat and gestured to the couch with an open hand. "I'll be right back."

She sensed his eyes on her as she left the room, the pleasant tingle on her back infusing a sway into her hips that she didn't walk with on a normal basis.

In the kitchen, she poured a generous amount of Château de Nalys Châteauneuf-du-Pape into two wineglasses and reveled in the deep, rich reddish-purple hue. The color emboldened her.

When she returned to the living room where Ayaan was sitting on the armchair, he stood to meet her and reached for the glass. Their fingers brushed. Soft and manicured neatly, his hands were strong, his nails square and unbitten—it was a pet peeve of Payal's when people chewed until their cuticles—and she wondered how it would feel to have their warmth on her body.

Heat rose in her chest again and she looked away, sitting on the other end of the love seat, curling her legs underneath her.

"How come our paths haven't crossed much before this?" he asked her, taking a sip. "Also, this is an amazing wine."

"Thank you." She raised her glass. "Well, actually, we can also thank my parents who sent me that lovely souvenir when they went to France last month. And to answer your question, I imagine it's because you've been entirely too busy color coordinating your skivvies."

He laughed. "Don't tell me you don't have funny habits or silly quirks."

"I can't go to sleep without washing my face."

"I sure hope you have good hygiene habits."

She stuck her tongue out. "What are yours, rainbow underpants? What random facts do I need to know?"

"I already regret telling you that information about my chuddies. But I'm ticklish."

"Mmm, so am I," hummed Payal. The wine loosened her tongue. "Especially on my neck."

"I'll remember that," Ayaan said. He unconsciously licked his lips as he set his wineglass on the coffee table, and Payal wondered what else his tongue could do.

Their knees were nearly touching now, the space between them bursting with electricity so strong that Payal's skin nearly burned.

"So...the app..." Ayaan mentioned. He leaned in a few inches. "What about it?"

"Well, you're successful, smart, and beautiful."

"I don't hear a question."

"You haven't been seeing anyone?"

"No," Payal said. "Relationships take work. Sex is easier."

Ayaan bobbed his head in assent. "You aren't wrong. It's easier to feel something hot and passionate and temporary than it is to value something permanent and stable."

"Creative careers are a roller coaster filled with inconsistency and instability. I'm finding my way right now. A relationship is the last thing I need."

"I feel that," he said.

"You were in a relationship, though. Why the app now?" she pushed. She set her empty glass on the coffee table.

"You know how it is. A new city in a new country. New potential. New opportunities...better weather."

"Oh, so you came over to talk about the weather then," Payal murmured, her face inching toward him.

"No...not at all," he nearly growled, sending shivers down Payal's spine.

The wine was forgotten as they crashed together like two

comets headed toward a collision course...and there was no more to be said for the night.

Two hours—and three mind-blowing orgasms—later, Payal felt her way along the wall, too lazy to turn on a light to guide her path from the bathroom to the bedroom. Ayaan had her spent.

In the dimly lit room, only brightened by her night-light—she wasn't *afraid* of the dark, she'd insist to anyone who would listen, she just didn't like it—she made her way back to the bed, satisfied and ready to crash.

Ayaan was slumbering, lying back on the left side of the bed against her pillow as if he'd propped it up against her headboard and drifted off without realizing.

She thought he'd have left by now, making excuses about how he had somewhere to be or something to do in the morning and allowing a clean break like most hookups. A sleepover wasn't the plan.

She reached for him, intending to gently shake him awake and remind him that this was fleeting—a lovely wave in a sea of lovely moments—and that it had passed.

But his lips had fallen into a relaxed pout, and a stray curl landed on his forehead, defying the product that had held his hair so impeccably in place for the evening. His only movement, the visible note that chaos lurked underneath a calm facade, was the way his eyelashes fluttered.

He was peaceful. Still. The polar opposite of the ravishing hands, insatiable kisses, and desperate hunger he'd shown for her only minutes earlier.

Payal couldn't place the tenderness that washed over her, but she pulled back her outstretched hand.

Instead, she climbed into bed, careful not to disturb him, rolled onto her side, and fell asleep.

Chapter Three

AYAAN

Payal was standing at the window, her back to him, wearing a diaphanous white robe that didn't appear, from where he was looking, to be tied in the front. The outlines of her body were visible in the light, and she might as well have not been wearing anything at all.

The arch in her back was pronounced above a pert behind, and the muscle definition in her long legs elongated them. She held a cup of coffee in her hands, and her long hair fell down her back, curling and waving at her waist. She hadn't noticed he'd woken up.

"Now that is a view," he murmured.

At the sound of his voice, she turned around, and the breath caught in Ayaan's throat. Her ease, the way she didn't move to cover her exposed nipples or any of her nakedness, struck him as confident. Even powerful.

"It is, right? I love the Upper East Side," Payal replied.

His eyes trailed from her slightly defined abs down to the smooth space between her legs that he'd tasted, felt, and been inside last night. He grew hard and wrenched his eyes up to her face.

"That view too." He smiled and winked, sitting up. "Why didn't you wake me?"

Her eyes brightened, surprised, and a smile coaxed at her lips.

"Well, normally, I would have expected you to leave right after, but you fell asleep and you were..." She blushed a little, and he found it endearing.

"I was what?"

"Sweet," she said simply. "Peaceful."

Ayaan was nearly naked under the sheets, but he might have preferred the vulnerability of nakedness to this. He was uncomfortably aware that, even if it was just in his sleep, he'd shown his cards and exposed himself.

And he wondered if Payal had the same drowsy recollection of Ayaan putting his arm around her in the indiscernible hours of the night and her nestling in to him, her head on his chest as they slept.

He was curious how she felt about it...if she'd liked the closeness that neither of them had claimed to want and if she'd felt the same comfort he had.

Growing conscious of the silence after her last statement, he gave his head a small shake to ward off the wayward thoughts. "I'm glad you thought it was sweet—much better than lying next to a serial killer."

"One night doesn't mean you aren't one, but I'll give you the benefit of the doubt," she said good-naturedly. "Would...you like some coffee?"

She sounded as though the words were foreign to her, as if asking someone to stay a little longer was so far out of her reach that she'd never fathomed making the request.

"I'd love some," he replied.

"Come out to the living room whenever you're ready, and I'll brew some in the meantime," she suggested.

He nodded and watched her push her sliding doors farther apart before heading toward the kitchen.

It was a much more peaceful morning than he was used to. He and Neha would either start off with a bang, an argument, or a rush to get started on their day.

He wondered if this was the type of life Arun wanted for him, of lazy mornings, warm coffee, and kind conversation, and if, perhaps, he was on to something. It was certainly better than yesterday's rude beginning, having to call his best friend, Kai, who luckily lived around the corner (though Ayaan wished their other pal Dharm, who lived in New Jersey and was too far away, could have rushed to his aid—he would have done it with less cackling laughter) to the stairwell in Neha's building to bring his clothes off the street, completely naked, and waiting twenty minutes hoping no one encountered him there.

The echoes of Kai's laughter would be burned into his eardrums for eternity.

Reminding himself to be present and pushing away thoughts of Neha or Arun, he pulled on his pants and buttoned up his shirt, rolling his tie into a ball that he stuck in his jacket pocket before emerging in the living room.

"Good morning," Payal greeted him as she handed him a cup of coffee.

"Good morning. This is a nice way to start the day."

"I don't usually do this," she admitted.

"What, make coffee?"

"Linger with someone after a night together."

"It helps that I'm dashingly handsome, doesn't it?"

She laughed. "Full of yourself, aren't you?"

"Only on a good day...and today's ego may be due to an amazing night," he confessed.

Payal passed him sugar quietly, but her soft smile told Ayaan she felt exactly the same way. "So what made you move to New York, anyway?"

"My family."

"Did they make you come here?"

"On the contrary, the fact that they didn't want me to probably pushed me to do it."

As they spoke, they moved back to the same love seat where they had begun the night before.

"I take it you aren't close, then?" An inexplicable expression crossed her eyes, like sympathy or maybe even understanding.

"We're...different." He shrugged. "We view life from polar opposite perspectives."

She gave a sympathetic smile. "I understand that more than you know."

"It sounds like you have some experience with it."

Shared experiences always created warmth in Ayaan. He and his best friends, Kai and Dharm, often spoke of their respective parents' experiences of seeing Indian faces in seas of white. Though Kai and Dharm were cousins who grew up in the U.S. and Ayaan's family had been based in the U.K., when their parents would stroll through a mall on a Sunday afternoon—miles and years away from the open-air markets they knew—and see another brown face in the crowd, they always acknowledged each other... A head nod. A small wave perhaps. Sometimes, even an enthusiastic greeting if they eavesdropped and realized the others spoke the same language of the hundreds in India.

Kai, whose family had emigrated when he was very small, had said something that resonated now: *You always acknowledged when you saw one of your own.*

Recognizing a kindred spirit in Payal—of someone British,

Indian, and whose family seemed to have as much discord as his own—was exactly what Kai had spoken of: the camaraderie that only those on the outside knew.

Payal seemed to understand all the overlapping spaces in Ayaan's identity Venn diagram...and it felt like a hug.

She fidgeted now, crossing her long legs and uncrossing them, as though perhaps movement would make her comfortable with what she was about to say.

"I'm an only child, so all the hopes, dreams, and disappointments are on me," she said with a shrug.

"Funny. I'm the second child and I'm still all the disappointments," he joked.

That earned him a smile.

"How do you like being here? What do you do again?" she asked.

"I'm the director of communications at a firm that manages lifestyle brands. But I always imagined myself leading my parents' company back home."

It was the first time he'd admitted it out loud. The recollection of his conversation with Arun nearly made him react physically, but Payal would have noticed. She was watching him closely, leaning in, focused on every word he was saying.

"Um, so, you have a day job, right?"

"I did. I was a director at a PR firm." She paused. "My dad wants me to take over the company eventually."

"Oh, so we're both destined for family businesses then!"

"I suppose so, though I hope more than anything my line is successful enough that I never have to lead my family's business or be involved beyond the compulsory board appointment."

"Why is that?"

"Because I want to *live*. And travel. I want to chase everything

I love at a million miles an hour…and if I went home, if I went back to London to the life I grew up in, I think I'd feel like I failed." Her eyes lit up as she spoke about her passions, and Ayaan saw brilliance in the light-brown hues…and watched it fade when she talked about being locked in.

He wondered how he appeared to her when talking about his family.

"How did you get into fashion?" he asked to change the subject.

"You'll laugh."

"Try me."

"I ripped a dress when I was probably ten years old. It was one of those tutu dresses with tulle everywhere and a velvet top—classic 1990s. My mom had tried to fix it, but because of the folds of the tulle, it wasn't an even stitch. Looking back, I was such an arrogant berk telling her that it was lopsided, but when she said, 'Could you do it better?' I said yes.

"She ripped the stitches out, handed the dress over, and said, 'Have a go, then.' I promptly failed. My nani said to teach me a little humility and show me what work looked like, so Ma put me in a sewing class…and it was the best thing for me. Throughout school and even college, I loved to sew outfits together in my spare time. I have a runner now who is far better with the details of fabrics, artisans and tailors who are far more talented—but for a little while, it was me and my sewing machine. What made you choose marketing?"

"I loved writing, speaking, debates, and convincing people what they should believe," Ayaan recalled, remembering nights of debate clubs and dissecting the spin the Royal Family put on their entire institution. "When I was younger, my family used to sit around the dinner table and we'd talk about the day's events. My parents would ask Arun, my older brother, what he thought about the market because he was such a whiz with numbers, but he lacked any practical knowledge. Then they'd ask me what I thought about politics, and we'd inevitably descend into the mechanism of the spin, how a person buys a narrative or the sale of a product, and how to grow visibility while maintaining authenticity. When I got to business school, it seemed like a calling to influence the thought processes of an audience for products I believed in."

"Well, you wouldn't have gotten to where you are without talent, so I think everyone was right on that count," Payal said.

The compliment soothed the lingering sting from Arun's words yesterday.

"So...Besharmi is your fashion line, right?" he asked.

Her eyebrows came together, and she cocked her head, puzzled at how he'd known.

"The logo is on the wall," he said by way of explanation, pointing at the wall in the corner where she brainstormed her designs.

"Oh." She laughed. "Yeah. Besharmi."

"Interesting name. What made you come up with it?"

She scrutinized his face before she answered. "My grandmother used to call me that every time I sassed her. She'd laugh, and it would be like music to my ears being called 'shameless' because there was so much power in being unapologetically bold. I had earned some form of approval when she said it with admiration in her tone. Other times, my mom or my aunts would call me or my cousins shameless with such disdain, like when we spoke up about something they didn't like. I remember my cousin mentioned she loved going to drag shows and my aunt called her 'Besharmi' and told her she was an embarrassment. In high school, I heard an aunty use it to describe a girl who wore a skirt above her knees. Suddenly, the very same word had become an insult, as though loving something or standing for something was, in fact, a weakness.

"I wanted people to own their stories...to rethink what this word, thrown around to make people feel terrible about themselves, meant. Because the truth is, it's weaponized to guilt them about having a spine. I wanted people who wore my designs to feel bold, empowered, unapologetically themselves, powerful, and in total ownership of their narrative. So...Besharmi. A line for people cultivating a statement life."

Ayaan reflected on her meaning. He had to hand it to her—the meaning behind the line added value to the way he thought of it. And he could see the streak of shamelessness in Payal, the unquestioningly confident way she approached the things that captivated her. He also appreciated how she'd owned a word that was often used to keep women in their lane in Indian families.

"I think you named it perfectly," he said firmly.

His stomach gave a loud rumble.

They both stared at his belly before sharing a laugh.

"Hungry?"

"Well, perhaps you've forgotten but I exerted myself quite a bit last night."

"I remember." Payal gave him a wink. "There are parts of me that got a workout in too, you know."

"Would you like to grab some brunch? The Smith is one of my favorites and it's not far from here."

She hesitated, and he wondered if he'd crossed an invisible line in asking her to carry on their time together. But just as he was about to add a disclaimer that he understood if she was busy and that it was a friendly offering, she nodded.

"I'd love to."

They stood, and when she offered to take his coffee cup to the kitchen, he insisted on doing it himself. She followed him into her kitchen, and he began washing his cup out, taking hers to do the same.

"Well, this is nice treatment in my own house. Maybe I'll hire you."

"You couldn't afford me...but I can think of payment." He smirked.

"I bet you'd like that."

She was five seven or five eight, only a few inches shorter than him. If he leaned in, he wouldn't have to go far to kiss her lips, run his tongue along them, and end up right back in the bedroom.

Payal shifted, her lips parting as though she were reading his mind. She gazed at him, and experienced as he was with reading signals, he knew she'd been thinking the same thing—the quick glance at his mouth before meeting his eyes again gave it away—but he detected hesitancy on her part when her shoulders hunched as she breathed out and pulled back slightly.

"Could I grab some water?" he asked to increase the gap between them and give her a moment.

"Yes. Yes," she said, looking relieved as she reached into the fridge for a water bottle.

He downed it in one go.

"I'll use the bathroom and we can go?"

"Sounds great. Let me change."

"I don't know, Payal, you could rock the barely dressed look." He grinned and she swatted his arm with a giggle.

"Get out of here."

He entered the bathroom and marveled at how many products lined the wooden shelves installed on the wall. Makeup products and skin care were arranged neatly, hardly leaving an inch of space for anything else.

It even smelled like roses.

He lifted the mouthwash bottle above his mouth and let some splash into it. He gargled for a moment, washing his face quickly as he did so, before spitting it out and running his fingers through his hair.

For a brief three seconds, he wondered if brunch counted as a date.

And he realized he wouldn't fight it if it was.

But Payal's words about a hookup, her reticence at growing closer again, her hesitant admission that she didn't do lingering feelings, and even her pause before answering on going to brunch all threw ice-cold water on any flames. This was temporary—and they'd enjoy it for what it was, even if Ayaan was understood for what felt like the first time in a very long time.

When he entered the living room, the words "I'm looking forward to the pancakes" died on his lips.

He should have peed into the water bottle instead of going to the bathroom. Evidently, every trip he took to relieve himself caused drama upon his return, and he knew the storm was coming when he saw the glare on Payal's face.

"'Girlfriend'?" She spat out.

Payal was holding his phone, and the look on her face was murderous.

Chapter Four

PAYAL

This son of a bitch.

Payal had picked up his phone, mistaking it for her own latest model of the iPhone, to text the CMC about the hookup and the potential date afterward. She anticipated their shocked reactions and the deviation from the typical Payal-had-another-hookup shrug they normally gave.

She'd been smitten. Ayaan had been a gentleman, and he ticked off boxes that she'd never known she observed in people to check, perhaps because they hit so close to home for her: London. Family issues. Indian background. She'd always been the odd one out in her group of friends, and every time her acquaintances posted on social media about their families, she experienced a stab of jealousy at their relationships. But now, someone got it.

Before she could register that the background on the phone wasn't the view from a villa in Santorini but rather a photo of a skyline, a text from a person labeled "Girlfriend" had caught her eye.

The feeling of betrayal, despite knowing that this wasn't going to go beyond a night's entertainment, lassoed around her heart in a way she couldn't understand.

"What're you doing with my phone?" Ayaan asked when he was confronted with the evidence.

"We have the same one! I thought it was mine. What does that even matter?"

Did he not see the problem? Why did he look so confused? Payal's fury was growing at an exponential rate at Ayaan's feigned cluelessness.

"'Girlfriend'?" He asked, puzzled.

"Look at your phone, Ayaan!" She tossed it to him—more aggressively than she'd intended, not that he didn't deserve having objects thrown at him.

"Oh," he said, making a face as he looked at the screen. And then he started to laugh.

Payal saw red. It was humiliating being the other woman, however unintentionally, and Ayaan found it hysterical. There was no other explanation other than him being a douchebag, or potentially psychopathic, that he could laugh at someone else's embarrassment rather than feeling ashamed.

Ayaan finally stopped laughing and put his hands up. "I swear, it's not what you think. Don't jump to conclusions."

The implication that it was her fault, her misunderstanding, and her stupidity that had led them here only made her more incensed.

"She's labeled as 'Girlfriend' on your phone! Obviously, she has some meaning to you."

"Neha must have put her name in my phone—"

"You're still with Neha?"

"No! She must have done it a while back and I never noticed—"

"You've had a girlfriend this entire time, haven't you?"

She didn't want to give him the time to come up with an excuse for his cheating ways. She didn't want to be on the receiving end of a speech about how he wasn't happy and he was looking for something different, and that was why he ended up in her bed.

"No, we broke up yesterday—"

"Yesterday? What the hell, Ayaan? Did you wait more than five minutes before looking for a hookup?"

His widened eyes, panicked at being caught, suddenly narrowed. An infuriating smirk appeared on his face. When he spoke, his voice dripped with derision. "Why does this even bother you? I thought you didn't want anything serious."

She threw her hands out, rankled at the obvious point he was missing. "That doesn't mean I wanted to be a home-wrecker! I love sex, but I have some morals, for God's sake!"

"You're the one who told me to come over!"

"And now I'm the one telling you to leave!"

"Fine," he snapped.

He marched past Payal and down the foyer hall, slid his feet into his shoes, and slammed the door behind him.

"Asshole!" she shouted, though she knew he wouldn't be able to hear her.

She stood, panting in anger, her entire body three degrees hotter than normal, staring at the closed door. What had been an enjoyable, pleasurable, even romantic night had turned into a sloppy mess.

The worst was the glimmer of hope she'd felt, particularly this morning, when he'd stuck around with no pretense and they'd drunk coffee together.

It was comforting.

And having a warm blanket torn off to let frigid reality pierce her was a rude awakening.

Ugh, screw him. It was his loss. Ayaan was a fool if he didn't see he was lucky to grace her bed or play a fleeting role in her life, and she wouldn't apologize for calling him on his games.

Her phone vibrated, and for a second, she thought it would be him.

Payal,
Call me.
Papa

Payal rolled her eyes. Would it kill someone to ask how she was or add any touch of humanity to a text? It was one thing if he was emailing his secretary or a business acquaintance he hadn't met, but she was sure even they received more cordial emails than she did because he was trying to make an impression.

Her father still hadn't grasped writing a text message without the greetings and formalities of email.

There was no pretending that there was much affection here—just a sense of duty and a vague loyalty, tied together by shared chromosomes and the same last name.

But ten minutes later, the phone actually rang.

"Why haven't you answered our text?" her dad said by way of greeting.

"I didn't see it."

"Is this how you act in your professional life? You don't respond?"

Payal rolled her eyes. "No, if it's work-related, I always do."

She didn't bother to add that her family rarely said anything of importance in their messages...just compulsory birthday wishes, travel itineraries, and reminders.

"Well, we need you to come back to London."

"Okay, when?"

"Tonight."

Payal pulled the phone away from her ear and glanced at it,

convinced it had glitched and she was hearing things. "Sorry, tonight? Is everything okay? Oh my God, is Nani okay?"

"We're fine. We have business to discuss, and I don't want to do it over the phone."

"Okay...but why—"

"Be on the red-eye tonight, Payal. Raj will meet you at the airport."

And with that, her dad hung up.

· · · · · · · · · · ·

AYAAN

"She threw your clothes on the street—"

"And then you hooked up with someone else?"

Kai and Dharm stared at him expectantly.

Ayaan was ensconced at a table in the Grey Dog in Chelsea. After plans had catastrophically fallen through with Payal for brunch, he'd decided he was still hungry enough to eat and called his two best friends to meet him so he could share his miseries with them.

Unfortunately, they were in the mood to take the mickey out of him after he recounted all the details of the most discombobulated twenty-four hours of his life.

"You should have seen his naked ass huddled on the stairs, waiting for me to bring his clothes up. Then he actually put on clothes that had been lying on a New York street." Kai laughed.

"To be fair, I'm surprised they were still there," Ayaan said.

"How do you even get into these situations?" Dharm asked.

"I think they find me."

"I think you let them."

Ayaan looked up from his burger and fries, frowning. "What does that mean?"

"How long are we going to sit around brunch and hear about how you and Neha broke up for the seventy-eighth time because she saw you say 'thank you' to a waitress? At what point are you going to be an adult and admit that these games are ridiculous? We're over thirty."

"I'm not trying to play games," Ayaan said coolly. "And not everyone finds their soul mate in college, Dharm."

"I'm not saying they do. I was lucky as hell with Maya. But you dated Neha for more than a few months, Ayaan. It wasn't unreasonable for her to expect things to progress."

"I know," he admitted. "I genuinely forgot...and in the moment, I was so flustered that I made it worse for myself."

"Kind of funny that you can talk to a boardroom of execs like you invented crypto, but a girl yells at you and you pee your pants." Kai shrugged.

Ayaan chuckled. "If you've seen Neha angry, you'd probably do the same."

Kai laughed too. "Dharm's not wrong, Ayaan. You could have handled the other girl, the hookup, better too. How hard would it have been to tell her that you and Neha had broken up and that the name on the phone was something you'd forgotten to change back?"

Ayaan nodded. Though they were admonishing him, the boys looked out for one another and he knew they would hold him accountable.

"Arun's call really threw me."

"He was an asshole about it, no doubt," Dharm said. "His holier-than-thou attitude can't possibly feel good to hear, especially because high school was so long ago."

"I don't want to talk about high school," Ayaan said sharply.

"Fair enough."

"Have you thought about speaking with your parents about a larger stake in the company? You are killing the game professionally. It might be time to prove yourself," Kai said.

"No... Well, maybe it's worth a conversation. But they've always held Arun in higher regard, and if they've offered it to him, maybe it's for the best."

"Ayaan, we're best friends so I say this with a lot of love. But you've got to grow the hell up, man, and more than that, you have to take what's yours. You've given up on yourself because you think they have—but you have a role in that company and in your family, whether you want to believe that or not."

Ayaan considered it. His relationship with his family hadn't been stellar in years.

Maybe it was time for a call to change that.

Chapter Five

PAYAL

As the plane rose above the clouds over Manhattan, Payal gave a small shake of her head.

How did we get here? A brief conversation without any emotion, a simple summons, was all it took to get her on a plane to London for a family she hadn't felt close with since she was a child.

The first time she could remember an extended conversation with Papa, they had been traveling to Vaishno Devi Mandir in India.

The business had been doing well, but Ma and Papa wanted to expand to three more locations. Thus, of course, came the idea for a family pilgrimage to temples across India where the one percent, the country's wealthiest, asked God for even more money and success to make these endeavors possible.

At ten years old, perhaps that was a cynical way to look at it. But as Payal locked eyes with another child outside the airport who was no older than her and clutching a baby clothed in rags, she didn't understand why her family had to fly home to ask for more when this child was on the street asking for food, without any parents around. It was a shame to ask for more when you had enough, but so it was.

After a night's rest at a hotel, a three-hour drive to Jammu, and a train ride from Jammu to Katra, they'd finally registered for the pilgrimage and sent their belongings ahead with the luggage carriers.

Of course, Ma and Papa had forgotten to mention the nine-mile trek up a mountain to get to the temple, a cave with ancient figurines that no one quite understood the origin of. They had sent Nani ahead in a vehicle so she would meet them at the top, but Papa had insisted the three of them make the pilgrimage to the temple.

Payal had been in no mood for these shenanigans.

Her legs ached as she walked, stopping only at the halfway point for a little box of Maaza, her favorite mango juice. And so they made their way slowly up the steeper inclines of crumbling paved road, through the fog that hid the surrounding mountains at random parts of the day, and dodged stepping in horse droppings from the hirable beasts that were steered by guides and whose hooves traveled precariously close to the edge of the unguarded side of the road.

Then she saw it.

The sight of the village erased any anger about the unexpected trek and the amount of traveling her family had done to get here.

Vaishno Devi Bhavan was set against a backdrop of mountains capped in snow. Little white houses with multiple stories were built like Lego homes into the side of the mountain. Payal marveled at the way they seemingly hung off the rocks and looked stable. The homes were concrete, white, and identical to each other—long structures that contained multiple apartments.

She'd paused for so long, marveling, that Papa turned around *and walked back the hundred meters that had opened up between them while she was staring.*

"Are you okay, Payal? What's taking you so long?"

"How did they build homes into the mountains like that?"

"I'm not sure. Perhaps it's God's grace holding them up." Papa smiled, as though his stress and thoughts about work had been left nine miles below in Katra and here he was just a father talking to his daughter.

"Look at those lines. The mountains are so jagged and rocky. But these buildings are straight lines. They're like toy houses." Payal barely blinked.

Papa looked at her strangely—not like she was a weirdo but like he'd heard about her before and had suddenly learned who she was.

"Why don't you tell me about it along the walk?" He reached out his hand.

She took it, the only time she could remember holding hands with her father after her younger years, as they talked about why it was so unique that these villages had popped up in mountainous terrains near the Himalayas and how no one could quite understand the way that multiple establishments had sprung up around holy sites in ancient days when they didn't even have the technologies the world had today.

She found herself wishing not for more riches and prestige like her mom and dad but for a life full of days like this.

And her parents' wishes on the pilgrimage must have been successful, because after that trip, the business grew and Payal's father became more and more formal, on the rare occasions he spent time with her at all.

Then as puberty struck, conversations decreased further. Her father had hopes of boarding schools and higher education, and

Payal had hit the age of slammed doors and a lack of understanding. The already-precarious relationship fractured more, aided by the distance between Payal and her mother...a bond that never seemed to get past "let's make sure your material needs are met and keep three miles of emotional distance between us." Payal couldn't understand why their relationship had never progressed.

Her thoughts turned to Nani, her paternal grandmother, who was her sole reason for calling their house a home. What if she wasn't okay? It wouldn't surprise her to know her dad had held back on the truth to ensure she would arrive as soon as possible.

After five hours of fretting, two bad movies, and a whiskey on the rocks to take the edge off, Payal landed at Heathrow Airport just as the sun was coming up.

Once she'd cleared customs, she looked for Raj, her family's driver, spotting him across the terminal in a simple black suit.

"Raj!" she greeted him warmly. He had become a member of the family over his years of service.

"Payal, it is good to see you," he said. "How was your flight?"

"I must be getting old. Flights don't feel as comfortable on my joints, no matter how much room I have," Payal said. She stretched her arms behind her and rolled her stiff neck.

"Listening to you tell me what old age feels like is like hearing a preschooler tell me they've discovered the cure to cancer with mud." Raj was like a second dad...or at least what Payal imagined a friendly dad would be like.

"In other words, I'm entertaining?"

"Life is always quieter without you, my dear."

Raj led the way to the black car, and Payal sank into the back seat, the same way she had as a child after a long day at school. The drive from the airport took forty minutes with traffic, and Payal watched neighborhoods fly by as Raj guided them to Wimbledon.

Papa had insisted on a home there. As a young student in India, he was fascinated by John Newcombe and Rod Laver, tennis players who had been at the top of their game in the '60s and '70s. As an immigrant who didn't know any better and had no care for social pressures (Payal couldn't imagine him being nonchalant, but Nani swore it was true), he had become certain that Wimbledon would be where his dreams came true too. Despite her father eventually being able to buy homes in Chelsea and Camden, Wimbledon had become Mehra family headquarters.

And as Raj drove up the driveway to the detached eight-bedroom home with the white stucco finish, Payal wondered if she'd been too hard on her family's history, on her parents, and on London itself. She had missed the house and the memories she had here: learning how to ride a bike on the front lawn, the summers spent drawing in the conservatory, and the fully loaded bar where she'd snuck friends in multiple times for parties.

She barged through the front door like she was thirteen, not thirty, and shouted "Nani!" as loud as she could. Her voice echoed in the acoustically favorable, high-ceilinged entryway, and she held her breath, hoping she'd hear a robust response that would quell her worries about Nani's health.

Her grandmother appeared from the kitchen in the back of the house, clad in her signature white and looking perfectly fine. Her hobble looked like it had improved since her knee replacement surgery last year.

"Payal, chutki, I've never been so happy to see you," her grandmother exclaimed, her voice warm and her eyes teary.

When they embraced, Payal inhaled the smell of cinnamon and cardamom and the faint hint of rose oil that Nani always dabbed behind her ears after she showered.

Nani was as healthy as a horse.

Now Payal well and truly missed London.

"Tell me about your life in New York City. You know, your nana always wanted to take me there, but we never got the chance."

"I know, you tell me every time I come back." Payal laughed. "But I'll bring you soon."

Nani steered her toward the dining room. "Well, tell me everything now, before your parents come along."

"What's the rush? I'll be here for a couple of days at least."

"Yes, but after this talk with your parents"—Nani lifted an eyebrow—"I'm not sure how keen you'll be on all the other elements of your life."

"Uh-oh," Payal said, frowning. "That sounds like a warning shot."

"More like a temple bell for extra prayers," Nani said.

"Thanks for the notice, wingwoman."

"The prayers are more for me. I have to deal with all of you." Payal laughed again.

Nani guided Payal to her chair. When she'd sat at the end of the table, Nani brushed the hair out of Payal's face, giving her face a long gaze. Her fingers tenderly caressed her granddaughter's cheek.

"I can't believe how much older you've become, chutki," Nani said.

"I feel the same way about you, Nani," Payal said teasingly.

"Chal hat!" Nani pretended to smack Payal, cupping her chin instead. "I'll be upstairs."

"I'll join you once we're done here."

Nani gave her a long look. "I'm sure you will."

When she'd left, Payal did a visual sweep of the room. Ma had a tendency to renovate the dining room and living room every few years, changing the paint color, the furniture, and the aesthetic based on what was trending. The room had been peach the last time she'd visited. Now it was a neutral gray, with mirrors on the wall and a combination of white and dark wood tables and chairs around the room.

It was similar to Payal's apartment, and the commonality made her want to find out if they had other shared preferences.

She tried to think back to their last family conversation in this room. It must have been the college admission talk.

"What do you mean, you aren't attempting to get into Cambridge or Oxford? They're close." Her father frowned.

"I don't know if I'll get in, and I want to see the world."

"So you'd rather go to the United States? And even then, you don't want to go to Harvard or Yale? You don't want the best?"

"I applied to those too." Payal took a sip of her water. "I will see where I get in."

"Why would you want to go so far away from us?" her mother asked.

Payal looked at her incredulously. Mumma spoke as if they were close, but they barely talked, and they lived in the same home!

"At any rate, going to the United States isn't 'seeing the world.' It's not very different from here."

Seventeen-year-old Payal thrust her chin in the air. She refused to admit that was exactly why she wanted to go. It was far enough away to count as a different country, as a foreign one, and for her to gain some points for going to school abroad. It was also similar enough that she didn't have to go that far out of her comfort zone. She just wanted to get away from what she'd grown up in and find her own person...or something like that.

She was nearly thirty now, and she couldn't help but laugh at the whimsical way she'd decided to go to the United States. She'd done her research and applied to the requisite good schools of course—the Ivy League ones as well as Berkeley, Stanford, UCLA, and her eventual alma mater, Duke University. But her sights were set beyond that to city life, to perhaps falling in love, and to finding new friendships that lasted a lifetime. All she'd known of New York life was from the movies, but it had seemed so glamorous that she'd had her mind set on it all year.

She was lucky everything had worked out without too many bumps and bruises along the way.

"It's good to see you, beta. I hope your flight was smooth." Payal's mom, who she looked so much like, glided into the dining room wearing an embellished kaftan. She gave Payal kisses on each cheek before taking the seat next to the head of the table on the other side.

She couldn't have been farther away. *So much for a family reunion.*

"It's good to see you too," Payal replied.

They sat in awkward silence for a few minutes.

Finally, Papa strode into the room like the king of the house he was. He appraised Payal over the papers he was holding, gave a smile and a nod. "Payal, welcome home. I trust your flight was smooth?"

"It was great. You know how it is... Sitting in one place is uncomfortable after a while."

She was a broken record. The repetitive edge of the conversations, the small talk, was an indicator of the distance between them. They didn't know how to close the gap with deeper questions than how the weather was, if bills were paid, or how traffic treated them.

"Didn't you fly business class?" he asked, frowning.

"I did."

"Why wasn't it comfortable?"

"It was a joke, Papa. The flight was fine." She fought the impulse to roll her eyes.

"I'm glad to hear it." Her dad took the seat at the head of the table.

"I'm listening. Is everything okay?"

"Yes and no." Papa sighed. "You've kept your distance from the company, and I haven't burdened you with it because I wanted to give you some time to build your fashion line and reputation as a leader. But we need you now."

"The company is all right, I hope?"

"We had a few bad investments and took a major hit...and we need to sell."

"What?" Payal exclaimed. "But, Papa, you've worked your entire life on this."

Her heart broke for her dad. For all his faults, he had been in business since college, and this must have come as a huge loss for him.

Papa cleared his throat. "Well, we found a buyer. The Malhotras' company, Veer, will buy us out and add us to their life-style brand to improve their home technology and, hopefully, aid with your fashion line as well with their considerable resources."

"That's great, Papa. What do you need from me? I'm happy to do anything."

"I'm glad you said that. As part of the negotiation, the Malhotras have requested that we form a rishta that goes beyond business. Their younger son, Ayaan, is a successful, educated young man who also lives in New York. To complete the merger, this match has to take place."

The words hung in the air.

"And by match...you mean..." Payal said slowly.

She had to hear it said aloud to confirm that the words came out of Papa's mouth.

"I mean that you have to get engaged to and marry Ayaan Malhotra to save our business."

Her mouth dropped open. "Ayaan. Seriously?"

This had to be a joke.

"He's a very good-looking boy," Ma said unhelpfully. "You know him, I take it?"

I've slept with him. And he showed his (damn fine, but still) ass in more ways than one.

"Uhh…you could say that," Payal mumbled quickly.

"Well, then, it shouldn't be a problem. He comes from a good family, and it will save our business, which is set to become yours. You have a lot at stake by saying yes," Ma said.

"No."

Payal rose to storm out, but her dad gave her a glare so fierce she sat down again.

"What do you mean, no?"

"I am not marrying Ayaan."

"Payal." Her dad sighed. "I can see why you feel blindsided. But I'm not sure where the question is on what you need to do."

"Are you kidding?"

"No. I don't understand why you're not willing to put your interests aside to do the single thing that will help our entire family."

Payal was aghast. "A single thing? You make it sound like you've asked me to go pick up a pint of milk! This is an enormous decision, and furthermore, it doesn't sound like you've offered me a choice in any of this!"

"How could it be a choice? You do what's right. The Malhotras are fine people."

"You don't even know Ayaan!"

"Do you?" her father asked pointedly.

We've seen each other naked didn't seem like the best remark to fire back.

"Exactly! How am I supposed to say yes to someone I don't know?" She dodged instead.

"Payal, you do what we all have. You say yes, and you get to know him as time goes on. You won't be getting married immediately," Ma placated. "You'll have time to date. This is only the first step."

"This is ludicrous!" Payal shouted, beyond the point of consolation and losing every semblance of calm with each passing second.

"It's you being ludicrous," Papa said with infuriating dismissiveness. "We've all made sacrifices, Payal. You said it yourself."

"And mine is my *life*? My fashion line? My dreams?"

"Do you like that beautiful apartment we paid for? The fine things you grew up with? Do you love this house and the memories in it? Because we're going to have to sell it all! Would you rather delay your dreams and protect all our assets or lose everything and start with nothing?" her dad shouted, pushed past the point of calm himself.

Payal raised her chin in defiance—the same obstinate gesture as she had used years ago when she'd wanted to break free.

"You think it's easy," Ma said now. "But when your father came here, he hardly had any money. He had exactly thirteen pounds in his pocket. He stayed with family friends, rotating on couches until he found a low-rent apartment. We didn't have toys for you as a baby. Three years later, after Papa had worked hundred-hour weeks, we had enough to have two bedrooms."

"You're forgetting our journey and convincing yourself you can do it. Not only are you incapable and completely ignorant of the suffering people go through, but we never intended for you to intentionally take on the burden of supporting yourself. We did all this for you."

"What was the point if you're only going to force me into the same customs you grew up with?" Payal asked bitterly.

"Because we need you to," Ma said.

"After all these years and all the sacrifice—" Her dad's voice cracked.

"You sacrificed your relationship with me for the company, and now you want me to save it?" Payal said.

The truth spilled out like oil. The source of her bitterness—that she was expected to protect the very system that had taken her relationships from her—was impossible to hide.

"It's going to be yours someday."

"I don't want it," she said stubbornly. "I don't want a company that I sold myself for before I ever owned it."

"Do you think I wanted this?" her dad shouted. "Do you think I ever wanted to give my daughter away, let alone in a business transaction?"

Payal recoiled. She'd never considered what her father had truly wanted for her, outside of accolades, entrepreneurial spirit, and success. She'd simply never known what was in his mind and hadn't grown close enough to him to ask.

To Payal's shock, heartbreak, surprise, and, inexplicably, her anger, her father had tears in his eyes.

Her dad took a stabilizing breath. "Payal, I know I'm asking a lot of you. I'm not a fool. I have thought through every outcome, every possible solution, and a buyout is the only way. It's old-fashioned, I know, to think about a marriage in the context of a merger. I always thought with all the freedoms we gave you, perhaps we could afford marriage being one too. Even I thought we were beyond those times, but it's become a necessity. All those people employed by us will lose their income. I'm at a loss. I am coming to you because you're my last option."

She softened infinitesimally, knowing that it couldn't have been easy to come to this conclusion…and considered the people who would lose their jobs. She thought of Harriet, who was a single mom and worked at the reception desk for Papa's office and baked cookies every time she knew Payal would be in the office as a child.

But she couldn't fathom how her entire life had to be wrapped up in saving the company.

"Ma, how can *you* even suggest this? As a woman."

"These agreements between families are nothing new, Payal," her mom said, gentler than she'd ever spoken to her before. "People sell themselves every day. They trade in integrity to get ahead at work, or they fire an employee and replace them with a friend. They pretend they've worked hard when it was luck that got them ahead. These arrangements aren't new—and I know they aren't modern or cool or as fun—but they can do a great deal of good for more people."

"And somehow, you ended up here, selling your daughter and feeling no remorse for it."

"No," her mother said, shrewdness in her eyes. "We didn't sell you. We did what it took to survive. Payal, I didn't want to marry your father when I agreed either. I thought about college."

This was the first Payal had heard of it, but she was too incensed to focus on the shared experience between her and her distant mother.

Ma seemed to take the silence as an opening to continue. "But my father looked to me to bring pride and, more than that, to fulfill his responsibility of getting me married. And I spoke to your father once. He mentioned he wanted to come to England and open a business. And I knew, listening to him speak, that he would do exactly that. I took the gamble. It paid off. I've never stopped thanking my father since. And you worry about getting to know Ayaan...but we found enjoyment in getting to know one another, learning how to grow together and how to build a partnership. We've created quite a life from nothing but those thirteen pounds."

Payal wanted to believe it. She desperately wanted a family—but how could she put her trust in people who didn't seem to understand the most basic of truths about her: that her freedom to make choices and live life on her terms was everything to her? How could she trust that Ayaan would be able to help her with that when the people who promised her to him couldn't do it themselves? They wouldn't know what to look for in the first place.

"You both have been miserable most of my adult life, Ma. I haven't seen you have a happy conversation in years. You're being remarkably revisionist about this beautiful history you have," Payal said.

Ma frowned but said nothing.

Her father's face fell, but his eyes were steely. He pushed himself back from the table, his drink still half-full, and stood. "Then get ready to say goodbye to your lifestyle. We will have to cut you off financially, stop paying for your apartment, and sell this house, because that's the only choice we have left."

"Then do it. I'd rather you sell the house than me," Payal said.

Determined to have the last word, she shoved herself from the table and marched to her room, leaving her parents in silence behind her.

Payal threw open the door to her room and slammed it, knowing the sound—an auditory indicator of anything less than perfect—irritated her mother and that such disrespect would irk her father more.

She was reminded of being a teen, rather than nearly thirty.

The room hadn't changed much since she was in school. She'd left a poster of the Spice Girls on the inside of her closet door, a tribute to her preadolescence. But even as she had prepared for college, knowing she wouldn't move home again, she had a sense of who she'd become. While the presentation might have changed, the hopes she'd dreamt of for herself were apparent even then.

Like her apartment, Payal's bedroom was light and airy, but it had splashes of color in places that Payal had deemed sophisticated and worldly at the time rather than the classy neutral she preferred in her surroundings now. A bright pink-and-orange bouquet of artificial blossoms in a golden vase on the corner of her dresser. Lapis-lazuli blue throw pillows against a white cushion on a bamboo papasan chair. Colorful beads from a street market in Jaipur hanging from her doorframe and leading into a closet.

Even then, Payal had dreams of travel, fashion, and a glamorous existence. In fact, she remembered, the inspiration behind the decor was a trip she had taken with her family to Marrakech over Easter break.

She unlocked her phone and texted the CMC: SOS. 911. Halp. I'm calling you.

Even with the tension around her, she was happy to be calling them. When she'd decorated her room at eighteen, she'd wondered what was ahead, and only months later, she'd met the CMC.

It was the first day of freshman year—move-in. Papa had come and left in one day, unable or perhaps unwilling to take more than one day away from work. He ensured all Payal's bills were paid and that her dorm was of high quality and then patted her back and left his baby girl across an ocean.

This was it. Freedom.

And while she'd had loosened reins from her parents at boarding school, the threat of her headmaster calling Papa and having her head torn off in a heartbeat was still imminent. Here, she was an ocean away, and as long as she wasn't too reckless, there was no supervision. No tattling. No fear.

She had thrust her B-cup chest outward, her hands on her waist in front of the mirror. Greatness awaited. Her Superwoman stance, however, was cut short.

"Uhh...am I interrupting something?" An alto voice with a husky undertone asked from the door.

Payal whirled around.

"Only the birth of freedom!" She grinned, banishing any red-faced shame at being caught in a power stance. She had nothing to apologize for.

"Ha, preach!" The girl leaned against the doorframe with a smile and a fist of solidarity pumped into the air.

"Come on in. I'm Payal. It's a pleasure to meet you."

"Sonam."

Sonam's curly hair bounced wildly as she walked over and plopped herself on Payal's bed without reservation.

"So there's this feminist meeting for freshmen later. I saw a poster on the bulletin board. Want to go?"

"Feminism, huh?" Payal neatly hung her cardigan. She didn't need the warmth quite as much in North Carolina as she did in England. "I'm down for that."

A few hours later, they'd picked up a quiet girl fresh from India, Kiran. Sonam and Payal had chattered their entire way to the meeting as Kiran, who Payal had accurately predicted was overwhelmed out of her mind, quietly observed.

Who is he? Payal had wondered when she saw the sole owner of a Y chromosome standing in the corner at the meeting, hardly

glancing at the girls who were giving him double takes left and
right, staring instead at his phone.

She'd lost her virginity in a sweet but uncommitted way to a
boy at a party last year. But she knew sex could be fun, and per-
haps with the lack of supervision, this boy would be the next one
to test the waters with.

When the three girls marched up to him, they did what fresh-
men girls do best: they found out information like they were CIA
operatives.

His name was Akash. His sister ran the feminist group they
were meeting at and had dragged him too because guys could be
allies. Yes, he was a freshman. No, he didn't know anyone.

By the end of the night, the smoking-hot boy had joined their
group and it was a bond that hadn't broken in over ten years.

She needed them more than ever.

She gave them a few minutes, then group video called all four.

"What's up?" Sonam was clearly still at the hospital, a bulletin
board behind her.

"Are you okay?" Kiran asked at the same time. Payal could
tell she was at Nash's apartment, far more neutral and minimalistic than her own.

Akash remained silent, staring intently into the camera, a
poster of the Avengers behind him, signaling to Payal that he was
the only one in his own home.

What she would give to be in her apartment, unaware and
apart from all this.

The wave of anger rose in her again as she recalled her parents' demand. But when she opened her mouth, the words couldn't
escape, trapped by disbelief that she had to utter them at all.

It was the anticipatory gazes from her best friends that
prompted her to finally speak.

"I have to get engaged."

A pause.

"Come again?" Kiran asked.

"That's what she said?" Payal managed weakly.

No one laughed. Instead, they waited, until Payal couldn't handle the quiet anymore.

"The company isn't doing well and my parents want to sell the majority and merge with another company owned by friends of theirs—and part of the deal is that I get married to their son."

"They can't do that," Sonam said. "Forced marriages are illegal."

"Only if you say no to it in the first place," Payal said. "And they aren't dragging me to an altar…"

"So obviously, you said no, right?" Akash pressed.

"I–I did. I want to. But…"

"What? Payal, no!"

Payal hadn't expected Akash to be the most volatile about the news.

"You can't get married!" he yelled. "You're not… This isn't right. This isn't *you*."

"The family is laying on the pressure," Payal said. "My dad worked so hard. He missed every significant milestone. He barely managed the small ones. He said this merger will save our family."

"At what cost?" Sonam asked.

"I've been asking the same question."

"Can you ask for time? Maybe tell them you'll circle back in three months and then use that time to figure out exactly how to pull the line off," Akash said.

"You can downsize your apartment, create a budget, be careful with your money…" Kiran suggested before her voice trailed off.

They all knew Payal couldn't; she was so accustomed to a lifestyle at a certain caliber. More than that, they all knew that the luxuries were her connection to her family. She couldn't lose the only material, tangible bond she had with them, give up her job, sacrifice the time and effort it took to start a line, and maintain her happiness. Greater people could.

Payal didn't believe she was one of them.

"It's like all my dreams are on the line," she said quietly. "Because if I say no, I do have to go back to a day job. I have to put on hold a dream that was accelerating. And I'd do it knowing that my parents would suffer too."

"It must feel heavy," Kiran responded in kind.

"Why do you sound so defeated? Say no. This is antiquated bullshit, and you are absolutely not giving in to this!" Sonam said.

"Do you even know this guy?" Akash asked. "Maybe you both can team up and argue with your parents about this. It's outdated to use your children's happiness as a bargaining chip."

"And cruel," Kiran said, no doubt thinking back to her own parents.

When considering her and Ayaan partnering up to fight their parents rather than each other or even teaming up at all, given their history, Payal couldn't help but let out a small chuckle.

"It's Ayaan."

The other three looked confused.

"Ayaan is the guy the family wants me to marry," she said.

"The boy from the café that one time?" Kiran asked, her excellent recall eliciting awe from Payal. "Wasn't he dating someone?"

She gave them a Cliffs Notes version of the one-night stand she and Ayaan had shared.

"Douchebag," Akash muttered.

"You let him sleep over?" Sonam asked, one eyebrow raised. "That's practically a proposal on your end."

Payal shrugged, trying not to think about how Ayaan looked as he'd slept. He was a liar.

"You might want to speak with him," Kiran suggested.

"What would she gain from that?" Sonam asked.

"A conversation. An ally. A sliver of peace to add to her face since she looks like she's aged twelve years overnight," Kiran said, smiling at the end.

Payal, unable to resist Kiran's softness, felt her lips turn upward.

"You have to buy yourself time, Payal. No decisions right now," Akash said. "Do whatever it takes to figure this out, and put off any decisions that risk your future. See if there are other financial specialists you can speak with about the company, perhaps."

It was the soundest advice yet.

Payal knew she'd been wrapped up in the emotionality of her decision, the surprise at being blindsided by such abrupt and life-changing news, that she'd lost her North Star and gotten lost in the chaos.

Now wasn't the time for action. It was the time for deliberation.

"Okay," she said, nodding. "Okay. No decisions."

"When do you come home?" Sonam said.

The word *home* brought Payal back, reminding her that she did have a family. She did have a home. It just wasn't here.

The thought lifted her spirits.

"I'll come back at the end of the week. Day after tomorrow," she said.

"We'll be waiting," Kiran told her. "Stay calm. Don't commit."

Payal nodded again.

They ended the call, and Payal was strengthened, as though the ferocity of her friends had energized her to fight on.

She thought back to what Kiran said and how her own mother

had mentioned the difficulties she and Papa had overcome. Maybe she did have what it took.

She could leave. She could find a place on her own and rough it for a few years until she met someone or rose enough in her career to afford the lifestyle she was used to now. She could beg for her PR job back and forgo the privileges her family had given her. She would miss the name brands and the exclusive way she could approach life without fear of money…but she could survive it.

But could she survive the guilt of letting her family lose the business they'd worked on for forty years?

They aren't family anyway if they'll pimp out their daughter.

Fury surged through her again. She'd put up with plenty—the recitals attended by Nani alone, the pitying looks from other aunties who muttered about her own mother working "too hard" to be there for her properly, the fact that she learned about her first period from her friends and a *Girls' Life* magazine.

Papa had even named the company Luxuriant because he'd wanted to evoke the same sense of awe, wealth, and status in people who owned products distributed by them. He had always wanted better, worked for wealth, and chased status at the expense of his own kid.

She'd done fine until now.

Why the family loyalty now? Let them drop dead. They hadn't given her anything aside from monetary support for her entire life. Love was something she learned from her friends, from fleeting moments in bed with whoever tickled her fancy that night, from watching strangers hug and kiss on the street. She learned it from Nani, who soothed her fevers and kissed her when she came home with an A. She didn't owe the two people who gave her genes a damn thing.

But maybe she owed Nani.

As she always did, Nani must have heard Payal's cry for help from across the manor. Slowly, she hobbled into Payal's room. Her white sari clung to her crepey skin as she moved. Payal could see the veins in her wrists now, loose from age. The white that had previously colored her hair in streaks had taken over.

"Nani," Payal croaked out. Her lip quivered.

This was the only place in London that truly felt like home, in Nani's arms now encircling her shoulders.

"They want you to get married," Nani said. "When did you get so old?"

"The same time you got old. Have you checked your sugar and blood pressure today?" Payal asked, concerned.

"Of course, or my girl will call me from America and let me have it." Nani smiled.

"How could they try to marry me to someone who—" Payal struggled with the right words to describe someone sleeping around.

After all, Nani was still her grandmother.

"Has a reputation?" she ventured instead.

"Your nana and I didn't know each other before we got married. Did you know he was arrested for shoplifting?" Nani asked.

"Nana *shoplifted*?"

"We were fifteen. What a rascal he was. But he wanted to give his sister sweets for Diwali and he had no money, so he took them. He insisted until the day of his death that it was a take now, pay later arrangement."

Payal chuckled. It sounded just like the stories she'd heard of her grandfather, a man she'd never met, who was said to have ironclad conviction and who, by all accounts, was a mischievous youth with a bright future as a businessman in Punjab.

"What does that have to do with me, Nani?" Payal asked

now, her mood shifting from amusement to disheartenment like a marble rolling down an incline.

"Reputations aren't everything."

"My parents are trying to get me married for theirs!"

That wasn't quite true, but Payal knew the embarrassment of losing the company weighed equally as heavily as the loss itself to her parents.

"Sometimes your future may surprise you, chutki, and while I don't agree with the reasoning behind your parents' wishes... perhaps you should give this boy a chance."

"I don't like him."

"Get to know him. Go for a coffee. Get used to each other. But do it with an open mind." Nani brushed a stray hair from Payal's face.

Payal rested her head on Nani's shoulder, the same way she did as a child. "Why are they doing this?"

Nani's eyes sparkled. "Maybe you need to look into what this could do for you...and use it to your advantage."

"What do you mean?"

"Payal, you're seeing your life as an ending with all this talk. *Think bigger.* Ayaan's family is wealthy. They are established. Ayaan, from what I understand, is talented at marketing. Your parents are desperate for this—and while I love my son and don't want you to be careless, you can certainly use your power here to make the life you want and the dreams you have come true. You can always say yes...*for now.*"

When Nani left the room, Payal was left on her own to ponder her future.

But slowly, a plan began to formulate with the pieces that seemed so haphazard minutes ago.

Payal didn't want to give up her dream of a fashion line, but maybe she didn't have to.

Ayaan was known for his marketing skills.

His family was loaded...and well-connected.

Payal had ten months until the fashion show, which, if done well, would inevitably get her more investors, press, and interest in her line.

The wheels began turning. This partnership didn't have to be in vain.

Though she had planned to seek out investors in the future and eventually gain independence from her family's money, this obstacle her parents had thrown her way had accelerated the plan.

I need more connections to invest in my line. And Ayaan's family had that.

Once she got enough investors, she would no longer need her family's support...or Ayaan's, leaving her free to live life on her terms.

She'd end the engagement after she'd gotten what she wanted and all the paperwork was signed...it would end up being win-win-win.

She'd been thinking she had to say yes to forever to save her family.

Perhaps she had to say yes temporarily to save herself. The clock was ticking on her dreams.

Payal couldn't imagine that Ayaan would want to commit to marriage—he couldn't even commit to a night—but perhaps it was worth speaking to him.

Chapter Six

AYAAN

Ayaan's mum was one of his favorite people in the world.

But his ringtone for his parents had always been a police siren.

Growing up, he was certain that she knew when he was up to something—like that time at school when he and the boys had bought cigarettes to try. The police siren would wail on his cell phone as a warning, typically scaring the hell out of him just as he was about to take a drag, and when he'd finally answer tentatively, she'd cheerfully reply on the other end, seemingly blissful and unaware that she'd just taken three years off his life and terrified him enough not to make the bad choice.

Now, even at thirty-two, the alarm would sound and Ayaan would sit at attention, conditioned like Pavlov's dog to expect a conversation about his latest antics.

It was no different today.

After the chaos of the women in his life and the real talk from the men, Ayaan was utterly exhausted, aching down to his bones. When FaceTime rang in the morning, he was half-tempted to let it go and call back tomorrow after he'd slept a full night.

But Dharm and Kai's words about growing up didn't escape him. He hit Answer.

"Hi, beta! How are you?"

"Hi, Mum! It's late. What are you doing up?"

"I was thinking of you, of course. I felt like you needed me."

"I always need you." He smiled, watching her face light up at his affection.

Mum had beautifully lined eyes that had stayed her most prominent feature even with age. Her hair was shoulder-length, layered, and always straightened or curled to perfection, dyed without a white strand in sight.

"Well, a mother loves to hear that. What have you been up to? It was a bank holiday, right?"

"It was," he said. "I spent time with some friends."

"Any girlfriends?"

"Mum..."

"I don't want you to be lonely, Ayaan!"

"What makes you think I'm lonely?"

"Aren't you?"

Ayaan was reminded of this same connection he'd felt with his mother as a child. He wondered how she'd known about his isolation without mentioning it.

"I'm fine, Mum."

"Always with the independence, Ayaan!" Another voice came on the line.

"Sarika!" He greeted her warmly.

"Hi, baby brother-in-law! How is the Big Apple?"

"Better when you're here! When are you coming to visit?"

"I was hoping to come in the summer. You better make room for me," she said.

"Don't bring Arun and we have a deal," he replied.

She laughed, knowing the contentious relationship the brothers had. "I needed a break anyway." ·

Her joy, the charismatic touch by which everything around her turned to gold and everyone became kind, reminded him of Disney princesses.

Was it any wonder Ayaan would never measure up when Arun had brought home a woman who could put a smile on Dad's face in the worst of times and aid Mum in dealing with the men in her life?

"What would we do without you, Sarika," Ayaan wondered, his thoughts slipping out.

"You'd be just fine." She smiled but the added twinkle in her eye from his compliment made his entire day.

As if he could sense that the sunshine was getting too bright, Arun appeared in the background of the camera, followed by Dad.

Ayaan's back instantly stiffened.

"Dad," he said stoically.

"Ayaan." The greeting was returned with the same formality.

Ayaan was tempted to bow and salute.

"What are Arun and Sarika doing over there, anyway, Mum? Did you make dinner? I could go for your aloo paratha right now."

"We came over to talk business," Arun interrupted brusquely.

"I'm glad you're on the phone. We all need to discuss something," Dad said.

"Everything okay?"

"It will be. The business is going toward the direction of expansion. We'll be buying out another company and growing another vertical. We'll need you on this."

His heart rate accelerated, thumping out of his chest. Possibility inflated inside him.

This was it. Ayaan would be asked to come aboard for the

company's growth, and he could prove himself. He didn't even have to ask for it. Dad had seen the potential and taken it upon himself to extend an olive branch to Ayaan.

His father had just given him the best news he could hope for...and hope had been in short supply the last few days.

"Yes!" Ayaan exclaimed. "Yes, I'd be happy to help with anything you need. I wanted to talk to you about being a bigger part—"

"This very much relies on you," his dad said. "Veer will be buying out a smaller company that started with tech imports and exports, moved into the lifestyle space with luxury home technology, gradually went into home goods, and also has a hand in fashion now."

"That's one hell of an evolution," Ayaan commented. "And we're adding them to our lifestyle portfolio?"

"Yes. They need some help—a few bad investments. But overall, their numbers are strong. Combined with ours, the potential for growth is enormous. It's a risk worth taking. Also, they're friends of ours."

His excitement grew to elation. He'd be leading this—the growth of this vertical would be attributed to him.

Ayaan thought about it. "This is a good opportunity. How can I help? The fashion line, in particular...I have some ideas already—"

"As part of the deal, we've discussed an engagement between you and their daughter to ground this business relationship in a personal investment too."

"What?" The balloon of hope, thrill, and belief inside him turned to lead and sank.

"Ayaan, you've been worrying us with your lack of stability. We had to take drastic measures. You said you wanted to be more involved with the company. This is how you'll do it—by being the bond that cements this merger and aids with its success."

"By getting married?" He gave a disbelieving laugh.

"The Mehras' daughter has gotten rave reviews for her up-and-coming line. She styled those two Bollywood actresses for Cannes, and she's been in quite a few print publications already. You'll work well together."

The Mehras.

Ayaan's stomach fell out of his butt.

"You set me up with *Payal*?"

"You know her?" Mum asked with hope in her eyes.

I've had sex with her.

"I... Yes. Sort of. What the hell is happening right now?"

"You're a wreck—" Arun started.

"We worry that you'll feel lost in the world, beta. Your brother has settled down, and Dad will be naming him CEO soon—"

"Thanks for the notice, by the way," Ayaan snapped.

"It's because we can't trust you yet," Dad said simply. "Since you were sixteen..."

"Someday you'll realize that accidents at sixteen don't define a person at thirty-two."

"No, but everything you haven't done after *does* tell us there isn't much to rely on," Arun chimed in.

"We want you to be happy, and we want you to have the same success and fulfillment that Arun and Sarika do. Every parent wants their children to be content with their lives, and I worry you don't have that," Mum said. "You need a sense of purpose."

"So you decided to marry me off to a stranger to fix that problem," Ayaan said.

"You can trust us on this," Dad said firmly. "And maybe if you do, we'll learn to trust you too."

He stared into the screen, seeing four faces reflecting back—and none were joking. Dad was grim. Mum was still hopeful that Ayaan would come around, dreams of a stable family future in her mind and, Ayaan thought, delusions that they'd all break bread together over Sunday dinners with multiple generations of Malhotras. Sarika showed doubts on her face, exacerbated by glances at Arun, who was a combination of stoic and smug at the conversation.

Ayaan couldn't take it.

He'd hoped to mend fences and then demonstrate the responsibility required to help his family's business out.

He did the most mature thing he could think of.

He gave them the finger and ended the call.

A few hours later, he sat at the Drunken Munkey. Inspired by British-Indian history, the food was spicy, flavorful, and a hybrid of cuisine that hit Ayaan in all the right places. And evidently, it made everyone in New York feel the same way, because the place was always packed.

Nestled away in a hole-in-the-wall town house, it was the perfect place for lunch and to inform his best friends that his life had been upended in minutes by his family.

"Why do you love this place so much?" Dharm asked, his nose crinkled as he looked around at the decor.

"Cheese toast," Ayaan said, with a mouthful.

"It's racist as hell, man," Kai said with a laugh.

"What?" Ayaan asked in shock.

Kai simply pointed upward to the chandeliers, with candelabras being held up by monkeys in British military uniforms.

"Oh my God." Ayaan's eyes widened. "How did I never notice that before?"

"You're not the most observant person sometimes. I know, I

know. It's a shocker. We'll do our best not to give you any more bombshells," Kai deadpanned.

"I think this one was enough. This is one of my favorite places to eat."

"Mission accomplished then," said Dharm.

"Actually...it might be me with the bombshell. And it could ruin my life."

"That's a surprise," Kai said. "Tell me: Did a girl throw your clothes out the window again, or did you find out you have a venereal disease? Some can be cured, you know."

"My parents want me to get married."

Dharm shrugged. "You're thirty-two. That's right on time."

"No, Dharm, they want me to get married in a business merger."

"That's some Bollywood-inspired goodness right there," Kai mocked, but he paused when he saw that Ayaan's grim expression hadn't shifted. "Wait...you're being serious?"

Ayaan filled them in on the conversation with his family, including the enraging smugness Arun wore on his face the entire time.

"Have you met the girl? Do you even know who she is?" asked Dharm.

Ayaan nodded, sheepish and unable to meet their eyes. "The girl is Payal Mehra. The girl I hooked up with over the weekend."

Kai's eyes widened. "The one who threw you out because you were an asshole?"

"The very same. And to be fair, she was a pain in the ass."

"She's not going to say yes after your shenanigans, so you basically owe me five minutes of my life back for listening to a story that didn't go anywhere." Kai laughed.

Ayaan toyed with the napkin on his lap. "Mmm."

"Do you want it to go somewhere?" Dharm asked.

Ayaan grew serious. Kai also settled down and his gaze fell upon Ayaan, waiting for a response.

Dharm's expression matched Ayaan's own, his brow furrowed, his lips pursed. Ayaan could tell that his best friend knew there was far more on his mind than he was letting on.

"I thought Payal was really great," he confessed. "She was funny, smart, and, like, a twelve on the hotness scale. I enjoyed our night, and I felt a spark. Then I blew it like I always do...and this giant grenade landed in my lap with my parents, which I'm sure will blow up any apology or effort I could make to fix things with her now."

Silence followed.

"That's a lot." Dharm said.

"I'm not sure what to do."

"Would you say yes to getting engaged?" Kai asked. "That seems like overkill, doesn't it?"

"No! I'm nowhere near that. I just liked her, I thought I could make it up to her if I reached out, and now my parents have brought this up and that means her parents have brought it up to her, I imagine, and either way, it doesn't bode well."

Dharm scratched his chin, looking as lost in consideration. "You could use this to your advantage, you know."

"How so?"

"You mentioned the other day that you wanted to gain more responsibility at Veer. You should negotiate with your parents. You'll say yes to this if they give you a big role...say, CMO."

Ayaan let the wheels turn.

"You're missing one critical element to this plan. Payal." Kai took a swig of his beer. "There's another family involved with this decision too."

Dharm was thoughtful. "You mentioned you had a vibe, right? This is your chance to do the right thing and to earn someone's forgiveness. Afterward, if she agrees to the match, then you'll be on your way to happiness. Her family's company is saved. You have a position of your own."

"And if it tanks?" Kai asked doubtfully.

"Then you handle it gracefully. Sometimes things aren't meant to be."

"Yeah, but the families will be pissed," Ayaan said. "The deal could fall through, and I could lose my role."

He wasn't completely callous. He knew what the implications would be if they didn't work out, and he didn't want to be the cause of another family's downfall. While he was used to screwing up and covering his ass, he wouldn't knowingly put an innocent family in his line of fire.

"Maybe. Yeah. True. But you'll have earned your parents' trust by then by working hard."

There it was again...*trust*. Ayaan wasn't sure this was the best way to go about it, but Dharm's shrewd plan wasn't out of the realm of possibility.

If he told Payal that he needed to get engaged to get a position in his family's company, he could already envision the mushroom cloud that would follow.

No, this had to remain quiet.

But Dharm was right—if he earned Payal's trust and simultaneously worked hard enough to earn his parents' faith, it would be a win-win-win.

"But do I really want her?" What did the real thing even look like?

"Didn't you just say you kind of liked her?" Kai asked.

"Yeah," Ayaan said as doubts grew stronger. "But she didn't believe me when I told her that Neha and I weren't together."

"Dude, it looked shady," Dharm said.

"I refuse to believe that people are so doubtful of the goodness of their fellow man that they automatically assume the worst in them. I didn't lie. I didn't cheat. She didn't give me a chance to explain. Why would I want to intentionally subject myself to that again?" Ayaan asked.

As he spoke, he grew more heated, the memory of Payal's smile fading fast, replaced by the vision of the girl with the angry eyes shouting at him to leave.

"Get a grip," Kai said. "Don't start with this goodness-of-their-fellow-man bullshit. You fucked up and you know it. She didn't know you from Adam, and you expect her to fall into your arms and trust you?"

"Maya met me when we were eighteen and drunk at a party. She had to get used to sober me—"

"Which is way less fun," Kai cut in.

"Truth," Ayaan said with a grin.

"Whatever. Either way, my point is that it took time to peel back layers and find something worth keeping. Maybe this needs to breathe." Dharm put his drink down with finality.

"I could ask for time to get to know her so that none of this is rushed," Ayaan said, pondering.

"Now you're thinking," Dharm said. "No harm, no foul. That might even protect her family's company if you take time to feel it out before getting engaged. They'll have the chance to look at other buyers before anything is set in stone...and maybe you can actually learn how to believe in each other."

"It sounds conniving. Maybe it is. But you can use it as a chance to redeem yourself," Kai said.

Ayaan was thinking the very same thing.

Perhaps it was the chance to grow. Second chances did exist. He had been given one hell of a reprieve. What was it Payal had said? *I want to chase everything I love at a million miles an hour.* Maybe this was his opportunity to do the same.

He'd read a quote once about humans' greatest fear being that they were powerful beyond measure. He never admitted it to anyone, but he believed that to be the case. He was certain the same psychology drove his own actions. After years of being told he was squandering his potential, he was terrified of finding out that he was, in fact, powerful. The knowledge would disrupt the status quo.

But he'd earned this. He had shown at his day job that he had natural talent. Veer could use him. And Payal was an added bonus.

This could be a win-win-win.

He just had to convince her to give it a go.

. . . .

Ayaan blankly gazed at his computer screen when he got back to work. His entire plan to have a productive day, sleep, and move forward from the Nightmare on Neha's Street was derailed by his parents' bombshell and his friends' scheme.

Looking over the stats from his team, however, he felt a modicum of winning.

In his time in New York—eight years, he realized with a start—he'd developed a better sense of success. Unencumbered by past mistakes and without the burden of his family's judgment, Ayaan had thrived on his own merit, and these tiny solaces reminded him of all the potential he possessed. Whatever Arun thought, heaps of praise about Ayaan's work were coming in from every campaign he worked on.

But he still wished his family could see it instead of holding the past over his head.

Despite wanting to stand tall, he sensed the hunch in his shoulders as he walked home, observing the occasional mask covering people's faces and feeling as though he too couldn't breathe easily today.

How could his parents ever have thought this would work?

How could he possibly have been convinced by Kai and Dharm, even for a fleeting second, that there was hope with Payal and that this entire situation wasn't effed up?

He growled in frustration, startling the woman he was walking by, who clutched her baby a little tighter as he passed.

He also hated himself for the little spark of curiosity that lit up inside him.

He climbed the stairs in the back of the building rather than taking the elevator, hoping that the physical exertion would force the demons from his chest and eliminate the doubts that continually flared up.

When he reached the apartment and closed the front door behind him, he felt nominally lighter.

His phone rang, and he pulled it from his pocket with a sigh.

Mum.

Despite contemplating hitting the red Decline button, he tapped the green one instead, accepting the call and pushing the phone against his ear.

"Mum," he answered quietly.

"Ayaan." Her voice was warm. "I'm glad you picked up."

"Mmm."

"Still upset, I see."

He leaned against the wall, untying his dress shoes and sliding them off. He neatly set them by the door, remembering Payal's laughing reaction when he'd done the same at her apartment.

"Can you blame me, Mum?" he asked quietly.

"Ayaan, jaan, you know love and dating can look different than you imagined. Look at your father and me."

"I know, Mum," Ayaan said, exasperated. "You chose Dad out of three family friends' sons—and let me clarify something: It's not a love marriage if you don't have much choice. Secondly, you love telling me you and Dad dated, but chaperoned dinners three times before your engagement don't count."

"Can you tell me your hesitation?"

"What's not to hesitate about? I've spoken to her once—" He bit his tongue immediately, knowing he'd slipped up.

"You spoke to her?" Mum's voice filled with joyful curiosity.

"Just once," Ayaan fibbed. "It wasn't a particularly charming experience."

"Well, second chances are always worth a pursuit. Your dad spilled soda on me the first time we met, and I was ready to—"

"Hit him with your chappal," Ayaan filled in dully.

"I need some new stories, don't I?" Mum said with a laugh.

He could picture her now—tossing her head back effortlessly when she was amused, her favorite diamond studs glittering in her ears, and her medium-length nails immaculately painted a deep red. She was so unaffected by his barbs, and despite himself, he loved her for it because he knew that his mother was genuinely interested in what he thought, how he acted, and who he was.

The verbal grenades he launched were always taken for what they were: frustrated outbursts by a son she tried to understand and loved even when she didn't.

It was more than he deserved, and the only thing he could count on.

"Mum, I'm sorry. It doesn't make sense to me," he said.

"Well, you wouldn't want soda spilled on you when you first met someone either, would you?" she asked easily.

"I'm not talking about Dad."

"I know, beta," Mum said. "What scares you?"

"Turning into Arun, for one."

"You are entirely too spirited for that, wild child."

Ayaan cracked a smile his mother couldn't see. "Payal and I don't know each other. Our first impressions were the equivalent of drenching each other in carbonated drinks. We may not grow to love…and if we can't manage that, my entire life is derailed for people I don't know. And if I'm saving Arun's ass in any way, then I'm throwing away my happiness for people I don't like."

"Be nice," his mother warned, but he sensed he hadn't upset her at all.

"Be honest, Mum. You don't like him either."

She laughed again. "I love you both…but that's where this is coming from, darling. I know that the prospect of business involved with relationships seems to take any fun or romance out of it all. You've had such fun in New York, and it's been a delight hearing about your accomplishments. But sometimes, you seem… sad."

Ayaan swallowed an unexpected lump in his throat and then cleared it as subtly as he could. "That's not true. I have an awesome life. Dharm and Kai are my best friends, I have a job I love, and dating was going fine."

But how "fine" could it have been if he never mentioned Neha to his mother?

"An awesome life and a full one aren't the same, Ayaan…and operating with a void, whatever that void may be because of, isn't how anyone should live. I worry about you. Since you and Arun stopped being so close—"

"Things change, Mum."

"Listen to me, beta. I know your father and Arun worry more about the perception of our family in public. I worry about you. You've fought against them and their beliefs so hard that I think you've gotten into the habit of throwing a punch in response even when no one is threatening you."

"I have no idea how you can say that this isn't a threat to my happiness. You've literally asked me to marry someone I hardly know for the sake of saving her family's company and for the growth of our own. How is that acceptable?"

"I know what Arun and Dad are asking of you. What I am asking is that you give it a chance. Speak with her. See if there could be a possibility. If there isn't...then you and I can tackle it together. I will always be in your corner. What's the worst that could happen?"

Ayaan couldn't sort out how to answer the question. On one hand, he had Dharm, Kai, and his mother insisting that the future could be bright if he'd allow himself the possibility of belief in himself and in Payal. On the other...this was a bananas way of doing it.

"I'll think about it, Mum."

"That's all I ask, beta."

He hung up, reflecting on his thoughts and the conflicting opinions of everyone in his circle.

What's the worst that could happen?

"Well, her family could lose her business, she could hate you, and your family could hold it against you forever," he said to himself.

It was his very hesitancy, his analysis paralysis, that he'd avoided at work to capitalize on ideas. He had to be decisive. Deliberate. Reactionary. Even with his family, who elicited a freeze response.

Perhaps it was time to take charge and direct his own life for a change. It wouldn't hurt to know where Payal's head was at after she'd heard from her parents.

He picked up his phone and typed out a text, erasing and retyping the words in an effort to sound as conciliatory and contrite as possible.

Ayaan: Hey, Payal, it's Ayaan. I'm sure you've deleted my number and rightfully so. Would you mind if we had a chat later? Do you have some time?

That's polite, he thought. Certainly better than the last time they'd shouted at each other. He had injected humility, flexibility, and an apologetic tone.

He checked his phone twenty times in the next twenty seconds, hoping for the read receipts to turn on and for her to respond.

Finally, thirty-eight seconds later, the receipt changed to Read and Payal began typing.

Payal: Hi, Ayaan. I agree. Are you able to call me after work?

He glanced at the time on the screen, and his stomach gave an unseemly grumble.

Ayaan: Do you have some time in an hour? If you'd like, we can meet for coffee.
Payal: I'm actually in London right now...but I can chat in an hour.
Ayaan: I don't want to inconvenience you. It's a bit late. Will you be up?
Payal: I'll be up.

Chapter Seven

PAYAL

Though Payal had no intention of following through on this plan of marrying Ayaan, the palpable weight of the decisions being made shifted the air. The trajectory of her life had been accelerated, transformed, and morphed into something she didn't recognize easily, and the size of those changes seemed far too big for a conversation with a person three thousand miles away over a five-inch screen.

Ayaan Malhotra.

It was unfathomable that his name, two simple words, had crossed her mind with the vaguest consideration just a few nights ago—that she had spent time staring at his photo with curiosity and attraction. In less than a week, they'd had an epic argument, and now she had to pretend they were going to get married.

It would make her laugh if it weren't so nightmarish.

She also had no idea what Ayaan thought about this development.

"His parents have spoken to him and it looks favorable" was all Ma had said to her this morning when she had inquired as to what the Malhotras had said about this entire situation.

It looks favorable. The prospect of marrying her simply being "favorable" was laughable. What happened to romance? What happened to choice without obligations?

What was wrong with these people?

And why on earth would it be favorable to Ayaan? She'd thrown him out the last time they'd spoken. What on earth could have changed his mind?

The possibilities were making her mind spin and, worse, the trust she had implicitly placed in her family and in the world all these years appeared misplaced. The doubt the last few days had sown screwed with her head, shaking up all the certainties she'd had faith in before. She wasn't sure who to trust or whether everyone was in this for their own gain.

Payal tried to recall the hours of debate clubs and negotiation courses she'd taken at Duke. Her goal was to convince Ayaan that she was in this for her family, for the company, and that she was open to building something—namely, her fashion line—with his help. She had to be charming but calculated, exude innocence but intelligence, and remain the paragon of a perfect daughter.

In other words, this time, she had to treat him like a one-night stand and a business contact but pretend to connect with him like a human.

She'd get what she wanted, and she could leave the others in the dust...let them sort themselves out.

Her FaceTime blared precisely at midnight, and she jumped, not expecting a video call.

Thank God she hadn't washed her face off or she'd already be at a disadvantage.

"Hello?"

The screen scrambled before coming into focus.

"Hey, Payal," he greeted.

"Hey," she said awkwardly, hating herself for still thinking his voice was sexy. "How's it going?"

"It's…umm…well, it's been an interesting few days."

"You can say that again."

Ayaan was in his apartment, from what Payal could see. The kitchen, a modern, modular type with shiny white cabinets that had no handles and gray counter space, flashed in and out of view behind him. His hair appeared to have been raked through multiple times, chunks protruding in all directions.

"Wait…isn't it nearly past midnight?"

"Yes, why?"

He made a face. "Why do you still have makeup on? Did you go out or something?"

"Yes, that's my life, a series of dates and one-night stands on weeknights."

"No, you're—" He rolled his eyes. "I didn't mean it that way. I was genuinely asking. I didn't want to bother you if you were busy."

"No, I was working late."

It was a lie—Payal put on makeup as soon as she showered and it felt like armor—but he didn't need to know that. *Who did he think he was, sounding so judgmental?*

"Well, I'm assuming your parents spoke with you. How're you feeling about all this?" Ayaan asked.

"You don't want to know the answer. I'm not sure I know the answer."

"Do you even believe in arranged marriages? That's not the path I would have seen for you." He didn't sound like he had an answer to his own question, but the doubt ignited anger in Payal.

What would he have seen for me? A string of one-night stands? Years of throwing people out of my apartment?

"Outside of the fact that our generation is largely borne of them, no, I don't. And you haven't seen much of me." She bit her tongue as she said it, already irritated at her stumble. He'd seen her naked, for God's sake.

Ayaan wasn't one to let that go.

"I've seen some of you," he said, and he smirked.

She wished she could slap the look off his face.

"Listen, Ayaan," she began, with an attempt at softness. "I know we started off as a casual fling and to say the last few days have been a surprise would be the understatement of the millennium...but my family needs me, and I'd like to be there for them. I hope we can approach this with consideration, even if we don't agree to getting married."

"Why?" he asked, and he sounded genuinely curious.

"What do you mean 'why'?"

"I didn't get the impression you were particularly close with them. It sounded as though you had a similar relationship to most of mine—" His sudden stop triggered Payal's Spidey sense.

"You aren't wrong," she conceded, trying to give him an inch. "But it means something to me to protect them. They're family. Regardless of what our histories are, how distant we may have been, their option at the end of the day was to turn to me for help, and that means a great deal to me."

"Mmm. I feel the same way. It's important when they place trust in you to do it justice."

"Why are you here?" Payal was curious. "We didn't exactly part on the friendliest terms. I thought you'd ride in guns blazing."

Ayaan laughed. "You judge me. But I believe possibility is always worth a conversation."

His humility and openness surprised her. He was so at ease with the strange circumstances, as though perhaps he was the one who'd wanted an arranged marriage all along. Speaking with him was becoming easier for Payal.

Maybe this would be simpler than she thought.

On the other hand, she wanted to shout, "Are you bonkers? They're trying to get us married!" but instead, she aimed at diplomacy.

"As complicated as our relationships are with our families and with each other, taking care of them is important, and I have to do what I can for them. My dad has worked his entire life for this company to come to the success it has."

"I understand that."

She crossed her fingers underneath the screen. She hoped she sounded straight to the point, trustable, and like her family's interests were driving the operation.

"I know this probably sounds crazy, far-fetched, and I'm asking more of you than I have the right to. But this is over thirty years of one family's history and hard work, and if you look at the numbers, you'll see that there is genuine possibility in the acquisition for Veer of both my family's company and potentially my line, if it will help my parents. An engagement seems sudden, but at the very least, I'd like to work on building the line with you so that Veer has the best chance if they choose to acquire it down the line. We can help each other." *Leave the ball in his court.* "Of course, I'll leave that up to you. Like I said, I realize I'm asking a lot of you."

Ayaan absentmindedly rubbed his chin as he nodded. "I'd like that very much. Growth for both companies is important, and we have the skill sets to help each other. My parents told me that they have always wanted me to be CMO, and I don't want to let them down."

Payal sighed with relief. "I never imagined you'd be open to this," she admitted. "I expected this to be a phone call where you'd tell me your parents were nutters and we'd fight through this."

"I considered it!" Ayaan exclaimed.

Payal couldn't help but laugh.

"But…you are right. They are our families and we have to do what's right, even when it seems completely out of touch. Veer is in desperate need of a revamp, and it's possible you're the key to it."

She made a sound of agreement. "For now then, for my family's sake and for the sake of this merger, I'd like to agree to this arrangement, and I can assure you I'll do everything in my power to make Besharmi as viable and successful as I can for the sake of yours. A tentative yes, if you will."

Maybe this would be easier than she'd initially believed; Ayaan certainly seemed less difficult than she'd anticipated, and as an expression of hopefulness crossed his face, he even seemed optimistic that the two of them would deliver results.

He may have been an idiot, but Payal was certain she was winning her case.

· · · · · · · · · · ·

AYAAN

It had been less than four days since their blowup, but it had felt like a million years. Ayaan was certain he'd aged ten years.

But Payal was being surprisingly amenable, and the ease with which this conversation was moving forward threw him for a loop.

Everyone is crazy! He wanted to shout about the way they were speaking so nonchalantly about an engagement. But instead, he pushed the gentleness.

"I know this wasn't a conversation either of us were expecting," he said honestly. "And I know I was the last one on the list of people you wanted to talk to ever again."

Payal gave a small shrug and a good-natured chuckle.

He grinned. "You didn't see this coming either, did you?"

"Not in a million years." She laughed awkwardly.

"I know. I was shocked too, but…"

"But?"

Ayaan intentionally glanced away, as though he was digging deep. "My whole life, I was against the idea of marriage as a transaction. But the more I thought about it, the more I realized it may have been a narrow view. We have an opportunity to do something wonderful for our families. Hearing my family say how much they believed in me and how they wanted me to take over marketing, and knowing I could help you, felt like a great opportunity."

He surprised himself with how easily the lie spilled out…how quickly he was able to omit *I just need to marry you to get what I want.*

"I also wanted the chance to explain myself and extend my apologies about that day," he continued, this time more genuine. "I shouldn't have laughed. I shouldn't have gaslit you. Neha and I broke up the day before. I should have been clearer about that. She must have changed her name on my phone the day or two before we broke up, and I never noticed because she never texted since, again, we broke up. I was in rough shape and didn't look at my phone."

"Well, that's a lie," Payal said swiftly. "It took you about ten seconds to get on a hookup app."

Ayaan tried to ignore her jibe but bristled with annoyance at being called out.

"Maybe I'm that much of a bonehead."

She had listened in silence until then but started laughing. "I'd agree. But I should have waited to hear your side before freaking out."

Relieved, Ayaan continued. It was here that he had to milk his story. While he was genuinely remorseful about their prior inter-actions, that didn't mean his future had to be set down the aisle... but he'd do what it took to get to his family and prove to them that they had overlooked him all these years. Emotional blackmail wasn't out of his comfort zone, and he needed Payal to believe his intentions were genuinely family-focused.

"The truth is, your comment about your family values just now meant a lot. It's really admirable that you're willing to put your family's needs above your own. You must care about them a lot."

"Very much," Payal hummed. "I want to make them proud. And it's nice to hear that yours trusted you more than you knew."

Silence ensued.

"Well, I had a conversation with my mother—who, by the way, is my favorite person alive." He couldn't lie the entire time. "And she reminded me that it's time to settle down and take life more seriously. She's not wrong. As you can see, I've screwed up quite a bit."

"You're not a screwup, Ayaan," Payal replied, sounding warmer. "We've all done things we aren't proud of, and some-times you need the right people in your life to push you toward the proper direction you were meant to go."

"I know this isn't what either of us imagined but our families need us, and for their sake, I'd at least like to explore getting to know you better, if that's okay. As you said, a tentative yes." *Just a little hesitancy to show you're nervous about it.*

She inhaled. "It's worth a try," Payal said. "I'd like that."

Mission accomplished.

"If it's okay, could we take it slow for about six months? Maybe longer?" She cocked an eyebrow.

Ayaan couldn't script this better. "I was hoping you'd say that." He laughed. "I've always found it shocking that our parents and grandparents said yes to their marriages after meeting once and, sometimes, not at all. I've always felt that some time was more prudent."

"I couldn't agree more," Payal responded. "Maybe something will grow. Either way, it's never a bad thing to line your ducks in a row for the future, whatever it may be."

You have no idea.

Chapter Eight

PAYAL

The more she thought about Ayaan, his family's resources, and sticking it to Papa and Ma (while outwardly looking like she helped them), the more certain Payal grew about the decision.

Taking a deep breath, she steeled herself for the conversation she was about to have. After this, there would be no going back on her plan.

She would be looking out for herself.

She tried to listen for the sounds of her family but couldn't pinpoint where they were. She searched, walking down the long hallways that she had run down as a child, constantly sliding along the wooden floor in her socks. She descended the long stairwell, remembering how, as a teenager, she used to slide down the banister to Ma's admonishment and Nani's shouts of "You'll break your neck!" She peeked into the kitchen, where she often did homework, hoping that her mother would come sit next to her and tutor her, but where she often ate alone or with Nani instead. The conservatory, where she'd had her first kiss at age thirteen with William What's-His-Name, was dark.

Finally, she stepped into the living room where her parents

and Nani sat on the L-shaped cream-colored leather couches. Nani was cross-stitching, a talent she'd possessed for so long that Payal had started an Etsy store for some of her designs. (Nani swore Payal's artistic talent came from her grandmother.) Ma, dressed in black leggings and a light-purple baggy sweater, was watching a Bollywood movie from the seventies with a glass of red wine in her hand. Papa absentmindedly gazed at the television hanging above the fireplace before turning back to his tablet and looking up when Payal entered the room.

He appraised her, raising an eyebrow. "Payal?"

"I want to talk to you all," she said.

"Have a seat," he said.

"I'll stand," she said. She didn't want to get too cozy. "I'll agree to this match."

Nani's eyes lit up. Ma smiled and gave a quick nod, as though Payal had finally gained membership into a secret club that only they were a part of. Even Papa looked surprised, his eyes widening and his mouth relaxing into what could be deemed a small smile.

"I'm very glad to hear that," he finally said.

"But I want a year until our engagement is formally announced."

Payal's assertive demand hung in the air for just long enough to give her hope before Papa countered.

"Eight months. I don't want to wait for an extended amount of time to see this through."

"Make it ten. Compromise with me," Payal said firmly. "You cannot ask me to marry someone I don't know. This gives us time to be certain."

"Why do you want to take so long?" Papa asked suspiciously. "We made our decisions in minutes and we've lasted decades."

"Well, you can do that or you can have a divorce on your

family's history, and you'll lose the company anyway. Why don't you choose which option looks better? I'll wait."

That was the golden ticket to winning this negotiation. Payal had saved the ultimatum for last, an appeal to her father's deepest worry about public perception and community shame. She would use his need to avoid any scandal or blight on his family's honor against him.

All was fair in love and war. And this was war.

Papa stared at her. Payal knew she had him, but he was thinking through alternatives to convince her to walk her proposition back and take a route more favorable to him.

It was Nani who chimed in. "Are you really going to fight her on this? She's already agreed, beta. You are being a stubborn donkey for the sake of winning a fight."

Papa glared at Nani before turning his gaze to Payal again. "Fine. Ten months."

He stood.

For a change, this final act of power didn't make Payal want to cower or run. Instead, she clenched her jaw, holding his stare until he finally shook his head, defeated, and left the room.

Payal turned and went into the kitchen, gleeful that she'd received what she'd wanted: to be able to smile without looking as though she was gloating.

Nani followed her.

"Well...now you've won, haven't you?" Nani clapped her hands together.

"I still only have ten months to organize this plan...and I can't fail," Payal mused.

"Hai Ram! You and your dad are more alike than you know," Nani muttered.

"What do you mean?"

"Exactly what I said. Neither of you likes to admit defeat... and when you win, you don't like to enjoy it. Instead, you think three steps ahead and find something else to worry about rather than trusting that your lives will line up."

"I have a lot at risk, Nani."

"So did he, Payal."

Payal refused to take the bait, to consider the others' priorities. "I respect that, Nani, but I have my own plan now. He doesn't get to determine how I do this."

Nani considered Payal's tone. She seemed to decide against pushing the subject further. "I'm proud you spoke up for yourself," she said instead.

"Me too. The rest of this plan is on me."

. . . .

AYAAN

Ayaan had also made a decision.

He couldn't bet on Payal. They had a lukewarm conversation, and it would take a Herculean effort to even try to get to know one another.

But he could bet on himself.

"Beta," his dad answered, his face coming into clearer view from a pixelated jumble.

"I wanted to talk to you," Ayaan said, willing his voice into a steady cadence.

"Is everything okay?" His dad frowned.

Ayaan wanted to be soothed, comforted by his dad's concerned tone, but the way his eyebrows crinkled together reminded him uncannily of the expression Arun often wore when Ayaan spoke.

He had to be on guard.

"I've been giving your proposition some thought."

"And what was that?" Dad asked.

Ayaan exhaled, reining in his temper. "Your thoughts on an engagement to Payal Mehra."

"I see. Do tell."

"Yes, do tell us your opinion," Arun cut in, coming into view.

If bets had been placed, Ayaan would have risked his salary on this happening. In fact, in a strange twist, it empowered him to speak up again.

"I'm open to getting to know Payal and getting engaged. Her family needs some support, and I'm happy to help our family in any way I can. I'm sorry for hanging up before. I was shocked, and I needed time to think about what this meant for all of us. But I'd like to earn your trust back for past mistakes and do the right thing for all of us." He crossed his fingers behind the screen.

Dad's eyebrows flew into his forehead. "Really?"

"You're going to say yes?" Arun asked with suspicion.

"In return, Dad, you'll name me CMO, and I get half the stake in Veer."

Silence followed his calmly conveyed condition.

"That's silly," Arun scoffed. "You're going to make a trade for your own good based on this girl's life?"

"How is that any different from what we're doing by buying out her company and including a marriage in the deal?" Ayaan asked.

"Well, that's completely different. It looks out for the future of our family's company."

"I'm doing the same," Ayaan replied.

"How? How is you being named CMO a good move for Veer?" Arun's voice began increasing in volume.

"Why do you want this, Ayaan?" Dad asked.

"You can't possibly be considering this, Dad!" Arun turned to him in disbelief.

"Oh, stop it, Arun," Dad scolded. "Ayaan is contrite for his past behavior, and he's acting with a lot of clarity right now. You yourself have complained about this before, so why are you fighting it?"

Arun spluttered but couldn't produce a coherent string of thought.

"Why now, Ayaan? Why should we trust you?"

"To answer your question, Dad"—Ayaan spoke over his brother's sounds of protest—"I've spearheaded the marketing campaigns for four different companies in the last year alone and yielded a minimum of 25 percent growth through programmatic marketing and 40 percent growth in sales from those transformations. I've also saved over $10 million combined for those companies with transformation plans and consolidation of their sales platforms. In addition, with the potential addition of Payal's fashion line and her family's company to our portfolio, brand management will be necessary across multiple verticals, and I have experience in that."

"That's very impressive," Dad said.

"Why do you want to be a CMO versus simply working at the company?" Arun challenged.

"The CEO and founder of Impact has noticed that I am good at what I do," Ayaan continued, gaining confidence in Arun's dour expression. "At this point, I'm happy to bring those considerable talents to Veer instead. To be frank, I'd much rather work at a family company and know I've had a hand in its success from a position that can affect change and lead the efforts in this transition."

"You'll have to work alongside me as CEO. The buck stops with me," Arun said.

"That's fine." Ayaan shrugged. "We can stick to our respective domains."

"And if we don't agree to your deal?"

"Then I won't marry Payal. I open my own firm. And you lose multiple avenues for growth. That's one hell of an accomplishment for a newly appointed CEO, isn't it?"

Dad had sat quietly until now, watching Arun's expression descend from cranky to murderous, but a twinkle crossed his eyes now.

"Ayaan, I must say I'm impressed with your initiative. You've clearly thought this through, and you've illustrated your success well."

"Well, I learned something from you about that." Ayaan smiled.

The flicker of pride in Dad's eyes was enough for Ayaan to know he had sealed the deal.

"Very well, then. I agree to this. You both will be announced as new heads next month. It's about time you take some responsibility. But this comes with a condition, Ayaan," Dad warned.

Ayaan's stomach plummeted.

"We'll announce the transition to CMO. At the engagement, you'll be appointed officially. Until then, you can remain in New York and ensure that Payal's company is successful, as we want to acquire a winner."

"But you won't renege on this?" Ayaan asked.

"No. I'm a man of my word. You will have CMO."

Arun rolled his eyes. "Ayaan, fine, whatever—come onto the team. But don't screw it up."

"I won't," Ayaan said firmly.

This is what I've always wanted.

Chapter Nine

PAYAL

TEN MONTHS UNTIL THE FASHION SHOW AND ENGAGEMENT

She was rolling her clothes into columns so they would fit neatly back into her suitcase when her phone dinged with a text message from Ayaan.

> Ayaan: Would you like to get dinner when you come back to the city?

She gazed at the phone, reading over the words again and again, as though an ulterior motive would present itself and scream, "Here I am!" for her to know his true intention.

But maybe he had meant it when he said he wanted to get to know her, and she was being a skeptic of genuine kindness now...and that was something she never wanted to be, the type of person who always looked for buried intents and never relished the beauty of a moment.

I'd love to, she responded. I come back late tonight, so perhaps tomorrow would work.

Great! came the response.

Payal thought for a moment before deciding that if Ayaan

would be kind, she could offer her own graciousness. I can choose a place to go if that works for you—7:00 p.m.?

Ayaan: Perfect. See you then.

Nani hobbled into the room and her eyes traveled over the bursts of color, travel trinkets, and pieces of memories decorating the room.

"What're you scheming, Nani?"

"I come in here sometimes when I miss you."

"But I'm right here."

"Yes, but you'll be going back today. It makes me sad. The house is always emptier without you causing trouble. Sometimes I come in here to feel your presence."

Payal couldn't help but smile. It was a common sentiment she heard so often from brown parents. Even Sonam's parents, for all her arguments and loud opinions, always stated that the house was emptier without her energy around.

"I didn't cause any trouble this time. I think it was the other way around."

"On the contrary, you were remarkable. Grace under fire."

"I don't know about that, but thank you."

"How are you feeling about this? Do you want to back out?"

"Is this a spy mission where you report to my parents how I feel, and then they can talk me back into it if I say I don't want this?" Payal asked, with full knowledge that Nani wouldn't betray her but deflecting anyway.

"No…it's checking on my granddaughter, who sometimes goes through life alone and shouldn't have to…at least, not at home."

"I do not."

"That's because you have me."

"Maybe that's all I need," Payal said.

"Now that I think about it, you might be right," Nani said with a wave of her hand. "But remember, sometimes life gives you unexpected stories."

"Are we still talking about our family?"

"Well, there was that story about your grandfather's cousin who thought he married a goat, but that's not what I meant. There was a flicker of something yesterday, and I hope that you let it light up your life."

"What do you mean?"

"Ambition. Hope. Being a strong woman who takes life into your own hands...and perhaps, a partnership."

"A partnership?"

"My God, child, have you never read a romance novel?"

"I'm not big on those."

Payal was lying; she'd read all Nani and Ma's secret stashes of Mills & Boon romances when she was thirteen and still loved a sexy, steamy escape into literature every once in a while.

"Have you ever read a book?" Nani's eyes sparkled. "Stories are made every day from ordinary moments, Payal. Someday, you'll learn that this has the potential to be the greatest decision you've ever made...if you give it a chance."

Payal tried to smile but she was unconvinced that this plot twist would lead to a happy ending. "If you say so, Nani."

"I do, my dear girl. Now...get to the airport before you miss your flight."

. . . .

AYAAN

It was seven ten. If there was one pet peeve Ayaan had, it was people who ran late and didn't text or call to let someone know.

He'd been waiting over twenty minutes for Payal to appear, and his patience was wearing thin from a combination of hunger, anticipation, apprehension, and annoyance. He'd paced the sidewalk, sidestepping other patrons and moving out of the way for people who were constantly trying to take up the spaces he was waiting in. He hadn't gotten to research this place at all. For all the stylish invites he received to go to new openings as an influencer, he was also a man of habit when provided with a choice, and he had a few favorites he loved to frequent when he could.

Knowing they would lose the reservation if he didn't make a move now, he approached the person behind the podium.

"Ayaan Malhotra—er, Payal Mehra," he said.

He was led upstairs to a dining room decked out with black tables and gray seats. Metal rods, fashioned into circles, hung from the ceiling with light bulbs ensconced every six inches, protruding into the air and dimly lighting the dining room. Creeper plants hung from vases suspended on the white brick walls.

Ayaan liked the lack of clutter, the minimalistic and happy atmosphere the restaurant provided. He couldn't stand places that were packed too closely together or whose decor overtook the room, but the intimacy of this place was nice.

"I'll have a Godfather, please," he mentioned to the waitress.

Five minutes later, he was sipping his drink, feeling the burn in his chest as he waited.

He wondered if he looked like a guy who had been stood up.

Crap. *What if I have been stood up?*

But then he saw Payal ascend the stairs. She was ready for business, or so it seemed, with her outfit—a tan sweater tucked into wide-legged, long black pants with black pumps that made her long legs even longer. A large brightly colored neon necklace draped around her neck, and she had a tan coat, matching her sweater, tossed over one arm while the other hand held a small black hand-bag. Her hair was in a side bun, tendrils framing her face.

"Hi!" Payal said cheerily, as though she hadn't made him wait fifteen minutes.

"Hey, Payal," he said, simultaneously amazed at how beautiful she was and irritated at her lateness.

They kissed each other's cheek, once on the right and once on the left. Hints of floral scents wafted through the musky, bold perfume.

"I'm sorry I was—" she started.

"Don't worry about it." He cut her off, trying to smile to make it sound more friendly. "I'm famished! Are you hungry?"

"I'm starving. I got a little lost in work today, and sometimes when that happens, I forget to eat."

"I thought I was the only one that happened to!"

"Definitely not."

They grinned at the shared quirk, and a flutter went through Ayaan.

"Okay. So. You're starving. Let's get some food."

They opened the menus a server put in front of them. As he scanned the listing of choices, Ayaan felt his irritation begin to reappear.

"I didn't realize this was a vegan spot," he commented, trying not to crinkle his nose and divulge that he wasn't impressed.

"Do you have a problem with veganism?" Payal asked.

"I mean...where is the chicken?"

"There are plant-based alternatives, you know." Payal seemed bemused.

"Are you a vegan? I don't think I knew that about you," Ayaan said.

Get real, Ayaan. You don't know anything about her. What did I get myself into?

"No, not usually. I ate a ton of junk food in London and I wanted something healthier. Plus, this place is delicious."

"Oh."

His tone, one of doubt, was clear. Ayaan didn't oppose veganism. For God's sake, he was Indian and many of his friends were vegetarian. But he didn't find a vegan restaurant to be the best choice when Payal should have known he was a meat-loving, Punjabi guy with a hearty appetite. If he had a preference, he wouldn't have chosen this spot. It would be too adventurous for a date that needed a little stability.

Shouldn't she have asked? Was that too much to expect?

"Wow, judgmental much?" Payal said, a small smile crawling across her lips as she took a drink of water.

"No, I thought... It's completely fine. This will be great." He plastered a smile on his face.

"You forgot to tell your face to agree with your words," she said swiftly.

"Our evening hasn't begun smoothly, I suppose."

"I was under the impression it was fine until now."

Ayaan contemplated whether it was smart to point out her lack of punctuality now. He tried to be gentle. "Well, it's not particularly considerate of other people's time to arrive late...at least without a text or call."

"Nor is it considerate of people who book dinner to complain about the choice without mentioning dietary preferences," she countered.

"I think the first is more egregious and the impatience from it can lead to the second."

"We can agree to disagree. Though I'm sorry I was late."

She certainly didn't sound it.

"If you say so," he said coolly.

The waitress appeared then, at a moment deemed by Ayaan as both timely and lucky, as he was certain Payal was contemplating leaving, dumping her water over him, or making a snarky comment back that would likely leave him scrambling.

"What can I get you both? Would you like more time?"

"No, he's lost enough," Payal said without batting an eyelash.

Touché.

"What can I get you?"

"I'll have a curried stuffed sweet potato with a side of brussels sprouts. I'll also have a Miss Casanova. Thank you. I think he would like an exit." She gestured to Ayaan with her chin.

Ayaan's head snapped up at the second jab. "Only if I find it for you, sweetheart. I'll have a margherita pizza, please."

"Ooookay," said the waitress, and given the snark at the table, she was a pro at being good-natured. "I'll be right back with your food, if you haven't found the exit by then. If you need it, it's just downstairs."

Payal gave a small laugh, and Ayaan couldn't help one either.

"You're witty," he said to Payal when the server had left.

"You sound surprised."

"A bit."

She rolled her eyes.

"So...how was London?"

"You know how it is. The weather goes through all four seasons in a day. Evidently, bombs drop about companies and marriages. The usual."

Her snark earned a begrudging nod. "I know that feeling."

"Indeed. But...you know. Family ties have a tighter hold on us than we realize sometimes, and we have to show up when it counts."

"It consistently catches me off guard that, based on what you and I talked about last week, we're expected to appear and grant wishes to family whom we aren't particularly close with."

"Yet they act surprised that we followed through on what they requested."

"My brother nearly peed his pants, I think."

"Is it any surprise if you haven't been dependable?"

He knew she was deliberately throwing punches to land. "It's about as surprising as I imagine it is for your family that you showed up for them at all."

Her eyebrows rose in surprise. Perhaps even admiration that she'd found a formidable foe.

He had to admit that the banter, the back-and-forth instantaneous sass lit a fire in him, as though he had to be alert and ready for sparks at any time.

And miraculously, Payal didn't look bothered by it either. Instead, her eyes appeared hungry, even craving some of the stimulation that came with being challenged.

Strangely, after the last weeks of highs and lows that seemed extreme, this somewhat brutal exchange full of barbs and intensity enlivened him rather than tiring him out. Payal's electricity made him want to see how he could outmaneuver her.

They sat in silence for a few minutes, occasionally glancing at each other, meeting the other's eye, and letting their gaze dart away to anything—the orange accents on the wall, the patrons around them, the waitresses bussing orders from the kitchen to the guests—to avoid connecting with each other any further.

The waitress returned with their food and Payal's drink after a few minutes of dodging eye contact.

"Well, I'm glad to see you're still here!" she exclaimed.

"The night is young," Payal said, but something in her voice was a touch more entertained than it had been before.

Ayaan picked up his fork and cut a slice of his pizza with his knife.

"Did you not pick up the New York pizza habit of actually using your hands?" Payal asked, amused.

"Not in a nice restaurant..."

"Ayaan. We don't see eye to eye on, well, basically anything, but I think you need to pick up that bloody pizza with your fingers. You're Indian, for God's sake. This isn't a new concept for you."

"Let's stop pretending that we both don't know exactly how good I am with my fingers, sweetheart."

He'd fired back without thinking but when he reluctantly put down his fork, satisfied at least that he'd quieted her down, he noticed her fighting back a smile.

Chapter Ten

PAYAL

She'd never cared what people thought before Ayaan came along and screwed with her head.

Yet she found herself, for possibly the first time in ten years, sitting at the Chaiwala café table fifteen minutes before the CMC was supposed to join her for chai. *They'll wonder what got into me.*

Ayaan hadn't asked why she was late—or he'd have known that the Uber she was trying to take to dinner had gotten a flat tire and her phone, which she perpetually kept charged, had gotten water in the charging port, rendering it unpluggable.

It was only ten minutes.

Her excuses hadn't been flimsy; they were real and irritating roadblocks that people faced every day. But instead, Ayaan had treated her as though she'd had no manners and had grown up in a barn, rather than simply asking her what had prompted the delay.

The nerve. He was so entitled.

She rolled her eyes.

A true mastermind learns everything they can about their victims...or at least, that was what Payal's love of true crime shows taught her.

Victim may have been a strong word here... Ayaan and her family weren't losing everything for Payal's gain. It was a win-win-win. But regardless, Payal had to learn as much as she could about Ayaan to ingratiate herself with him, create a believable story, and build some credibility in his eyes.

Social media was the best insight in today's world.

She wasn't curious. No, she told herself, this was purely research.

Pulling up Instagram, she stared at his profile. Five hundred thousand followers? *Who was this guy?*

Holy shit, she was engaged to...er, dating...forget it... She was somehow strangely involved with an influencer. *What did you just get yourself into?*

He had a couple of thousand posts but as she scrolled, endlessly, it seemed, to the bottom of his feed, she realized he knew what he was doing. He'd gotten on the bandwagon prior to anyone else, and he'd become an original influencer simply by the quality of his photos and the way he displayed his lifestyle as aspirational.

She even saw a photo of her neighborhood posted from the day he'd come over. Unbelievable.

She examined a photo of his—a throwback shot of his high school friends, all in uniform.

Payal didn't even know he had gone to boarding school, let alone a school like Harrow.

Sadness struck her. In this arrangement, they'd missed all the beautiful moments that set up a relationship for success: learning about favorite cuisines through trial and error, finding out why someone had a scar on their left thumb, telling stories about their first trip to the beach, and hearing words that they couldn't pronounce when they were little and that had stuck around in family lore, like the way Payal's family still sometimes called tomatoes *mo-tay-ters* because Payal swapped the syllables when she was learning to talk.

Their story not only had spoilers about how it would turn out, but it was as though they'd started reading the book with the last page.

Worse, the fact that they didn't know the little details and didn't care to learn made the idea of pulling off this charade—making Ma and Papa believe that she had tried her absolute best to make it work before she called it off—even more daunting.

Determined to learn what she could and perhaps to make herself more miserable, she continued scrolling through his Instagram grid to uncover any of his other interests.

He had a photo at a shooting range, with protective glasses over his eyes and his taut arms aiming a pistol toward a target.

Ugh. She hated guns and couldn't understand the American fascination with them.

In a photo of a meal—at the Drunken Munkey, not too far from Payal's apartment and one of her favorite restaurants—Payal found a common thread. Perhaps their love of food would be the catalyst to carry their chemistry forward. They were Indian, after all. Food was the center of everything. Maybe just not a place that didn't offer chicken.

But Payal's eagle-eyed observation registered another detail. A hand had made it into the shot, and it belonged to the person quite clearly sitting next to Ayaan…with long, manicured, dark-maroon fingernails and gemstone rings on most of her fingers. Payal had to guess it was Neha's subtle appearance that had made its mark on the shot. She imagined Neha laughing or moving suddenly as Ayaan took the photo of his food, perhaps making fun of him for doing such a basic thing, before he'd done it and not recognized she was in it.

Neha probably showed up on time.

No. She wasn't going to play this game, the comparison championship that often crowned one woman's accomplishment over another.

Instead, she hit Follow on Ayaan's Instagram.

"Payal?" Kiran asked incredulously.

She looked up, met by three completely shocked faces.

"Are you early?" Akash asked from beside her. "I'm hallucinating."

"Whatever you took, I must have taken it too, because by God, I also see Payal in front of us," Sonam said.

Payal rolled her eyes. "Very funny."

"Well, I say we make it a habit," Akash said as he pulled a chair out and plopped into it. "It's a pleasant surprise."

Something about Akash's words coming so soon after Ayaan's prompted Payal to ask, "Is it really irritating? I know it's not the best habit."

Kiran shrugged. "It doesn't bother me. You show up in every way that matters."

"Honestly, we've gotten so used to it that I don't think about it," Akash said.

"You show up fifteen minutes early professionally. It's just a quirk with your personal life, and we all operate on IST sometimes," Payal said.

"Why the sudden ask? It hasn't bothered you once in the last ten years," Akash asked.

"I was late to meet Ayaan yesterday and he was clearly irritated by it."

"You met Ayaan?" Sonam asked, with an eyebrow raised.

Payal recapped the trip, the conversations with Nani and her parents, and the date with Ayaan.

"Sorry. Did you just say you agreed to get engaged?" Sonam asked.

"I mean, in theory. I don't bank on it happening."

"So...you got engaged to save your parents' company. But you don't intend on going through with it," clarified Kiran.

"Do you realize how ridiculous you sound right now?" Akash asked, cutting in.

"It sounds a little crazy, I suppose..."

"Because you're a wackadoodle who just agreed to get married to 'save a company' for a family that sold you off in a deal with a guy you've slept with and who regularly shows his whole ass?"

A beat passed.

Payal stared at Sonam's incredulous face and then moved to Kiran's open-mouthed and scandalized expression at Sonam's outburst. Then she burst out laughing.

"What are you laughing at?" Sonam said, her voice rising a few octaves. "This isn't funny."

"No," Payal gasped. "Nani had asked if I ever read romance novels and I said no. But the way you described this...it's so ridiculous."

Sonam gazed at her and a smile began splitting her face. Kiran let out a giggle at Payal's mirth.

"Only you," Sonam said, shaking her head. "Only. You."

Payal spoke again after they'd recovered. "He's an ass, though. This won't last."

"You have to try in order for it to," Kiran said softly.

"What do you mean?"

"Payal, I don't even know if I agree with what you're doing. But I do know that tough times happen. 'Shit hits the fan,' as Sonam would say. There are greater stakes here between your family and his, and the two of you, than you're willing to admit.

And with great risk comes great reward if and only if you make great effort to match."

"And if you can't, you have to back out...and soon," Sonam advised. "This isn't logical or smart to try and draw out. If you get too far ahead in this, you might be signing life away to unhappiness. Worse, there are a lot of people with their life's work on the line. Be careful."

Their words dwelled in the air, creating heaviness around them. The girls knew not to criticize one another's decisions too much, whether or not they agreed. They simply offered advice and hoped for the best. Akash, on the other hand...

"I cannot believe you're agreeing to this," Akash said. "You're bonkers."

"Stop it, Akash," Payal snapped.

"Do you hear yourself?" he challenged back. "You are literally saying yes to a *marriage* for a leg up...and for a petty revenge mission on your family. What in the actual hell are you thinking?"

"And if I was a guy who was doing what it took to get a leg up, you'd call me ballsy or bold."

"I think I'd still call him an idiot too."

The quiet painfully hung in the air.

"Wow, I could cut the tension with a knife in here," Sonam commented.

They all gave light laughs.

"Akash, you don't have to agree with me on this. My family isn't like yours or Sonam's, or, for all the crap they gave her for dating Nash, like Kiran's either. I have never been close with them. They asked me to sacrifice everything to save them. While loyalty calls every once in a while, because they're still my family nonetheless and we share some DNA, I need to look out for myself because no one will. Ayaan's family has money, connections, and the potential to help my family. They have access to wider distribution channels. I don't know what will happen but right now, I have no choice but to trust myself and hope that I can walk away without too much damage down the line."

"The hell if I know what you're doing," Akash said, raising his hands up in the air.

"The hell if you know what any woman is doing," said Sonam.

"This is so far-fetched," Akash said. He shook his head, tiring Payal with his disbelieving expression.

"This is desperation," Payal said firmly. "It is a Hail Mary."

"You're not Catholic," Akash said.

"Then it's a hai Bhagwan, but whatever it is, I need it to work," she snapped.

Even as she said the words, uncertainty plagued her, eating away at her conscience.

"How are your parents, Kiran?" Sonam seemed to read Payal's expression before deciding a subject change was the way to go.

"They hung out with Kirti again last weekend," Kiran said, a fond smile crossing her face.

"I cannot believe you went all the way to India, found your estranged sister, talked said long-lost sister into a reunion, pulled it off at a hospital, and then managed to save your relationship at the same time," Payal said.

"Well, when you say it like that...suddenly, your comment about your far-fetched life seems to apply to me too," Kiran pointed out.

"It was quite the Bollywood movie. But you'd sacrificed so much. It was time for mending bridges," Akash said.

"I'd do anything for my family," Kiran said quietly. "And for Nash."

"You're your best when they're their best," Sonam said.

Payal didn't respond. The discussion had hit closer than her best friends realized. Sacrifice, family, and doing what it took to bring the disparate elements of her life together...Payal admired Kiran for taking the plunge and doing whatever it took to get to an end result, even if her parents had been douchey on their way to reconciliation.

Inspiration was everywhere, she'd tell herself when she was designing. But maybe it existed for everything.

• • • • • • • • • • •

AYAAN

Ayaan stretched out on the long side of his black, L-shaped couch. Though he was a social creature, he loved the occasional night in, spent in his little apartment. It was his quiet oasis.

Except when Kai and Dharm were also there, grilling him about his so-called date with Payal.

"I don't understand why you're still so damn grouchy about the whole thing," Kai said.

"You wanted a second chance and you got one better. Both of you, by some act of God, agreed to get engaged and now you have ten whole months to make a good impression," Dharm said. "I fail to see the problem."

"Well, maybe she didn't make a good impression on me," Ayaan said.

"If she was actually forgettable, you wouldn't be sitting here thinking about her," Dharm said.

"I'm annoyed it didn't go smoothly."

"You mean that she didn't fall into your arms, forgive you instantly, and then have sex with you?" Kai asked.

Ayaan glared at him. "Shut up. No."

"Okay, jokes aside...how did it go?" Kai asked.

"Well, she showed up late."

"Yes. Definitely worthy of the guillotine," Dharm said.

"You know how I hate that."

"Did you ask her why?"

"No..." Ayaan felt a touch of heat in his cheeks, as though he was being chastised by Arun.

"That may have been a good move. You never know if it was a one-off." Dharm shrugged. "We show up late to dinner all the time. It's practically the Indian way...and the New York way because of trains. And, I don't know, an occasional human flaw to have a problem that sets you back on time."

"Then she took me to a vegan place."

Kai and Dharm gazed at him expectantly. "And?"

"And she said she'd eaten so much in London, she wanted to be a little healthier for a day or two to recover."

"Smart move. I eat so many samosas every time I go home, I always come back feeling as though I've gained a pouch." Kai patted his stomach.

Ayaan rolled his eyes. Kai went to the gym every morning at five, and he was entirely too vain to let himself develop anything that didn't resemble a six-pack.

"I figured she'd ask where I wanted to go or ask about cuisine or pick something universally liked, even if it was boring."

"You're really looking for this to fail, aren't you?" Kai asked incredulously.

"What? No—"

"You put more genuine effort into choosing your shoes in the morning...or, I don't know, taking the right picture of our dinner to put it on Instagram," Dharm said.

"I feel bad for her," Kai said.

"Why?"

"Because she has to put up with you nitpicking at her. For the love of God, you acted like a big man taking charge of your life when you said yes—you literally got all the things you wanted—and now you're going to sabotage it for the dumbest reason I've ever heard."

"That's not—"

"It's true and you know it." Dharm cut him off. "Own your choices. You're being ridiculous."

Ayaan was incensed. Though he knew Dharm and Kai were always willing to call him out on his childish behavior, he was restless at the accusations they'd leveled at him. He wasn't being ridiculous. Could they really blame him for having cold feet at the idea of getting engaged to a virtual stranger, even if it was for his own interests?

Was it wrong to be afraid of something, even if a piece of you wanted it?

When the boys had left, he stewed about it, irritably picking up takeout boxes and shoving them into a garbage bag. Once he'd taken it down the hall and thrown it down the trash chute, he came back to his now-silent living room and threw himself back into his comfortable spot on the couch.

Still aggravated and wanting to rewind to a week ago, before any of this had happened, he picked up his phone and opened a text.

Hey, he typed to Neha—whose name he had changed back from "Girlfriend" as he stormed back to his place from Payal's—and sent it before he could think twice.

He waited for a second, anticipating that regret at the impulsive choice would catch up with him.

But his tolerance for impulsivity must have increased after

telling his parents yes to Payal, because he didn't feel anything. Instead, righteous anger boiled over.

This wasn't his fault.

Between his family igniting both ambition and anger in him, his aggressive move for CMO, the expectations of his parents and his brother, and now, the way he was forced to make Payal a part of his life, he was flying blind, scrambling to make a move without being able to come up with a plan.

As though the universe had heard his innermost thoughts about chaos, his phone vibrated in his hand.

Neha: Hey...I'm in Italy for vacay for the next week, but let's
   get together when I come home. Maybe we can fix this.

Ayaan nearly got a hard-on thinking about the reunion they'd have...and he knew Neha had the same reconciliation in mind. Sex was the Band-Aid in their relationship, the fix-all for a moment gone wrong.

Deep down, he knew that wasn't the way to handle any discontent happening now.

I don't care, he told himself. *For tonight, I can distract myself, and I'll figure it out tomorrow.*

With those final thoughts and a sliver of hope about the coming days, he fell asleep.

Chapter Eleven

PAYAL

NINE MONTHS UNTIL THE FASHION SHOW AND ENGAGEMENT

Payal shot up from the couch where she'd dozed off and stared at the fire alarm, wondering why it wasn't blinking to alert her of any danger, before she realized the sound was coming from her phone.

Shaking her head and rubbing her eyes with the heel of one hand, she picked it up off the coffee table and answered, knowing that the only person who would call this early on a Saturday was Ma.

"Hello, Payal. How are you?" Ma's crisp voice floated through the line.

"A bit tired. I must have dozed off while sketching." She fought a yawn. "How are you?"

"We're all fine. I wanted to talk to you about this upcoming weekend. Is there any way you and Ayaan can fly back for a three-day break?"

"Sorry, what?"

"We'd like the families to meet formally, now that you both have agreed to the engagement."

"This seems somewhat rushed, don't you think?" Payal tried not to panic at meeting the Malhotras, with the added pressure of Ayaan in the room as she was put on parade like a show pony.

Ma seemed to have other ideas. "No, I think we need to get to know one another. At any rate, this merger will need to be discussed, but it's important that we thaw any ice as soon-to-be relatives to ensure that this process goes smoothly on all fronts."

"I can speak with Ayaan..."

"Good. Let me know by tonight. We'll need you to arrive on Friday night so we can schedule a Saturday dinner."

Ma hung up without so much as a goodbye.

Payal groaned, tossing her phone on the couch. She dropped her head on her chest. Sleep had rapidly run away from her in the short minutes that this conversation had distracted her.

It sounded naive, but Payal hadn't thought this far ahead. In all the plans of faking affection, going on dates for show, and pretending to adore Ayaan, she hadn't factored in that she would have to meet his family for real and pull the veil over their eyes so soon.

She'd barely gotten to know him and what she'd learned wasn't endearing.

They'd have to call each other fiancé.

But she couldn't see a way out. Perhaps she had to speak with him. They could even team up against this development and push it off for a few more weeks, until they'd settled into this routine and it didn't feel so foreign.

She waited a few hours until a reasonable time—10:00 a.m. was reasonable, right?—before calling Ayaan.

"Payal, this is a pleasant surprise," he greeted her.

"Hey..."

"What's on your mind?"

"Our parents are having dinner on Saturday night and would like us to fly back and attend."

Silence.

"Are you kidding?" Ayaan asked, sounding gobsmacked.

She was relieved to hear her own disbelief echoed in his response.

"Evidently, because of the merger, they'd like to accelerate the meeting-the-parents element of this courtship," Payal said.

"Accelerated is right. Zero to two hundred, our families are, aren't they? We've had dinner once."

"I could say I have an investor meeting that can't be moved," Payal suggested, hoping he'd agree.

"They'll only push for the next weekend after that," Ayaan replied.

She knew he was right.

There was no escape.

"I'll book the tickets," Ayaan filled in for her. "We can take a red-eye on Friday night."

That was how they wound up booked on a JetBlue flight, sitting across the aisle from one another in first class.

Ayaan and Payal hadn't arrived at the airport together. Payal had delayed leaving her apartment until the last possible second despite knowing that Ayaan would judge her for being the last person on the plane.

But Ayaan had arrived even later than her. Perhaps he'd had as many doubts as she did about flying into a crisis.

"Hey," he said, breathing heavily and shoving his bag into the overhead bin.

"Long day?" Payal asked in surprise. "Aren't you usually a stickler for time? I would have imagined you to be at the gate hours ahead of departure."

"I try," he said shortly. "But work got in the way."

They sat awkwardly as the plane began pulling away from the gate, and Payal had never seen anyone as intent on watching the flight attendants demonstrate safety practices. She had a feeling he didn't want to talk about what was on his mind, and she didn't probe.

After all, she was carrying her own baggage—both literally and figuratively—tonight.

"Excuse me, ma'am, may I have a whiskey on the rocks, please?" Payal asked the passing flight attendant.

"It's a bit early in the flight, don't you think? Aw, hell—you know what, I'll have one too." Ayaan shrugged. "How was your week?"

"It was good," Payal said.

It had, in fact, not been good.

Two weeks ago, she had received an email confirming that she had netted a meeting with Manish Menon, an investor in fashion who had supported some of the biggest South Asian designers coming up.

On Monday, she'd been ready, born for her moment to shine.

Payal had ensured every stitch of her samples was perfect, that her materials were impeccable, that her designs were cutting edge, that the sketches for her future work were detailed, colorful, fluid, and drawn with enough vision that anyone who saw them would know she was a woman with a mission.

She'd spent hours putting together a presentation with her sales, comparative figures against other designers, photos of the actresses at Cannes who she had styled, and breakdowns of her financial spend and income projected over the next few years.

She'd fretted all week about the impending response, though she was certain she had nailed it.

And just as she'd climbed into the Uber to arrive at the airport, convinced she'd hear next week and that something must have come up on Manish's end, she'd received an email.

Payal,

Your designs are perfection and your talent is undeniable. You're early in your career, however, and I need to see you receive positive reviews at industry events in order to feel confident about where my money is going. It's a no from me for now...but a possibility for the future, particularly after your next few showings.

Payal was playing the words in her mind, dragged down by each one as they flashed before her eyes, and she recalled the sinking feeling in her stomach as it repeated itself now. Ayaan's voice broke through her saddened reverie.

"You should tell your face that," Ayaan replied, echoing her words from dinner. "Are you okay?"

Though his legs were stretched in front of him and he leaned on an elbow as though he didn't care about a thing in the world, his eyes were intently focused on her face, awaiting an answer.

"I had a setback with the line," Payal said. "I'll be fine."

"What was it?"

She paused. "Do you want to know?"

He nodded, not looking elsewhere. "I do."

Payal explained how much she'd prepared, how she'd envisioned a yes and amped herself up for one but hadn't gotten it. "It feels like a huge failure."

Ayaan had leaned toward her as she spoke, his head in the line of fire for anyone walking up the aisle. "I don't think you can view it as a failure...or, as I suspect you do, a reflection of who you are."

"Why?" Payal asked, curious now at his seemingly fresh interest in her.

"He never shut the door on you. He took the time to write a note, and based on what you and my family have told me, you're set for a show soon. Which means he's keeping an eye on you to see what you come up with. This isn't a no. It's full of potential. And even if it is a no, fashion is subjective. Unknown designers need one hit to give them a boost. They need the right marketing or the lightning strike of success to become a household name. You're doing all the right things. Your storm is brewing. Momentum is building. The strike simply hasn't happened yet. Did you mention that Veer is interested in you? We may not be acquiring your brand now—just your family's—but the leverage exists."

Her gaze, which had fallen to her hands, snapped back up. "No...I didn't."

She knew, deep down, that was her biggest mistake. She didn't present the outside interest in her brand. Admitting any connection to Veer made it all the more real...and she wasn't ready for that.

"That's a selling point, you know. For as awkward as this impending engagement feels right now, it credits your marketability for investors to know other companies love you too."

Payal knew he was right. His pep talk was certainly empowering, a surprising shot of energy coming from an even more unexpected source. But she wanted to mope. She wanted to have a cry, to feel the pressures of the last weeks, and to sit miserably with them.

It wasn't logical, but then again, life wasn't.

"Thanks," she replied.

"What, that's it? I thought the pep talk was pretty good."

"What, do you want a cookie?" Payal snapped.

Hurt crossed his face as he recoiled a little, but his recovery was so quick, Payal didn't have a moment to feel sorry for her overreaction.

"Fine," he said quietly.

He put his headphones on and turned his head to the screen in front of him, and Payal felt a jab of guilt at the way she'd treated him for being kind. He'd offered a moment of connection, and she'd whipped him with the very olive branch he'd extended.

"Ayaan," she said.

But he didn't turn his head.

Payal reclined her chair and folded her legs underneath her, letting her head collapse against the back of her seat.

What felt like minutes later, she was awoken by a sensation on her forehead, her neck, and her chest like a fly kept landing on various parts of her body. She swatted her hand around her face without opening her eyes, but the persistent light hits against her forehead finally pushed her to open her eyes.

When she looked down, annoyance burned under her skin.

"Are you throwing peanuts at me?" she hissed across the aisle.

"Well, if you're going to set the example of being a toddler, what's stopping me from doing the same?" Ayaan growled back.

"Behave!"

"Then quit being a pampered princess."

"You stop being an entitled prick."

A peanut hit her squarely in the forehead.

"You know what, fine. Toss your nuts around." Payal glared at him, rage building inside her at his increasingly amused expression.

Ayaan smirked. "Hey, you said it, not me."

She simultaneously cracked a smile and wanted to throw her carry-on bag at his head.

"See, there's a smile."

"It wasn't because of you."

"If you say so," he replied, infuriatingly cocky.

"I want to be sad about it. I'm allowed to be sad about it." Payal grabbed the pillow from her big, leather carryall. Her neck ached from the awkward way she'd fallen asleep.

"You aren't allowed to let it slow you down," Ayaan said.

Irritation crept up at his words. He was right, of course, but the fact that Ayaan was the one being logical through a crisis felt like the universe pouring salt in a wound.

"The fact that you think I'd slow down is proof that you don't know me well," she said with finality, and she put the pillow against her right shoulder and turned away.

They didn't speak for the rest of the flight.

As they advanced through customs and stepped through the baggage claim into the space where families welcomed their relatives returning home, Payal spotted Raj.

"I'm that way," she said to Ayaan.

"Well then, I'll see you tomorrow," he said awkwardly, tucking his hands in his pockets.

"Listen, Ayaan—" Payal started, hoping to apologize for her behavior.

"Don't worry about it." He offered a half smile. "You were stressed. A red-eye is tiring. Humor wasn't what you needed. It happens."

She tried to smile, but he turned away, throwing his duffel bag over his shoulder as he walked in the opposite direction from her.

She didn't even know how he was getting home.

Payal thought about him for the entire drive, barely answering

Raj's polite questions until he stopped asking them, knowing her mind wasn't in the car.

It wasn't until she had sunk into her bed for a nap, exhausted by the day's events and the flight, that she realized the date that she'd be meeting the Malhotras.

It was Valentine's Day.

. . . .

AYAAN

"It's a big day!" Sarika had cried out, pulling open the curtains in Ayaan's blackened room. "Rise and shine!"

"What're you on about?" Ayaan asked, feeling bleary-eyed and rubbing his eyes as the room came into focus.

He sat up in bed, leaning over to yank a T-shirt off the floor and pull it over his head.

When he'd arrived at the family home in South London just past nine in the morning, only Mum and Sarika had been there.

Their hugs had been the best thing about the week.

"How was your last day?" Mum asked. "Was everyone sad at your going-away party?"

Between Payal's crankiness, the flight, and jet lag, Ayaan's going-away party at work felt like a distant memory. Among the hugs and congratulations on his new venture at Veer, he'd felt a mixture of sadness, excitement, and anticipation at the prospect of this new phase.

He had felt so overwhelmed at the idea of leaving a good thing behind for uncertainty that he'd stayed too long at the party and had to rush to the airport to make his flight to London.

Then he'd stewed about whether it was the right choice.

"It was bittersweet," he recalled to his mom now. "Where are Arun and Dad?"

"They went to their Saturday morning tennis match," Sarika said apologetically. "Papa said to take a nap and be ready to make a good impression."

He shouldn't have been surprised. He had been apart from his family during the pandemic for nearly two years, and even then, when he'd finally returned home, Dad hadn't been home.

Giving a small nod, trying not to be disappointed, he went to bed.

Four hours later, as Sarika puttered around his room and asked him questions about New York, he wasn't sure he was ready to make an impression on anyone.

Payal had been so frustrated. He could sense it from a mile away, and on some level, he had empathized with her anger at herself and the roadblocks to success she was facing.

He'd believed, erroneously, that if he showed her he had faith in her and made her laugh, perhaps she'd warm up and she'd know he was trying to make up for their fiery dinner date. He couldn't blame her one bit for not trusting him.

It had backfired. And Ayaan was tired.

"How is it going getting to know Payal?" Sarika asked, always reading Ayaan's face like a book.

"What made you think I was thinking about her?"

"I can see it."

"I think I bit off more than I can chew."

"With Payal or with life?"

"With every single bloody thing."

Sarika's sharp features softened and she sat on the end of Ayaan's bed. "Tell me about it."

He recounted the dates he'd had with Payal—even admitting they'd hooked up prior to any of this—and explained how he kept viewing these opportunities as fresh starts, only to dig himself deeper into rather than out of the hole he was in.

"Aww, Ayaan," Sarika said softly. "That doesn't sound easy."

"It's fun figuring that out, when no one has confidence I'll do well at Veer either."

"Hey!" she cried, indignant. "I believe in you!"

He gave a tight smile but didn't say anything.

"Be you," she said. "You get in your own way trying to be someone else. You're exceptional when you're effortless."

She stood, gave him a quick kiss on the forehead, and left the room.

Ayaan stretched his arms above his head.

His room was a snapshot of the life he'd lived in London.

He loved to read—a little-known fact about him that people didn't seem to pick up on because they assumed he was a partying frat boy who didn't care about literature. But two floor-to-ceiling bookshelves chock-full of colorful spines stood one on either side of a big-screen TV that was a few years old now.

His MBA diploma from NYU Stern—the reason he'd moved to New York in the first place—hung here instead of his apartment in Manhattan, as though he had to ensure his family saw it and knew that he was accomplished and dependable.

The memory of his days at school caused his eyes to drift to the corner he didn't often observe—a bulletin board full of photos of his group of friends, including a few mutual friends he'd shared with Payal, medals from football matches that he'd won, and concert ticket stubs from his favorites: Coldplay, Death Cab for Cutie, and U2.

He turned his gaze away, determined not to dwell on the past.

Today was one more chance to start anew.

Chapter Twelve

PAYAL

Of the small talk Ma had greeted Payal with, she only added one statement of any value: "Dress nicely."

Of course, Nani had responded with "Payal always looks nice," which had heartened her, but Payal had understood the message.

Her cobalt-blue kurta didn't hit her at the knees but was at midthigh instead and skimmed her waist. Glistening glass beadwork formed the shape of a peacock up the left shoulder of her top, tightening around her chest and baring her right shoulder. A small bow of beaded georgette tied her top on. Her pants, a bright parrot green, were cut like a dhoti around her legs. She had fashioned them into a feminine statement, as she often did, having her tailor stitch the folds into place and embroider each fold with beads.

A dupatta draped over one shoulder and down her arm—and this was the piece of work she was most proud of. The dupatta served as the embroidered feathers of the peacock adorning her tunic. Decorated with teal and blue beadwork, with silvery middles, the plumage was set against a thin, green georgette stretch of the scarf. The dhoti bottoms were baggy, comfortable, and contrasted with the tightly fitting top, giving Payal a good balance of dignity, tradition, and fashion-forwardness.

As always, no matter how foul her mood was, her attitude transformed slowly as she dressed in Indian clothes. She was hardly a wreck, even on a bad day, but wearing clothes from India lent her a touch of royalty that she carried with her.

She'd designed this one herself, stitched by her family's tailor in Delhi, who knew exactly how Payal loved her fit—tight but breathable—and whose skill matched Payal's vision to a T. This tailor had linked her with family members who worked as artisans, and now the entire group fulfilled Besharmi's orders at fair prices, working with Niyathi on fits and with Saachi on design to pull off the entire effort.

Payal brushed her long hair, smoothing it down with a touch of oil and adding a twist from her side part to just behind her ear. She did the same on the right side and brought the two twists together, effectively tying her hair half up and letting the rest cascade down her back.

She'd decided to incorporate a soft glam face into her look for the evening. She smiled wryly, knowing that what most people considered a soft, natural look often was created with more product than could ever be considered natural at all.

She spread some primer over her smooth brown skin before adding foundation, concealer, setting powder, and blush. She brushed eye shadow over her lids—gold, with deep plum in the crease—and carefully painted eyeliner along her lash line. She used her favorite mascara, a thick coating that turned her big eyes from beautiful to exquisitely sultry.

Raj drove her family to Ayaan's home, which also happened to be in Wimbledon on Cottenham Park Road. Despite their families being so close in distance, she hadn't met them often, though she'd recognize their faces in a room.

As they pulled into the driveway of the sleek, white home, she glanced up and thought the Malhotras had lit up the entire house like it was Diwali.

They were fifteen minutes past the start time of seven thirty, and Payal's stomach sank looking at the clock, glowing in the front of the car.

When they rang the bell, Bhoomi Aunty answered the door, dressed in a shimmering purple sari with gold paisley print.

Ayaan's mother had the friendliest face...round, a little less firm than it was twenty years prior, but she had soft features that made Payal think of kindness. Her eyes drooped slightly in the corners, and her full smile, which only got bigger when she saw Payal, crinkled her eyes, making her crow's-feet more prominent.

"Hello, hello! Welcome!" she cooed.

"Hi, Bhoomi!" Ma practically sang back. "We're so sorry we're a bit late."

"No worries at all, Roopa. We all operate on IST. I can't remember the last time I was on time for anything!" Aunty replied good-naturedly.

Payal watched as Aunty greeted her mother, commenting on the parrot-green shade of her sari, telling Nani she had missed her homemade rotis that reminded her of home, and giving Papa a namaste and telling him she was very happy that they were able to take a night off from work to come discuss all their future ventures together.

There was no doubt: Ayaan's mom was the peacemaker, the angel, the kind person sent to allay any unrest.

"We're happy to be here. I look forward to meeting Ayaan and knowing the happiness he'll bring to my daughter," Ma said, as though she had any idea what made her daughter happy in the first place.

Nani put a reassuring hand on Payal's back and patted it gently.

They all trudged into an enormous living room, adorned with white couches and pillows decorated with silver and gold embroidery. A fireplace protruded into the middle of the room, contemporary in style, with glass on either side of the fireplace allowing anyone nearby to see through it to the other side.

As the others took their seats, Aunty and Payal had lingered, the last to enter the room.

"These are for you, Aunty," Payal said softly. "Happy Valentine's Day."

She handed Aunty the bouquet of two dozen roses of red, orange, and pink hues, ornamented with baby's breath.

"These are stunning!" Bhoomi Aunty replied. She handed them gently to another woman Payal had vaguely recognized as Ayaan's sister-in-law, who'd seemingly appeared out of nowhere.

"Can you take these and put them in a vase, my dear? Let's set it into the middle of the coffee table so they're seen."

"Yes, Mummy," she said with a smile.

"You know, Payal, we are so happy to have you in our family," Aunty said warmly. "We're thrilled you made time for us this weekend on such short notice. It's been so long since we've seen you!"

"It has," Payal replied. "Thank you for having us!"

Her heart lifted an inch or two. In her mind, everyone had an end goal or bottom line related to this marriage—including her, she supposed, with the promise of not having to go back to work—but Aunty's eyes were different. Rather than projecting images of a merger contract being signed, work situations being sorted out, or money changing hands, Payal simply saw her reflection.

Someone was happy she merely existed. What shouldn't have felt like a revelation was indeed one of epic proportions. Payal took Aunty's hands gratefully.

"Thank you," she said again in a whisper.

"I know my son has had…missteps. But I knew when I heard that you were living in New York, had a degree from a great school, and a wonderful job—and now Ayaan says you are pursuing another dream of fashion—that you might be just what he needs."

"How?" Payal couldn't help but wonder.

"Sometimes people with wild hearts or who wander too much just need a little guidance. Someone to help them along. Ayaan is a smart boy and he's always done well, but I hope that he'll learn to take things more seriously with you around. I hope you can find magic together while discovering some stability."

Aunty had such hopes for their future. Payal pretended to smoothen the eyeliner under her bottom lid to ensure her tears didn't fall in front of all these people.

You're pursuing a dream of fashion. How often people hid their passions behind their backs instead of owning them for all to see. While Payal was fearless and confident with anyone else who'd asked what she was up to, speaking to elder Indians somehow didn't prompt the same brazen attitude. She had tucked away her dreams instead. "I'm working PR for a major firm right now… andrunningafashionlineontheside," she would rush through, as though if she said it quickly or quietly enough, no one would catch it and be able to judge her.

But Aunty had sounded so proud, as if breaking out of the box of acceptable professions was admirable and exactly the kind of relentless dream-chasing Ayaan needed.

The motherly warmth was so foreign to Payal that she simply smiled and nodded.

"Come, come. Let's introduce you all... Ayaan! Your fiancée is here!" she called up the stairs.

The word *fiancée* nearly made her flinch. Payal was reminded of being a teenager, when her parents or Nani would have to call for her to come downstairs before she'd leave the sanctuary of her computer, internet, and DVDs.

Kuljeet Uncle, Ayaan's dad, and Arun joined the others first.

Ayaan's dad, like Papa, was wearing a tailored suit, as though this family gathering was, in fact, a battle between lions in the wilderness. Payal would bet money on the competitive instinct in the room driving both of the older men to act like alphas, determined to dress, act, and present themselves as the best.

Arun wore a simple red kurta. The warm tones complemented his wife's peachy salwar suit.

"Neeraj! It's good to see you!" Kuljeet Uncle bellowed, sticking his hand out for Papa before pulling him into a warm hug.

"Uncle, hello." Arun gave a warm smile and touched Papa's feet in a traditional sign of respect before touching his heart. "This is my wife, Sarika."

Sarika stood again. "We've met already, Arun. Roopa Aunty and I were just talking about how delightful Mummy's cooking is and how she's worked all day on dinner."

One thing was for sure...the manners in this family were impeccable, the tradition strong. *What the hell had happened to Ayaan?*

As though he'd heard her, he descended the stairs, swinging around the end of the banister as his footfall landed loudly on the floor.

"Hello, everyone," he said. Pausing for a moment as everyone watched, he clumsily put his hands in a namaste before going directly to Papa and shaking his hand. He touched Ma's feet and she gently patted his head as he rose.

"Look at your manners, Ayaan. Bhoomi, you did wonderfully with your boys."

Payal nearly pulled a muscle fighting an eye roll.

As Ayaan passed Arun, she heard Arun mutter, "Really? Jeans and a dress shirt? You couldn't bother with a salwar or a suit?"

Ayaan closed his eyes for a heartbeat and clenched his jaw before opening them and seemingly plastering a smile on his face as he strode to Payal.

"Hi." He parked himself in front of her, blocking her view of the others.

She could feel their eyes on this interaction.

"It's nice to see you," she said.

Ayaan went for a hug just as Payal reached for a handshake.

"Oh—er—" she mumbled.

"Sorry," he said.

He stretched his hand out right as she moved to hug him, and his hand stabbed her stomach.

"God, I'm sorry—"

"It's okay. It's okay," she said, forcing her face not to wince.

"Well, clearly, Ayaan is smooth," Arun joked.

"Just some jitters, eh, Son?" Payal's dad said, marching up behind Ayaan and patting his back.

"Anyone would feel jitters with Payal," Nani said.

Everyone in the room laughed except Payal, who scanned the room for a window to jump out of. Ayaan's chuckle had seemed perfunctory.

She would have told Kiran or, better yet, Sonam to utilize the emergency system women often used to get out of a bad date, like texting them "911" to receive a sudden call faking an emergency, but she could tell her parents all her best friends were in various hospitals sprinkled across the United States, on the verge of meeting their creators, and Ma would probably request they stifle their death rattles until dinner was over.

Nope. She would have to endure.

As they sat around a colossal dinner table that seated nine people with ease, Aunty glanced at the ravenous faces scouring the table for what they'd be eating.

"I made chicken makhani. You know, it's a British-Indian dish from colonial rule but Ayaan loves it so much. I'm certain he was a carnivore in a past life. Probably a dinosaur." Aunty laughed. "I try to make it anytime he's home."

Payal met his eye for a second, knowledge dawning on her about his preferences and why he'd looked uncomfortable at the vegan dinner. He was a comfort-food kind of guy.

"Payal used to say warm Horlicks made her think of me at boarding school," Ma recalled. "I believe food memories are real. Think about how home cooking doesn't just remind us of our own homes but of India itself."

She glanced at her mother in surprise, shocked that she'd remembered that time when Payal was fourteen and she'd tearfully requested the drink from the cook at school because she missed home.

Then she remembered she was at a dinner with a family she'd been promised to and that it was not actually her mother who had provided the warm Horlicks for most of her adolescence. The nostalgia evaporated quickly after that.

"So, Payal, tell us about the line. What are you working on? What inspires you?" Sarika asked, doling out dal makhana, sarson da saag, the chicken, and karahi gosht with remarkable efficiency, all while keeping her attention engaged with Payal.

Ayaan followed her and handed her each person's plate, surprising Payal with his willingness to help.

The eyes shifted to her, and she grew warm, aware that her answer was not just an expression of her latest project but a projection of her potential.

"I was accepted to Fashion Week a few weeks ago for a runway show," she started, to the sounds of impressed murmurs. "It'll be a part of an ensemble show with feature designers. They aid in PR, interviews, and provide hair styling and makeup, and I'll present eight outfits. My outfits are largely inspired by the South Asian diaspora and different traditional wear from India, while balancing concepts of the West. For example, I've taken Kancheevaram saris from South India and created power suits and blazers in brighter colors and with gold borders at the wrists and ankles to emulate jewelry and royalty of old. I like mixing styles because I'm mixed in terms of culture," she said.

"Not so out of touch that you wouldn't do this for your family," Aunty said.

If only you knew I had to do this for me.

"How do your sales look?" Arun asked rather abruptly.

He was clearly not one for the touchy-feelies.

"I've made quite a few bespoke pieces so far, and an influencer recently bought one of those power suits and put it on her social media, so I've received a sizable bump of about twenty-five additional bespoke orders in the last month or so. It's growing."

"That is impressive. Ayaan will be a great fit for you then, as his marketing skills can take some of that responsibility off your hands."

"Mmm," agreed Payal.

Ayaan nodded along. "I look forward to it."

"Do you like living in New York?" Arun asked. "I always wondered what the appeal was. Ayaan hasn't sold it too well, I'm afraid."

Payal tried not to frown, though it was as if Ayaan had personally affronted her. "I like apples, so I figured moving to the biggest one was the best idea," she said with a laugh.

It was a dad joke that they ate up.

"Seriously, though, I'd love to hear your thoughts," Arun said when his own chuckles had subsided.

"You all know what it's like to feel your potential, to grow beyond your boundaries, to build something and watch it shine. Everything I've experienced from university at Duke to life in Manhattan has been a living example of that same feeling. I can't ask for more than to know I've fulfilled a greater purpose. The traffic is atrocious, but are we going to pretend Central London is any better nowadays?"

"She's right. It took us twenty minutes to go less than a kilometer the other day," Uncle conceded.

As Payal fielded questions and built a rapport with these strangers, she grew less conscious of herself...less like she was facing an interrogation and more comfortable in her own skin and the role she quite literally had at the table.

She couldn't remember the last family meal she'd had around the dinner table at home.

"Uncle, how's Veer? You seem to be quite determined yourself, given its impressive portfolio."

"Well, my dear, you have to be to get anything done in the world."

"Do you ever want a break?"

He laughed. "I don't know what I'd do with my time."

"I think you've earned a flight to Fiji and a drink in your hand, don't you?" Payal teased.

"Why else do you think I'm passing Veer on to Arun and Ayaan? Both the wealth and the stress should be distributed to my boys!"

Payal laughed. "I'm sure Ayaan and Arun are more than capable. They'll be glad to take it off your hands."

"She's not lying," Arun said with a grin. "I'm excited for the new role."

Ayaan nodded and offered a small smile but said nothing.

The boys, despite their similarly handsome features, had differences that came out in telling ways.

Arun was handsome. Just as Ayaan had a head full of hair, Arun was coiffed within an inch of his life. If he put any more product on his head, he'd look like Jimmy Neutron. He had narrower eyes than Ayaan—where Ayaan's were large and almond-shaped, Arun's were downturned. Ayaan's smile was shyer than Arun's—as though Arun was used to throwing his head back when he laughed while Ayaan looked down and chuckled into his chest.

Most of all, Arun looked like he wanted to be here...and Ayaan looked like he wanted to be anywhere else.

Payal wondered if they got along and if they shared the types of conversations she always imagined siblings having. It was a bond she never got to experience because Ma had been so ill during her pregnancy that her parents had decided not to put her through it again. But she saw Sonam fight with her brother with all the love in the world, Akash's sisters treat him like a baby, and Kiran go on a mission to find her sister and end the family rift just to understand what to do about her own relationship...and Payal longed for the same.

But she felt the pull of family tonight, of nights around a table and togetherness. Sarika had been in this family for some time now, and Payal wanted to pick her brain to understand what it felt like to be surrounded by laughter.

"Sarika, what do you do?" she asked.

"Everything," Arun said simply before Sarika spoke. "She is

everything. I'd argue she's one of the best things to happen to our family."

The pride in his eyes put a lump in Payal's throat.

"Hear, hear," said Ayaan, and he showed more enthusiasm than he had all night. "Sarika is the best."

"Well...if I'm allowed to speak." Sarika laughed. "I work at Veer now in the PR department, but when Arun and I were first married, I worked as a publicist for Disney. I did my MBA at LSE."

"That is impressive!"

"She was at the top of her class. Sarika is a champion at keeping her head in crisis," Ayaan said.

"We're very lucky," Aunty said, blowing Sarika a kiss with both her hands. "She keeps Arun's temper in line and supports Ayaan's ideas."

"That's amazing. You're a superwoman. Oh my God, Aunty, this karahi is to die for." Payal groaned as she closed her eyes and relished the flavors of the lamb, cream, and spices coming together on her taste buds.

The rest of the room laughed.

"Look at this poor girl. We're barely letting her eat," Aunty said warmly. "Everyone leave her alone so she can enjoy her naan in peace."

As the conversation carried on among the others and she learned a little about each member of the family, Payal noticed that she was the one commanding the room, whether by her explicit involvement in guiding the conversation or the implicit need of others to include her. Her parents had barely spoken, watching Payal interact with unrecognizable expressions on their faces. Papa had been watching Payal chat with Uncle about business, and his face had a genuine smile most of the time, occasionally defaulting into an unconscious frown. Was he puzzled at his daughter's ability to be loved? Proud? And Ma had done what she always did: laugh, sit, and chime in occasionally but largely remain on the outskirts of involvement. Nani had injected wit when she could.

It was Payal who was at ease, deftly handling the attention and loving the laughter.

What a welcome sensation it was to feel powerful.

· · · · · · · · · · ·

AYAAN

Ayaan couldn't stop staring at the clothes everyone was wearing—funny, since Payal, who was making a living off designing them, didn't seem to be fixated upon them at all. After years of attending South Asian events, he knew exactly what clothing conveyed—and it was never as innocuous as families tried to portray. Like everything he'd experienced so far in life, and in particular with this matchmaking scheme, these relationships were transactional.

Both the fathers were dressed as though they were attending a business dinner…which, he supposed, they were. The mothers had worn saris with just enough embroidery to convey social status and financial security but simple enough to be deemed approachable, warm, and maternal.

Arun had worn a red salwar kurta as the paradigm of the prodigal son, alongside Sarika who looked like the ideal daughter-in-law in a beautifully embroidered coral salwar kurta with a pale-green dupatta covering her chest. The image of Arun appearing the traditional, kind older child benevolently wishing the best for his brother gave Ayaan the impulse to laugh, and he coughed as he choked it back.

Payal questioningly glanced at him before deeming him unworthy to pay attention to.

They had chattered their way through dinner, with Payal handling the questions as though she were dodging a media firestorm. She was graceful, humorous, and relaxed in the face of a tough crowd. Yet Ayaan still wanted to run out of the room.

This was *work* pretending that they'd had positive feelings toward each other, when the reality was that the two of them couldn't seem to find the same page to land on. Every time Payal pushed, Ayaan pushed back. When she pulled away, he wanted to run. Weren't relationships supposed to be a balance?

At the very least, the people involved had to be fighting for the same thing to make something succeed.

His mother's shout of "Your fiancée is here!" had made him want to piss his pants. How was this normal?

And with the pressure of their parents watching them, Arun shooting glances at him every time Payal said something funny, like "Look at what you're missing out on appreciating!" and Sarika's occasional penetrating gaze to see how he was doing, Ayaan felt forced, as though someone were gripping his head in place and forcing him to watch the scene.

His panic was reaching peak momentum when Arun said, "Well, when you and Ayaan get engaged, we'll have to go to Sussex for a wine tour. A friend of mine from business school is a sommelier and his wines are exquisite."

The prospect of a double date with Arun (but Sarika!) made Ayaan need to get some air.

"Excuse me," he said, and he pushed his chair back and stepped into the kitchen. "I'll get another bottle of wine."

That was what he needed to take the edge off. By the time the bottles on the table had made it to him, he was nearly taking in fumes rather than drink, and it was the perfect excuse to knock back a few glasses alone.

But he couldn't bring himself to drink his anxieties away. Instead, he filled a glass with water and dropped half a glass of ice cubes in, relishing the coolness as it froze his throat, slowed his breathing, and soothed the torrent in him.

The freeze of cool water was far better than the burn of a drink.

The family's kitchen was one of Ayaan's favorite spots in the house. Airy, bright during daylight hours, and, given the enormity of the house, a relatively cozy country-style room with beams in the ceiling, this space held some of Ayaan's best memories.

He remembered sitting on the counter as a little boy while his mom cleaned and plastered his deeply scraped knee when he fell off his bike. He and Arun had grown up doing their homework at the island, next to each other, and he could distinctly remember asking his older brother for answers. Arun would give none on principle but instead would spend immeasurable time walking Ayaan through processes for answers.

Their grandmother, Mum's mother, had lived with them until he was fifteen. She'd died before he'd gone away to university. But how many nights had he rolled out rotis with her because she'd insisted the boys should learn to feed themselves?

He'd been in the kitchen getting a glass of chocolate milk, his I-had-a-bad-day indulgence, when Arun had called from the hospital to say she'd passed away.

He gave a shiver, trying to shake out the remnants of the memories that made an already anxious mind turn down a morose road.

The door to the kitchen closed behind him and he jumped.

Arun stepped into the kitchen and moseyed over to the wine fridge, opening the door painfully slowly and pulling out a bottle of pinot.

"It astounds me how many bottles we go through at these dinners," he said, looking at the bottle in hand and giving Ayaan a shrug. "But at least everyone is having a good time!"

His tone was surprisingly soft.

"I know. Wine doesn't feel like alcohol when we're drinking it though—at least until the next morning," Ayaan said.

"Tell me about it. Remember how we used to drink a bottle in an hour and feel great the next day? These days, I won't drink a thing and I still feel as though my body has started cracking in new places every time I roll out of bed."

Ayaan gave a small laugh.

Arun set the bottle on the counter and awkwardly paused there. Ayaan gave him a questioning look, unable to read his brother's mind—and filled with memories of days at this counter when he thought he could.

"Are you happy?" Arun asked suddenly.

"Do you only talk to me to antagonize me?" Ayaan snapped, unable to hold back a visceral, angry response to any prodding.

"No," Arun said, and for once, he didn't seem like he was trying to poke a bear. "I was genuinely curious. Obviously you're committed to this farcical situation, but since you seemed to be all in, I figured you'd be spending more time with her. I had hoped you'd be happy or, at the very least, not look like someone was skinning you alive."

Ayaan was stunned that his brother was perceptive enough to recognize that he was out of sorts.

"And that begs a question... Are you doing this to get back at me?"

Anddd we're back, Ayaan thought.

"What the hell—"

"If you're doing this as a retribution thing, I have to say,

Ayaan, you're being a selfish prick. You and I don't see eye to eye, and we both can come to terms with that. I haven't made it easy on you either, and I'll be the first to admit it. No, I mean it," Arun added when he saw Ayaan's accompanying eye roll. "But please, don't put two family businesses at risk for this game you're playing. I can't believe I have to say this to you. No matter how much shit I give you, I thought you'd be better than that."

Though he was firm and admonishing him, Arun was astonishingly placid in his delivery.

He took the bottle and left his younger brother in the wake of his words.

A light flickered inside Ayaan.

When his friends had called him on his self-sabotaging behavior and his attitude, he'd let it roll off his shoulders. Their opinions held value, but he felt comfortable living his life on his terms regardless.

But when Arun, the brother who had held Ayaan to a higher standard and berated him when he didn't meet the bar and whose approval Ayaan quietly and desperately wished for, mentioned that his behavior was unkind...that struck a nerve differently, more rawly than Ayaan had experienced before. This advice was coming from the Arun who Ayaan had idolized and been best pals with for his entire adolescence, the one who always encouraged Ayaan to be better...the one who inspired Ayaan rather than inciting riots in him.

Payal didn't deserve to be collateral damage in his scheme.

And the truth was that she did deserve better.

She had risen to the occasion beautifully, despite reservations he knew she had to have too. She had mentioned multiple times she was doing this for her family, and Ayaan couldn't imagine that type of sacrifice.

Maybe she did deserve more credit for what she was giving up. Payal Mehra was a pain in the ass, sure, but she'd still done something noble for someone else so she couldn't be all brat, right?

He heaved an enormous sigh, willing perspective and level-headed calmness to shape his next move.

He returned to the dining room where the families were mid-guffaw about a story from Arun's childhood when he visited the petting zoo and got kicked by a donkey.

"Ayaan, you've been awfully quiet tonight," Payal's dad said.

"I was just thinking about how the moment that Arun landed ten feet back, permanently imprinted by those hooves, was the pinnacle of my life," Ayaan joked.

"Who knew I could fly?" Arun laughed.

"So, Payal, what did I miss?" asked Ayaan.

She appeared surprised, her mouth dropping a bit. She recovered quickly and, with her eyes darting around the room, conscious of her reaction, she replied, "We're talking about your childhood experiences. Arun was saying you were the perfect child when you were younger."

"Yeah, when you were younger," Arun joked. Miraculously, instead of going into detail, he continued. "But I guess that's everyone, right? Ayaan really hit his stride at LSE and NYU—he's found his niche over the last few years. He's still a superstar when he puts his mind to something."

Ayaan gave him a grateful smile. He knew, deep down, that those words weren't for show, and the swell it gave his heart suddenly made him ravenous.

"Did anyone have a favorite tonight? Because I think my mom is right. Her chicken makhani is one of my all-time, go-to dishes."

"I agree," Payal said. "It was an exceptional meal, Aunty."

"Well, we still have dessert...kheer and some Hyderabadi sweets I picked up," Mum said.

"Mum grew up in Hyderabad since her dad worked for the railways," Arun explained.

"It feels like home to me!" Mum said warmly.

"And we got the benefit of eating all the good desserts." Ayaan laughed.

Payal smiled. "When I was little, Nani used to raid the fridge with me and steal the burfi in the middle of the night. We'd sneak back to our rooms and eat, always laughing because it was our little secret."

"Your parents knew," Payal's nani said.

"They didn't!" Payal's eyes widened.

"Yes, we did," Aunty said. "You weren't quite as stealthy as you gave yourself credit for."

Payal frowned and made a face like she was disappointed she had been disillusioned about her childhood memory.

"If it makes you feel better, Arun actually stole all the candy I received on my birthday from my piñata, but he did it little by little, so one day I opened my secret hiding spot and it was all gone," Ayaan offered.

Payal's lips curled upward.

"He thinks it was a secret hiding spot. He put it in his piggy bank and left it on his bedside table," Arun said.

"I thought the piggy bank was smart!"

Arun laughed.

"You boys seem so close," Neeraj Uncle said. "Have you always been that way?"

"They were inseparable when they were younger," Dad said. "You know how it is between brothers. They distance themselves a bit as they get older."

That was certainly sugarcoating it. Awkward silence followed Dad's white lie. Ayaan felt Payal's gaze on him and grew warm under her keen observation.

"Well, I don't have siblings, but I'm not sure I'd be smart enough to hide anything either," Payal offered, and to Ayaan, it sounded as though she was sweeping in to make him more comfortable.

As they finished dinner and leaned back, satisfied, Mum offered to clean up and serve dessert in the living room.

Ayaan stood and as the others moved to the other room, he lingered, collecting plates so his mother wouldn't have to do it alone. When he turned, he nearly ran into Payal, who had her hands outstretched for the pile he was holding.

"I can take it," she said softly.

Ayaan noticed how exhausted Payal looked. While her makeup was impeccable, there were light bags visible if one looked closely enough, and she seemed to deflate once she wasn't surrounded by people.

He wondered if he was contributing to it.

This was what he'd always wondered about—what it would be like to feel comfortable at a family gathering. What it would be like to have someone who fit into the chaos, saved him when he needed a rescue, and completed his team. Tonight had turned out well, to the surprise of all those involved.

When he handed the dishware over, feeling her fingertips gently graze his, their eyes locked and an unspoken agreement seemed to pass between them. *I'll try if you will.*

Chapter Thirteen

PAYAL

All in all, it hadn't been a horrible experience. In fact, Payal had even enjoyed herself. She would be the first to admit the notion surprised her. She'd never imagined herself actually feeling relatively comfortable in a family meeting without dating first, never mind with a setup by her *parents*.

But her cousins had arranged marriages and it couldn't be all bad. Her friend from high school, Esha, had a bouncing baby girl with her husband, who she'd been set up with right out of college. And Payal didn't judge the way they met when they got married, so who was she to think she was above the same situation?

But she *was* above this selling out for her family's business, no? Any woman was above this.

Then again...Ayaan was pleasant by the end of the night. He was funny. He seemed at ease with himself, and that was the biggest weakness in a man for Payal—someone who effortlessly found his place in the world and who would conquer it with her.

But what had prompted the change?

She had noticed that he was quiet for the first half of the evening, subdued and near jitters. She could relate to the nerves, though she'd come out on top of them. She'd also sensed the contention between Ayaan and Arun, a push and pull of respect and disdain that changed rapidly, and she couldn't quite put a finger on.

She had to take it for what it was…an evening full of community that had led to a sense of understanding between the two of them by the time her family left the Malhotras' home, well past two in the morning and only after multiple rounds of desserts, chai, and drinks.

They'd discussed the merger as well—a brief conversation revolving around the word *engagement*. She'd watched Papa and Uncle do a handshake deal on the fact that their children were now unofficially engaged…that the engagement would be formalized in ten months, by which time all the contracts establishing the merger of Veer and Luxuriant would be completed.

The notion that Veer would acquire Besharmi wasn't explicitly discussed but it was insinuated that if she and Ayaan got engaged, the partnership was potentially on the table.

"Do you…maybe want to do something in the city?" Ayaan had murmured to her as they watched their parents say a long goodbye in the foyer, as Indian families often did—drawn-out goodbyes that sometimes led to one more chai or coffee before terminating the night for real.

"Sure. I'd like that," she replied cautiously.

"And Payal…happy Valentine's Day," he'd said just before they'd left the house.

Endgame. You have to think about what's in this for you.

Nani woke her the next morning, gently pushing her shoulders until she opened her eyes.

"You have a flight to catch tonight, and I wanted some time with you," she said, putting a cup of chai on the bedside table.

"I haven't even brushed my teeth, Nani." Payal gave a small laugh.

"It's okay. Drink the chai. Your parents' rules about hygiene before breakfast aren't meant to be followed if they can't see you breaking them."

Payal took a sip of the sweet masala chai, pursing her lips together and giving a contented sigh. "This tastes like Kiran's."

"I think you mean Kiran's chai tastes like mine."

"Obviously…you are the original."

"How are your friends doing?"

Nani had heard all about her and her friends' exploits in college and the less wild but equally unforgettable nights that they'd shared as adults in the city. In some ways, Payal suspected Nani lived to hear the stories as much as she loved to tell them…for someone who hadn't been afforded the freedom to be educated and who was married off and weighted with motherhood by her early twenties, Payal's tales of adventure must have come as vindication that at least one woman in the family had been privileged enough to chase her life rather than be caught up in it.

And to Nani's credit, she had never judged the decisions Payal and her friends made.

"Akash slept with a girl and then she dumped him," she'd said once in a raw moment where she'd forgotten her audience and the double standards rampant around sex.

She had covered her mouth then, terrified she'd betrayed Akash's secrets and, worse, shamed a woman for having a healthy hookup, all to her grandmother who had grown up in a conservative society.

Instead, Nani had responded, "Good for her. Akash is a good man, but perhaps she needed better."

Since then, the filter was nonexistent.

"Kiran and Nash are happy," Payal said now. "Akash is dating around but he hasn't found anyone yet. Sonam is busy with her residency and hasn't dated anyone since college...or ever, really."

"How did they handle your news about Ayaan?"

"Oh, they all hated it. Akash took it the hardest."

"I always thought he had a thing for you."

"No," Payal said firmly. "We are just friends. But he is protective."

"Well, don't be too hard on him for it. He's looking out for your best interests."

"Is Ayaan my best interest? I can't tell."

"He certainly seemed nice to you by the end of the night. He seemed apprehensive at first."

Payal rolled her eyes. "I have no idea how I feel about him."

"Well, I can't imagine having six pairs of eyes on you was easy...but the benefit is that you both live far away. While I personally despise that fact, you have some freedom to be kind and know each other away from prying eyes."

Payal nodded absentmindedly. "Our definition of family is so strange sometimes."

"Family is what you make of it. I saw how you warmed to Bhoomi quickly last night. Feeling a little motherly bonding?"

Nani's knowing glance hit too close to home for Payal and she looked away, choosing to take another sip instead.

"Payal, some mothers don't have the instinct. Yours still loves you. She doesn't know how to show it, that's all."

"I'm aware."

"But if you find camaraderie in Ayaan's family, perhaps it's worth exploring, and you'll be able to fund your line. Ultimately, your happiness matters more than anything else. If you decide Ayaan isn't worth it and he isn't supportive or you don't have chemistry, don't hesitate to walk. I will always flank you in a battle. You'll never be alone."

A lump formed in Payal's throat. "You'd fight for me?"

"You keep acting as though my old age keeps me from raising hell."

"No, I know better."

"You should. I raised your dad, after all, as well as his brothers. I grew up on a farm, for God's sake. I'm no delicate flower."

"You're very tough," Payal said, humoring her but knowing that her grandmother was 100 percent correct about her tough skin.

When Payal waved goodbye to her family who, for the first time, came to the door to wave her off as Raj drove her off to Heathrow, she felt a spark of optimism that she'd be okay with whatever future came for her.

Ayaan would fly back the next night after finalizing some business with his dad and the company. Payal was on her own for this flight, and she used the time to message with Niyathi about the next designs she'd conceptualized and make appointments to meet with Saachi.

When the flight landed at JFK and she'd arrived back at her apartment, Payal went to her bedroom and peered under her bed frame.

No one had ever noticed the musty old box underneath her bed at Duke or tucked into the back of her closet in her Manhattan bachelorette pad. She liked it that way. It was a hokey old thing, something no one would ever guess she'd buy, what with her penchant for Prada and Chanel. But when she saw the gently battered keepsake box on a tampon run to a generic retail store, something about it spoke to her.

The gold paisley on pink-and-lavender-watercolor print reminded her of the embroidery work she'd seen on her cousin's wedding lehengas. Maybe it was the nostalgia of an Indian wedding itself, which she hadn't been to in a few years. She wasn't sure, but a compulsion to buy it overwhelmed her, and before she knew it, she walked out of the store $19.99 poorer.

First, she'd placed her jewelry in it—but the outer facade of the box didn't suit the jewels inside. On a whim, as she went through her semesterly routine of replacing the photographs on the mirror of her vanity, she tossed them in the box and felt as though the box had come to life, containing pieces of her heart that were the closest to her.

And so it became the holder of her deepest desires, the one she didn't speak of to anyone. A photograph of her family—the people she never wanted to admit she missed. A cutout from one of those hokey Bollywood magazines of an advertisement displaying a family adorned in wedding wear—the family she wished she had, happily smiling at nuptials in resplendent outfits and thrilled at one of their own tying the knot. A picture of the CMC at a bar for someone's birthday—Kiran's twenty-first, maybe? She had been the last to turn twenty-one, nearly a year younger than the rest. A photograph of Payal with her parents on the day of her Duke graduation, where Papa had uttered rare positive words about her: "My daughter graduated from Duke! This proud papa will be happy to hand over the company now."

It was one of the only times in her life that he'd said he was proud of her.

The box had remained something only for Payal until recently when she divulged its existence to Kiran—Payal had used it to tell Kiran, during the depths of her struggle over her family's lack of acceptance of Nash, that in a twisted way she had been jealous that Kiran had a family who loved her so very much.

Ayaan *had* that family. Aunty's eyes lit up when she mentioned him. Sarika—God, what would Payal have given to have someone so sweet as a role model in her own family? Even Ayaan's dad and brother seemed to welcome her home with more warmth than her own parents.

She imagined him having those dinners every time he was back in London, basking in the light of his mother's glow and belly-laughing with his dad about the latest antics he'd been up to in New York.

She wanted that. And she'd enjoy it until she no longer could.

. . . .

AYAAN

The flight back to JFK was endless and he hadn't even left the runway yet.

Plagued by mechanical issues, the flight had been delayed first by an hour, then by two. Now, thanks to a delay-ridden traffic jam, the flight was tenth in line to take off at 7:30 p.m., putting his arrival at nearly midnight.

Ayaan pulled out his phone, thanking his stars for internet access. He clutched a soda in his left hand as he opened Instagram and mindlessly scrolled through photos of his friends and strangers with his right.

A photo of Payal had come up with her grandmother, both of them laughing at a joke he wouldn't ever hear. Nani was wearing a white sari and Payal's white salwar was beaded. Her dupatta draped gently over her chest and shoulders, and the composition of the photo was bright, as though it had been taken in a sunroom, with couches in the background but abundant light everywhere.

Out of curiosity, Ayaan pulled up Payal's profile. He hadn't viewed it yet, determined not to care about her or tie himself to her in any way, including social media connections...the weakest and strongest links there were in today's society.

For as social and business savvy as she was, he would have expected more frequent posts, a profile full of videos, photos, and information about the intimate details about her life. He didn't know why he thought she'd be the type to share the minute details of her day, but he had fully anticipated her documenting the coffee she drank in the morning, the brand of dress she wore to lunch, a photo of her outfit of the day, a sketch about her latest design, and a video talking about the most recent fashion faux pas.

Instead, he saw that she posted once or twice a week, all about her line and her life, but still unreachable somehow...*kind of like she is in real life.*

Payal was still a bit of a mystery.

Her bio read: "London bred, New York bloomed. Founder of Besharmi. Fashioning a statement life."

Catchy.

He scrolled through her profile, clicking on various photos and learning what he could, impressed by her aesthetic: a combination of black-and-white photos and bold colors that had been edited to appear more raw and ragged.

The same three faces appeared in the occasional photo of her with anyone else—two girls, one with sharp features, long hair, and a kind smile, and another with short hair shorn at the shoulder and a rounder face. A dude was in them too, a handsome guy who looked to be about five eleven and the type that Ayaan would have detested. Payal had photos of the gang of four at a winery in upstate New York, at lunch in front of a greenery wall, and in front of the Brooklyn Bridge with pizza slices.

One particularly sweet photo, even by Ayaan's standards (his feed was primarily food and travel), featured them looking years younger at what appeared to be a basketball game, decked in Duke University gear. Payal had a thick Duke scrunchie around her high ponytail and wore a blue crewneck sweatshirt with "Duke" written across the front and blue jeans. She had a fake tattoo or sticker on her left cheekbone.

These friends had been around a long time. He wondered if they knew about him.

The rest of the photos he scrolled through were a mix of highlights of her career and cityscapes of both London and New York. And the highlights were impressive. There were images of clients who were styled by Payal during her stylist days, and within the last year, she'd begun wearing many of her designs out and about, serving as her own marketing department.

She had been invited to the premiere of a Hulu show based on Hindu mythology and wore a lavender sari dress, strapless and cinched at the waist with the ornate gold border embellished with sequins and beads hitting her midthigh. Gold glitter pumps had elongated her legs so she looked like a model.

In another, she was dressing Sheetal Pandya, a Bollywood actress who had recently crossed over to Hollywood and who had worn one of Payal's designs to her movie premiere.

All in all, Ayaan thought, Payal was impressive even if inconsistent with broadcasting her achievements and processes.

He could work with that.

His conversation with his dad the night before, the reason for his delayed return to New York, hinged upon one critical point: that his CMO position was guaranteed only if Payal's company was acquired and successful in the meantime. He had his work cut out for him...but the conversation had inspired Ayaan to take charge.

It was risky to take charge in this way—to spread the word that Payal's line would be related to the expansion of Veer. He couldn't come out and mention the acquisition openly in case the entire plan fell through. Neeraj Uncle didn't seem like a man who would go back on his word about selling his company, but then again, contracts weren't finalized and Ayaan knew better than to assume it was a done deal.

Opening a text message, he typed out a simple message. My friend Payal has an incredible fashion line for South Asian women that I'll be doing some work for. Would you do me a solid, follow her, and share her profile if it fits your aesthetic? He hit Send to all the acquaintances and friends he'd chatted with, whether he'd met them at Neha's fashion shows or through parties.

Then he opened up his laptop and opened a new email to all the marketing contacts he knew.

He drafted an announcement similar to a press release, crafting a message around his work for an upcoming fashion brand and that he wanted to tell people about it, given how stunning it was. He catered the message to women, particularly those in their twenties, thirties, and forties, and ensured that he mentioned the gifting possibilities fashion provided for people who had no idea what to buy the loved ones in their lives.

"Good evening, folks. We're next in line to take off and we appreciate your patience…"

Stowing his laptop and phone away, Ayaan hoped that there would be a slight bump for Payal's fashion line and that he, in turn, would get the cogs moving on developing a larger presence and successful sales strategy.

As the plane crossed the western border of the United Kingdom an hour later, he began doom scrolling again.

Neha had posted a photo at one of their favorite rooftop spots, the Press Lounge, in Hell's Kitchen. She was wearing a black strapless dress, and she was surrounded by a number of friends, all of whom were involved with the entertainment industry in varying capacities and whose names Ayaan only remembered because he could call on them for favors.

He added them to the text list.

Then he glanced at the photo again, noticing that Neha's arms and legs were endless, displaying her tanned skin and proportions. If there was ever a revenge photo to post, this would have been it.

Except they hadn't talked about the fact that Ayaan was being pressured into committing to Payal. They hadn't even met up since their last blowout fight—and Ayaan suspected that if they followed through on their recent text exchange, sex would have been an inevitable consequence of the reunion.

Perhaps it was better to remove temptation. Payal deserved some level of commitment, even if they weren't in a relationship. At the very least, she certainly didn't deserve him sleeping around with his ex-girlfriend whose manipulation of his phone had gotten him into trouble in the first place.

He hoped Payal was doing the same, turning down the suitors—and Ayaan had no doubt there were many lining up to impress her—out of...maybe not affection. But hope. Respect. Anything at all other than nonchalance.

He found himself not wanting to have the conversation with Neha over text, an instinct contrary to all the times over the previous year where they would have long text messages go back and forth to discuss their feelings, involved enough to want to argue and uninvested enough not to do it in person like adults. The only times they wanted to talk in person tended to lean toward more of a physical reunion and less of an effort to quell any mental unrest.

It felt childish all of a sudden. Indirect and cowardly.

He admired that Payal, for all her brazenness and stubborn attitude, wore her emotions on her sleeve and didn't hide them when she was upset or angry. He wasn't used to it. He also didn't lack the self-awareness to recognize he himself didn't do the same. He was a runner and he knew it.

Taking a deep breath, determined not to screw up one more time, he messaged Neha.

Ayaan: I'm back around midnight—do you have time to chat on
the phone?

Neha replied quickly. I can come over.
Ayaan responded, I'm not sure that's the best idea.

Neha: If you're going to end it one more time, don't bother
with a phone call.

Ayaan dropped his head in frustration. He was trying to do
the right thing, for God's sake.

Ayaan: I'm sorry. I have some family commitments and changes
happening with life. I want to do the right thing.

He could hear the rage in her voice and recall the cold stairs
against his ass as he read her response.

Neha: Please. You've hardly ever made the right move in your
life. And we always do this song and dance—you realize
you miss me and I, for whatever godforsaken reason, miss
you and we end up together again. Let's see how long this
lasts, Ayaan.

He began typing a response, one that was calmer than perhaps
he would have responded with even a month ago, but he changed
his mind. He wouldn't drag this out. He wouldn't go back. He had
to do the right thing.

He had to give Payal a chance.

Chapter Fourteen

PAYAL

During the next week, Payal noticed a sizable bump on social media—shares of her posts and mentions of her account had shot through the roof, and her followers across all platforms had increased by nearly *eight thousand*. The power suits she'd described to Ayaan's family were the biggest hit, with comments on the posts talking about the luxury, style, and East-West fusion of the pieces being memorable.

And a photo of Payal—wearing a lilac sari jumpsuit with the sleeveless top half and the bottom half designed to appear as though a dhoti had wrapped around her legs, belted with a silver sequin oversized belt she'd bought from Promod on a trip to London and minimal jewelry save for the shine of the silvery-white border—went viral, earning another few thousand people following her. It was one of Payal's favorite photos, editorial in nature, with bouffant hair and dramatic eyes, in an alleyway in the West Village where it hadn't looked like anyone had passed through since the eighties unless it was to do drugs. The stark contrast of the darkened walls, brick path, dumpsters, and fire escapes to her glowing, light-filled look was captivating.

Sometimes it took one person to share an image they'd seen of a brand or entity they liked, and the middle of the Venn diagram they'd create between the liker and the brand would get bigger and bigger with more exposure.

Payal couldn't sort out who the influencer was behind the scenes, but her name was getting out there. She was flooded with requests about pricing, and in just one week, Niyathi had been given so many assignments that she'd brought on another assistant to help her with the workload. Saachi had hired more tailors.

Then, on Wednesday evening, about ten days after she'd arrived back from London, an email pinged in her inbox.

Dear Payal,

My name is Tarika and I'm on the hunt for a dress for the summer premiere of Karmic Connection, a show on ABC that follows five single South Asians on their quest for love. I recently saw your design with the purple sari dress (you called it "the Sonam" on your photo, if that helps— it's so bold!) and I'm OBSESSED. I was wondering if you could create a bespoke one for the premiere, preferably in a mint green, for me. I would be happy to post it all over socials as I'm a content creator as well. P.S. I heard about you from Ayaan Malhotra if that helps.

Ayaan?

Payal frowned. They had texted a few times since they'd both arrived back in the city, mostly memes or quick check-ins to make sure nothing worthy of a missing persons documentary had happened to the other. They hadn't even been bothered to schedule the dinner date he'd proposed.

He had never mentioned this.

She hoped he wasn't telling people about the acquisition yet. This was all behind the scenes until the engagement and announcements.

She unlocked her phone, opened the app, and went to his profile. The image of the dress, the one that had gone viral, had been posted to his account with the caption "If there's a brand that nails culture and class, it's this one. Besharmi by Payal Mehra is one to watch... I'm calling it now." It had over sixty thousand likes and each little double tap was like a hug.

He'd posted it a week ago, at the same time that he'd started following her—Payal had tried to be nonchalant about it when she saw the notification—which meant that this bump very well could have come from him.

Was he sorry for all the barbs they'd thrown at each other? Was he doing this to showcase his talents for Veer?

Obviously he has some stake in this. But they'd never talked about it. He had no idea what direction she wanted to go in.

Annoyance flicked at her insides. *Of course he would act without asking her what she wanted for* her *line.* But the irritation faded quickly, replaced with something resembling gratitude. He'd done nothing but post about her line. He'd shined a spotlight and utilized his networks to help her, and despite her suspicions about his motives for the assistance, he had lifted her nonetheless.

She responded in the affirmative to Tarika and asked her for her availability to talk through her thoughts, get her measurements, and toy with some fabrics. Then she called Saachi and Niyathi, certain that all of Manhattan had heard their excited cheers about landing this bespoke opportunity.

Then she texted the CMC.

Payal: So…Ayaan posted about me on his Instagram and he
  has 500K+ followers.

Akash: I have 300. No self-respecting man cares that much.
  He's a douche.

Payal: My sales are up and Niyathi had to take on an assistant
  to help her fulfill them all since he posted.

Akash: Okay, so he's a douche with sheep.

Kiran: I think it's kind. He talked you up and people saw the
  talent.

Sonam: Agreed…and can I just say once again this is weird?
  Anyway. Whatever his motive and whatever he posted, it
  helped you and that's the endgame.

Payal: What do I do now?

Sonam: The nice thing to do would be to thank him.

Akash: Yeah. Thank him for helping you, and then while you're
  talking, tell him you aren't down for an engagement.

Payal: Not an option right now, but thanks.

Kiran: Perhaps you can take him to dinner or something since
  the last was not the best impression.

Sonam: Maybe you can actually get to know him while you're at it.

Payal set her phone on the couch next to her and turned her
head to stare at her work space in the apartment.

The corner was covered in framed prints of fashion
illustrations—long, lithe watercolor images of brown-skinned
women in sky-high heels, with big hats, flowy dresses, and global
locations spread behind them. Among them were cutouts from
magazines and printouts of flowers, quotes, skylines, and all the
little things that sparked life in Payal's imagination and caused her
to draw. This corner, the messiest in her otherwise pristine apartment, was her home. It was where her dreams came to life.

And Ayaan had helped her inch a little closer to the life she'd wanted.

At the very least, she owed him a thank-you.

Picking up her phone again, she called him.

"Payal! Hello!" He sounded cheerful.

"You posted about me," she said.

"I did."

"Is it any surprise you'd do that without actually talking about where I want to take the line?" she asked, and she hoped he'd take her teasing to heart.

"It boosted you, didn't it?" he asked.

"More than you know. Thank you."

"You're welcome. You deserve it. Your line is stunning, Payal. I hope you don't let anyone tell you differently."

"Why are you being so nice to me?" She couldn't help herself.

He paused and quiet fell on the line in between them. "Because I know this situation is strange…and you were wonderful with my family. Because I felt terrible about our last dinner. I can write you a list if you'd like."

She gave a giggle. "Well…that's a good start."

"I mean it."

"Well, I'd like to thank you and I was wondering if you'd go to dinner with me. We can do something afterward. To repay you for your kindness and the opportunity you sent my way."

"I'd love to."

Payal released the breath she was holding. "Sounds great. Friday night?"

"It's a date." He must have realized what that sounded like to two people who had been forced together and then he corrected, "And by that, I mean it's on my calendar and we shall go to dinner…and something else."

On Friday evening, Payal waited just inside Baar Baar NYC. She was ten minutes early this time.

The restaurant had an aesthetic that Payal's entire brand could get behind. Upon entry, her eyes were drawn to a beautiful circular chandelier, designed so that the light bulbs formed leaves of a vine growing from its metal base. Plush velvet booths in mustard yellow and teal curved around wooden tables. The far wall had a giant art print of a fierce South Asian woman with a sari turban, bejeweled with a heavy matha patti, jhumka earrings, and an impressive nose loop. The ferociously determined expression on the woman's face, her eyes outlined with black kohl, was like hearing a rallying cry.

Not that Payal really needed it today—her outfit made her feel like a boss. Under a black leather moto jacket, she wore a red cap-sleeved sheath dress. Black high-heeled boots reached her knees, boosting her frame to nearly six feet. She'd finished her look with smoky, bronzed eye makeup and a deep red lip color that matched her dress.

"Ah, so you do know how to be on time," Ayaan commented.

"You'll never let me live it down, will you, chicken makhani?"

"Did you just call me chicken?"

"Yes...and for the record, I've vetted this menu and I think you'll be thoroughly satisfied."

A mischievous smirk crossed his face, and Ayaan opened his mouth but then appeared to think better about making a smart comment back. "I really like the look...and I vetted the menu myself."

"What, you don't trust me?" Payal teased.

"Maybe I wanted to make sure it went smoothly instead. Their catchphrase about Indian heritage through a New York lens was catching."

He'd read the website. A flutter went through her. "So...you haven't been here?"

"No," he said.

"I'm surprised!"

"I stick to old favorites."

"That's interesting."

"Why?"

"Because you're the kind of guy who loves trending topics and fleeting ideas. You thrive on the next one! I guess I anticipated that you would be the person who attends every opening of a brand, gala for a cause, and restaurant on a watch list."

Ayaan fidgeted and gave what Payal could only imagine was an uncomfortable laugh. "Not quite. I have attended all those—and I pay attention. I find trends really fascinating. How they rise. How they fall. If they don't fall, then what's keeping them ahead of the game? It's more about the strategy and the thrill associated with it than it is about the trend itself. But for my own personal experiences, I'm a creature of habit. Maybe because my brain is wired most of the day to look for anything but."

It made sense to her but... "I can't relate. I like being kept on my toes."

"Evidently, since you never quite stop keeping people on their own." He gazed at her.

A shiver went through Payal, warm and full, at his voice and intensity.

She hadn't noticed before that the black dress shirt he wore over his deep-blue jeans were making his skin glow and that his eyes, normally dark brown, seemed to have taken on a lighter tone underneath the dim lights.

"I try," she replied weakly. "So...what do you want to eat?"

His gaze lingered on her lips before going back to her eyes.

The same naughty look from before appeared across Ayaan's face again. He cleared his throat before he answered. "Why don't we share a few different dishes?"

Payal had grown warm under his watch and had known exactly what he was thinking. After all, she had wondered about his abilities at using his tongue, just before remembering exactly how it felt. She looked down at her hands and counted to three, breathing in and out in time.

"That sounds great," she said.

After a meal of avocado and green chickpea bhel—"ugh, veggies," Ayaan had moaned before proclaiming it "delicious"—and lamb keema Hyderabadi—"Now this is what I'm talking about!"—and finally, their entrees of paneer pinwheels and beef short-rib curry, Payal could hardly move.

"I'm stuffed," she proclaimed, shifting her weight to accommodate the fullness in her stomach.

"Me. Too. How do people come up with creative ideas like these? I never would have thought to mix some of these ingredients."

"I guess that's what happens when you grow so familiar with your craft."

"You'd know best. How do you come up with your designs?" Ayaan asked. "What made you get into design once you grew out of your sewing machine?"

Payal leaned back, still tasting the different tangy, spicy, sweet, bitter, and savory flavors on her tongue and envisioning herself putting together designs with the same ability to combine elements. "I realized how different outfits made people stand differently, walk with more elegance, carry themselves with power that they hadn't owned before...and I put together designs from looking at...well, everything. The violet of the clouds when it's just rained and the sun is setting. The power and vulnerability of a priest when they wear a dhoti and invoke God. The way a red dress feels like a power move." She gestured down her body with her hands.

"It was an effective one," he said. "And I find that fascinating."

"You do the same, you know. You capture lightning in a bottle and light the way for people you're working for."

"That's an impressive way to put it," he murmured, not breaking eye contact.

There it was...the electricity passing between them and the light it ignited inside her. But maybe it was something new: mutual admiration. The gentle tug of respect pulled at her heartstrings.

"Speaking of design...are you ready to go to part two of our thank-you night?"

"Should I be nervous?"

"No...I think you'll find it very cool."

After paying for their bill—Payal brought out the credit card and insisted on covering the tab this time—they called an Uber to ride the admittedly short distance to Chelsea.

The wondrous wide eyes and open-mouthed awe on Ayaan's face as they walked into Artechouse in Chelsea Market were worth a million dollars.

A combination of art, technology, and design, the dark rooms and displays focused on the construction of fractals, mathematical formulas creating shapes and dimensions. While Payal couldn't follow the exact science of it, she valued what the fractals were being used to do.

The famous painting *Nighthawks*, by Edward Hopper, was digitally superimposed along one wall with an animated hologram depicting the same bar in the current day. The juxtaposition of history from the 1940s and present day were what Payal loved about London and New York, and seeing them live in a renowned painting filled her with awe.

Ayaan walked slowly along the same wall, his eyes seemingly hungry for every small detail.

"This is so cool," he murmured as Payal walked next to him. "And look at this fractal stuff...who knew?"

He stood in front of a display that sensed the movement of people's hands, curling his fingers and using them to pinch and push air as fractals on a screen in front of him transformed according to his movements.

"I don't understand," Payal admitted, frowning at the screen.

"Here, let me show you," he said. He stepped slightly behind her right shoulder.

He took Payal's hand and pried her fingers apart gently, coaxing them into circles and showing her how colors and details shifted.

Payal tried to ignore the goose bumps on her arms and hoped he didn't notice.

"It's strangely hypnotizing, isn't it?" Ayaan murmured, and his breath tickled her ear.

Payal didn't answer. She was too busy holding her breath, attempting not to be hypnotized herself.

When others entered the chamber to toy with the same demonstrations, they broke apart.

"Want to go downstairs?"

Both Ayaan and Payal had deliberately avoided looking at their right side as they'd viewed *Nighthawks*. If they'd paused to look, they would have spoiled the magic of a massive room being enveloped by color, loud and soothing instrumental music, and art.

Holding out until now was the best decision they could make;

Payal inhaled sharply as they descended the stairs into the room and were sucked into a dystopian world of color.

"I've never done a hard drug in my life, but if I did, this would be the place," Ayaan said.

Payal laughed and shushed him, gesturing to the benches in the back of the room, where they sat.

"This is..." Ayaan's voice trailed off.

"Yeah." Payal filled in.

It was as though they were traveling through Alice in Wonderland's skewed fantasy of odd shapes, movement, and not-quite-real landscapes full of color. The projections encompassed all the walls of the room and the music pulsed through them, making them feel like they were flying through a foreign world.

"The CMC would be tripping out watching this," Payal said without thinking.

"What's the CMC?" Ayaan asked with a frown, turning to her.

"I have three best friends. They're like my family. We call ourselves the CMC—the Chai Masala Club."

"That's cute. What are they like?"

"Sonam is an explosion of a human being. People have called her too much, but I think she's so much. She's loud, bold, and funny. Kiran is soft, sweet, and currently dating an American named Nash. That's a story for another day, but it was drama!" She flicked her hand to embellish her tale. "Then there's Akash. Neither of us will ever admit that we're basically the same person."

"He's the only guy?"

"Yep. Poor thing has to deal with all of us, and we gang up on him sometimes, but he's a pro. Besides, he has sisters and he understands it's a woman's world and he's living in it."

"You've never dated?"

Payal paused, knowing the question was coming. It always did, because the idea of a guy and girl simply being friends was never simple enough for most people. She also felt the heat rise in her cheeks, aware that her ability to lie was questionable at best.

"No...but we may have met because I flirted with him."

Ayaan laughed, but not unkindly. "And he didn't take the bait? What was wrong with him?"

Payal grew amused. "We were better being best friends."

He seemed to speak without thinking, not even looking at her as he continued watching the colors around them. "He missed out."

Payal couldn't help but smile, and she turned away, staring at the current landscape projecting all around them: a strange world of rolling hills of green with rainbow orbs floating above each mound. She was reminded of being on a golf course.

"Who are your friends here?" she asked him.

Their bodies were so close, the heat from Ayaan's warmed Payal's skin.

"My two best friends are Dharm and Kai—Kairav," he corrected. "Except no one calls him that. I have known them since business school at NYU. They're cousins. But it's funny, I never feel like I'm the odd one out when I hang out with them. It's like I'm that third cousin they've been missing the entire time, and I know so many of their childhood stories."

Payal nodded.

"I'm sorry. I must be boring you," he said.

"No. Not at all. You remind me so much of myself when I talk about my best friends. I'm just marveling at how similar the feeling is...of a found family and how you can belong in a group that wasn't around since you were born but know you better than the people who were."

"Exactly!" he exclaimed. "A found family…"

Ayaan frowned and Payal wondered what had crossed his mind. When he spoke, he surprised her.

"My former boss, Greg, is getting married in a couple of weeks. I have a plus-one. It was supposed to be Neha—" he said this last part with hesitancy. "But I'd love it if you could come with me."

The softness, the uncertain question coming from a person who was perpetually cocky, prompted Payal to smile. "I would love to."

And she was surprised at how much she meant it.

Chapter Fifteen

Ayaan remembered the marble lobby of Payal's building and how furious he had been when he'd charged out of it last—but he was the opposite of angry this time. Instead, he carried a small bouquet of bodega flowers he'd picked up around the corner.

He didn't know what type she liked, but he'd seen lilies in her apartment before, a detail that had stuck with him, and he'd hoped that the half dozen he was holding would be received well.

He knocked on her door, exhaling deeply to release any jitters.

Footsteps resounded in the floor, thumping underneath Ayaan's feet. The door opened.

Payal was breathtaking.

Her body was accentuated by a long dress with pink, orange, and red abstract flowers adding a pleasantly colorful effect to the dreary winter months they were in. The dress was pleated at the waist, and Ayaan had to draw his eyes away from how perfect her breasts looked. Her hair was parted in the middle, slightly wavy and down over her chest. She wore a blue cashmere scarf over her shoulders and draped over her arms.

"Wow," he breathed.

"You're not too bad either," she said with a radiant smile and a wink.

He'd spiked his hair in the front, spent more time than he would ever admit on his skincare routine, and worked out this morning, knowing he'd look stronger if he felt stronger. His smoky-hued suit only added to his swagger.

"I tried. Sadly, sweatpants weren't appropriate," he said, pretending he hadn't thought through every detail. "I got these for you, by the way." He thrust the flowers out to her.

She lit up, her cheeks reddening. "These are my favorites."

"I noticed the lilies by your bed last time. Thankfully, the flowers aren't apologies or bribery, so we're off to a better start."

To Ayaan's pleasant surprise, she laughed. That mentions of their inauspicious start now brought a chuckle rather than irritation was progress.

"So how awkward was it asking Greg not to put Neha's name as a guest and to put mine down instead?" Payal teased as they settled into an Uber after making small talk about the weather and how March had been a little more pleasant than they'd anticipated.

"Greg is super chilled out. He probably expected chaos."

"And Zara? What's she like?"

Ayaan marveled at her memory. He had mentioned Greg's fiancée's name only once and Payal had kept it close. Strange how these small gestures seemed to mean the most.

"She's elegant. Not uptight. The few times I've met her, she's been so cool. I am certain that tonight will be beautiful, if not for Greg's taste, for Zara's."

"I love weddings!" Payal burst out.

Ayaan observed her childlike uninhibited enthusiasm as she

clapped her hands together. "Let me guess… You've had yours planned since you were a little girl?"

Payal grinned. "Not one. Damn. Thing."

"Really?"

"I love weddings for other people!" she corrected. "I love the way two people look at each other—usually, because I did go to an Indian wedding a few years ago where the groom had taken celebratory shots and couldn't walk in a straight line…dangerous when you're going in circles around a fire, and the bride yelled at him and then the priest actually poured water on his head—but the optimism they usually carry when they look at someone else who just promised to spend their entire lives making them happy. I think babies and weddings are two of life's celebrations that give people immense hope for the world, even if it's not a decision that's right for everyone. I like basking in other people's wins… but I've never been able to envision it for me."

"Payal Mehra, closet romantic. Who knew?"

"I always thought…" she said slowly. "If I'm meant to be with someone, I'll want to make the effort. Life won't be only about me and my interests anymore because I'll be making his better too."

She'd put words to his yearning. He'd wished for the same on nights when he'd seen Arun and Sarika laugh, a tenderness appearing in his brother that didn't present itself to anyone else but that Ayaan knew to be the best of him.

They pulled up to the venue, thanked the driver, and Ayaan walked around to open the doors and help Payal out of the car and onto the curb.

Her hands were like butter, and her fingers were long as they curled around his. She let go as soon as she'd stabilized herself.

The wedding was taking place in the Glasshouse, with the ceremony on the fourteenth floor and the reception on the twenty-first.

White cement walls were broken up by floor-to-ceiling windows and provided triple exposure to the Hudson River, downtown, and Midtown. It was a simple, classy space for someone who had the clarity of vision to turn it into whatever they wanted.

Zara's elegance was on show for the guests, in the form of long baskets with white roses, flickering white candles, and more white and blue flowers in gold-trimmed mason jars neatly lining an aisle. Chiavari chairs sat on either side of the aisle in front of a white platform stage holding a square backdrop of what looked like a gold wire bookshelf—except it was massive and the shelving was made of mirrors. Candles sat on the mirrored shelves and were punctuated with more white dahlias in golden mason jars.

Fairy lights twinkled from the ceiling, as though the event was being held under the stars, and they were cocooned further by the sweeping views of the Hudson River with the twinkling lights of New Jersey in the distance, Midtown with all its hubbub, and downtown with all its power.

Ayaan couldn't help but marvel at how beautifully the photos would come out against a setting like this.

"Wow," Payal whispered as they stepped into the dimly lit, romantic room.

"Tell me about it," Ayaan whispered back.

They chose seats on the left side of the room on chairs wrapped with a white, shimmering bow across the back.

Ayaan placed his hand on the middle of Payal's back to guide her to their seats. When she started and turned to him, he pulled his hand back suddenly, apologetic and hoping he hadn't crossed a line, but her smile, one of reassurance, warmed him and he put his hand back, daring to move his thumb against her toasty skin visible in the dress's split back.

He could have sworn she gave a shiver, and it was so reminiscent of the night they'd spent together, of the responses she had to his tongue in places no one here would ever see, that he had to do long division to keep himself from getting a hard-on.

The lights dimmed, the way they would at a theater before a show, and the murmurs did a decrescendo to the occasional whisper.

The doors opened and Greg walked in with his four groomsmen—his brothers and cousins, from what Ayaan had gathered at work—and they took their standing positions on the stage in front of the audience.

Greg made eye contact with Ayaan and gave him a glowing smile and a nod.

He wore a black tuxedo, a bow tie at his neck, and his grooms-men were in matching sleek black tuxedos, with bow ties in a blue that reminded Ayaan of Mykonos.

When a gentle piano tune breezed across the room and the bridesmaids had gracefully completed their coordinated walks, Zara glided into the room in a resplendently white gown.

"That is a *dress*," Payal whispered.

Ayaan looked at Payal again, and her eyes were slightly narrowed in an expression he had seen not in her but in himself. Her wheels were turning, and she was building something in her mind.

Payal's eyes hungrily took in every detail of Zara's one-shouldered beaded dress that clung to her bronzed body near her chest and cascaded loosely down the rest of her as she floated down the aisle with her father.

Not wanting to interrupt Payal as she designed something, Ayaan turned back and they all sat again to witness the ceremony.

As Greg and Zara said their vows in front of their loved ones, Ayaan shot a quick glance at Payal and noticed tears in her eyes. Pulling a handkerchief from his pocket, an antiquated habit that he had learned from his father, he handed it to her and she glanced at him with grateful humor as she dabbed at her eyes.

"Why are you leaking?" he whispered, leaning over.

"Be good," she murmured back, so quietly he barely heard her.

"You don't like that."

She stifled a giggle and continued to watch the couple at the altar.

"On my worst days, I will seek shelter in you, and on my best, I will lift you to your greatest heights," Zara was saying.

Ayaan hoped that wishes came true, even when wished for through glass windows and on other people's promises...because if he ever made one, it would be for the very same thing Zara was vowing now.

Payal, next to him, was enraptured, her glassy eyes slowly blinking back tears, a faint smile on her face, nodding along with every proclamation the couple made to each other as though she approved of every word and was prompting the next.

"I present to you, Mr. and Mrs. Burton!"

The guests stood, clapped, and cheered, all while tossing rose petals that had been provided in cones tied to the chairs in front of them. Ayaan couldn't help but be endeared by Payal celebrating the union of two people she didn't know as though they were her closest friends.

Servers glided around the room with platters full of spanakopita, Brie and fig jam on crostini, and mini quiches for a cocktail hour before guests were seated for dinner.

"Are you always hungry?" Payal asked, amused, as Ayaan took another serving of the crostini.

"I'd say I'm a growing boy, but I just eat a lot."

The next hour was a whirlwind of speeches and thank-yous and the most delicious chicken dish Ayaan had ever tasted.

As people began to move to the dance floor, Payal and Ayaan lingered at their table, taking in the atmosphere.

Greg and Zara approached Payal and Ayaan as they made their rounds.

"It's so nice to meet you," Greg said, shaking Payal's hand.

"We've heard wonderful things about your line," Zara added.

"From Ayaan?" Payal shot him a surprised glance.

"He's been telling all of us, his clients, his friends... I think you have a fan," Zara said.

Ayaan's cheeks burned and he tried not to meet Payal's eye, watching the bar instead. He was afraid that if he looked at her and saw gratitude—or worse, for whatever reason, any bewilderment—he'd feel something greater...that he'd see potential in her eyes, and when he inevitably screwed up, he would break up these beautiful memories with ones of disappointment.

"Well." Payal spoke again when Ayaan wouldn't look at her. "That's sweet. I'm glad I have him on my side."

He snuck a look at her then, and a smile passed between them like a secret.

Payal turned back to Zara. "Your dress is stunning, by the way...and, Greg, you look incredibly dapper."

"For the one and only time in my life, I'm afraid," Greg responded.

"Untrue, but I'll let him believe it so his head doesn't get too big," Zara said.

As they headed toward the next table, Greg gave Ayaan a fist bump and said, "I like her!" as he pointed at Payal.

Something about the compliment, that had nothing to do with him and everything to do with her, stirred a swell of pride in Ayaan's chest...especially when he saw that Payal had heard, her expression growing softer at Greg's words.

"Well, well. You are a hit."

"I try, sir." She curtsied with her long gown.

"So…now that they've gone on to the next table, and we don't need to be on our best behavior…"

"Want to get a drink?"

"I totally thought you were trying to lead this conversation, and potentially me, elsewhere."

"I'm virginal, so I have no idea what you're talking about."

"Yes, and I'm the pope."

The teasing and banter continued as they went to the bar.

"I'll have champagne, please," Payal said.

"I'll have an old-fashioned to go along with that," requested Ayaan.

They stood in comfortable silence until the bartender passed them their drinks.

"Do you want to dance?" Payal asked.

"You know that stereotype about Indian people being able to dance or sing?"

"Yes…?"

"I am the exception."

"You are not. Everyone can dance."

"I can't."

"Maybe not *well*. But you *can*."

Ayaan rolled his eyes. "Oh, so you're going to catch me on semantics."

"Yes. Because it matters what you think you can do!"

"You're a pain in the ass."

"Coming from the guy who has shown his ass multiple times, is that saying much?"

Ayaan couldn't figure whether he wanted to fire back or laugh.

She had downed her champagne and gestured to the bartender for another, flashing him a giant smile as he passed it to her.

"Okay, fine. My shoes might be killing me. We may need to sit." She winced and rolled her ankles.

"Aren't you into fashion? Shouldn't you know that kind of thing about what you're wearing? Functionality versus...style...or something like that."

"Functionality doesn't always make you feel good."

"I think the entire purpose of functionality *is* to feel good."

"No...think about a good—" She struggled to find an example, and he suspected that the alcohol was already going to her head.

"Oh! Think about a vibrator."

"Come again?"

"Exactly."

He rolled his eyes.

"Some vibrators are built for functionality. They're small. They have one speed. They're meant to be used discreetly. Theoretically, they're perfect. But maybe they don't feel good or fill you up or vibrate the way you need. Maybe you need the one that looks nice, or has a wonky shape, or does something a little different... and when you get it, this funny-shaped, unconventional vibrator, it rocks your world."

"Vivid description," Ayaan said, trying not to let his imagination run wild.

"Functionality doesn't meet your needs then. You need the fancy one."

"Your shoes are the fancy vibrator."

"My shoes make me feel sexy as hell," Payal finished with flourish.

Ayaan considered it.

"Okay, I concede."

"Good. Let's sit down."

"So...do you have a vibrator?"

"Wouldn't you like to know?" Payal asked with a twinkle in her eye.

She gestured for one more champagne flute before they went to their dinner table.

After having chattered away for the last few minutes, the silence from Payal was a little disconcerting. Ayaan wanted to hum "Yankee Doodle" or tell a terrible knock-knock joke just to fill the quiet.

"What did you think of—" Ayaan started.

"You know what I loved the most today?" Payal said at the same time.

They laughed nervously. Payal gestured for Ayaan to go first.

"What did you think of the wedding? I figured you would have an opinion since you turned the waterworks on," he teased.

She laughed but she was subdued. She wrung her hands lightly and her shoulders drooped a little.

Ayaan began to grow alarmed that he'd done something wrong—though he couldn't figure out what—before she spoke.

"It was absolutely beautiful," she said softly. "Have you ever looked at two people and thought 'My God, there is no denying you're meant to be'? That's how I felt looking at them. And the elegance of the decor...this beautiful city surrounding us. It was the perfect setting."

Ayaan filled with pride as though he'd had a hand in tonight's beauty. It was inexplicable. The awe in Payal's voice at the glimpse into Ayaan's life—however peripherally or through his friends—was so novel.

"Someday, at my wedding, I'm going to have giant carts of

Indian street food, Mexican tacos, Thai noodles, and no one will have a sit-down dinner because they'll be too busy stuffing their face on all the good things we grew up with as party foods instead."

The sudden turn in conversation stopped him short.

"What about naan, tandoori chicken, roast meats, and alcohol? People can't have all that and still only have street food. They need a solid meal," Ayaan protested. "And a place to sit."

This felt like a funny argument. They were supposed to be getting engaged...fake, of course, and certainly not happening, yet they were talking about weddings without any implication of their future at all. Odder still was the way they disagreed, like a married couple might.

Ayaan's mind spun.

"I'd have places to sit. I'm not a heathen!" Payal said. "But they won't be tables. They'll be laid-back couches and chaises strewn about a garden, where people dance and lounge and see the stars and eat and chat with friends."

"That's so many things at once," Ayaan said with a laugh. He sipped his drink.

Payal nearly slurred her words, already four champagne glasses in. "Because *I'm* so many things at once."

"You're not lying," he said.

She was so close to him. Her body heat, that soft skin that had made him crazy only a short time ago, was inches away.

But she proverbially and literally stepped back, sitting up straight again and adding distance between them. "But marriage probably won't happen for me."

The air sucked out of this moment, this tiny, happy place that they'd escaped to for a few minutes. Ayaan tried to recover.

"Why do you think that?"

"I've never been in love," she confessed, swaying in place. "I wouldn't even know what it looks like."

"Ever? Even like puppy love?"

"Nope."

"Why do you think that is?"

"Not the right person. Not my thing. Not what I'm used to." She shrugged. "There's an endless list of reasons."

"But Kiran and Nash, and exes, and your parents—you've seen love before."

"My parents." Payal laughed, part bitterly and part just used to the truth. "They hardly talk. And yeah, my friends have a lot of love. I don't deny it exists at all. It just never happened to me."

"Do you have hope it will?" he murmured.

"I do," she whispered back. "Someday."

Tingles crept up his spine. He didn't believe in déjà vu or psychics, but there was something, a change in the air, that tickled his senses.

The DJ's tunes were deafeningly loud and the bass pulsated through the floor like a heartbeat. But the intimacy of confiding their hopes created a bubble around them—one that Ayaan didn't want to burst.

Chapter Sixteen

PAYAL

SIX MONTHS UNTIL THE ENGAGEMENT AND FASHION SHOW

Payal crossed off the first two weeks in March as complete on the calendar stuck to her fridge.

She had six months until the Fashion Week show. Six months until the engagement.

Every waking moment she had, she'd spent sketching, on the phone with Saachi about fabrics, and talking to Niyathi about what she envisioned for the show, the food people would be served, the musical talent, and the logistical moves Niyathi would have to make on Payal's behalf.

Creatively, she was exploding.

She'd done research into the many ways that women tied saris in India, sometimes with six-yard fabrics and other times with nine. She'd spend countless nights wrapping chiffon, silk, and cotton around herself in twists and pleats to produce new takes on the same styles that women had worn for centuries, turning them into dresses, dhotis, and occasionally, when zapped with inspiration, repurposing the cloth into Western pants and blazers and tunics.

Niyathi had spent hours pinning the folds, measuring, and

taking photos to show Saachi, and the three of them had strategized endlessly on which designs were the best to put on sale on the website versus save for exclusive showings at the show.

Now, she was prepping for a meeting with Misha Singh.

Misha was the next obstacle Payal had to overcome in her quest to acquire enough funding to land Besharmi where it needed to be. Funding was required to create samples, hire another tailor full-time, and distribute. A venture capitalist who focused on both technology and fashion startups such as South Asian clothing rental companies and women's health technology apps, Misha was a Harvard grad with an impressive portfolio working for major banks across the globe before beginning her VC career.

And she was interested in Besharmi.

As Payal sat at her newly bought desk in the corner of her room, she stared at the social media and sales growth over the last month and a half and took a sharp breath at the results.

Ayaan's involvement and his calls to various pop-ups, boutiques, and influencers and website tweaks he suggested had led to 60 percent growth in only six weeks. He'd gotten even more followers and sales by filming her behind-the-scenes, encouraging her to do more video content, and utilizing more trends that she told herself she didn't have as much time to do before he came along.

She didn't want to do this without him.

She thought about the last few big outings she'd had between dinner and Greg's wedding and stared at the rose that Ayaan had swiped on the way out, now hanging from the corner of the bookshelf, laid out upside down to preserve its white color.

"What's this for?" she had asked at the door.

"You," he'd answered simply. "You can remember our night when you look at it."

She hadn't kissed him. He hadn't made a move. But the rose

reminded her every day that they could connect and that fire could still ignite in her heart when she looked at him...during the moments when she didn't want to throttle him.

Those moments of tolerance, even sweetness, seemed to have increased lately.

Whether she was "dating" him or not, one thing was certain: Ayaan was good for Besharmi. And he deserved to be in on the meeting.

"Ayaan!" Payal greeted him when he picked up the phone.

"Payal!" he echoed. "What's up?"

"I have a meeting with Misha Singh tomorrow."

"The investor?"

Payal could practically see Ayaan's ears perk up. "Yes."

"Do you need any help?"

"I was wondering if you wanted to be there with me."

"I would love that!" Ayaan sounded elated.

"Want to come over and we can sort through it?"

Two hours later, he was at her door.

"It's funny being in here," he commented, following her to the kitchen.

"Why?" She pointed at the wine she was uncorking at the counter to ask if he wanted some.

He nodded. "Because last time, if you'd had wine in your hand, you would have poured it over my head."

"You aren't wrong. But you have been exceptionally sweet lately, so you have earned yourself a free pass."

"I deserved that," he said with a grin.

"You can rest assured I won't throw you out this time," she said, handing him a glass.

"I appreciate that, thanks. And on a side note, I really appreciate you pulling me in on this meeting."

"Ayaan, there has been a huge bump in sales, in ideas, and in possibility since you began helping. It felt wrong not to let you be a part of the success that you're cultivating."

Ayaan's cheeks turned pink. "Thank you."

"Now...let's get to work!"

"I guess the moment passed, huh?" Ayaan laughed. "You couldn't even let me enjoy the compliment before you decided to run me ragged."

"Hard work never sleeps," Payal said, quoting Papa. She gave a small laugh at the unexpected reference. "My dad used to say that."

They sat in the living room, graphs and presentation slides printed in front of them.

"To be fair, I think all Indian dads follow that principle," Ayaan said.

"Do you think they ever knew how to live in the moment and forget the responsibility?"

"Maybe. I have to wonder if they had an intense work ethic because they couldn't quit...not because they didn't want to be in the moment. They probably felt so much fear that they'd lose everything from the prestige of being the first in a Western country, to the shame of being unable to care for their families, to sheer pride that they were the chosen ones, that they were unable to stop even if they wanted to. Then you get hardened by it and you don't know a different life."

Payal wondered if he was speaking from his own experience of wanting success or whether he was disappointed by the collateral damage of his dad's. Either way, Payal felt the urge to soothe the chaos in him and wipe away the expression of contemplation on his face.

"Well, maybe it's our turn then to take it on and let them take a break," she said. "Let's do this."

Payal showed Ayaan the graphs of the growth he'd fostered, and his eyes widened at the impact. He mouthed, "Wow," as he flipped through the pages of information carefully collated by Payal and her accountant, and when he glanced back at Payal, she knew that he had forgotten any sadness and that it had been replaced with inspiration.

They ordered Thai food and got to work.

It was near midnight when he slipped on his shoes again. She leaned against the front door, closing her eyes for a split second.

"You're exhausted," Ayaan murmured. "Have you been sleeping?"

"Sometimes," Payal said with a small smile.

He closed the gap between them, taking a step closer to her. She straightened up and met his eye.

"You are doing great," he said. He put two fingers under her chin and tilted it up to look at him. "But, Payal..."

She blinked slowly, willing her eyelids to stay open and fighting the beckoning of her warm bed. "Mmm?"

"Put yourself first. You can't sacrifice your health and the other things that matter to you for this dream. Stay in the moment."

His smoldering gaze drifted to her lips, and for a second, she thought he'd kiss her. He leaned in, and she tilted her chin up, closing her eyes and giving in to whatever happened with him.

He pushed his lips softly against her forehead. "Get some sleep," he whispered.

Ayaan put his hands on the doorknob behind her, and she moved out of the way, flustered as the air whooshed between them again and he brushed past her.

"Good night," she said.

"Sweet dreams. We have a big day tomorrow."

And with that, he was gone.

The next day, Payal was ready. She wore one of the dresses she'd designed, a shift dress in a deep red with gold brocade leaves that wound themselves around her. She put on a black blazer over the dress, hanging subtle gold hoops in her ears as accessories and tying her hair in a low, loose bun with tendrils that curled and framed her face to soften her look. Simple black pumps completed her outfit, and she looked like a million bucks. She quite literally was.

Ayaan had inadvertently matched her, she realized as she met him outside the nondescript building on Fifty-Fourth. He wore a dark-gray tailored suit with a maroon shirt in a shade similar to hers.

"Oh my gosh, we're twinning," Payal said, unsure whether to feel dismay at their identical look or to be amused.

"I prefer the synergy, which is what we'll need more than ever today," Ayaan said as he gave her a quick hug as a greeting. "You ready?"

"Born ready."

They entered the marble lobby and hopped onto the elevator, riding up to the thirtieth floor in silence. Before they entered, Ayaan turned to her and steely determination simmered in his dark eyes.

We're together and we are a powerhouse, they said.

Payal stared back. She knew her expression said the same thing.

Misha Singh was smaller than Payal had imagined, a woman of five feet and a short bob that reminded Payal of Sonam's. She wore a sleek black suit, cropped at the shin, on top of a hot-pink pair of heels...a bold accessory Payal loved. She already felt comfortable here.

"Thank you both for coming," Misha said. "It's lovely to meet you."

"We're so thankful for this opportunity," Payal began. "Let's get started."

Five minutes later, she was lost in her pitch, flowing seamlessly from one point to another in a nearly spiritual experience where her journey, her ethic, her work, and her ambition came together fluidly.

"Investing in us, you'll get a two-for-one deal. Besharmi has been building its credibility over the last three years through styling and design, and while that's half the average length of a retail brand before they approach investors, Besharmi has one unique element: Veer, one of the UK's biggest lifestyle brands, has shown interest in picking it up for their portfolio. Not only will you have access to South Asian millennials in the United States, but the UK will also be a viable market if an acquisition occurs and we can negotiate shares and interests among multiple companies."

Payal could feel it in her bones this time. Unlike during her previous meeting with Manish Menon, her words stuck every landing, and Misha appeared engaged, fascinated, and warm about the potential of Besharmi now and in the future.

"I'd also like to introduce you to the next CMO of Veer who is consulting on the marketing for Besharmi," she continued. "This is Ayaan Malhotra."

"Ms. Singh, I have to say that Payal is one of the most talented designers I have ever seen," Ayaan said.

Payal willed her face not to betray the satisfaction she felt lighting up within her.

"Her brand is approachable but glamorous, traditional but modern, respectful but bold. It is, in every way, a brand that lives up to its name: unapologetic and shameless. Veer is very interested in acquiring Besharmi in the fall, and your involvement would allow a stake for you in a growing company and a market share in UK lifestyle brands. Let's walk through the numbers."

Payal was gobsmacked. Ayaan was eloquent, funny, and charismatic to the point of being undeniable. She couldn't take her eyes off him.

He was gentle with his hands when he spoke—a flaw Papa had always told her to fix about her own presentation, where he often said it looked like Payal would flap her wings and fly away. Ayaan used them only to emphasize a point or to gesture and create connection between his audience and himself. His speed was moderated and his tone was smooth, a cadence that soothed a listener into believing whatever he said.

Ayaan was right about his skills: he'd been born with whatever the "it" factor was for success.

Finally, after what seemed like an hour of speaking between him and Payal, Ayaan said, "I really appreciate you inviting us here and hearing what we have to offer."

Misha pushed her glasses back onto her nose, smiling, and slid the handouts she'd been given closer to her.

"Payal, Ayaan, firstly, thank you for sharing all your work and the growth of Besharmi. I'm very impressed. I'll be honest… Your designs, your projections, and the team you've assembled so far are exceptional. There is no question. But from one insider to another, I will warn you about something."

"Yes?" Payal asked, hesitant to know but hungry all the same.

"You're going to have to work doubly hard. The unfortunate reality of being brown is that there is, at the moment, limited space for success of all upcoming South Asian designers in the West. As with Hollywood, literature, and politics—anything that requires selling your face along with your product, whether it's yourself or your ideas—the world has advanced but is still leagues behind giving fair footing to everyone. I see it myself when I'm excluded from meetings or consideration for opportunities because a team has already made a diversity move and doesn't want to have two of us in the room. Some roadblocks to success are out of your hands.

"Be prepared for that. But do not let it get you down."

Payal soaked it in. She'd already known it would be a tougher road for a newbie, let alone someone who was using her culture to move forward in a world that told her she didn't belong. But the pragmatic words, cushioned by a nudge to keep going, were still ones that Payal knew she'd cling to.

"I want to think about this for a day or two. But I'll let you know the moment I decide."

"I can't ask for more than that," Payal said. "Thank you for your time."

She and Ayaan packed up their binders of information, stowed away Payal's laptop in her bag, and left, walking out of the building with their heads held high.

The second they hit the pavement outside, Ayaan turned to her.

"Well, how do you think it went?"

"You were one of those guys who went over the test twice, weren't you? Once when you took it and the second time when you asked all your mates what answers they got so you could figure out your score," Payal teased.

"Yes. Yes, I was," Ayaan said, throwing his arms out and owning his habit. "Now...how do you feel?"

She was calm. At peace. For all her teasing, she would usually go over the presentations herself.

But this time, with him by her side and with the way they pushed out the messaging of Besharmi, she was rooted in confidence.

"I feel great," she said firmly.

Ayaan grinned. "You did great. I'm so proud of you."

With a hug, they parted ways.

Her phone already had a message from Kiran on their group thread.

Kiran: How did it go?!
Payal: WE KILLED IT!
Akash: And the frat boy didn't ruin it?
Sonam: Don't ruin the moment! Congratulations, Payal!
Akash: Congratulations, Payal. You deserve this. I hope you
　　land Misha's investment.
Kiran: So...on another note...how is it going with Ayaan now?

Payal paused, elated at her victory and warming inside at her friends. Their text message threads never got old, never ceased to fill her with happiness, and today, when she felt so content, she had so much goodness to pass around.

Payal: We've had an amazing time lately. It's like seeing a
　　whole different side of him.
Kiran: You're still certain you want to do this? You're showing
　　you can earn money for your line and succeed without
　　your parents... Maybe you can give it a chance with Ayaan
　　without the engagement being a part.

She thought about it—but the success of today was pervasive and it bred recklessness. Payal, high on one victory, wanted to see how much she could push another.

Payal: I'm sure...I can't screw too much with the deal on the
　　table yet. But at the moment, I don't want to kill him, so I'd
　　say we're making awesome headway.

And though she wouldn't say it out loud, even to the CMC, she wasn't sure if she wanted to give up on Ayaan yet.

. . . .

AYAAN

She was extraordinary.

Payal was dignified on a good day, consistently elegant even when she was flustered or furious. She had the presence of an old-time movie star: stylish, aspirational, and charming. Everything about her brand was embodied in her, and her number one selling point, her authenticity, was in lights.

To see her turn on the magic—in her element, invested in the success of her project, and free from the confines of family and friends—was breathtaking. Ayaan was reminded of watching tennis matches at Wimbledon when athletes at their prime performed under pressure and played with grace and litheness when at their most powerful. It was like an art form...and Payal was the same type of muse.

He was touched by a tinge of guilt then. For all the help he'd tried to offer, genuinely interested in her brand's success and wanting her to shoot for the stars, he knew he was still doing this for CMO and to get what he believed he deserved from his family.

The trade-off, despite being a win-win in the end, was manipulation to get there, confounded further by how he was beginning to love Payal's company. Her wry humor, her drive, and the way she didn't judge the weight he carried about his family whenever he inadvertently distributed it to her were peaceful reminders that he did have a place in the world.

Mum called as he sat at his desk in his apartment, stretching out and relishing how he felt.

"Ayaan, beta, how are you?"

"Payal and I had an investor meeting that went really well, so I feel like I'm on top of the world," he said.

"Ah, so you and Payal are doing well, then."

That wasn't quite his point, but in typical motherly fashion, Mum got right down to the details, and they were all about Payal.

"How did she do? What did she wear? Is she good at public speaking? How does she feel about you?"

He should have anticipated the ambush of questions, but he was too amused today to be irritated by the interrogation. He recapped the dress she wore, in which her professionalism, culture, and brand were on full display, explained how he felt like he learned something about her as she spoke and that she was a gifted businesswoman who exuded values he held close.

"It sounds like you've grown on each other," Mum said.

"Somewhat," Ayaan agreed.

"Well, seeing as you were terrified before, even this much agreeability feels like a victory to me."

"It is. You aren't wrong."

"Is this where I get to say, 'I told you so'?"

"If you must."

"No, I'll spare you this time," Mum said sagely, as if she was being benedictory.

"Her business has grown so much. I think if this engagement works out—er, at the time of the engagement," he corrected, "we might be able to convince her to let us acquire her. But even if not, she's the next big thing. I can feel it."

"Trust your instincts, beta. You have good ones. And I'll say this: it is so heartening to see the way you and Payal have come together to nourish something and share in something you both love. These are the experiences that strengthen you."

Ayaan, for all his ruminating, hadn't thought about it that way. "I guess you're right."

"I'm always right. I'm your mother!"

He laughed. "How are Arun and Dad? Have you spoken with Payal's family lately?"

"They're ironing out the details of the acquisition with her dad on a daily basis and consulting with the lawyers. Aunty seems excited about you. Also, Arun and Sarika will be in town in a couple of weeks, so make sure you put it on your calendar."

"Oh, I get to hang out with Sarika?" Ayaan exclaimed. "Yes!"

"And Arun."

"Yeah, him too," Ayaan said with noticeably less excitement.

"Ayaan," Mum said sternly. "Build bridges, don't burn them."

"I think that ship has sailed."

"These water-based analogies are already tiring me out, so let's just settle on you going to dinner with Arun and Sarika, okay? Preferably with Payal."

Ayaan rolled his eyes.

"Okay. I'm off to have coffee with Payal's nani."

"Her grandmother? Why?" Ayaan couldn't picture the old woman and Mum spending time together.

"That woman is the most fun I've had in years. I think I'll trade in all my friends for her company," Mum said.

He recalled Payal's mentions of her. "I've heard she's feisty."

"Trust me. This is where Payal gets her spunk from."

Ayaan understood instantly. "Then I imagine she's wonderful. Have fun!"

The phone rang again almost immediately after he had set it down.

Ayaan didn't look at the screen, assuming it was his mother forgetting something minor. "Yeah, Mum?"

"AYAAN!" The screech at the other end of the line was deafening.

"Uhh...Payal?" he asked, wincing. He hoped there wasn't any permanent ear damage, and he would bet that every dog in her neighborhood had just begun barking.

"Misha said yes! Misha is willing to invest $100,000 in Besharmi! Oh my God, Ayaan!"

His heart leapt through his chest.

"YES!" he exclaimed. "Payal, congratulations! You sealed the deal!"

"*We* sealed the deal!"

He could practically hear her grinning on the other end, and he was certain that she could sense the same energy radiating from him.

We. The word held magic—perhaps because it wasn't in the context of being a couple. Perhaps Mum was right...that nourishing Besharmi and building its future together had bonded them more than he'd realized.

They had done this together and Ayaan brimmed with pride at the way they had riffed off the other's strengths, sold their teamwork, and landed a respected investor. *We* had a power he hadn't understood before.

He couldn't wait to see where it took them next.

Chapter Seventeen

PAYAL

The joint victory tasted different. It was magnified somehow, stronger and bolder than it would have been if Payal had succeeded in getting Misha to say yes on her own. It was as though their talents had multiplied and the results had grown in tandem.

After the last few dates and the investing meeting, Payal finally felt the saplings of something new inside her: genuine hope that she and Ayaan might work out for the better.

She didn't want it to take root so deeply that she became convinced that they would grow into a permanent partnership. She wasn't that optimistic...yet. But the sliver of happiness this victory provided her, the glimpse of what their potential could be when combined, and the victory that it had led to were worth a celebration.

Ayaan seemed to read her mind.

"You know what? Let's celebrate!" Ayaan said now, his voice filling the joyous quiet on the phone line. "Dharm, Kai, and I usually get dinner once a week to catch up."

Payal frowned, confused at what he could be implying. Why did he want to celebrate if he couldn't go out tonight?

"Come with me," he said.

"You want me to come to dinner with you and your best friends?" Doubt replaced the hope. *Was this too soon?*

"Come," he said, and there was an urgency this time—a near-growling command that simultaneously turned her on and challenged her.

Then again...Why not?

Two hours later, she was at the door to the Penrose on the Upper East Side. She'd been here before—always for brunch or happy hour but never for dinner. It was a cute bar, industrial chic, and buried unceremoniously on Second Avenue and Eighty-Second.

Her black pumps clacked against the hardwood floors of the back room, where booths with camel-colored leather benches lined the wall and a long picnic table sat in the middle of the room. Her eyes scanned and found Ayaan sitting with his two friends, and he stood when he saw her. His friends turned their heads, broadly smiling when they made eye contact.

"Hey, Payal," Ayaan greeted her. He kissed her on the cheek.

When she replied, "Hi," her voice came out softer than she'd intended, betraying her nerves.

One of his friends slid out of the booth, towering over Payal. His hair was neatly trimmed and parted to the left with a neat wave in the front. His forehead was prominent, a slightly receding hairline beginning to show on his square face. Thick, straight eyebrows sat above his kind eyes, and though he had a short, clean beard and mustache, when he smiled, Payal could spot dimples that immediately made him look younger.

"I'm Dharm," he said, reaching for her hand.

The other friend, who Payal now knew to be Kai, slipped out of the booth behind him, tripping on the leg of the table and causing a loud clatter. Some of the other patrons turned to see where the sound came from.

"Smooth," Ayaan commented before turning to Payal. "And this is Kai."

"I like making an entrance," Kai said without skipping a beat, and Payal was surprised to be greeted with a warm hug.

"I think you've succeeded," she said, and the boys laughed.

As she joined them all, sitting next to Ayaan and wedged toward the wall and away from the rest of the room, she felt her nerves dissipate, and the cocoon of the booth provided some comfort.

"I hear you both have known Ayaan since B-school," she said.

"Yeah. We did what everyone does: spot another Indian in class and sit next to them," Dharm said.

"Then make fun of him endlessly when he asks where 'the loo' is," Kai chimed in.

Payal laughed. "To be fair, my friends did that too."

Ayaan looked pained. "Okay, there are plenty of Americanisms to make fun of…like fanny packs."

"Why is that weird?" Dharm asked.

"Besides the fact that no one has worn one since 1980," Kai said.

"Categorically false," Payal said. "I'm a designer and they've been making a comeback. Also, 'fanny' doesn't mean what you think it does back in England."

"What do you call them?"

"Bum bags!" Ayaan said with rather more vigor than anyone anticipated.

Dharm and Kai burst out laughing.

"You would get heated about the bum, wouldn't you?" Kai chuckled.

Ayaan's face turned a light shade of pink. "Shut up."

Payal laughed delightedly. "He struck me as the 'anything that moves' kind of guy." She nudged his shoulder with her own.

Dharm bellowed a laugh. "You're not wrong."

"Okay, I think it's time to order, don't you?" Ayaan said, shifting his weight and busting out the menus.

Payal playfully pushed her leg against him under the table, and his cheekbones rose as he fought a grin.

They ordered their dinners—Kiran came to Payal's mind, and she ordered a macaroni and cheese in honor of her dairy-loving pal—and as the waitress left to get their drinks and place their food orders in the kitchen, Ayaan stretched his arms above his head before dropping them abruptly, his eyes widening.

"Uh...mate..." Ayaan spluttered, interrupting Kai's story about the best macaroni and cheese he'd ever had.

"What?" Kai asked.

The boys turned, and when Payal saw their eyes collectively grow bigger, she followed their gaze.

At the bar, dressed in a killer black pencil skirt that accentuated a perfect butt and a tank top that made her boobs a solid eleven out of ten, stood Neha.

"Well, since you've been so subtle, I'm sure she hasn't noticed you," Payal remarked.

Her comment prompted them all to snap back.

"Maybe she didn't." Dharm shrugged.

Payal noticed movement in the corner of her eye and knew that wasn't the case. "Don't look now but I can promise you she did."

"Hi, guys!" Neha said cheerfully, greeting Kai and Dharm but not taking her eyes off Ayaan.

"Hey...hey, Neha," Ayaan said.

"Good to see you," Kai said. "Last time our paths sort of crossed, Ayaan was naked in a staircase."

If looks could kill, Ayaan would have murdered Kai with his.

Payal frowned, unsure whether she wanted to follow up on

this tale later, before deciding to introduce herself. Glancing at Ayaan, she saw his discomfort—his rigid posture, the slight frown teasing at his eyebrows, and the death grip he had on the bench.

As subtly as she could, she covered his hand with hers to say, *I got this.*

He squeezed her hand back gently and gave a nearly imperceptible nod.

"Well, we've all been caught in compromising positions, haven't we?" she asked cheerily. "I'm pretty sure my roommate nearly caught my first boyfriend with his pants down around his ankles at boarding school."

Neha stared at her.

Payal moved her hand back to her lap.

The subtleties in Neha's body language were impossible to miss. Her back straightened infinitesimally. Her fingers brushed a stray hair off her face and smoothed out the long length over her shoulder. Her eyebrows rose by a hair.

Payal knew what was happening—this was the Size Up... the unconscious and unnecessary comparison one woman made against another that inevitably either led to feeling inadequate at the end of the night or basking in superiority. It was the measurement of an adversary.

She wanted no part of it.

She could recall with painful detail what it felt like to be teased mercilessly for the Indian food Nani packed in her lunch, being called an outsider, and having whiter, blonder girls tell her to eat her smelly curry in her own country instead. She distinctly remembered being told that she wasn't invited to Poppy Wellington's birthday party because she was too much of a slut—when the reality was that she hadn't been kissed yet and the rumor had been started by a girl who hated Payal for outranking her on an exam. She could remember the games she played with her own head, watching her best friends get ready for parties in college and wishing she had the same bounce in her hair as Sonam or the same dignity as Kiran.

In other words, the girl-on-girl crime that society often brought to the table with no consent from its participants was a place Payal didn't want to sit, as either the victim or the perpetrator.

While she certainly wasn't comfortable with the idea that this girl had been with Ayaan—simply for the purposes of business and this fake engagement, of course—she had no reason to be unkind. Neha was a part of Ayaan's past. And she was part of Ayaan's future...maybe.

This wasn't a competition. Hell, they weren't even playing the same game.

She gave a genuine smile. "Hi, I'm Payal, by the way."

"Neha. Nice to meet you."

"Likewise! How do you know—" She bit her tongue. "Do you frequent Penrose often?"

"Not often, but my friends had a happy hour they wanted to go to in the area and then wanted some food."

"Well, that sounds like a delightful night—" Payal said.

"And we don't want to interrupt it—" Ayaan started.

"I've seen you on Instagram with your line," Neha remarked suddenly.

I saw you make out with Ayaan at a café once, Payal wanted to say, but she figured that would be awkward. "Oh, I'm glad those ads are paying off!" she bluffed.

"And, of course, I saw you on Ayaan's feed."

Dharm and Kai looked like they were watching a ping-pong match at a million miles an hour.

Ayaan sat back, seemingly chilled out about this unfortunate interaction. But his persistent tapping on the bench, rattling against Payal's thigh like a drill, gave him away.

"He's been helping a lot with the line," she said easily.

"Is that all you're doing?" The doubt in Neha's gaze and the way her voice took an uptick at the end of the question told Payal far more than Neha had likely intended.

"I don't think we need to discuss that," Ayaan said suddenly. "Our families are friends and I'm helping her with marketing."

Payal couldn't explain the sting from the omission of...what, exactly? Was there anything to omit?

"Yeah, business has been steadily rising lately," she said. She swallowed, jutted her chin into the air with confidence, and flashed what she hoped was a radiant smile.

"A word of warning to the uninitiated," Neha said to Payal. "Ayaan can't commit to anything. Whatever he's told you about wanting to be with you, I can assure you he doesn't intend to follow through."

"This isn't—" Ayaan started.

"People change, Neha," Dharm said, and the authority in his voice was so visceral and protective that the table fell silent. "Payal is a talented designer, and she doesn't need to be wrapped up in this tonight."

"I highly doubt he has changed," Neha said. "Be careful, Payal, or he'll break up with you via text message like he did to me ten days ago."

Ten days ago? Judging by the sharp looks of confusion on Dharm's and Kai's faces, they were equally as taken aback by this new development.

"Luckily, I don't have to worry about a breakup." Payal laughed, deflecting. "It's all business. If he doesn't end that partnership by text...or ever, we'll be just fine."

Neha glared at Ayaan. "I hope so. Have a good night, guys."

As she stormed away to her friends, Ayaan slouched into the bench and exhaled.

Kai finally asked the question they were all wondering.

"Ten days ago?"

"We haven't seen each other since the breakup two months ago," Ayaan said shortly. "Trust me, it's over."

Payal's relief was palpable but so was her continued discomfort. She couldn't wrap her head around the dynamics between Neha and Ayaan, let alone herself and Ayaan. But she wasn't one to give in, to admit any kind of defeat, and she certainly wouldn't expose any weakness now among his friends.

No. She would hold it together and get to the bottom of this game.

. . . .

AYAAN

Ayaan hated to admit it, but he'd been nervous in the hours leading up to dinner. High off the victory of landing Payal an investor and amped at the feeling of success—if Arun was ever right about anything, it was that success was addictive—he'd acted impulsively by inviting her to dinner with Dharm and Kai...exactly as he had when he'd texted Neha to begin with. He expected that there would be some awkwardness with the new group dynamics—but he hadn't expected that Neha would show up and that the awkwardness would be his own, while Payal shined under pressure, winning over his friends in the process.

Dharm was watching her with admiration in his eyes, and Kai had raised his eyebrows more than once as Payal offered kindness for each of Neha's attempts to embarrass him for their past.

The waitress reappeared with their drinks.

It was impossible to believe it had only been a few minutes since they'd placed their orders. Ayaan was certain it had been years.

"Thanks for handling that," Ayaan murmured to Payal as his friends claimed their drinks and took their first sips, commenting on the taste to each other and drowning out his voice. "That could have gone a lot worse if you hadn't been so relaxed about it."

"Ten days?" she whispered back, and he could see the questions percolating on her face.

"Can we talk about it later?" Ayaan asked, meeting her eye. "I can answer your questions as soon as we're alone."

Kai had taken a swig of his drink, unaware of the conversation happening in front of him. "You were a champ, Payal," he said. "That couldn't have been easy, and you were really dignified."

"Grace under fire," Dharm said.

"Thank you," she said. "I know she's probably hurt from whatever history she has with Ayaan. There's no reason to be mean. It wasn't personal."

"It must have been awkward talking about the line's success, especially since so many of Ayaan's fashion contacts came from meeting them at Neha's shows, but you were really nice about it," Kai said.

"Sorry...what?" Payal asked, shocked.

Ayaan cringed. "Some of the people I contacted about your line and who were sharing your social media posts were people who I met at Neha's shows... She's a model."

Payal closed her eyes and breathed in, like she was trying to control herself. "So our paths will likely cross at some point in the future."

"It's possible."

Ayaan snuck a look at Dharm, whose unamused face consisted

of a straight mouth and eyeballs that were about to roll out of his head.

Their food came then, and there was a flutter of utensils being unwrapped from napkins, the clink of dishes, and first bites (and accompanying groans of delight). Ayaan glanced over at Payal, who was pushing her macaroni and cheese around on her plate, only taking a few bites before setting her fork on top.

"You okay?" he asked.

"Not too hungry," she said with a smile.

When Dharm asked her how long she'd lived on the Upper East Side and what college was like at Duke, she answered with the same enthusiasm and kindness as she had at the beginning of dinner, but Ayaan sensed an undercurrent of disappointment beneath her collected facade.

"Thank you for dinner," she said when Dharm insisted on paying and they had all exited the restaurant onto an active Second Avenue.

"It was my pleasure," Dharm said, leaning in and giving her a hug. "I've been wanting to meet you, and to say we're glad tonight happened would be an understatement."

He gave Ayaan a quick hug and Kai followed.

"I like her. Don't fuck it up," Kai whispered before clapping Ayaan once on the back and stepping away.

"I'll walk you to your place," Ayaan offered to Payal, and she didn't protest.

He watched her as she walked, realizing he associated the sound of high heels with her now. Her long legs had an equally long stride as his, and it was refreshing to walk alongside someone without having to adjust his gait.

They weaved through patrons of other restaurants and people lingering around outdoor seating, where heat lamps warmed their skin as they ate in the chilly air. Flushed servers ran between them from the kitchens and back to the dining areas. The energy of the streets was buzzing in the air.

But Payal was distracted, and Ayaan could tell her mind was elsewhere.

"You're quiet," he said.

"Indeed."

"Okay, I know you're mad, but please talk to me."

They turned onto Seventy-Sixth Street where the crowds dispersed, and the sidewalks were emptier than the avenues.

"Now you want to communicate?" she snapped, whipping around in the middle of the sidewalk.

Ayaan knew he deserved the jab.

"Do you have some crazy radar that makes you an asshole the second someone trusts you? Like, 'Oh, it looks like I made someone happy today. Maybe I should ruin it.'"

"No, of course not—"

"Then why do you keep doing it to me?" Payal shouted.

Her voice echoed down the street, making Ayaan wince. The space between them, six feet at most, became an ever-widening chasm.

He answered her, knowing that his truth would only fuel her anger. "You have every right to be mad and I'm going to be honest with you, okay? I texted Neha after our first dinner together... It was a bad day, and I had doubts about whether we would make this work and how, God, how ridiculous all this feels sometimes."

"Ridiculous," Payal scoffed.

"Can you deny it?" Ayaan challenged. "Our parents set us up, Payal. I'm not a cruel person. No, don't shake your head. I'm not a mean person. But you can't blame me for having doubts. Can you honestly say you've been all in? You haven't had a single question about whether this will work?"

For the first time, Payal looked shamefaced. He hadn't meant to shame her but to find solidarity. Slowly, she nodded.

"Yeah, I've had doubts."

"It's not *you*," he said, and he emphasized it again to drive it home. "It. Isn't. You. You are beautiful, smart, funny, and one hell of a clinic in staying calm when the entire house seems to be going up in flames. But this is intense and neither of us saw it coming. I know for a fact that you never saw a future with me. You said it yourself the first time I came over: 'Relationships take work. Sex is easier.' I had a different mentality: relationships were fine as long as they didn't go anywhere. Then suddenly, the most permanent relationships we have—our families—were sealing us into a deal with the things we wanted most—security and success—and wrapping those goals up in each other. I got a little spooked, okay? I'm sorry."

Payal's jaw was taut, as though she was grinding her teeth to hold back her thoughts.

"Then I saw you with my family, and I saw you try nonetheless. You had been hit with the same ambush, and you were still willing to give it your best. And I saw how happy you made my parents...so I decided I'd end it with Neha. I hadn't seen her since our breakup. I didn't want to carry on with the games. If you were going to try, I would too."

Payal nodded slowly, seemingly taking in his words and letting them sink in. When she spoke, there was far less vitriol than Ayaan had expected she'd hurl at him. "Okay."

"Okay?"

"Yeah. Okay...but you can't keep pulling the rug out from underneath me," she said. "Don't you get tired of apologizing? Because I'm tired of being on edge and of putting my trust in you if you're only going to break it."

"I have no idea why you're sticking around," Ayaan said softly, hoping she'd fill in the silence.

"Because I don't have a choice," Payal said simply. "You have these moments of light where I think you're a great guy and that we have this...spark. But if I walk away, my family loses everything. I have to be in this until"—a strange look crossed her face—"I mean, unless I want my family to lose Luxuriant. So yeah, I thought we could try for a while and make the best of it. But your lies make me wonder why. It's humiliating and I'm better than this."

"I didn't mean to lie to you," Ayaan said quietly. "I thought I could handle Neha by myself, end it with her, and move forward with you. I didn't expect it to get sloppier than that."

"You might have seen it coming given your ex is a model and your..." She let her voice trail off, avoiding the word. "I'm a designer."

"You might be right."

A hurricane of emotion flooded through Ayaan. He was sincerely apologetic about the damage to Payal's pride. No one wanted to attribute their success to their partner's ex. And he was sorry that he hadn't mentioned the on-again, off-again nature of Neha's and his relationship, catching Payal further off guard. But he couldn't get the thought of CMO out of his mind when he thought of the future—and he couldn't let Payal walk away if he wanted that dream fulfilled.

"I'm sorry," he said again. "Payal, I'm in. Just stick around. I promise, you'll see that I'm not a total moron."

"You have one more chance, Ayaan Malhotra," she said with a small smile.

"I'll take it," he promised. "You won't regret it."

Chapter Eighteen

PAYAL

FIVE MONTHS UNTIL THE ENGAGEMENT AND FASHION SHOW

She wanted to trust him.

But in the week after their fight, Payal couldn't settle into a holding pattern with Ayaan.

It seemed as though every time she wanted to trust him, the earth shook under her and decimated her belief in him...and every time she felt the least stable, their families seemed to have the Payaan (Sonam's moniker for the two, which made Payal think of *pile-on*—which was also accurate) radar tuned to sense any rumblings happening across the pond...just to interfere, with or without knowing that they were doing it.

> Hi, Payal! It's Sarika. I got your number from Ayaan. I'll be in town for a girls' weekend next week and would love to grab a coffee and take a walk if you're available!

Payal did enjoy getting to know Sarika at their family dinner. Her calm demeanor and easy personality were refreshing in a room full of people out for their own interests.

She texted back telling her she would love to see her new friend while she was in the city, and they could grab some coffee and walk around Central Park.

"Hey, stranger," called out Payal.

She had walked up the stairs in the Shakespeare Garden in Central Park, where she found Sarika sitting on a bench, waiting.

"My goodness, look at you!" Sarika exclaimed. "How do you manage to look like you're coming off the runway all the time?"

She gave Payal a warm hug, careful to avoid Payal's hands holding two coffees, and left the lingering smell of vanilla around Payal when she pulled away.

"You're too kind. It was a jeans and flats kind of day." Payal laughed. She handed Sarika the venti mocha she had requested. "Your order, my dear."

"Arun teases me for loving Starbucks so much. He thinks it's incredibly American."

"It is, but I won't lie. There is no guilt, just pleasure, about it," Payal said, tapping her drink against Sarika's own and toasting to the love of the coffee chain.

"Isn't that the truth?"

"Why did you choose this place to meet? I have walked this park a thousand times, and I don't think I've ever paused here," Payal said.

"Well, outside of choosing a landmark named after the most famous English poet of all time, my parents brought me here when I was little and the memory stuck," Sarika explained.

"That place for me is the Cotswolds," Payal said.

"Great taste you Mehras have," Sarika said. "Let's walk. I love this spring weather to wander in." She pulled her light-pink belted trench coat a little tighter.

"So what brought you to New York? You said a girls' trip?"

They started walking along the stone path toward Belvedere Castle, pedestrians passing them by occasionally but still relishing the oasis of quiet in the middle of a bustling city.

"My best friend had a business meeting in the city. We all decided to work remotely for a few days and take a little vacation while we were at it. Arun is going to join me late Saturday for two days and we'll take a red-eye back on Monday night."

"That sounds lovely! How did you meet, if you don't mind me asking? Ayaan has mentioned in passing that you've been together for years."

"Our paths crossed sometimes in London as children. We had a number of common friends, and my cousin, Chandni, lived in Wimbledon—"

"Hey, I knew her! We were neighbors when we were younger!" Payal exclaimed.

"I did my recon," Sarika said slyly. "I knew you went to the same school, and she said you were delightful...and she's never wrong, quite obviously."

"Why, thank you. It's so funny how even the biggest cities in the world can be like villages when we examine our networks."

"I think the rule surrounding six degrees of separation is more like two or three with our communities."

"It is uncanny. But please, continue. I rudely interrupted," Payal said, gesturing at Sarika to carry on with her story.

"Chandni brought me to a Diwali celebration when I was thirteen, and Arun and I talked about comic books and video games the entire time...and football, of course. She didn't tell me until later that she endured three years of Arun asking about me, so I didn't have a bloody clue that he had any interest. When we were sixteen, he was like a boy-band star. Don't laugh, I had a type! All the girls wanted him, but he was so quiet and broody when we were together at parties, and I found his mystery a little endearing. We finally got together when we were seventeen and haven't looked back."

"He seemed really nice at dinner. I can see the charm," Payal admitted, thinking about how kind he was to everyone...seemingly, except Ayaan. "I like that he's assertive and confident. It puts people at ease."

"It's a Malhotra trait. I love it. Don't get me wrong. But I'm telling you, I'm so convinced that sound, healthy friendships with other strong women can drive the world. As much as I love my husband, these last few days were much needed, and I feel capable of taking on the world after the recharge and remembering who I am without the identity of being a wife hanging over my head."

Payal thought of Sonam and Kiran—though Akash also counted as a powerful ally—and bobbed her head. "I know the feeling exactly."

"How is the line coming along? Are you preparing for this show in September?"

"I'm nervous," Payal admitted. "The growth has been huge, largely thanks to Ayaan lately. But any big dream comes with its risks and there has already been a lot of change this year."

"Indeed. How are you both doing?"

Comfort surrounded Payal and no hesitation crept up before she answered honestly. "We're...a work in progress."

"Ah, so you have no idea what you're doing!" Sarika said.

Payal laughed. "None. We take two steps forward and three steps back each time. Navigating this hasn't been easy."

"I can't imagine. I was shocked you agreed to this."

Payal grew warm under the spotlight, wondering if Sarika knew more than she was letting on about Payal's true intentions when she agreed to the match.

"Sometimes, I am too."

"What have some of your struggles been?"

"We have some issues with trust." Payal danced delicately. "He...doesn't always make the best decisions and I can never grow confident in the ground I'm standing on."

"Have you been spending time together?"

"We do. We got in a big fight last week, so it's largely been text messages asking how the day is going or discussing social media strategy."

They stopped in front of Belvedere Castle. Children screamed as they pretended they were kings and queens, and Payal relished the peace of the water in front of the castle, reflecting the blue skies above and the budding greenery around.

When Sarika wasn't looking, Payal gazed at her. She had beautiful, large, almond-shaped eyes that were lined but not heavy with shadow. Her brown eyes were dark, but color still shined through, nearly reddish in the glumness of the gray day. Her thick, black hair was in a high ponytail, ends curling, and her round face gave her a childlike quality. In her light-pink trench coat, she wouldn't be mistaken for anything over twenty-five.

"May I ask you a question?" Sarika curled both her hands around her cup and interrupted Payal's admiration of her.

"Yes, of course," Payal said.

"Do you think you can be happy with Ayaan? Or are you forcing yourself to do this?"

Besides the CMC, no one had asked Payal that question. Her mind rushed with her true intent of using the Malhotra connections, the nights she'd enjoyed spending with Ayaan, and the sheer heaviness of connecting with someone while simultaneously being unable to rely on them to come through.

A sound escaped her, a cross between a croak, a "What?" and an "Umm."

"You might have to repeat yourself," Sarika said lightly.

"What, I didn't make sense?" Payal jested. "I feel chemistry with him, Sarika...but I'd be lying if I said it was easy to feel taken care of by Ayaan. And I'm not foolish enough to think that you can sign your future away on potential."

"That's what our moms did," Sarika observed. "I don't know how."

"Have you ever thought about that?"

"Every day," Sarika said, throwing her cup away in a nearby garbage can. "Sometimes I think the women in our mothers' generation—most of them anyway—were uprooted from their fathers' homes and replanted in their marriage homes, all on the hopes that someday the man they married would fulfill those promises...but they weren't watered, cultivated, and taught to grow on their own."

Payal stared at her feet. "If we don't do what our parents want, we're disrespecting the journeys and the sacrifices they made to uproot themselves. But if we do, we turn our backs on an opportunity our mothers never had."

"I had doubts when Arun and I were dating," Sarika confessed, digging the toe of her boot into a crack in the pavement. "He was so focused that he was inadvertently selfish, and his condescension could be so cutting. I didn't want to say yes until I'd seen him change and witnessed firsthand that he wasn't going to keep up with the behaviors that would push me away."

"But you loved him, Sarika. From what Ayaan has mentioned in passing, you both dated and had time to observe patterns. I don't want to negate your journey...but I don't have the benefit of time to make that demand with Ayaan," Payal said gently.

"Payal. Of course you do. Maybe not time. But you have the right to demand kindness," Sarika said. "I know that your parents are so worried about what will happen to their hard work, and Mummy and Papa on the Malhotra side are concerned about Ayaan settling down and Veer's growth. But you need to look out for you. No one else will."

"What are you saying?"

Sarika gave Payal a penetrating stare. "I'm not saying anything about what you need to do. I'm saying you have the right to demand what you need. And while Arun might disagree with me for saying this out loud, you can say no to this match with Ayaan."

Payal let the words sink in. It landed differently when a peer said it. Further, Sarika was inside the circle. When her friends said it from the outside, it was with the bias of knowing her for years, of not knowing the Malhotras, of distance from the situation despite their closeness to her. Sarika, on the other hand, was in the thick of it and, from what she'd shared, had the same doubts on her own journey.

"I'm not sure I want to say no yet," Payal said quietly.

"Then don't."

"I don't know if I can say yes either."

"That's okay too. Just don't forget that this is your life. And that for the women who came before us and the women who come after, you making a choice for yourself is a win either way."

"Can I ask you a question?" It was Payal's turn.

"Of course! I just picked your brain, didn't I?"

"Did I sense tension between Arun and Ayaan at our family dinner, or was that my nervous jitters reading into a situation?"

Sarika gave her a knowing look and a soft smile. "Arun and Ayaan haven't gotten along since Ayaan was a teenager. Ayaan got into some trouble in school—you'll have to ask him about it because I don't want to betray his confidence if he doesn't want it known yet—and the family was hard on him about it. Arun, especially, has given him a lot of grief over the years. I'm not sure it's fair, to be honest. In Arun's eyes, his younger brother was the star of the show until that point, and this one stupid, childish night was a fall from grace that he never recovered from.

"To me, one stupid, childish night is simply a reminder that no one is perfect and it teaches you that life isn't easy. Ayaan recovered and went on to do good things...but somehow, this black mark is one that Arun has clung to and held over his young brother's head. Every minor misstep since, like coming home drunk or not settling into a long career at one company or failing a class, seems to magnify Arun's perception. It isn't fair. I wish it didn't exist. They used to be impossibly close."

"Really?" Payal's interest was piqued. "I wouldn't have guessed."

Sarika's voice grew animated. "Oh, yes! Ayaan was the younger, more charming, more outgoing brother and Arun was serious, focused, and smart. But they encouraged each other. In fact, it was Ayaan who asked me to meet him for coffee and told Arun the same thing—and proceeded to bail so we were stuck at the same shop together. He texted Arun from home to tell him that if he didn't tell me how he felt, he'd break Arun's video game console...which is how we got together when we did. Otherwise, I'd probably still be waiting for him to tell me he liked me."

Payal laughed, delighted at the imagery of a young Ayaan being so authoritative with the brother who now dictated his choices.

"Somehow, that story illustrates Ayaan perfectly."

"It does, doesn't it? I know you're on the fence, so I don't say this to sway you. But Ayaan is a good one. His heart is kind. Mummy thinks he's lost, but I don't believe that either. Not all who wander are lost." She gazed meaningfully at Payal for a split second before turning away. "Now...tell me about you. What's with the curiosity?"

"You know how it is. Due diligence for the man I'm supposed to marry and who I hardly understand, let alone know well enough to dedicate my life to," Payal fibbed.

The truth was that she was curious about the way Ayaan ticked and why he seemed to run from the goodness in himself. But perhaps when the people closest to him seemed to rarely see it, he'd convinced himself it didn't exist. A self-fulfilling prophecy of sabotaging his own reputation before anyone close to him could be let down.

She felt pity.

Then her fingers closed tightly around her cup, unexpected anger coursing through her at the way Ayaan had been treated.

The damage the families had inflicted on their own members had an undeniable ripple effect. Every relationship was impacted by the decisions made on behalf of other people, erasing their voices but building resentment.

Payal didn't want to be a part of a cycle like that. She wanted to decide for herself.

And for now, she would stay.

· · · · · · · · · ·

AYAAN

Ayaan wasn't sure that the Indian American Association Gala was quite where he belonged, seeing as he wasn't fully Indian or at all American. But when Arun had called last week to tell him that Veer needed a representative at networking and fundraising events in New York and that a family friend was on the board of the Indian American Association, Ayaan got up from the dinner he was sharing with Sarika in his living room, left it uneaten on the coffee table, and put on a suit.

"Leave it to Arun to kill the fun," she said as she rolled her eyes.

"I know. I never get time with you. He's probably jealous." He weaved his tie through his deft fingers, forming a Windsor knot perfected from years of boarding school.

She gave a husky laugh. "You missed one big thing, you know."

"What's that?" He patted down his jacket, checking for his wallet, keys, and phone and that his tie was in place.

"He knew he wouldn't be here in time for it, and he trusted you to go."

He considered what she said, dropping his hands and putting them in his pockets. He watched Sarika, who didn't break her gaze, one eyebrow raised, challenging him to fight the goodwill gesture that he knew his brother had extended.

"Yeah. I guess you're right," he conceded. "It's a step forward."

"Good. I'm proud of you. Now...while you go eat on the company's dime, I am starving and get to eat your food too."

She picked up the containers, putting them back in the paper bag they came in, and tossed her coat over her forearm.

"I'll walk out with you," she said.

Gotham Hall was a lavish venue for a proportionately luxurious party. Modeled after Roman amphitheaters, the former bank stood on Broadway and Thirty-Sixth, bringing antiquity to the modernity of Midtown. A vast domed ceiling showcased a hexagonal pattern around a central oculus, from which a chandelier featuring candle-like lights hung, high above the crowd. An enormous ring hung around the lights, supporting speakers that were loudly playing Bollywood music. The high walls were largely empty of windows, save for decorative ones.

Ayaan felt like he was in an underground, covert lair...that happened to be in the center of New York City. Banners hung from the walls, with the names of three charities on them that the association donated to on an annual basis and that events like these helped raise funding for. Ayaan recognized the names of an educational charity, an NGO related to period poverty, and an organization dedicated to providing clean water to rural India.

Appetizer tables and buffet tables lined the outer ring of the room, while fully occupied table rounds dotted the central expanse of the chamber.

A rumble resounded in his belly. God, he was starving. Making his way to the appetizer service, he picked out the mini quiches from the selections and had the server place three on a white porcelain plate for him.

"Finally," he said to himself. He opened his mouth to shove in an entire quiche.

"Ayaan?" a voice asked from behind him.

He stiffened, gathering his thoughts and wishing he hadn't given in to his growling stomach. *Goddamn quiche.*

He turned.

Neha stood in front of him. Her prominent, heavily lined eyes looked even larger on her equally heavily made-up face, which had been contoured to emphasize every angle.

"Hi, Neha," he said. "Are you—are you stalking me?"

He'd meant it as a joke, but she narrowed her eyes.

"Of course not. Every professional in the city comes to these events."

"Evidently. Well, it's nice to see you."

"No girlfriend here tonight?"

He planted a smile on his face. "Nope. I'm here on Veer duty."

"That's unfortunate. She seemed…nice."

Ayaan could tell it bothered her to say so.

"So," he said, looking around for an excuse to leave the conversation politely. "What have you been... Oh."

A tall stranger had appeared at Neha's elbow with a fruity-looking, bright-green drink.

"Here, baby," he said to Neha, handing it to her.

"Oh," said Ayaan again.

A sense of relief that Neha had moved on flooded him. And so did a prick of jealousy.

But it was dulled. Two months ago, Ayaan would have had the urge to remark on her bad taste or roll his eyes visibly enough that she'd know she'd gotten to him.

Instead, he felt the tiny ache of sadness one got when realizing that the happiest phases they'd experience with someone were now in the past and that they would have to venture into a new dynamic now that didn't have the same thrill. It wasn't Neha that he was upset about losing. It was that the door had finally closed, and the resounding thud had shocked his system.

"This is Ayaan," Neha said, gesturing to him while winding her arm around her date's elbow. "This is Deep."

"Nice to meet you," Ayaan said, shaking Deep's hand.

"How do you two know each other?" Deep asked.

Jesus, take the wheel.

"Oh, our paths crossed in the past. Nothing important," Neha said sweetly. Her eyes were full of fire and brimstone, despite her sugary tone.

But Ayaan simply smiled. "If you'll excuse me, I have to meet with someone quickly. See you around, Neha."

He left her standing with Deep, puzzled at the lack of reaction, and walked to the other side of the room to do a visual lap of the guests. He shoved a piece of quiche in his mouth and chewed frantically, savoring the buttery goodness as his gaze wandered, once again drifting to the architecture of the room.

Payal would love a fashion show here.

The abrupt diversion to thinking about Payal caught him by surprise.

But the flashing lights, the music echoing off the walls, and the people gathering for a good cause were beginning to give him an idea.

"Ayaan!" a booming voice hit him from behind.

"Pankaj Uncle," Ayaan greeted him with a handshake and a warm hug.

"You look more like Arun every day, son," he said.

"Oh, don't say that, Uncle. I'd like to keep my hairline for a while longer."

Pankaj Uncle guffawed. "How are you, beta? Your father says you'll be taking on CMO in a few months and that you're engaged! Congratulations!"

Ayaan tried to ignore the word *engaged*, but it was inevitable that as news spread, it would become common knowledge...and that as much as he fought it in his mind, Payal would be considered his fiancée, whether he was ready for it or not.

"Thank you! We have a lot of exciting developments happening. This event has been beautifully coordinated, by the way. How is the fundraising going?"

"Exceptionally well! We're already planning another event in about three months. If you have ideas on entertainment, you let us know. The younger generation is always far more in tune with what kinds of creativity are brewing."

Ayaan calculated the time frame. The upcoming event would be in July...two months before Payal's show, the engagement, and the CMO announcement. The opportunity to feature her gave him a thrill, and the chance for growth for Veer—for himself and his career—jolted him with energy.

He had to shoot his shot.

He smiled, put his arm around Uncle in a gesture of closeness, and pretended to think.

"So...Uncle, how would you feel about a fashion show for entertainment and a sponsorship from Veer to fund it?"

Chapter Nineteen

PAYAL

> Ayaan: Arun wants to have dinner with us tonight. I know it's
> short notice…but it won't last long as they have plans
> tomorrow and they fly out in the evening.

Payal wasn't sure she wanted to spend time with Ayaan after
their fight, but he had begged for a second chance and promised
he wouldn't let her down.

*When had she become a girl who gave so many second chances
to be treated well?*

> Payal: I can be there.
> Ayaan: Are you sure?
> Payal: Yes, it'll be nice to spend time with him and Sarika.
> Ayaan: I was really hoping you'd tell me you were busy so I had
> an excuse.

She couldn't help but laugh, but it was an exhausted one. She
couldn't be angry with him. He'd messaged her earlier to tell her
that the Indian American Association wanted to work with her on

a charity fashion show, good practice for the one during Fashion Week. He had promised the support of Veer too, for cross-brand promotion.

Landing Misha's investment provided some financial help in creating the samples for the show, and she couldn't have done that without Ayaan's help either.

Yet she still hurt.

Payal knew she had no claim on Ayaan. She didn't even want him! But when he was charming, self-deprecating, and kind, she couldn't help but find him endearing. Then he'd demolish any goodwill between them, and she'd be back at square one. His ill treatment of her had to be an indicator of how he valued her, right?

Then again, the spark when they spent time together was undeniable. When Ayaan was around, he brought out the version of her that was sharp, on her game, and alert at all times...even if he also brought out the worst in her.

And she'd enjoyed her coffee with Sarika so much. Both his family and the insights they provided softened her heart toward him. She understood more whenever she spent time with them, and it illuminated some of the murky darkness she couldn't see through when he was around.

That evening, she took an Uber to Ayaan's apartment in FiDi.

Knocking on his apartment door on the sixteenth floor, she exhaled through her teeth, shaking off the jitters.

Ayaan opened the door holding a beer in his hand and, Payal had to admit, looking criminally good in a plain black tee and blue jeans that hugged his hips and were torn at the knee. Behind him, she saw that the door led directly into a galley kitchen with a small entryway space for a closet and coat rack.

"Hi," he greeted her. "Thank you for coming at the last

minute. My mom reminded me they'd be here and told me I had to meet up with him for dinner." He leaned closer to her and whispered, "Obviously, that meant I forgot and tried to get out of it."

Payal grinned. "And clearly, you were successful."

She unbuttoned her camel dress coat and shrugged it off. Ayaan put his beer on the counter next to them and moved behind her, taking the coat into his hands as she dropped it.

"Thank you," she said, taken aback by the manners.

"You haven't been here yet, so I might as well give you the full treatment and tour," he replied. "This is the kitchen..."

They walked through the contemporary white space, a long kitchen with lightly stained pine floors, which led to a large living room.

"And the living room...and Arun."

"Payal, it's so good to see you!" Arun exclaimed warmly.

He came over and wrapped Payal in a big hug. He wore a plaid shirt, the collar neatly folded over the neck of a tan crewneck sweater, and dark-blue jeans without a hole in sight.

"Likewise!" she told Arun. "Ayaan, your place is beautiful."

She looked around, taking it all in. Ayaan's apartment was a corner unit, and large windows ran the length of the room on the left before turning the corner and wrapping across the back wall.

"Wow," she breathed at the view.

The city's lights enveloped the building and both windows looked out into the twinkling metropolis. High-rises reached into the sky all around them, and Payal wondered about the lives of the people she saw through the windows of their apartments. Maybe those ant-sized people had breathtaking moments of clarity every time they looked out their windows too, surrounded by the city's buzzing buildings.

Ayaan's decor was similar to Payal's. While she had utilized grays and creams as her neutrals, Ayaan had thrown in lots of blacks. His black leather couch was a squishy-looking leather sectional that followed the corner of the room, allowing anyone who sat there to feel as though they were immersed in city lights.

She tried not to think about what his bedroom looked like, or she knew she'd wonder about his bed too.

"Haven't you been here before?" Arun asked.

"No, not yet," Payal said. Upon reading Arun's doubtful face, she replied, "Ayaan usually comes over to mine. The neighborhood is a little quieter, and we like to be away from the bustle when we can."

The last part was a lie, of course, but Ayaan shot her a grateful expression.

"That makes sense," Arun said. "I like the quiet too, actually. That's why I couldn't bring myself to move to Central London even though our offices were there."

"You and your brother have that in common, then," she said, hoping to keep the peace.

"Payal!" Sarika said, emerging from the bedroom, where Payal deduced the bathroom was attached.

Seeing Sarika again was exactly like having the sun shine down on her face after a long hard winter. They embraced like they hadn't seen each other in years, and if they hadn't been surrounded by the boys, Payal was certain she would have jumped up and down and had a childish reaction to Sarika's appearance.

Unlike the other day when she'd been dressed more formally, Sarika was now in ripped, light-washed mom jeans and a baggy gray cable-knit sweater. Her hair was curly and natural, and her makeup was so minimal, Payal wouldn't have known she was wearing any if her face hadn't shimmered just a little in the light.

"Payal, what's your favorite cuisine?" Sarika asked.

"Thai, hands down."

"Look at you, Ayaan. You got it right!" Sarika exclaimed, nudging him.

Payal gave him a frown and a smile. "How did you know?"

"You ordered it when we hung out once. Lucky guess."

Payal flashed back to the night they'd worked on Misha's presentation and remembered the fleeting moment of closeness they'd shared as the night ended. "Oh, yeah, that time. Great memory!"

As they gathered around the couch, Ayaan pulled some chairs from the small dining table in the corner of the room for more seats, and they dug in. It was relatively quiet, only punctuated by the sounds of Sarika asking for a water bottle or Ayaan getting up to get more red chili flakes for everyone.

Yet the company still felt warm to Payal, a cozy change from the norm.

"So...I have a game," Sarika said after they'd cleaned up the remnants of dinner. She produced a small box from the gray handbag next to the couch.

"A game?" Arun asked.

"Okay, not quite a game, but my friends brought this deck of cards from some novelty store. They're just questions to get to know one another better, but I thought it could be fun to learn about each other."

"I'm not sure if that sounds fun or nerdy," Ayaan said.

"It's not so bad," Arun said with a laugh. "We actually use them sometimes to make life more interesting."

"Please don't tell me that there are sexual questions on there or I might need to hurl myself out the window, thinking about my brother's sex life," Ayaan said.

"No!" Sarika burst out laughing. "They're fun questions to ask on a relaxed night, and your brother and I have been together for nearly twenty years. We need a jump every once in a while."

"He's so uptight, he could use a jump to loosen up, amiright?" Ayaan joked.

They all laughed, though Arun's seemed forced.

"I'm in," Payal declared.

Sarika doled out cards to each of them.

"I'm only handing out two each because we're going to have to leave shortly and if we get lost in these, we could easily be here until midnight. We spent four hours once talking about these questions between my friends, Arun, and me. Just read the question to the person on your left."

"Okay, we can start in a minute! I need to use the loo. Hang on," Ayaan said. He stood and went through the bedroom.

When he heard the door close, Arun turned to Payal. "How's Ayaan doing with Besharmi? Is he making an impact?"

"He just volunteered Veer to be a sponsor for the Indian American Association Gala, you know. And with that snagged a fashion show for me. It's impressive." She couldn't help but notice the hint of pride that slipped into her voice.

"Well…it was a win, I suppose." Arun shrugged.

Arun hadn't said anything particularly cruel. He wasn't being snide. But the dismissal of Ayaan's wins irked Payal deeply. No matter how they'd ended up having to partner up, Ayaan had demonstrated that he was a reliable and talented marketer, and his expertise had gained opportunities for both the Mehra and Malhotra families that didn't exist prior to his involvement. While Payal wouldn't be the first to defend his behavior in affairs of the heart, she certainly wouldn't let an insult against his business efforts slide.

"Arun, I don't know the history between you and Ayaan. I don't need to. What I do know is that he is insightful, careful, thoughtful, and intelligent when it comes to what he does. You may know the ins and outs of Veer, and I respect you very much for that, but Ayaan has ideas for marketing that would bring Veer's profile into the spotlight...particularly with the acquisition of Luxuriant. If I were you, I would trust in his ability. I do."

Arun appraised her. "I was sure you were only giving in to the whims of my tempestuous brother, but perhaps you do care about him more than business."

I do. Payal reined the words in, forcing them to lie calmly inside her.

The same anger from Central Park, frustration at the lack of belief in family, dissolved the warmth she had demonstrated until now.

"I think your brother is talented, and perhaps it's time you recognize it," she said coolly.

He raised an eyebrow, and she got the distinct impression that he considered her formidable.

"I'll try," he said finally.

Sarika had quietly been watching this encounter but had given a subtle nod to Payal as Arun spoke. Payal knew that she had her approval, and she knew that no matter what happened with Ayaan, when it came to his talents and his purpose, she would go on protecting him for as long as she could.

· · · · · · · · · · ·

AYAAN

When he returned, the room was a few degrees cooler.

Payal and Arun were watching each other as though they had never seen each other properly before. Sarika was quiet.

"Did I miss something?" he asked.

"Only Payal and Arun talking business. Trust me, you didn't miss much," Sarika said lightly.

Ayaan shrugged. "Sounds good. Let's do this."

"Okay," said Arun, taking the first turn as always and reading off his card. "Sarika, was there something your parents refused to buy you as a kid that you really wanted?"

Sarika touched her chin before her eyes lit up. "Oh my gosh, yes! When I was about six, my parents took me to Disney World in Florida for a week. It was our last night and we were in the gift shop in the Magic Kingdom, and I fell in love with a four-foot-tall Mickey Mouse stuffed animal. He was bigger than I was. And I asked my mum and dad, and they both said no. We couldn't fly back without buying the thing a seat of its own! I can't remember another time I threw a tantrum in a store, cried, and made a scene—"

"Until you insisted upon your engagement ring," Arun cut in.

"Oh, shut up," Sarika said, gently smacking his arm. "I did not. You're going to make me look like a diva! Now, Ayaan, what types of things have you collected in the past?"

"Conquests don't count," Payal said wryly.

"You're not funny," Ayaan said. "Actually, you mentioning Disney World reminded me of this, Sarika. I used to collect Christmas ornaments."

"I remember that," Arun said fondly. "He had so many, and he'd always be sure to stop in a gift shop on his way out of a new place."

Ayaan caught his breath, unaware that Arun remembered this quirky childhood habit.

"Do you still put up a tree?" Payal asked.

"No...we all grew up, I guess, and stopped decorating each year. I still bought ornaments through college, but I guess once we stopped putting up the tree, it lost its purpose." Ayaan shrugged.

Sarika's sympathetic gaze touched his skin softly, and he did his best to avoid it. "Payal, what is an adventure you'd like to go on?"

"Well, you both have mentioned Disney and I've never been there!"

"Really?" Arun, Sarika, and Ayaan asked at the same time.

"My family didn't take too many vacations together. We weren't quite as warm as you guys are...but now that I'm spending time with you all, maybe it's time!"

"We can go," Sarika said. "We'll go someday."

Payal blew her a kiss, then picked up her card for Arun. "What was your favorite news story of the last year?"

It didn't take a breath for Arun to answer. Completely straight-faced—even Ayaan had to give him credit—he said, "Last year, scientists created a 3D model of a discovery they'd made that a dinosaur had an all-purpose orifice."

Payal nearly choked on her water. Sarika's face split into a giant smile, and she covered her face as she laughed herself to tears. Ayaan, who couldn't manage the poker face his brother had kept up with, asked, "Did you enjoy looking at the 3D, all-purpose orifice, mate?"

Even Arun started laughing.

"Okay, Sarika. You're going to have to be honest about this one," Arun said. "What is something your significant other introduced you to that you now like?"

Sarika opened her mouth and Ayaan knew in a split second that she was about to make a dirty joke.

"No sexual innuendo, for the love of God!" Ayaan bellowed in jest and Sarika stuck her tongue out at him.

"Your maturity always stuns me, baby brother-in-law. I was going to say...classical music."

"You didn't like classical music?" Payal asked.

"I was a bit of an emo girl when we met," Sarika confessed. "I liked loud music."

"She was basically a metalhead. Don't let her fool you," Arun said.

"You changed it. I work to classical music now. It's your fault."

"Hey, me too!" Payal said.

"It's soothing, isn't it? Okay, Ayaan, your turn." Sarika held the card out in front of her. An indescribable expression crossed her face, and her eyes flashed to the box before looking at Ayaan again. "What event in your life taught you the most about yourself?"

Ayaan froze. Payal didn't know the root cause of his entire family's strife with him and how one night when he was sixteen had changed everything. To lie or to tell the truth?

He'd already partaken in the biggest lie of all when agreeing to this engagement, hadn't he? Now he had promised he wouldn't hurt her...but if he told this story in front of everyone, or God forbid, if Arun blurted it out, he would lose the narrative and maybe lose her too if she agreed with the rest of his family that he wasn't worth the time of day.

"I don't know if you have one event that changes you," he said. "I think...sometimes you go through one thing, and it splinters into a million other things, and all those pieces can hurt you or help you in whatever way they're meant to. Everything can teach you about yourself."

He glanced at Arun, who had a curious expression on his face. He half expected his older brother to make a remark like, "I know what changed you, Ayaan!" but instead, Arun nodded.

"I agree with that," he said.

Ayaan cleared his throat. "Payal, what was the greatest feat of your childhood?"

"That I survived it," Payal joked. "I was a handful and a bit of a tomboy. I did more daredevil things than I ever should have."

Everyone laughed.

"No...my biggest bragging point when I was younger was that I flew to India all by myself when I was six to spend a summer with my nani before she came to live with us permanently. I thought I was so cool because I'd done it alone—except at that age, you have flight attendants who watch you like a hawk and accompany you everywhere, but I was sure it earned me some bragging points."

"You were fearless even then!" Sarika said. "I cried on my first flight alone, and I was twenty-two."

"And, Arun...last question." Payal paused, and Ayaan couldn't determine whether it was for dramatic flair. Then she looked up with a smile on her face, as though her expression hadn't fallen mere seconds before. "It's the moment of truth. Is there something you initially hid from your partner because you were worried it would ruin your chances?" Payal asked.

Ayaan felt the heat from the question though it hadn't been posed to him.

What am I hiding? The fact that I used you to get a job...and now if I tell you, I'll lose you.

"I hid that I liked her! We were so close as friends that I was terrified of changing the dynamic and the possibility of failure. It wasn't until Ayaan gave me pep talks every day and then staged a coup that I confessed."

Sarika's eyes softened, and Ayaan wondered if Payal would look at him like that—sustained, undeterred from the obstacles life threw their way, and resistant to time.

"That's all the cards," Sarika said, sounding mildly disappointed.

"That was actually really fun!" Payal said. "I didn't think it would be so random and insightful. Those aren't things we learn every day."

"Likes random questions…check," Ayaan said. He marked an invisible check in the air.

It didn't take much longer for Arun and Sarika to call it a night. It was only nine thirty, but Sarika wanted to cram in more sightseeing before their early evening flight back the next day, and she insisted on getting some rest.

"We'll see you in two weeks for your trip to London! We only have you for a fortnight to plan an entire engagement party. This is going to be fun!"

Ayaan tried to smile and he watched Payal register that they'd be together for two weeks, curious whether she would show any apprehension that they were racing toward this party.

But she simply smiled and nodded, a sphinx when it came to how she felt.

Sarika and Arun put their shoes on, swung coats over their shoulders, and hugged Payal and Ayaan.

"Thank you for tonight," Ayaan murmured to Sarika. "You always make life feel lighter."

"I brought those cards so you both would have a chance to learn about each other and take the pressure off," she said back, keeping her voice low and shooting a glance at Arun and Payal, who were in conversation about the logistics of the upcoming London trip. "Trust yourself."

He had never loved his sister-in-law more.

Payal and Ayaan waved the two off, and she began collecting her own belongings, returning to the living room to pick up her bag and pulling her coat off the hook by the door.

He didn't want her to go. After a shaky few weeks since their fight, tonight was the first time their conversations were warm and anywhere close to normal. Well, to be fair, normal was griping at each other. But the inexplicable connection they had shared at the wedding and in electric moments throughout the last few months...he was reminded of the sparks tonight.

He missed them when they were gone.

"Hey," Ayaan said, touching her wrist as she headed toward the door. "Can I be honest?"

Payal paused, raising an eyebrow. "If you're about to tell me you had a one-night stand with Neha, you're about to quit marketing to open a taco stand in Harlem, or that you and Kai are secretly the people who walk around in Sesame Street suits in Times Square, then you don't have to be honest. You can see yourself out."

Ayaan didn't see that coming. He burst out laughing. "It's my apartment! But no, none of those things."

"That's okay. I could still make you leave," she teased. "Anyway...I'm all ears."

"I heard what you said to Arun," he admitted. "And I wanted to thank you."

Her eyes widened. "How did you know?"

He laughed. "Payal, I live in a one-bedroom apartment the size of a matchbox. There isn't much that can be said in the living room that can't be heard in the bathroom."

He had heard every word, feigning ignorance when he'd returned. Typically, it would have taken all he had not to fire back on Arun, but the manner in which Payal had stood up to him had fallen over Ayaan like a warm blanket.

Her loyalty, despite the fuckery he'd put her through, and the fact that she hadn't turned her back on him was everything. He didn't have words for the springs of butterflies that had erupted inside him.

Not to mention, a woman putting Arun in his place on his behalf was sexy as hell.

Payal flushed and answered, "I wanted to protect you. You worked really hard."

"Thank you. I appreciated you standing up for me."

"It's not fair how Arun talks about you," Payal said heatedly. "I know he's your family and I like him a lot. I do," she added once she saw Ayaan's expression. "But you have to give credit where it's due and share in the wins of your family...or at least, that's how I always imagined it should be."

"Well...for all the family vibes we give off, there are a few elements lacking, and faith in me is one of them."

"If it makes you feel any better, I have belief in who you are and what you can do."

"Really?"

"I've seen it," she said simply. "The way you breathe life into the things you love. Only a fool wouldn't see that, Ayaan Malhotra."

She kissed his cheek.

He wanted to turn his head, meet her lips, and not let her go, but instead, he reminded himself that she hadn't given him a clue that she felt the same way...and that she couldn't, after all he'd done. He was only doing all this to get the stake he wanted in Veer, right?

But as he waved her off, he knew he was lying to himself.

Chapter Twenty

PAYAL

FOUR AND A HALF MONTHS UNTIL THE ENGAGEMENT AND FASHION SHOW

This time, they rode to the airport together.

Payal had been on plenty of trips with her friends. She and Kiran had taken a road trip after college where they'd witnessed a memorable moon rise over Nashville at a bar high above the city lights. The CMC had gone on a weekend trip to Chicago once and eaten so much deep-dish pizza that Payal was sure she'd rolled back onto the plane on the way home.

But there was something different about being on a trip home with someone you felt something for.

The past two weeks, since their night at Ayaan's apartment, Payal had gone back and forth, running circles around all the different conflicts this situation had presented.

The fashion show was now four and a half months away, and so was the engagement party.

And if she ended it, the deal with her parents would fall through, damning them all to this life of distance and dysfunction. Though if she continued, she might not be happy, and Ayaan's track record with trust was abysmal.

Sometimes, the fraud felt like too much.

She wasn't sure she wanted to walk away from Ayaan, but she also couldn't imagine starting an engagement, a marriage, without the certainty of being in love with someone or knowing those feelings were reciprocal. There was loss associated with the planning of this engagement party too...as though she was wasting efforts and this should be a meaningful thing with someone she loved. Now, the romance of planning colors, venues, menus, and decor had also become collateral damage in a power move.

If she ever got engaged for real, then all this wouldn't be new and magical.

Then she'd circle back to the butterflies she inexplicably felt when a text came from him or she knew she'd see him, and the reflection on where her heart was only muddled her thoughts further.

"Payal, are you sure you haven't fallen for him?" Kiran finally asked on a group video call one day.

"No!" Payal protested. *"How could you think that?"*

"I don't know," cut in Sonam, sounding bored. *"Maybe because you don't stop talking about him."*

"He's annoying!"

"You also just spent a night with his family that you loved," Kiran said patiently.

"But that doesn't mean I like him." But she sounded, even to herself, rather less convinced.

"Good. Then fake break up with him and end the madness," said Akash.

I don't want to lose him, Payal wanted to say, but she knew she'd saturated the conversation with the same arguments, and she allowed Kiran to switch the topic to her and Nash instead.

Ayaan and Payal had talked about marketing on the way to the airport and rehashed the last couple of weeks, during which

Payal was busy and Ayaan had gone on a few days' trip to visit Kai's family with him in Boston. The silences were growing more comfortable, and Payal felt less pressure to fill them with chatter.

He'd bought her a coffee when he noticed her yawning while looking at her laptop.

"It's like overpriced mud," he'd commented with a laugh as he handed her a cup from the shop two gates down. "But I thought you could use it."

The thoughtful gesture turned her head toward him, beginning the cycle of confusion all over again.

The plane rose over the clouds, and Payal pulled her sketchbook from her bag, doodling a figure absentmindedly. She liked to draw through the mental block that creatives often faced, like the lack of words on a page or the designs that mimicked the twenty that had come before because the well of originality had dried temporarily. Pushing through the discomfort seemed to be her MO these days.

The plane bumped and dropped suddenly, eliciting some shocked gasps and shouts from fellow passengers.

"Damn," she mumbled. The bump had caused her to scribble across the figure on paper, and the sketch was unsalvageable.

As she flipped the page, hoping to start anew with better ideas, she looked over at Ayaan.

He was gripping the armrest like he was trying to break it off in his palm.

"You okay?" she asked.

"I don't like turbulence."

"I don't think anyone likes the feeling of being tossed in the air," Payal said.

"Mmm." He exhaled heavily, closing his eyes and pursing his lips as the plane lurched once more.

"But if this helps…it's like hitting a road bump. Nothing violent. Like taking a speed bump too fast in the air."

He grunted a response and Payal laid a hand on top of his.

His fingers were rigid, curled so tight that Payal was certain they would remain stuck that way if he didn't loosen them up. His jaw was clenched. The cabin shook again.

"Sorry, folks, we seem to have hit a rough patch. We'll be moving to get out of it in the next few minutes but hang in there until then and stay in your seats," the captain's voice announced.

"We figured out it was rough, thanks," Ayaan mumbled.

Payal ran her fingers over his knuckles absentmindedly. She wouldn't be able to draw anyway, so she turned on the screen in front of her, putting on a random movie she'd seen advertised.

Ayaan's hand gently loosened under hers, the sinew moving from taut to relaxed as his fingers began moving apart. Payal's fingers found the gaps in his and gently filled the spaces as she watched the movie. When Payal glanced over a few minutes later, Ayaan's eyes were closed and he was snoring lightly, his hair fluttering slightly under the air-conditioning and his face finally relaxed.

Though she had hoped to draw, she let her hand sit in his.

He awoke with a start an hour later, and when Payal turned to him, he glanced at his hand, still open-palmed on the armrest, tangled up in hers. Meeting her eye, he pulled his hand toward himself quickly and gave her a small smile, blushing slightly.

"Well, the bumps seem to have lessened," he said, not looking at her.

Payal startled a bit at the unexpected pull away from her. "I'm glad you got some rest."

"Were you able to sleep at all?"

"No…"

"Why? Everything okay?" He searched her face and she felt the heat rise in her chest.

"I'm so tense right now," she growled. "I can't focus on my designs because I'm thinking about this engagement party and all the decisions that will need to be made for that. But when I think about the party, the business pops back into my head and I think about investors who need to fund the line. Which then brings me back to the designs that need to be completed." *Not to mention how I feel about you.*

"That...is a lot of feelings."

Payal narrowed her eyes at him in response. She stuck her tongue out and turned back to the sketchbook she had just brought to her lap.

"I mean it," he said sincerely. "It sounds overwhelming."

"So much is changing. Most of my life, I've embraced that. Now, I'm...a little tired."

"What are you scared of?"

"I'm anxious. About the line and the show and success I want so badly." *For reasons beyond fame itself,* she wanted to say. "Of this party. Seeing my family. Planning this event. All of it."

The plane jolted, turbulence outside shaking the inside, but Ayaan didn't flinch or take his eyes off her.

"How do you feel about this engagement party?"

Payal tried not to show any surprise on her face about the flyby question and her conflicted feelings about it. "Why do you ask?"

"How would you feel about going smaller rather than bigger? You have so much on your plate... I know Indian families often have enormous parties, and with ours being in businesses, our networks are even larger. But what if we make it intimate?"

Relief flooded her. "Really? You'd be okay with that?"

He shrugged. "If it takes the stress off your face and allows us to ease into the announcement, why not? I can bring it up with the parents."

"Did you just volunteer as tribute to take the heat on a decision you know they'll hate?"

"I did. I'll do it for you." His cocky smirk sent butterflies zooming through her. "And what if I plan a relaxing night out?"

"Like a date?" Payal asked dubiously.

"Yes," Ayaan said simply. "Let's get to know each other better...and maybe even London. Home turf. New company. What do you say?"

He was earnest, and after the hit he was about to take with their families, Payal couldn't help but feel endeared to him.

"Okay," Payal said. "Let's do it."

"Well, we did do it that one night, but we can do it again," he said without missing a beat.

She felt her face settle back into grumpiness. "You're not funny."

But when she turned away, she gave a chuckle.

· · · · · · · · · · ·

AYAAN

Meetings with multiple hotels around the London area, florists, event planners, and decor vendors for the August engagement party was one of the most exhausting endeavors Ayaan had taken part in.

Why would anyone want to get married if this was what the festivities entailed? But then, typical Indian events were never small. The tiniest wedding he'd been to was a hundred people, and the bride and groom had upset their extended family by leaving second cousins off the list. Arun and Sarika's wedding had four hundred attendees.

Payal and Ayaan had whittled their list to one hundred for the engagement party. Ayaan had managed to convince his and Payal's family to keep it smaller under the pretense that between the acquisition and engagement, plenty would be celebrated, and they could do a large wedding as a culmination for the year.

He also didn't mind going to bat as the white knight protecting Payal from additional stress.

But he wouldn't be getting married, at least according to the plan, and this smaller party allowed for less damage across the board.

Yet as he spoke to Payal, laughing over their shared dirty humor and finding himself texting her through her day just to see what she was up to, he noticed his resolve becoming shakier. Perhaps marriage to Payal was a step further than he wanted to consider, but a future with her...

He wasn't opposed to it. Rather, he began to look forward to it, wondering if perhaps they were better suited than they'd believed.

True to his promise but later than he'd hoped, he had set up a night out for the two of them on the Saturday after they'd arrived, at the halfway point of their trip home. The May weather in London was chillier than New York, but they were still experiencing all four seasons in a day. He hoped the skies would hold on their night out.

He looked up. The sky was clear, stars twinkling faintly against a navy sky. Ayaan held a bag of takeaway Indian food from his favorite restaurant in the area.

"Quite a trek out here, isn't it?" Payal's voice rang out.

Ayaan grinned. "Am I the only one who finds it funny that trekking across London is a long distance for Brits while Americans regularly say they drove six hours and don't bat an eyelash?"

"I used to find it so odd when Sonam talked about how her family drove from New Jersey to North Carolina to see family!"

They watched each other for a moment, their lips playing at smirks.

"Hi," Ayaan said finally.

"Hi," Payal replied, and she stepped in for a hug.

Though they'd only seen each other two days ago, at a frenzied food tasting where Payal's mother and Mum had lectured the staff on how exactly they'd gone wrong on every flavor, this reunion rang differently. The marina around them was quieter, the sounds of water lapping against the boats and the murmurs of passersby echoing only as background noise. The peaceful ambience of the area lulled them into contented calm.

Payal wrapped her arms around his neck and Ayaan breathed her in, the scent of musky jasmine emanating from her hair and filling him up. When she stepped back again, their eyes met and the air between them sparked and crackled.

"So...what are we doing? You aren't taking me out on the Thames to drop me in, are you?"

"No...you look way too good for that," Ayaan replied before he could stop himself.

She blushed and looked down, brushing some of her long hair out of her eyes.

Payal was dressed simply—for her, anyway—but the relative simplicity of her outfit, a black blazer over a white tee and dark-blue jeans, was a turn-on for Ayaan. He'd only seen her in a full face of makeup and fashionably styled, except for the morning after they had hooked up...but she looked different now, lighter somehow. Ayaan could see her vulnerabilities and she'd slipped off her armor for tonight.

"Now...are you ready?" Ayaan held out his free hand.

Payal took it, and Ayaan led her to a small yacht docked at the end of the path. A refurbished wooden boat straight from the canals of Venice, the *Regina* was now a vintage yacht with a contemporary cabin fitted with luxurious cushioned seats, a romantic espresso dining table with candles, and a captain who greeted them as they climbed onboard and stepped a few stairs down into the space they would occupy.

The roof of the cabin had been fitted with glass windows, allowing guests to view both sides of the Thames and the starry sky from the yacht.

Romantic, chilled out, and luxurious, all at once. Ayaan couldn't have asked for better.

He helped Payal step down, steadying her as she found her balance on the gently swaying vessel.

"This is beautiful," Payal said breathlessly.

"Well, I hope it's delicious too, because I brought some food for us to have a little dinner as we cruise along."

Her eyes lit up. "You didn't!"

"I asked Nani what your favorite Indian dishes are," Ayaan boasted, thinking of Nani's exclamation about how he'd be making Payal's day and how he was such a good boy.

"You are unreal," Payal said with a clap and a laugh. "Thank you so much."

"Let's eat. The captain is going to move us along."

They took their seats on either side of the dinner table, and Ayaan waved to the captain to get started. The boat gently pulled away from the dock, and soon they were floating down the waterways leading to the Thames.

Ayaan opened the bag, neatly placing all the takeaway containers in a line in front of him and announcing each dish. Then he produced two paper plates and paper cups. Two wineglasses had been placed on the table already, presumably by the boating company.

"Tandoori chicken, because I'm on this date too. Medu vada, because South Indian cuisine is some of the best I've ever had—"

"My best friend Akash's family is from Karnataka. Trust me, there has been a lot of Kannada fare in our apartments. Continue."

"Mumbai chaat, because you mentioned you love street food. And…mutton curry, which Nani told me you loved, and vegetable biryani because that's your other favorite. Also, enough roti to feed half of London."

She put her hands on her heart. "This is so thoughtful."

"You sound surprised."

"Pleasantly," Payal teased.

"Oh, wonderful, so you've joined the ranks of my family in underestimating me!" Ayaan said sarcastically.

She laughed. "Maybe I'm impressed!"

"Then you're nothing like my family."

"I can assure you that's not true," she said kindly. Instead of going along with his self-deprecating joke, she watched his face intently.

"What are you looking at?" he asked.

"You," Payal said simply. "You have a really lovely smile."

He offered it again, his high cheekbones rising. Instead of responding, he stood and went to the mini fridge, where he brought a bottle of red wine out.

He poured them a glass each, and Payal took hers, lifting it to her lips.

Ayaan wondered for a second what it would be like to kiss her as he watched her take a sip.

He cleared his throat. "Let's go out to the front."

They exited the cabin and settled into the cushioned benches on the bow of the yacht. Drifting slowly for a bit, the engine quietly whirred beneath them. Ayaan breathed in the smell of summer—river odors and all—and the crispness that the air by the water always held. City lights glowed lining the river, and the towering buildings seemed to form a protective wall as the yacht floated along.

Payal's shoulders relaxed, and she rolled her neck. She sighed, leaning back and stretching her long legs before curling them underneath her, which Ayaan noticed was her characteristic comfy move.

"You look infinitely more relaxed," he commented.

"I feel it. Thank you for arranging this. Sometimes the weight of expectation is so heavy and you don't realize how long you've carried it until moments like this."

"You carry it well, Payal. Don't let anyone tell you differently."

"Where has your mind drifted off to tonight?" Payal asked. "What's your happy place?"

"Tonight, I think it's here," Ayaan said honestly. "Water. A pretty girl. A boat. Some seclusion. City lights. It's lovely."

Payal blushed. "I have to agree...though I usually zone out to the beaches of Cancún when I need a place to imagine I'm in. This is a nice second!"

"I'll take it. Are you a beach person?"

"I'm a beach baby. I love the sound of water and the smell of salt in the air. I don't mind being hot."

She hadn't meant it as a commentary on her own beauty, but Ayaan inwardly agreed that she was, in fact, very hot. Her breasts looked particularly perky too. Hoping she didn't catch his eyes drifting to them, he forced himself to lift his eyes. "I like your necklace," he said lamely.

"I've been very into pearl jewelry lately."

"Did you just say you liked pearl necklaces?"

It took Payal a moment to recognize Ayaan's hidden meaning

and that this was no innocuous question. He watched as she frowned before meaning dawned in her eyes, and they widened.

Payal choked on her wine. "Ayaan!"

"You can't blame me for going there."

"Why are you such a prepubescent boy?" she exclaimed, but as she said it, an enormous laugh burst out of her chest. "I really set myself up for that."

After witnessing the wrinkle that had seemingly carved itself into her forehead over the last week, Ayaan was relieved to see her throw her head back and laugh. Her hair bounced on her shoulder blades and he wanted to rest his hand there, feeling the curve of her back as he slid it down.

"If you could dress anyone in a Besharmi design, who would it be?" Ayaan asked suddenly.

"Kate Middleton. The Duchess of Cambridge. Prince William's wife." Payal said immediately.

"Funnily enough, I do know who Kate is without the clarifications."

"She deserves all the styles and honors and clarifications on earth."

"I think she has them—she's a royal. What about Meghan Markle?"

"A goddess. If she wore my designs, someone would have to pick me up off the floor."

"They could wear them someday."

"Please. On what planet would they need to?"

"Hey, you never know. Dream big. Royals have diplomatic events. You could be the next Anita Dongre."

Payal let out a wishful sigh. But she looked down, and her soft smile told Ayaan that she was imagining it and that someday, she'd make it happen.

As though the universe had heard them discuss royalty, their boat passed by the Tower of London, its gray stone turrets protruding into the night, aglow from the spotlights.

They both watched it from the water, awestruck. Payal's mouth dropped open, and Ayaan felt the same sense of wonder at a sight they'd both seen a thousand times.

But the world looked different tonight, no matter how many times they'd seen it before.

"Well...I wouldn't have seen a wonderful night like this coming a few months ago," Ayaan said finally.

"What was your first impression of me?" Payal asked, turning her head to him. "Should I even ask?"

Ayaan laughed. "Well, we met on a hookup app..."

"Oh, so you thought I would be easy!"

"One, there is nothing easy about you, and two, I quite honestly don't believe that about anyone. People have sex. It's not a big deal. But no..."

"Then?"

"Can I be honest?" he asked.

"You promised me you would be," she murmured, and she leaned toward him, putting her empty glass on the wood panel built into the seating.

"I was wrong about what I thought you'd be," he said so quietly, he barely heard himself over the splash of the waves. "I thought you were beautiful. And it's true. And I thought you were temporary. But you're so much more."

The air between them crackled, as though London's magic had weaved itself through the air and lit them both up from the inside out. He could swear Payal's eyes nearly glowed in the dim light on the river, and in that moment, he knew she felt the same way about him.

Chapter Twenty-One

PAYAL

Payal woke up on Saturday, two weeks after they'd arrived in London and the day before they would leave it, with a smile on her face.

The trip had been smooth…easy, even, with Ayaan's input.

It was amazing how easy it had been to convince him that a small engagement party was the way to go. She wasn't faking the stress she was under, of course, but a little manipulation went a long way, and she was thankful that Ayaan had also wanted a minimal celebration.

It took the pressure off, that was for sure.

Whatever their current strange situation, Ayaan had proven himself a fun companion. In fact, Payal thought, he had demonstrated he was more than that. He'd been fun, thoughtful, and someone who Payal genuinely enjoyed spending time with.

The funny thing was that it wasn't the wealth, good looks, or connections that Ayaan's appeal lay in—though they were certainly bonuses and the entire driving force behind this operation. No, his vulnerabilities were like a door into a world Payal wanted to explore further.

Payal: Want to go for a walk?

Ayaan: Like a date? He was echoing her own doubtful question on the plane.

Payal: Yes.
Ayaan: I'm a hard sell.

I know exactly how hard you get, she typed back after a moment, with a mischievous impulse and a winking emoji.

Ayaan: LOL okay, sold. Let me know when.

They settled on Wimbledon Common, a large green not too far away and without bells and whistles.

They met at the Wimbledon War Memorial, the easiest landmark to identify and one of the many obelisks dotting London's cityscape.

"What, no wining and dining?" Ayaan called out as he crossed the street.

"And here I thought you'd enjoy my company. Do I have to woo you?"

"A man likes to be wooed sometimes."

"Shall I buy flowers and gifts and only take you to the fanciest places for meals?" She remained straight-faced.

"I'd settle for nothing less."

His cheeks twitched as he walked up to her now.

He looked *good*. In dark-blue jeans, a black crewneck sweater over a black-and-gray-plaid collared shirt, and with black sneakers on his feet, he was preppy and put together. His hair was gelled into intentionally disheveled spikes in the front.

She loved the way he walked, his back straight and his chin up as though the world was a catwalk and he was the only one onstage.

She had a distinct feeling she treated the world the same.

"It's nice to get away from the families and chaos of work sometimes, isn't it?" she asked.

"It's lovely. This was a great idea."

"Why, thank you, princess."

He rolled his eyes.

As they began walking north with no destination in mind but quietly accompanying the other, Payal breathed in the air. The mulch crunched under their feet. Houses lined the right side of the street, and the left was full of green grass and trees, not a building to be seen. It was as though they were toeing the line between civilization and wild.

"Have you ever noticed that we've never spent time not doing anything?" she asked.

"What do you mean?"

"Well, outside our initial meetup, we've always had dinners or family events or done something that requires our attention. We've never met up to simply walk or chat."

Ayaan thought about it. "I suppose it's easier, isn't it? When you're at dinner or out in the city somewhere, it doesn't require you to rely on yourself to create a connection. You can always find a commonality in the busyness or make small talk. Genuinely being alone with your thoughts or with someone you feel something for forces you to be yourself and be comfortable."

Payal tried not to focus on the fact that he'd said *someone you feel something for*.

"You're right," she said instead. "Our families have also led a lot of our conversation by forcing us to interact...not that I mind being with you. It's been really enjoyable, actually."

"I agree with you," Ayaan said. "It's been surprisingly wonderful."

They walked in peace for a while. Payal was distinctly aware of his hand swinging close to hers. She could convince herself that she felt the warmth of his skin and the tingle of the almost touch. She was tempted to take his hand.

"When we go back to New York, you should meet my friends," she said suddenly.

"You have friends?" he teased.

"I can go and leave you here with none," she retorted.

"So much for being enjoyable together, then." He chuckled. Then he added, unexpectedly, "The CMC sound like a great bunch. I'd love to meet them."

"They're my found family," Payal said proudly. "I'm sure they'll adore you."

"Speaking of family, tell me about your relationship with your parents," he requested. "You've mentioned you aren't close, besides Nani. I never hear you call them just to chat or see them call you. What's your story? If you don't mind me asking..."

Payal steeled herself, digging as far as she could to unearth the years of rumination on why her relationships with her parents were distant. It was a physical lift to move her reflections on them and push them out of her body.

"My dad used to be kind when I was little. We spent more time together, and he used to be at home more often. Then the company began growing, and as the internet exploded, so did business. After that, it was like his mind was elsewhere all the time even when he wasn't."

"That must have been hard...though I can relate."

"Was Veer always a priority?"

"We were very close until sixth form," Ayaan said. "Then it...it fell apart in many ways. But I relate to being forgotten sometimes.

Even through the pandemic...I hadn't seen them in nearly two years, but when I arrived in London again after borders opened up, only Sarika and my mom had a warm homecoming. It was as though I'd erased myself from Arun and my dad."

Payal made a face. "We all had so many losses through it. It must have been painful to come back and feel as though we'd learned nothing about the value of relationships."

"Some people found it easier to survive than thrive, I suppose," Ayaan said. "But I've hijacked the conversation and I apologize. What about your mom?"

"My mom's mom died early," Payal said. "Her family is more traditional. They married her off young, at twenty, because they didn't think she needed to be too educated. That's exactly why Ma insisted I went to the best schools.

"She advocated for me often when I was younger and I won't deny that...but I don't know if she knows how to be a mom outside of providing basic needs. And it wasn't the money or the opportunity I needed—not to be ungrateful—but the softer things like dinner together or a hug when I was sad or those motherly chats people rave about. The trauma of losing her own mom never let her be a mom to me...and the fact that she didn't have a say in her life as a girl made her not want one.

"My mom wanted a boy so badly. I don't think Nani was the one putting pressure on her. She loves me so much that I can't imagine her making Ma feel as though she had to have a boy to add value to the family. That's an effed-up notion anyway. But like I said, when you see your world devalue someone because of their gender, it influences whether you'd want to put someone through that...and we carry all the garbage and trauma our parents carry, so when I hit twenty-five, she began getting on my case about marriage because she was taught it's what you do. At thirty, she was ready to sell me to the highest bidder, which in this case..."

"Was my family," Ayaan said quietly.

"I saw it that way at first," Payal admitted. "But now..."

"Now what?"

She didn't know why they were whispering—in the evening air with traffic and London's nighttime walkers.

And while her mind said, *Now you're a worthwhile connection to have*, her heart simply didn't agree with the logic. Ayaan wasn't simply a contact being used to elevate the brand.

"Now you're becoming more than that," she murmured without thinking.

Ayaan slowed his walk upon her words, as though the words had a hold on him, and when Payal snuck a side glance at him, he had a soft expression on his face, his lips curling slightly.

Then, as though he was reading her mind and studying her, his hand found hers.

She opened her fingers, letting him wind his through them, and she stepped six inches closer to him. And on they walked, around a park in London, hand in hand, finally comfortable simply being together.

Chapter Twenty-Two

AYAAN

THREE AND A HALF MONTHS UNTIL THE FASHION SHOW AND ENGAGEMENT

In the week since they had arrived back in New York, Ayaan couldn't help but think of something his mother had said before he'd left: *"You need a girl like her to bring you light. Selfishly, I wasn't sure we'd end up with another daughter-in-law like Sarika, who adds buckets of joy to every well she dips into. Now, we'll have two!"*

Now, when he reflected on her words, annoyance with himself followed.

He wasn't supposed to have let it get this far. Somewhere in all this, he was supposed to let Payal know he didn't feel anything or, better yet, she would walk away. Instead, they were holding hands, sharing vulnerabilities, and growing so close that he didn't want to let go.

Which was why he was arriving at Payal's apartment to meet her friends over a dinner she'd said she'd host.

"Are you cooking?" he had asked, surprised.

"I can't make noodles without setting the kitchen on fire," she replied.

"I haven't even mastered pancakes properly. I'm sure our

children won't mind having takeaway every night," he said without thinking, and he froze at the slip.

But Payal didn't react visibly. Instead, she shrugged. "They'll live. Besides, they'll be dressed impeccably, and if they're your kids, they'll have Instagram sponsorships by the age of three, so we'll have already given them a reason for therapy. What's one more?"

They laughed.

"And it's good we have Nash for that, correct?"

"You studied my friends," Payal said. She formed a heart with her hands, just over her chest, and pouted as though the words were the most aww-inducing she'd ever heard.

"I like to know my audience," he said.

"I'm glad you do. And for the record, I would love to learn how to cook. Maybe we can take a class together."

He'd said yes and grown excited before he could stop himself.

The side of him that had its heart set only on the position at Veer was ringing the alarm at meeting friends and mingling circles. But the pull of wanting to know everything about Payal was growing stronger by the day. With every look, every moment of shared vulnerability, every joke, and every success, Ayaan knew he was falling for her.

"Nervous?" Payal asked as she let him in.

"Not until you asked," Ayaan said with a laugh.

"You're smart, sarcastic, and nice. It'll be fine," Payal said, giving his arm a squeeze reassuringly and guiding him to the living room. "Guys, this is Ayaan," Payal said. "Ayaan, these are Sonam, Kiran, and Akash, my best friends—"

"Soul mates really," a curvy girl with a black cropped, chin-length wavy bob and with one leg over the armrest called out before bounding out of the seat and extending her hand to Ayaan.

Sonam wore square-rimmed glasses, but Ayaan could see she had beautiful teardrop-shaped eyes behind her frames. She wore ripped boyfriend jeans, black flats, and a black tee...a simple look that told Ayaan she knew exactly who she was.

"Stop, Sonam. You'll scare the guy," the girl who Ayaan now knew had to be Kiran said with an Indian lilt to her accent. She stood from the love seat, came over, and gave him a hug. "I've heard wonderful things about you!"

"That's what nice people say when they don't want to tell you the bad things," Ayaan said.

"Absolutely not!" Kiran said. "And I'm a terrible liar so you can trust me on that."

Kiran had a square face and long black hair that reached past her waist in gentle waves, and Ayaan liked her already.

Lingering in the background with quiet gravitas and a penetrating stare was Akash.

He looked like a typical Wall Street guy: preppy, hair spiked, and probably wore a suit to the gym.

In other words, Akash was, admittedly, a good-looking fellow who took care of himself.

"Hey," he said now from his spot near the love seat. He made no move to come over.

Ayaan could recognize the power move from a mile away, a gesture that required him to be the bigger man and to utilize effort to fit in. Glancing at Payal, who smiled with a hopeful expression on her face, and not wanting to disappoint her, he decided to give in.

Stepping around the love seat, he walked over to Akash and raised his hand to shake.

Akash's sight dropped to Ayaan's extended hand, and he paused for a second before taking it and giving it a tight, firm shake. The two men's eyes locked.

"Good to meet you," Akash said finally.

"Likewise, man."

They hadn't let go, and Ayaan was sure this stereotypical moment of machismo would lead to one of the men breaking the other's hand.

"Akash, you want another beer?" Sonam asked.

Akash let go and Ayaan thanked Sonam on the inside, wishing he could rub his hand without appearing like a delicate daisy. *That guy totally hates me.*

He was, however, astute enough to realize he also didn't trust Akash worth a damn. Payal was beautiful and smart—and seemingly surrounded herself with the same. It seemed impossible to believe that they hadn't dated.

People can be friends without dating, he heard Kai's voice in his head. *Trust her.*

"So...the CMC?" Ayaan asked, bringing up the nickname of the group.

"In college, we spent our first night getting to know one another over Kiran's cup of chai..." Sonam started.

"Oh my God, that chai is divine," Payal said.

"I'll make some later," Kiran said with a smile.

"As I was saying, Kiran's divine cup of chai brought us together and we realized later that we shared masala about our lives over the experience. It became a tradition. The name is silly, of course, but saying 'Akash, Payal, Sonam, Kiran' is a waste of time, and when we were eighteen, it sounded exclusive." Sonam finished with a shrug that seemed dismissive but Ayaan suspected was full of pride at all the years they'd stayed close.

"You guys basically created a secret society," Ayaan said.

"It feels like it sometimes," Payal said.

"That entire phrase about 'spilling the tea' started with us first," Sonam said. "Quite literally. I think Akash gave me third-degree burns."

"I did not, and you tripped me!" Akash said.

"So, Kiran, where is Nash?" Ayaan asked when they'd sat down with their food, a couple of pizzas that Payal had ordered from a place called Vinnie's.

"His aunt is visiting for a week and they're off doing all the touristy things," Kiran said.

"You've been together for how long?"

"Nearly two years now," Kiran said.

"Don't ask her when she's getting married, or she'll tell you that you're being like her parents and may curse you out in Hindi," Akash said.

"The pressure is real. I can sympathize," Ayaan said.

"So you and Payal are getting engaged officially, huh?" Akash asked.

Ayaan willed himself not to sweat. "Indeed. End of August."

"It's all been kind of quick, no?"

"It has," Ayaan admitted. "You never think you'll go from an engagement to liking each other rather than the other way around, but I suppose that's what our parents have been telling us from the start."

Payal nodded. "Nani loves telling me how she and Nana had to figure out each other's tastes and learn how to fall in love. But there's not a day that goes by now that she doesn't mention a funny story or something she loved about him."

"You wouldn't have been the one I imagined having an arranged marriage, though," Akash pushed.

"I wouldn't have either but here we are," Payal said firmly.

"I'm in the same boat," Ayaan said.

Payal smiled at him from across the room as though she was

telling him she had his back, and her easy grin replaced any apprehension Ayaan had with happiness.

Akash didn't appear mollified, but Kiran chimed in, "Well, we're all happy for you and that given your...inauspicious beginning, you've ended up here."

"Oh, man, she told you?" Ayaan exclaimed.

"We're basically in a relationship with you too, pal. You might have to get used to it," Sonam said.

Ayaan laughed. "Quadruple the love, I guess."

"Nash says the same thing."

"I think my family feels the same way!" Sonam said. "It's not like we don't have friends of other backgrounds, but there's something so unifying about a shared experience. Who else is going to understand what it was like being made fun of for bringing Indian food to school for lunch, or being called a terrorist, or the way people mispronounce your name and act as though it's your fault they can't wrap their tongue around it?"

They all made sounds of assent.

"And don't forget the good things," Kiran said. "Who else will understand the log kya kahenge mentality and make fun of it with you? Or fight against some of the ingrained behaviors like your friends? We're taught to follow blindly, and despite best efforts, sometimes you catch yourself continuing cycles of outdated thinking or unfair practice without realizing. And it's nice to have people to call you on it and help you stand for what you believe in."

"I'm a little jealous," Ayaan said. "I have two best friends I see all the time, but being a social butterfly when I was growing up meant that I flew alone a lot between groups rather than having one base to come back to. This is much like a home you can rely on."

"It is," Payal said. "Sometimes that's what you look for...stability, love, and a home. I'm lucky I found it."

"I'm thankful you've brought me in," Ayaan said genuinely.

The night was a fun one. Ayaan was in awe of the circle that Payal had cultivated with her friends over the years, the inside jokes they knew, and the laughter they shared. Even Akash broke the ice eventually, sharing stories about his upbringing in New Jersey and how he and his friends once ended up in a fight with a burly-looking group of guys, all over a piece of gum.

Much like Ayaan felt with Kai and Dharm, the instant camaraderie was warm and welcoming. It reminded Ayaan of the same feeling he'd had when he visited relatives in India. No one left the home without an offer of dinner first, guests were constantly invited to spend the night even without enough beds because someone would simply adjust for the night and sleep on the floor, and everyone knew everyone else's business and, despite any disagreements or gossip, offered help before ill wishes.

One niggling doubt lingered, however, as the CMC left the apartment and Payal and Ayaan were finally alone.

"Are you sure you and Akash haven't...you know. I don't know. Anything."

Payal appeared amused. "You'll have to be clearer."

Ayaan gave her his most exasperated look. "Have you guys boinked?"

She laughed heartily, throwing her head back, and though Ayaan couldn't help but smile along with her, his question remained.

Payal took a deep breath.

He knew his instinct was right—but he had to wait an ungodly amount of time before Payal considered what she was about to say. When she finally met his eye, he knew there was a story in their history that he wouldn't like.

"Even Kiran and Sonam don't know this," she said quietly. "And this is something we agreed to bury."

He waited.

"When we were in college, Akash dated a girl seriously. He might be more liberal with what he wants now, but back then, he was a monogamist to the bone, and he had dated her for three years—the final two of university and our first year in New York. But she was younger. She ghosted him. And..."

Payal gave a nearly imperceptible shudder, her eyes glazing over. "We've never seen him like that. Ever. He was ready to fly back to Duke to get her to talk to him before we talked him out of it. He'd lost weight. Eventually, he refused to talk about her because it hurt so much. We learned quickly not to mention it or ask how he was doing even, because he was so angry and the only moments when he seemed at peace were the ones when he could distract himself with a laugh or an outing or his job. Maybe that wasn't the right move on our parts, but it was all we knew and we were so young.

"It was about four months later, and he and I hung out one night. Sonam was at home. Kiran was sick. It doesn't matter, they weren't there. One bottle of wine turned into several, which turned into a drunken conversation. He mentioned how he needed a distraction and how he missed physical intimacy with someone whose face he loved, and I thought 'Well, I'm here, we're young and a little drunk, and...'" She shrugged with a half laugh.

"So...you've hooked up."

"I would hardly call it that! He could barely get it up and I practically fell asleep. It was sloppy, on edge, and nothing we ever repeated." She put her hands out like, *What else am I supposed to say?*

Ayaan valiantly tried to put off the roaring jealousy in his heart. He could relate, couldn't he, to the feeling of aimlessly hooking up to forget a reality? After all, he and Payal wouldn't have met had that not been the case.

He kept secrets too, after all. He had to give her credit for admitting that she and Akash had a history, one that they hadn't even told their two closest friends about. Ayaan's heart opened, basking in the trust Payal had placed in him with the confession.

If love was trust, he had to do the same.

Chapter Twenty-Three

PAYAL

Payal had meant to walk Ayaan out from her place...but she'd walked him to the lobby. Then he'd lingered before suggesting they take a walk. Somewhere along the way, he offered her his jacket.

Now, as they sat on the grass of a park, Payal had asked Ayaan to tell her a secret.

"It always makes me anxious to go back to London," Ayaan confessed.

"Why?" Payal nearly whispered.

"They haven't seen me the same way since...well, we had a situation in high school, and they've believed I'm a screwup since then," Ayaan said quietly. "It's not true. I mean, I don't think it's true."

"It's not true," Payal reassured him, placing her hand on his. "What happened?"

The memory of Sarika mentioning an incident came back to her, and she knew that he was about to tell her and that this was the time to listen. To be supportive. To remind him that whatever happened in his past, they were building a new future.

Ayaan searched her face for a few seconds as though he was looking for a sign that she was trustworthy.

Then he took a deep breath.

"I was about to begin sixth form at Harrow. My friends and I were a bit wild, and we were staying with my friend Parag's family for a weekend in the summer. They lived quite close to school. We snuck out from home late on Saturday night, and a bunch of us got a bit drunk at the local pub. Parag had hardly drunk all night, so he was fit to drive. We thought about a taxi, just in case, but it was late and we were tired."

Payal's skin rose into goose bumps, knowing where this story was going.

Ayaan's face contorted as he recalled what happened next. "I don't remember a single thing after that until I woke up in the hospital with a concussion and a broken left arm. The authorities had told my parents that the drive had gotten a little wild, that someone in the back had distracted Parag somehow, and he'd rolled the car over the side of the hill by accident."

"Was anyone else hurt?" Payal whispered.

Ayaan nodded, his gaze quickly darting away when it met Payal's. He played with the button on his shirt cuff instead. "Parag. Everyone else had bumps, bruises, fractures, or concussions. Injuries but mild ones in the grand scheme. Parag had to learn to walk again. He spent nearly a year in a rehabilitation facility. He still walks with forearm crutches."

"Oh, Ayaan..."

"His parents were so noble about it. I wish they weren't; we didn't deserve it. But they kept saying it was an accident—that the road was winding, that a group of boys was bound to have something stupid happen to them, and that it was terrible luck. They're wonderful people, really."

"Do you keep in touch? With Parag, I mean."

Ayaan nodded. "We do. He's as kind as ever. We aren't as close, but given all that's happened, I would never expect to be. Sometimes you go through something life-changing and you can't ever find your way back to the person you were before it."

Payal got the impression he wasn't talking about Parag anymore.

"Sarika mentioned that your relationships with your family shifted after that."

He nodded again. "My parents were horrified, of course, during the day or two in the hospital. Mum fretted and Dad repeatedly called doctors who probably wondered what they were doing in my room—a nephrologist isn't going to know the details of a concussion, is he?" He tried to give a small laugh, but it resembled a cough. "Then...as we were all released, word began to spread, and people looked for blame. I think my family began to do the same. Log kya kahenge, you know? 'What are people going to say and how are we going to cover for you?' Then Harrow got involved. They are quite strict, you know. People have been thrown out for drug use even during off-term."

"I remember," Payal murmured, recalling the news stories surrounding that very issue.

"The headmaster contemplated expelling us too. The gravity of the rumors was becoming too much to bear for the school. But between Dad, the other boys' families, and even Parag's parents, who spoke up for us, we weren't thrown out. It was sheer luck."

"You didn't do anything, Ayaan. It was an accident."

He clenched his jaw, the muscle twitching. "I know."

"And you weren't expelled either."

"No...I wasn't. Until the accident, my grades were stellar, I played tennis competitively, and Arun used to joke that I would outshine his records. I actually did end up winning one more award than he did. But they seem to forget that now. Everything fell apart after that night. It was like Gabriel falling from heaven or all those asuras we learned about in Hinduism classes that were punished for becoming too arrogant. I don't think my parents thought I was redeemable. I'd grown sullen too, and I'd lash out when they tried to speak with me. I failed a big exam in college and had to repeat a class. Showed up drunk to a family event that I'd forgotten about. Just a series of mistakes that weren't huge but felt colossal to everyone. Eventually it became a game of pins and needles. Then it became easier to avoid each other altogether."

His face fell and his shoulders did too, and Payal desperately wanted to prop him up, to remind him that he had more to him than an accident from nearly twenty years ago.

She put her hands around his face and lifted his chin so their eyes were level.

"That's not true," Payal said firmly. "You still shine. Your parents are wrong."

He stared at her. "You know your parents were too, to set this deal up, yet you supported them. We do strange things for the people we love. We're willing to believe the worst in ourselves simply because they say it exists."

She nearly recoiled at the intensity in his gaze. His eyes sometimes took on a shade of brown that reminded her of whiskey bottles in the sunlight. He'd touched upon a bruise so deep inside her that it took her breath away. He had held a candle up to the corner hidden away from the world: the disconnect she felt between the loyalty to her parents and all she wanted, and the happy medium she was unable to find.

Until now...when she saw his understanding face and the kindness in his eyes, observing her reaction and somehow knowing exactly what she was going through.

"Maybe my parents were onto something when they told me to do this," she whispered, not moving her hands.

He breathed a sharp intake of breath, and his face brightened. "Maybe when my mom said I needed you, she was right."

A spark traveled from her heart to every part of her body, leaving trails of tingles that lit every nerve on fire.

An eyelash sat on Ayaan's pronounced cheekbone. Without thinking, she moved her fingers to it, gently collecting it between her thumb and forefinger. He closed his eyes in response to her touch, and when his lashes fluttered open again, she'd taken his hand, slowly flipped it over, closed it into a fist, and placed the eyelash on the back of his palm.

"Make a wish," she whispered.

"Why?" he asked.

"Because Nani said so," she said, recalling her grandmother's gentle encouragement of wishing on everything from candles to eyelashes to rainbows.

He closed his eyes.

Payal fervently made a wish of her own: that she could capture these fleeting seconds of hope and belief and lock them away forever inside her. She wished she could remember Ayaan this way, innocent and believing, in a gesture as small as making wishes on eyelashes.

"Now, keep your eyes closed and blow on it," she said.

"Am I allowed to make a dirty joke?"

"You are not, sir," Payal said, a smile cracking her facade and bringing lightness to the otherwise sweet moment they were sharing.

"Okay...I'll believe you on this." He took an unnecessarily large but endearing inhale and blew on the top of his hand.

Payal closed her eyes alongside him, wishing for a third time. *I hope he gets what he wants.*

When they both finally looked at the back of his hand again, the eyelash was gone. Payal was still holding his fist, and Ayaan made no move to pull away.

Instead, like he did in London, he wound his fingers through hers and dropped their hands between them, their elbows resting on their knees.

Payal's focus closed in on Ayaan's beautiful face before dropping to his lips. He licked them unconsciously, like he knew what she was thinking, and they moved slightly toward each other.

Her heart thundered in her chest, unlike it ever had before with any of the many men she'd kissed, and the breathless anticipation came out in a small sigh as they inched closer.

Her eyes began to close, knowing soon she'd only feel his lips on hers, and an ache developed far south of her chest.

A dog barked nearby and they pulled away quickly, jumping at the growling sound interrupting the night's peace.

A woman strolled by, pulling on a leash with a curly-haired puppy whose giant ears flopped around while he explored and he barked here and there at absolutely nothing at all.

"Well, that scared the hell out of me," Ayaan said. His chest rose and fell quickly.

"My heart is pounding," Payal said with a laugh.

"I always wanted a dog named Huckleberry."

Payal paused. "Huckleberry..."

"Yes, I read the *Adventures of Huckleberry Finn* when I was young, and it stuck with me. A little rapscallion sounded like the perfect person to name a puppy after."

Payal laughed, but the image of a small Ayaan's eyes lighting up, just the way they were now, at the notion of bravery, adventure, and a bouncing dog gave her a flutter.

"Let me guess: your dog would be a giant, hundred-and-twenty-pound beast who walks you rather than you walking him."

"Huckleberry, my future cockadoodle, is offended at your insinuation that size matters."

"Well, we know size doesn't matter with you," Payal said without thinking.

Ayaan raised an eyebrow. "What was that?"

Heat rose in her chest, but Payal gazed at him defiantly. "Nothing."

The air between them simmered, and their bodies leaned in, leaving only inches between them. Payal sensed the heat from Ayaan's skin on her own, and goose bumps rose like peaks as every fiber on her body reached for him.

"A cockadoodle?" Payal asked, dissipating the electric air between them.

But even the word *cock* in the context of something entirely unrelated to sex made her mind race with flashbacks to their first night.

"What? Oh...yeah." Ayaan gave a small shake of his head as though he had to get the same dirty thoughts out of his mind. "There's a small problem with my dog wish. I'm quite allergic and the notion of hypoallergenic dogs is a myth."

Payal burst out laughing again. "That's not a small problem! How bad is the allergy?"

"There was a hospital incident at boarding school once. Anaphylaxis. No big deal." But Ayaan's lips were curling.

"I've never had a dog," Payal said. "My mom is afraid of them and wouldn't let me have one."

"If you could have one, what would you name him?"

"Who says it would be a 'him'?"

"Okay, him or her..."

Payal thought.

A minute passed. Ayaan didn't take his gaze from her face and Payal didn't sense any rush as he waited for an answer with the patience of a kindergarten teacher awaiting a correct answer.

"Mulligan."

Ayaan appeared taken aback. "*Mulligan?*"

"You think adventure is worth a tribute. I think second chances are."

The knowing glow in Ayaan's eyes told Payal that he knew they weren't talking about puppies anymore.

"Fair enough. Maybe we can get them both someday. Huckleberry and Mulligan."

Someday.

The mention of a future, the certainty of the two of them conquering the world together, becoming dog parents and maybe even real parents with a family of their own, wasn't foreign. It wasn't out of place tonight.

It felt like a reality, like an inevitable certainty that the two of them, underneath the stars tonight in New York, could be in the wilds of Bora Bora and would still be together as a team.

It brought an involuntary, heartfelt, enormous smile to Payal's face.

Ayaan was still waiting expectantly, as though his nonchalant mention of their future hadn't rocked her world. Payal was heartened that it didn't seem to rock his, that perhaps his mind had wrapped itself around their future so easily that it wasn't shocking for him to accept it.

"Huckleberry and Mulligan. They sound like a law firm," she said.

"Or a cartoon...the *Adventures of Huckleberry and Mulligan.* It could be a children's show on Netflix."

"Can you even imagine? We'd be such terrible influences if we were behind a show."

"I think we could do it." Ayaan grinned. "Look at us. We can do anything together."

Payal couldn't stop herself.

She moved suddenly and shrunk the space between them, crashing her lips against Ayaan's. As her eyelids fluttered shut, she caught Ayaan's surprised expression before he melted into her, pushing back with equal enthusiasm.

He lifted his left hand and placed it on her neck, pulling her closer as he held them both up with his other. His lips—Payal had forgotten how soft they were—parted, and his tongue softly ran over her bottom lip, urging her to part her own.

She let him in, and their kiss deepened, their tongues dancing together.

Payal's hands ran up his chest, feeling the muscle underneath her palms, and her fingers curled, pulling on his shirt and trying to bring him closer to her.

Despite being in a park and knowing people could see her enthusiastic display, she didn't care. Uncrossing her legs and shifting to her knees, she climbed onto Ayaan's lap, extending her legs behind him and bending her knees to support him.

Without breaking their kiss, a hungry and nearly ravenous mix of months of wanting and needing the other, he stretched his legs out underneath her and leaned back, holding up both their weight, moving a hand to her waist as though every part of him needed to be touching her.

When they pulled apart, they both let out a small laugh of delight.

"What was that for?" he whispered to her.

His hands were still gently cupping the back of her head, his thumbs tracing circles on the skin right on top of her pulse. She was certain he could feel her heart pounding through her body.

His eyes were searching hers as though she could offer a logical explanation...and she knew she couldn't. She'd never be able to find the words to formulate the paragraphs, the chapters of tributes she'd need to tell him what his faith in her, his belief in the two of them, and the hope he'd sparked had done to transform her.

Her deepest fears, of not being good enough, and her greatest sadness, of not having a family, had been put to rest with Ayaan's slow and steady persistence.

"It was for you," she said.

His eyes lit up in surprise, and Payal wished she had a camera to capture the beauty on this man's face, the utter delight he showed at being praised and seen.

"Well...it looks like I got my wish," he said.

She didn't know how she had ever wanted to ignore him.

. . . .

AYAAN

Once he had tasted Payal's lips again, he craved them again and again.

Casual sex was good and dandy—a quick solution to a temporary problem and without the pressure to work through the crises. There was an escape before anything ever got to the point of effort.

But being consumed by someone, overtaken by their smallest quirks, was new...and Ayaan was taken aback to find out how much he loved that he'd fallen for Payal.

They'd taken to spending evenings walking around the city, often around new neighborhoods. Sometimes they stopped for coffee and leisurely strolled about unfamiliar streets. Other times they walked for a short break between social media strategy and business development ideas, using the march around the block as a creative boost.

It had been two weeks since their kiss. They'd stopped for a glass of wine and dessert at an Italian restaurant in Chelsea tonight, a welcome break from the workload. A walk afterward seemed appropriate given the sugar coma they were verging on.

"These walks are the best part of my day," Payal said. "I've been in the design cave so much lately but it's become a literal one lately. My skin feels like it hasn't seen sunlight unless you're dragging me out."

"You're practically a vampire," Ayaan said.

She laughed. "To be fair, today might not have been the best day to seek out the light."

The weather was temperamental this week, and thunderstorms were on the horizon. The gray, ominous clouds were hovering low above the skyline, and they looked as though they would burst any moment.

"You are like the light sometimes, you know. You're always so positive even when you're tired or coping with our families. There's a lot to be said about that."

Payal blushed and looked down. Her inability to take a compliment was endearing.

"So I know we always talk about marriage within the context of our crazy families...but if you did it your way, what would it look like?" Payal asked.

Ayaan considered the question seriously.

"It wouldn't be a test," he said.

"What do you mean?"

"Relationships can so often become transactional, you know?

People want something out of the other person—an engagement, a marriage, then children, or a house. Even teamwork can become a competition if you don't learn to value the other half's talent enough. I always envisioned marriage as the single relationship in your life that didn't have a power dynamic. Instead, I'd form a powerful unit that could be tested but wouldn't break. Two halves of an inseparable team." The wine had loosened his tongue. "Sometimes I can see that with you."

"Sometimes?" She put her hand on her chest, pretending to be offended.

"Well, when I'm not screwing it up," he said.

She laughed. "Your track record lately has been pretty good."

"What do you picture marriage as?"

Much like Ayaan, she didn't seem to have an answer ready. Her lips fell into a pout, considering her answer.

"I never believed love would be a completion of another person. That implies you're missing a piece of yourself...and it seems lonely to me, walking through life with a part of you wandering out there and perhaps never finding it. I've always believed I was already complete and that if I had the privilege to fall in love, we'd multiply. Love would be an additive property. We'd grow together. We'd be complete separately."

Payal was spot-on. She'd done a better job of illustrating his own thoughts than he had.

In fact, to him, it sounded as though they'd both described what they were already creating.

"I don't know that I ever saw marriage in the cards for me," Ayaan confessed. "I know we touched on that when we first met, but love, commitment, and marriage all seemed terrifying."

"I can relate," Payal said. "But I've felt a shift lately...as though with the right person, they could all be a beautiful journey."

"Yeah...I know what you mean."

They shared a look, and Ayaan wondered if the knowing twinkle in her eye was an invitation to kiss her again.

Engrossed in their conversation, they had found themselves near Thirty-Third and Seventh, a loud area full of businesses, hotels, and tourists on their way to Penn Station, eager to walk over to the Macy's on Herald Square or Madison Square Garden.

Thunder roared in the sky above them. Lightning flashed, drenching the streets in shadows and light as it streaked across the sky.

"We should probably get inside," Payal said.

"I'm...not sure we have much time for that," Ayaan said.

He felt his eyes go wide as he observed the skyscraping tower ahead of them fade in a wall of rain.

"Ayaan!" Payal shrieked as the rain began to pour heavily from the sky right above them.

There was something so breathtaking about Payal without any inhibition, vulnerable and raw in the rain. Her light-blue shirt had become transparent and her black bra was showing through the fabric, turning Ayaan on. Her hair, pristinely tied into a low side bun, had become wavy as it grew wet and little curls appeared around her hairline, disrupting the flawless style she had spent time on before showing up.

And the glow on her face, laughter etched upon it as the rain came down in sheets upon them, could have lit up New York City.

Ayaan could feel the chill of his skin as it soaked in the collapsing clouds. His hair, carefully styled into place, began to melt onto his forehead. He looked down and his jeans were spattered with water, darkening his thighs as he stood in the storm.

"We have to go inside," Payal sputtered again. "We'll catch pneumonia!"

"That's not true," Ayaan said with a grin.

"Is this the time to correct me?" she said with a disbelieving laugh. "Really?"

"I can think of something better to do," he said.

And he pulled her close, his face dripping over hers, and covered her mouth with his. The rain poured over them, soaking them to the bone, but they stood in the middle of the sidewalk, their arms wrapped around each other's bodies.

Chapter Twenty-Four

PAYAL

TWO MONTHS UNTIL THE ENGAGEMENT AND FASHION SHOW

Payal had had more I'm-in-over-my-head moments today than she had in her lifetime.

The Indian American Association had decided they wanted to choose their own members to serve as models, a choice Payal had been on board with because of the different body types—until she'd spotted one name she hadn't expected on the list delivered to her only two weeks before the show: *Neha Dev.*

"New York has eight million people and we had to choose this one, eh?" she'd mumbled at the time.

"I'm sorry, I didn't think that would happen," Ayaan had said apologetically. "Do you want me to have them choose someone else? I'm sure we can find a way to blame it on Arun."

His hopeful expression at putting his brother in a tough place made her giggle.

"It's fine," she lied. "But if I push her off the runway, I'll blame it on you."

Payal had dealt with Neha's cutting gaze with as much kindness as she could muster and stayed distracted from the fray with fittings, makeup, vision, and coordination with the event planner who had wanted to have a dinner, fashion show, and dance as part of the charitable endeavor.

Since she'd worked on eight original outfits for the Fashion Week show, she had decided to roll out a few of her summer and fall designs before they hit her website. Yet despite artisans already working on the outfits and a huge amount of legwork completed, the logistics of the show were plenty to handle, as evidenced by Niyathi, who was still impossibly, impeccably managing the day-to-day of the line as well as the logistics of the show.

"I think we need another assistant," Niyathi said, breathless from running across town between a fitting and a venue check.

"You're welcome to hire someone for day-of help. Get a helper, Niyathi. You do more than your fair share on your own. We can afford it."

"It's literally the day before the show!"

"And it's only a few hours…ask around and see if our contacts have any fashion students who want to gain experience. We can pay them, feed them, and write a reference as needed. Just be sure they've done a show before."

Niyathi thanked her and was off to the races…which was how they'd ended up with Jess.

Now, in addition to Neha's coolness, Payal had another problem on her hands.

Jess was a blond, blue-eyed girl, appropriately dressed in all black to blend in, who looked around the room with the interest of watching paint dry.

"So…this is Indian fashion?" Jess asked as they frantically began steaming outfits that had wrinkled in transport to the venue.

"Yes." Payal gritted her teeth. It wasn't the poor girl's fault for asking questions. She bit back the headache that was sneaking up on her and attempted to maintain patience with everyone speaking with her.

"Is it traditional?" Jess asked. "Because I heard that model Neha make a comment earlier about how it was fusion, but she sounded kind of judgmental about it."

The Lord is testing me, Payal thought.

"It is fusion. Much like everyone's identity onstage, including Neha's," Payal said. "It's wonderful that we get to mix together two cultures we love, don't you think?"

"That is a great outfit," the young woman said, staring at a passing model wearing a lehenga.

"Thank you. It's a lehenga, and South Asian women—"

"Actually, I bought something similar at ASOS," Jess commented. "It was a two-piece with similar beadwork. Were you inspired by them?"

Payal recoiled. Fighting the glare threatening to obliterate any goodwill, she spoke as gracefully as she could. "No. In fact, I daresay many of the larger retailers are inspired by other cultures and don't recognize their origins in product descriptions. While I'm certainly not egotistical enough to imagine anyone would copy my designs, specifically, larger retailers do have a history of appropriating meaningful dress and selling to the masses by masking any history. What you saw and bought was a lehenga, a traditional piece from South Asia. Bindis, yoga, chai lattes, and mala beads are also appropriated from South Asian and East Asian cultures."

"I mean, I love wearing bindis to Coachella." The girl shrugged. "I appreciate how beautiful they are. I'm all about feeling like a goddess!"

"Perhaps," Payal said. "But I also doubt you've been spit on when riding the subway for wearing one."

The girl's smile faltered. "I didn't... I'm not... I just like the looks."

"I'm sure you do," Payal said kindly. "What's not to like? I'd love to walk you through them and give you some background if you've got time later."

"I'd like that," Jess said, and for the first time, she appeared interested. "How did you get so many people to come? Marketing is tough these days."

"My...boyfriend?" Payal couldn't help but end the statement in a question, but it didn't feel wrong either. "He is quite good at these things."

Ayaan walked up to Payal at that moment, a cell phone in his hand. The sight of his face gave Payal a burst of energy she didn't know she needed.

"What's up?" she asked.

"How's it coming?"

"Oh, you know. Your ex. Twenty-seven things that need to be done. No sleep. I'm dandy."

He gave her a sympathetic smile and squeezed her shoulder. He paused for a second, then leaned and kissed her forehead. "You're doing great," he whispered.

He noticed Jess then.

"Hi, I'm Ayaan," he said, extending his hand. "I've been helping with marketing efforts for Besharmi."

Jess was interested now. "I follow you on Instagram!"

"Nice to meet you."

"Wait...are you guys dating? Payal just mentioned her boyfriend being good at marketing."

He turned to Payal, an eyebrow raised.

Payal felt her face grow a degree warmer. She thrust her chin in the air and locked eyes with Ayaan, raising an eyebrow of her own.

"How did you two meet?"

"Our parents, actually..."

"Your parents set you up?" Jess's ears perked up.

"It's not uncommon in our culture," Payal explained. "Neither of us saw it coming but it was a pleasant surprise."

She didn't want to go into detail, but in the chaos, she didn't have the energy to lie about how they'd met either.

"Wow, you know, I'm not sure I would have seen that coming," Jess said.

"We didn't either, but we're passionate about similar things and he's kind of hot," Payal said with a shrug and a wink.

Ayaan shook his head with a chuckle.

"You always read about arranged marriages, and I can't imagine being passionate with someone your parents set you up with."

"You realize that an arranged marriage doesn't mean missionary-style sex for the rest of our lives, right?" Payal asked.

"Well, no, but you come from a part of the world where women aren't exactly dominant or given much freedom, right? How do you know you're passionate about the only option you have?"

Ayaan's mouth had actually dropped.

Be it the chaos of the day, Neha, the pressure she was cracking under, her confusion about Ayaan, or simply the arrogance of a girl who couldn't be bothered to be open-minded—no, actually, to not be racist—Payal was incensed and she unleashed.

"Okay, Betty—"

"My name is Jess..."

"Okay, Lucy. Here are some fun facts for you. There are over one billion South Asians on earth. I promise you: women are having sex. Maybe even good sex. And if you want proof of that, our heathen, undeveloped culture gave you the gift of the *Kama*

Sutra, the divine art of pleasure through sex about two thousand years before the West figured out how not to drink their own sewage and die of cholera. Let's not pretend the Western world has any claim on being more forward-thinking, okay?"

Jess's mouth opened and closed a few times.

Payal crossed her arms, not breaking eye contact before smiling. "Now...let's focus on the show, shall we? Can you check on the lineup? We go on in twenty minutes, and I'd like to get these dupattas styled."

Red-faced, Jess left.

"I have never been so attracted to you in my life," Ayaan deadpanned, his eyes enormous.

"She might have done us a favor in coming to help with the show, but the attitude toward the culture was unnecessary," Payal muttered.

She didn't feel bad. Hell, she didn't have time to. Now, she had to get ready to put these models on the stage.

"Payal! A surprising number of non-South Asians came tonight," Pankaj Uncle said as he passed by and came to check on how preparations were going. "Mention fashion in New York and people come out of the woodwork to see what the latest trend is. Payal, I would highly suggest making the rounds at some point. There are even some press outlets that could be good publicity for you."

"Thanks, Uncle," Payal said.

"We don't want to send you back to that job, now do we? This line has to be successful!"

She tried to appear confident. "Indeed."

"I hear you and Ayaan are engaged now as well. Congratulations! I know your dad from our school days and Ayaan's family from our time in London. What a small world. It was very convenient that they came together!"

Whether he was remarking on the serendipitous connection or implying that it was shrewd to pool their resources, she couldn't read...but the mention of the engagement and the weight of this show and its success, as well as her family's ties to Ayaan's, all took the words from Payal's mouth.

"Thank you," she managed. "It was."

"You have ten minutes, Payal," a show runner called out.

There wasn't time to dwell.

Frantically pinning a dupatta on a model wearing patiala pants with a crop top, she swung a side eye at the rest of the models lining up. Niyathi was walking along the line doing a once-over on all the details: the intentionally messy braids and half updos accentuated with flowers, the pinning details, whether wrinkles had been steamed out, and whether makeup was heavy enough to withstand the lights.

Seemingly satisfied, she said, "We're good," to Payal just as she finished the pin job across the model's shoulders.

Payal paused before each model, doing a second look-over to follow Niyathi's.

The lights dimmed.

It was go time.

Each model ascended the stairs with her head held high. They sashayed down the runway, struck poses that made them feel comfortable—Payal had given each one a suggestion, based on the outfit they were wearing and whether pieces like lehengas needed to be swung around to show off their spin—and then strolled back.

Seven models took less than twelve minutes.

Before Neha climbed the steps, she turned to Payal. "Trust. Me. I know what I'm doing."

Though Payal wanted to push Neha off the end of the elevated runway, she had to admit Neha knew exactly what she was doing. As an actual model, she was the final one to walk, wearing the most important outfit of the night: a pair of pants designed like a dhoti, with gold stonework creating spiraling designs up the tie-dyed patterned legs. The blouse was a hot-pink sleeveless crop top, and Neha had a gold sparkling, sheer kaftan over it. The draping, the summery colors, and the resort-wear look made the outfit something Payal knew instinctively would sell well.

Neha walked with the grace of an apsara, her feet barely hitting the ground and nearly gliding down the catwalk as though she was being propelled by an unseen force.

She rounded the end of the catwalk, stopped, leaning on her back leg, then did a half turn and struck one more pose. The bone structure in her face was impeccable, and the way her jawline fell into the perfect pout was effortless. She and the clothing complemented one another, each pushing forward the image of a modern, cultured, and global citizen ready to conquer the world.

They may have shared Ayaan but there was no memory of that now; instead, Payal grinned at the way Neha carried herself and the transformation in her body language. She hoped every woman who wore her designs would have the same visceral shift in her demeanor: a straight back, a proud chin, no more dropped gazes, and shoulders back.

Payal couldn't help but release a "Woo!" when Neha got off the catwalk.

As the models lined up for a final walk and Payal joined in at the end of the line for her own entrance, she sucked in a gulp of air.

It was over. And the applause was deafening.

The eyes were on her as she walked in between the four models each on her left and her right. She waved and the applause increased a few decibels.

And then it was really over. The guests returned to their meals and Pankaj Uncle thanked her on the mic for presenting her designs, advertising her website and mentioning that the show was sponsored by Veer.

She was met with flashbulbs as she reached the backstage press area, where photographers and press lingered to capture the magic and report back about the happenings of the night. Some of the influencers invited to the show were posing on the step-and-repeat red carpet set out for them and speaking to interviewers.

But Payal was only looking for one face...the person who had gotten her this opportunity and reminded her how much she loved what she did.

"Ayaan!" Payal couldn't help but shout when she spotted him.

He was standing alongside the wall, scanning the room himself. When she heard her shout his name, he scrambled through the crowd, pushing people aside unapologetically as he made his way toward her.

"Over here!" she yelled again.

"I'm so proud of you!" he shouted.

Before either of them allowed the setting to sink in and determine their actions, Payal threw her arms around his neck and, in a total lack of inhibition, bounded off the balls of her feet into the air.

Ayaan caught her, and as her legs wound around his waist and she hugged him close, he supported her weight with his hands.

"Hi," she said breathlessly.

He was still holding her and the intimacy was staggering, a public display that she would never have partaken in had she not been elated at this momentous occasion in her life.

"Hi," he replied back, tightening his grip.

The penetrating surveillance of cell phones, cameras, and all the showgoers closed in on them. Feeling the prickle around her neck, Payal unwrapped her legs from his waist and planted her feet on the ground.

"Sorry," she said quickly, looking down and feeling the heat rise in her chest.

"I'm not," he responded. "I'm so amazed by you."

A camera clicked and the white light that exploded from its flash doused them both in radiance.

He was holding both her hands. Ayaan's face, under the Technicolor lights, looked awestruck. Pride saturated every pore.

"Come here," he said suddenly.

"What?"

"Let's take a picture."

"Why?" she asked before she could stop herself.

"Because you did this. This is your day."

"We did this."

"Then let's mark it one for the books and document it…for us."

He switched his phone to selfie mode and pulled her close.

Payal breathed him in, the scent of his cologne filling her, and she tried to ignore the ache in her chest from wanting him.

Click. The phone made a sound and the images of them froze on the screen.

"Sooo…for such a frazzled day…it didn't turn out so bad, did it?" he asked with a grin.

Payal turned to him, certain that she was standing three inches off the ground. "Tonight was perfect."

. . . .

AYAAN

"*Besharmi by Payal Mehra is a love story between centuries of South Asian culture and contemporary New York,*" an article on Urban Underground's website stated the next day.

"*Up-and-coming British-Indian New Yorker Payal Mehra is a*

global designer with South Asian roots," a Time Out New York reviewer wrote. *"Her visionary takes on styles from different geographic areas in India and her application to modern bicultural identity is one to watch."*

Of the publications and websites that had covered Payal, every single one had deemed her extraordinary. Even the least enthusiastic had still described it as "clever."

She and Ayaan had also made it to a less savory, more speculative, filmy site that earned clicks off reporting gossip on influencers and their moves.

"Payal Mehra is achieving new heights, aided by British lifestyle company Veer, and in particular marketing whiz kid and influencer Ayaan Malhotra. Besharmi employees have said they spend so much of their time together, they could be a married couple. Whether or not business has turned to pleasure remains to be seen, but for now, all that matters is that Besharmi's star is on the rise."

Arun FaceTimed from London, as usual before 9:00 a.m.

"What's up, Arun?" Ayaan asked as he sipped his coffee in the kitchen after his shower.

"Ayaan…" Arun let his voice trail off, visibly taken aback that Ayaan was up, ready, and energized.

"Why do you look like you've seen a ghost?"

"I feel like I have. Did you sleep?"

"I did. A solid five hours, in fact."

"I'm impressed. How did the show go? The articles online are raving."

"I've seen. They're so positive! I've already gotten multiple emails from people who have read them and want to collaborate with the brand on shoots, in print, and I have"—he checked his phone—"two…no, three investors who want to meet up."

"Sabyasachi took time to grow investors. He's one of the greatest designers in contemporary Indian history. Make sure you aren't jumping the gun. Ensure the brand remains the same throughout."

"Maybe Payal needs to be a disruptor. Every designer's path is different, just as any company's is," Ayaan said.

"You're not wrong," Arun said contemplatively. "This is new territory. There are a lot of new designers coming up, but what you've done with her social media presence, pushing it to two hundred thousand followers and over a million in revenue this year, is remarkable. I want to be sure you aren't growing faster than you can keep up. Keep reevaluating."

"Arun, I know...but Payal *is* remarkable. She's working like a maniac. They've hired more artisans to keep up with demand on designs. They have grown the number of tailors. They're scaling properly."

"What do you have in mind?"

"Digital consults. Rental platforms. Collaborations with other smaller designers. Perhaps a bigger storefront rather than the small studio they're operating out of."

"I'm glad to hear it. We have to figure out how to get ahead of that article about you and Payal dating, though."

Arun never missed a thing. His tenacity was admirable, Ayaan admitted to himself, albeit begrudgingly.

"It's just a gossip site, Arun. No one is going to pay attention."

"That site gets hundreds of thousands of views a day. The comments are always trash. But speculation is enough for people to leak merger news and we should announce this as cleanly as possible, without the added drama. Let me think about it."

Ayaan knew better than to argue. "You let me know. These things can get out of hand so I don't want to be too dismissive. I'll follow your lead and talk to Payal."

"She's trusting you, trusting us, to take care of this. Don't let her down...and know that you're doing solid work."

It was the closest thing to a compliment Arun had given him in years. Ayaan hung up the phone feeling as though he'd shed years of weight off his person.

He'd never felt so confident. Pride in himself, in Payal, and in what they were achieving swelled up inside him, and he was sure he'd burst.

Gratitude flooded him when he pictured Payal last night, the way she floated into his arms like there was nowhere else she'd rather be...and how he couldn't think of a single place anytime or anywhere in his life that he had felt so at home.

Payal had infused every part of his life—from his family to his profession to his own perception of himself—with joy, laughter, and confidence. She had taken a chance on his ability and allowed him in, trusting him with her work and her own journey in life.

He had fucked up time and again, but she had given him hope and something to work for, and they were reaping the benefit now. Her words came back to him about love being additive.

She had added so much to him.

He had to see her.

He didn't know what propelled him out the front door, in an uncharacteristically casual gray hoodie, black jeans, and black-and-white Nike sneakers—he would have rather worn this on a grocery run—but his heart was pounding, and a force pushed him toward the subway, down the stairs, and onto the next train heading uptown.

In the twenty minutes it took him to go from his apartment in FiDi to the Upper East Side, jumping transfers, and walk the few blocks from the Eighty-Sixth Street station to Payal's place, he felt no doubt.

He'd never been so sure of anything in his life.

When she opened the door, wearing the same white satin robe that he'd first seen her in, he had never been so happy that all the roads on this wild and crazy ride had led him here.

"Hi," she said as though she'd been expecting him.

"Hi," he breathed.

And without waiting, guided by his gut and the inexplicably strong burst of love he felt for this girl, he stepped in and kissed her.

Chapter Twenty-Five

PAYAL

Payal had known it was Ayaan at the door from the second the rapping noise had rung out across her living room.

She hadn't jumped at the sudden sound. Instead, a sense of certainty swiftly settled upon her and she knew she was exactly where she was meant to be.

"Hi," she said, opening the door.

"Hi," he responded.

Before she'd breathed in and opened her mouth to reply, he kissed her.

And the world snapped into focus, as though every single fuzzy thought she'd had about Ayaan, her family, the last few months, and her career vanished in a split second and was replaced with only him and the soft way his tongue rolled over her lips.

The urge for him grew inside her, spreading from her heart to the tingle on her lips to the hollow between her legs.

Deepening the kiss, she pulled him closer, pushing the door closed behind him.

It wasn't until midafternoon that they both stirred, unaware that they'd fallen asleep after the third time they'd come together.

"Good morning?" Payal said, looking up at Ayaan.

She was still in his arms, her head resting in the crook of his shoulder and his chest.

"Amazing morning, indeed." He laughed, and she felt the deep resonance of it against her ear.

"That was...unbelievable," she said.

"You're unbelievable," he replied, kissing her forehead.

He wrapped his arm around her, and she nuzzled in, resting her arm on his chest and rolling her fingertips in circles, spelling random words.

F-A-S-H-I-O-N.

"Hey."

"What?" she asked.

"Be my girlfriend."

"What?"

"Payal, our families agreed to our engagement. I know we were fiancés in their minds and in the public. But we never talked about it. We never got to *feel* it. But you're here now. We're together. And you make me so happy. Let's be together...officially. On our own terms."

She smiled against his chest and snuggled in. His heartbeat thumped against her ear.

"Okay," she whispered. "Yes."

"Besides, you already called me your boyfriend to that piece of work at the show."

Payal giggled. "I did, didn't I? But in my defense, what the hell else was I supposed to call you?"

"'That guy' would have worked," he joked.

"You're not just another guy," she murmured.

"Would you have imagined us here that first night?" Ayaan asked her.

Payal had wanted to tease him about those circumstances, but she couldn't bring herself to mention anything but the fact that life had handed them their greatest blind side.

"Never," she said instead. "But I'm so happy we are."

It was funny...she'd imagined lying with someone in post-coital bliss, whispering sweet nothings about the first time they realized they were meant to be together. But it had never felt right when she'd imagined it before. The face of her imaginary boy-friend was always hazy, and the feeling of wanting those conversations wasn't certain enough to convince Payal that such bliss was meant for her at all.

But now...she hung on every word.

"Wow," Payal said.

"What's that?" Ayaan stirred and opened his eyes again.

"I went from business partner to girlfriend to bedmate in a night," Payal said with a wry smile. "What else is in store?"

"Well...tomorrow, you'll officially be my fiancée," Ayaan said.

He turned his Apple watch toward her, and a text message glowed on the screen from Arun: Announcement tomorrow at 9:00 a.m. about merger to capitalize on good press. Announcing earlier than anticipated and preponing the party. Social media post about engagement to follow in coming days.

"Oh, wow," Payal whispered.

She gave a nearly imperceptible shudder. Her heart banged against her rib cage like a wooden spoon against a tin can.

"What?" Ayaan grew alarmed, his eyes widening and his back turning rigid underneath her. "That didn't sound good."

"No...no, I'm just..."

"What is it?"

"I'm...scared. This is a really good thing right now. Speeding ahead to an engagement, our families, the merger... I know I said yes. But that was out of necessity and it's so soon and impending and—" Her words were racing and Ayaan sensed her body shift, becoming stiffer and more guarded. "I don't want to ruin a good thing. What if letting people in ends up ruining this?"

"Hey. Hey," he said, rubbing her spine at the curve of her back.

She loosened up immediately.

"Payal, listen to me." He gazed at her, seemingly unwilling to break eye contact until she understood. "We *are* in a really good place. That won't change. This merger does add pressure, and I understand that it's scary to jump ahead to an engagement that involves the public and our families when we just got to a really safe place between the two of us. It feels like we're jumping the gun. But I promise you, if you doubt this or we have reservations, we can always work this out. I promise you I will not hurt you. This will not be an arrangement of convenience. I'm here for real. I know you are too."

His words loosened all the coils she'd wound up in her chest, all the fears, the lies, the worries she'd had about the line, the families, this relationship, and how she felt. Somehow, it had all made sense in the end, and they had arrived at this place, in bed together, waking up to each other's morning bedhead and naked skin.

There wasn't anything to lose. She had it all and nothing could weaken it.

"I trust you," she said, and rather than be surprised the words were escaping her, she settled in them, allowing her faith in him to warm her like the blanket they were lying under.

"I know Arun mentioned social media... Am I allowed to post something about us?" he asked. "I loved that photo of us yesterday."

"Did you just ask if we could make it social media official?"

Payal paused. "It sounds awfully juvenile when I say it that way, doesn't it?"

"Is it juvenile to tell people when you're happy?"

Warmth grew in her. "Are you?"

"I could shout it from rooftops. That's why I asked."

Payal thought about the people who would see the photo, the rumors it would start, and the fuel it would add to the announcement coming in only a few short hours.

But Ayaan was right. What did it matter if it was now or later? They were happy.

And this was one thing they could do on their own terms.

"Yes," she said, and she nuzzled back into her place on his chest. "Shout it from rooftops."

L-O-V-E.

Chapter Twenty-Six

Drunken Munkey was buzzing tonight. People lined up outside in groups, and the tables inside were set so close to one another that people had to excuse themselves to move past other guests and get out of their seats. It was a consistent game of Tetris to find comfortable space and still eat to one's heart's content.

"How goes the escape plan?" Kai asked smugly as he sipped his drink. "You look awfully into the goings-on."

"I...er, I mean, I'm going to..." Ayaan sputtered.

But he wasn't going to do anything. There was no escape plan. In fact, Ayaan had jumped all in. But a gnawing thought crossed his mind, not for the first time, since he'd asked her to be his girlfriend.

Dharm and Kai were gazing at him expectantly, as though they knew exactly where his thoughts were leading and what his hesitancy meant.

"Change of heart?" Dharm asked lightly.

Ayaan leaned on the table, his hands clasped underneath it.

"Would there ever be something Maya could confess to you that would have kept you from proposing to her?"

Dharm frowned, caught off guard at the question. "You didn't, I don't know, sleep with Neha or something, did you?"

Ayaan gave a scoff. "No, not at all. I barely even talked to her at the fashion show, and that was the last time I saw her."

"Then no, barring any cheating, I can't imagine a situation where I wouldn't propose to Maya because of something she said."

"I'm stuck on whether I should confess something. I may have embellished my family's desire to make me CMO and acted as though they intended on it the entire time. She has no idea that I negotiated it in exchange for this engagement...or that I never intended to follow through. It was like a date-and-ditch situation that has now taken me for a spin."

"You should—" Dharm said.

"You shouldn't—" Kai started.

They stared at each other.

"That was helpful, guys, thanks," Ayaan said lightly. "Very clear directive."

"How do you feel about her?" Dharm asked. "You don't seem to be running for the hills."

Far from it...

"We're officially together and I could see an entire life with her."

The words seemingly froze the room.

Kai's face changed, as though he'd been doubting Ayaan this entire time, jesting and teasing as though he couldn't be taken seriously, and only now had seen him clearly.

Dharm's eyebrows had risen, and he appeared impressed, letting out a whooshing whistle.

"That's really big, man," Kai said. "I'm... Wow."

"Is it that hard to believe?"

"I'm proud of you," he said simply. "All this time, we've made fun of you for not having your head on straight, and you've always been the friend who has killed it professionally and been a mess personally. And now...I mean, Payal is incredible. You've been shining. This is really good."

"That's exactly the reason I've been toying with telling her the truth about how this started. Because I don't want this secret hanging over my head. But if I do, then she could walk and I don't know how to get through that because I cannot imagine losing her."

Given that he'd just come close to advising Ayaan to tell Payal, Dharm surprised him now by shaking his head.

"I was about to tell you to. But what Kai just said about shining...he's right. This is really good for you. Payal has been really good for you. And perhaps it doesn't matter how you got there. It matters that you did. You dated Neha for nearly a year, and you couldn't remember that you had to meet her parents. I've seen you do a double take at a pharmacy because you've seen Payal take a particular brand of allergy meds and you're afraid she's run out. The change in you has been remarkable, Ayaan. If it ever gets out, you can trust that to fix it. But you don't have to rock the boat."

Ayaan took that advice in, pausing as he let the words soak into him.

"I'd like to draw attention to the fact that Dharm said I was right about something," Kai said.

They all laughed.

"In all seriousness...spend the rest of your life making it up to her, A. She deserves nothing but the best from you. But this version of you also deserves happiness and all the good things that come from building a future together. Don't risk it," Kai advised.

Ayaan listened. He *had* changed. Everything in his life was better now. Even his family seemed to be coming around. The gripes from Arun had lessened. His dad had called him just to chat the other day. Mum was lighter, as though her already-tinkling laugh had elevated an octave by releasing the weight of her family's strife.

Revealing that he'd never intended to marry Payal would only mar the fact that it had become the truth.

Payal was the truth.

Nothing else mattered.

Chapter Twenty-Seven

PAYAL

ONE WEEK UNTIL THE ENGAGEMENT PARTY
FIVE WEEKS UNTIL THE FASHION SHOW

"Wow, so the announcement went out," Sonam said. "How do you feel?"

"Like I've aged forty years!" Payal exclaimed.

They all laughed.

"Well, you look happy," Kiran said with a knowing smile. "You're glowing."

"Payal always glows," Akash said.

"Thank you," Payal said, squeezing Akash's hand.

They were at the Chai Spot, a teahouse in Little Italy that served Pakistani chai in little glasses reminiscent of the roadside dhabas in the motherland. Brightly colored ottomans and rugs in Turkish prints were spread out around the room, setting up a desi space that Payal would have dreamt of as a child.

"The release about the merger went out," Kiran said. "It's a done deal. Veer congratulated both of you on their social media accounts."

"Well, we all had to follow the accounts for this craziness and watch it play out," Akash cut in.

"The question remains to be asked... Are you still considering backing out?" Sonam asked.

"I don't want to back out," Payal said. "Ayaan and I are in a good place. We're officially together."

Sonam laughed suddenly. "It blows my mind that you had a one-night stand with a guy, he was a jackass, you did this to save your parents' company but really to save your own ass, then you ended up falling for him. It's like a rom-com."

Payal joined in Sonam's laughter. "Well, he turned out to be much better than I ever imagined."

"I don't like him."

The three women turned to Akash, whose voice was filled with disgust.

"What? He's arrogant. He seems nice enough. But he hasn't seen stability a day of his life. His penis is like a welcome mat at a revolving door."

"And if you were standing in front of a mirror, Ayaan would be your reflection," Sonam cut in.

"No!" Akash's eyes sparked.

"I can't lie, Akash." Kiran gave a small smile and a shrug of concession. "She's kind of right."

"I am not a womanizing asshole with—"

"You are smart and nice, and you have a close family and a head the size of Russia," Sonam said.

"And by that, she means the one on your neck," Payal said before adding, "unlike Ayaan, who possesses another head that is particularly large..."

"Gross." Akash scrunched his nose.

"I agree with them, Akash. He might not have started off with the best first impression but Ayaan comes from a great family, and he's handsome, intelligent, and charming."

"When you put it that way, he sounds like those marriage ads in newspapers back in India that our parents used to have to peruse to find a partner," Sonam said.

"When I put it that way, I mean he's exactly like Akash."

Payal thought to correct Kiran's misplaced notion that Ayaan and his family were very close but found herself unwilling to betray his confidence.

"I like him," Payal said.

"Well, I don't," Akash pushed again. "You deserve better."

"I chose him," she said pointedly. "And I wouldn't have if he wasn't worth it."

"I don't trust that," he replied, and it cut her deeper than she cared to admit.

Did the others feel the same? Payal watched them. Akash was the only one fidgeting in his chair, but Sonam and Kiran remained calm despite the sharp remarks being thrown around.

Payal examined them as she asked, "Do you guys think I'm making a mistake?"

Kiran spoke first. "No. Life gives you surprises. Ayaan turning out to be an emotional lifeline rather than a financial one was yours."

"I had my doubts," Sonam confessed. "I thought you were being a damn fool putting so much at stake…but like Kiran said, it's worked out. He looks at you like you hung the stars in the sky. And he's pushed you to be even better than we already knew you were. He's good for you."

"It does feel wrong not to come clean," Payal admitted, despite wanting everyone to support her choice.

"Payal, why would you? Perhaps it started dishonestly. But

that doesn't have to be brought to the light if you end up where you're meant to be...together," Sonam said.

"Don't you think we're starting with a lie?"

Sonam paused. "No. Because now, when it matters, you're in love with him. Anyone would expect you to be apprehensive about an engagement to someone you hardly felt anything for— and you both had a rough start to begin with, what with your sexual escapades and throwing him out."

Payal laughed, still disbelieving that they'd started there and ended up here.

"Ultimately, you grew to love one another. That's what matters most," Sonam said.

"I disagree," Kiran said. "You don't have to confess that you were using him. I think that would hurt him. But you could say you did this to save your family—"

"He knows that, though," Sonam cut in.

"Would you want to know if he was using you for something?" Akash asked. "And let's be real, he probably is."

"What could he use me for?" Payal asked. "His family is in power here. Ayaan's doing just fine."

"I don't know...but if he had any reason, would you want to know?"

Payal thought about it. On one hand, she had just argued that transparency was important to her. But on the other...Sonam was also right. At the end of the day, she and Ayaan had fought through their preconceived notions, and it wouldn't matter what it had taken for them to end up together as long as they'd become a couple and learned to be happy.

She also suspected Akash had more reason to talk her into saying something that would upset Ayaan. If she followed his advice and Ayaan grew furious, Akash would have every reason to say, "I told you so," and as much as she loved her best friend, Payal didn't want to give him the satisfaction of being right.

"I would be fine with it. We're happy now," she said. "As long as he didn't sleep with someone else or anything like that…"

Though she wasn't sure if Ayaan would feel the same way about her deception being irrelevant, she wasn't convinced she should unleash a tsunami of potential damage. Instead, she thought, she'd tell him if the time was right. Perhaps it would turn into a joke in their future, as they sat overlooking a beach with a successful company behind them, and she could say, "Hey, remember when I agreed to marry you because you could help me with my company?" And they'd laugh because they'd come so far and it didn't matter.

"Fine, your choice," Akash said and he got up. "This is ridiculous."

"Where are you going? Sit down," Sonam commanded.

"No, Payal's being an idiot," he said. "It's one thing to like him. Fine, you grew into your feelings for each other. But an engagement? Us flying to London this weekend to celebrate with you? Don't you think that's premature? What if you break up? Now that you're 'officially'"—he flashed air quotes with his fingers—"together for real, what if you get hit with reality and can't back out because your companies are entwined too?"

"People are allowed to change their minds, Akash!" Payal said, exasperated. "I thought he was a jerk. I thought this would be my way to play my cards. But it worked out. Why can't you just be happy?"

"Because I seem to be the only one with any sense."

Sonam, the most pragmatic of the bunch, stayed surprisingly quiet. Kiran, who had seen what risks came with love and pursued it anyway, would give Akash time to simmer down before she told him off gently for being a jerk.

Payal hated the silence, so she turned to him, imploring him to agree with her. They hardly ever disagreed, and Akash leaving in a huff wasn't the way that she wanted to start off this experience of celebrating.

"Come on. Sit down."

"You're making a mistake," he said finally, and to the sounds of Kiran and Sonam's sighs, he swung his bag over his shoulder and left.

· · · · · · · · · · ·

AYAAN

The engagement party may have been small but the celebration was a three-day affair. As they always did with major life events, the family priests had determined the most auspicious times and dates for the events.

Luckily, the engagement had fallen on a Saturday. And in true Indian fashion, the families had decided it would become a three-day affair with a welcome party on Friday, the pooja on Saturday afternoon, and a reception to celebrate afterward. Sunday would conclude with a farewell brunch to send off the guests in well-fed style, hopefully exclaiming, "The Malhotras and Mehras throw the best parties!"

The venue was about an hour north of London, a historic nineteenth-century home-turned-hotel. The families had rented out most of the estate to house their guests and hold the party.

Kai and Dharm had joined Ayaan in his room to get ready for the Friday night welcome party.

"I'm going to propose to her," Ayaan said as they buttoned the cuffs on their sherwanis.

Silence followed his proclamation.

"Well, I believe this is your engagement party, so we might be celebrating that very thing, mate," Dharm said. "You seem to have lost the plot."

"Shut up," Ayaan replied, giving Dharm's arm a whack. "I want to get down on one knee and propose to her after this welcome party."

"You just decided to officially start dating a few weeks ago."

"Yes, but I fell for her long before that...and I know she felt the same. I'm in this, Dharm. I have no fear. She's the one for me. How many people get married in Las Vegas after two weeks and make it work for years? Our own parents met once and they've been married for ages. Your parents are so sickly cute and they met on their wedding day."

"This is true," Dharm said.

"I want to do this right. The grounds are beautiful. I can ask her to marry me...and then we have this party and start our lives together the right way."

"Leave it to you to go backward and sideways on every step." Kai chuckled. "This is the most out-of-order relationship ever."

"And that's what I'm going to fix. She deserves it to be perfect."

He went to his suitcase, rummaging in the zipped pocket for the tiny box containing the ring.

Feeling the edges of the box, he pulled it out and opened it.

Kai and Dharm peered in.

"Well...that's pretty," Kai said. "And the most expensive thing I've ever seen you buy that wasn't for yourself."

"We're happy for you," Dharm said.

He pulled Ayaan in for a hug, patting his back.

"Now, let's go see that girl of yours and get drunk."

The Long Gallery, a hall with wood paneling and an old-fashioned warmth, had been decorated with market lights and uplighting that made Ayaan feel as though he'd walked into a circus.

Large, lighted marquee lettering spelling "LOVE" sat in the corner of the room with a tabletop set upon them, serving as a bar. The tablecloths were glittery, and large floral arrangements, decked with crystal garlands, sat in the middle of each table, making the room look as though it were dripping with diamonds and sparkles.

It was luxurious and cozy all at once...very on-brand.

Payal was already in the middle of the room, surrounded by the CMC, and she was a vision in a blush-pink lehenga with a unique style, like a caped two-piece gown.

When she spotted him, she stopped speaking, her face lighting up, and immediately joined him.

"Kai, Dharm, you both look dashing."

"We tried," Dharm said with a smile. "Maya sends her apologies for not being here. Her mom has the flu."

"I'll send her flowers on Monday," Payal said. "Now, both of you, go get drinks."

"You don't have to ask me twice," Kai said with a laugh. "You look beautiful, by the way."

When the two left, she turned to Ayaan and his heart fluttered.

"You are breathtaking," he said to her.

"You're not so bad yourself," she said. She put her hands on his chest and his heart thumped against her palm, through the gold brocade on his sherwani in the same shade of blush as her lehenga.

"Actually," she said now, "you're the best-looking guy in the room, and I can't believe you're mine."

Ayaan glanced around, ensuring no prying eyes were watching before giving her a quick peck on the lips.

The volume of the bumping music lowered, and Payal's dad came onto the middle of the floor, mic in hand.

"Ladies and gentlemen, we wanted to thank you for coming tonight," he said over a mic. "Payal and Ayaan have achieved amazing heights. I'm not just talking about their efforts with Payal's line, Besharmi, but with each other. Payal has always been driven—she is my daughter, after all."

The audience laughed. Payal rolled her eyes good-naturedly.

"But lately, when she's visited London, she's been lighting up from the inside. When she goes out with Ayaan, she comes home with a smile on her face. In addition to the merger with Veer, cementing our relationship on a personal level means a great deal to our family. Witnessing their happiness is a parent's greatest dream, and the Mehras thank all of you for being here to eat, drink, and be merry on the engagement of our children."

The guests clapped and tapped forks against their glasses.

Ayaan glanced at Payal, who had a smile on her face that didn't quite reach her eyes. "You okay?"

"Oh, you know how it is. They hardly speak to us, yet they claim our success," she said. "He did get one thing right, though."

"What's that?"

"I do come home with a smile on my face when I'm with you."

"Well, then, let's forget what they put us through before and raise our glasses to the fact that we're here tonight. Because I would rather be with you than anywhere else."

As they finished dinner and the DJ's music changed from light piano tunes to more upbeat Bollywood beats, guests began making their way to the dance floor.

"Hey," Akash greeted them as Ayaan and Payal moved to the center of the room.

"Hey," Payal said. *Was that hesitation in her voice?*

"Well, congratulations on your engagement. I'm really happy for you both."

Akash seemed to be speaking more to Payal than him, and when he glanced at her, Ayaan noticed that her cautious smile was turning into a genuine one.

"Thank you," she murmured.

"Now...I'm going to get another drink. And maybe that bartender's number," Akash said, locking in on the girl behind the bar before giving Payal's arm a squeeze and leaving them alone.

"What was that about?" Ayaan asked. "You seemed tense."

"Nothing. We had a little disagreement, but it looks like it's water under the bridge," Payal said.

Though he wanted to ask more questions, Kiran appeared out of nowhere and shouted over the music. "Congratulations, Ayaan and Payal!"

"You landed the best when you got our best friend," Sonam said, arriving next to her.

She was already a few drinks in, judging by her glassy eyes and singsongy voice, but Ayaan knew she meant every word...and that if he forgot it, she'd hunt him down.

The music grew louder, and people started cheering. The Punjabi roots in both families came to the forefront as the alcohol began to flow freely. Payal's dad began shedding pound notes in line with the family tradition of showering money on celebrating guests, and dance moves that only saw the light around Indian family and friends showed themselves in guests who showcased their bhangra skills.

The bursts of color were the happiest thing he'd ever seen. Rhinestones from saris cast small beams of light across the room. Rich colors shone under the lights on silk outfits, and gold thread shined amid the rainbows of hues.

Kai pulled Ayaan into a dance-off in the middle of the circle, and Ayaan knew his joints would feel a healthy early-thirties stiffness in the morning while his spirit would feel twenty-five for-ever when he was with his friends.

Surrounded by the people who had made him who he was—then and now, broken and whole—he was stunned by the support of the people who had come here to wish them well.

As the party wound down, Ayaan was hit with emotion that he hadn't been able to wholeheartedly feel since he was sixteen years old.

He was *home*.

When Payal looked up at him and smiled, grazing her hand against his chin and gazing at him like the world was in his eyes, he knew he was about to make the best decision of his life.

"Do you want to go for a walk?" he asked.

Chapter Twenty-Eight

PAYAL

"Do you want to go for a walk?" Ayaan asked.

Payal nodded, observing the dwindling crowd and the line awaiting Ma and Papa to say good night. The night had clearly concluded, fading into peaceful silence after a roaring party.

She had felt like royalty in a one-shoulder gown with stonework stitched in lines from the top of the dress to varying lengths past her waist, cascading like rain. Her chunni was unique, one end tied around her neck with two thin rhinestone ribbons, with the rest of it draping along her left arm and trailing behind her, all the way to her right wrist where the other end buttoned around the wrist like a shiny bangle. The effect was meant to give guests the impression she was wearing a caped gown before the traditional appearance of a chunni appeared. Her hair was neatly tied back into a sleek, rounded bun that sat at the nape of her neck. Diamonds glittered at her collarbone and dangled from her ears, a set Nani had bought for her when she had turned sixteen and that she'd saved for a special occasion.

Lifting her lehenga and stepping gingerly on her now-aching feet, she walked slowly next to Ayaan as they stepped into the night air.

"Are you still wearing your heels?" he asked. "Your feet must hurt."

"Please." Payal made a face. "I put on juttis the second the dance floor opened."

"I kept wondering how you were managing elaborate dance moves in stilettos."

She paused, lifted the edge of her skirt again, and stuck a foot out. Silver-and-gold-beaded juttis sparkled.

"Smart girl."

"I try."

"What did you think of the night?" Ayaan asked.

Payal reflected on the room full of people she loved and the glow on their faces as they looked at her like they'd never seen her before. The clear emotional investment in her and Ayaan's success was evident as they hugged the couple and showered blessings on them.

She couldn't get past how handsome Ayaan looked. His pink sherwani was embroidered with colorful beaded flowers in reds, blues, and greens, and the padded square shoulders elongated him somehow. He wore a three-strand pearl necklace, accented with ruby-colored stones. His favorite gold Breitling watch gleamed on his wrist. *Put a boy in a sherwani and he becomes a prince.*

And he was *hers*.

"A friend of mine once told me that weddings are such a strange and surreal experience because you see all the important people of your life in one room and your best friend from when you were five years old gets to meet your boss...and that a room will never be so full of love again because they've witnessed your journey. And for us, we get to experience that *twice*."

A curious expression crossed his face. "Between an engagement celebration and a wedding, you mean?"

"Can you even imagine?" Payal said with a laugh. "I thought I'd explode today from joy. I think at a wedding, I'd be a fluff of confetti and sparkly things from the emotion."

The implication fluttered between them and didn't seem to dissipate into the air. Instead, Ayaan wound the fingers of his left hand through hers and gave them a squeeze that seemed to say, *It's all coming for us.*

They came upon a red bridge crossing over a sparkling creek. It stood as part of a Japanese garden and Payal slowed to a stop as she stood in the middle of the structure. It wasn't grand or enormous, but the beauty of it, the simplicity in its design and the peaceful sensation it evoked, elicited a sigh from her. Twinkly Christmas lights were wrapped around it.

Underneath the stars and walking the beautiful grounds with Ayaan, dressed in their Indian finery and sharing a comfort she'd never experienced before after the high of being surrounded by her loved ones...a bubble of calm enveloped her, and she was invincible.

She was a queen, commanding the universe to do what she asked and gracious enough to accept all the surprises it contained.

"Have you ever had a moment when you feel like you've received everything you could ask for?" Ayaan murmured, gazing at her now.

Her thumb traced circles along Ayaan's own in response. His heartbeat pulsed through his veins and she was reassured by the thumping underneath her skin, as though the night was confirming it was real and that he was standing in front of her...hers.

"Tonight was everything, wasn't it?" she whispered. "And the journey hasn't even begun yet."

Ayaan cleared his throat and turned his entire body toward her.

"It's funny you say that." He gave a small laugh and looked at their hands entwined. "Payal... I..."

His nerves, sometimes adorable, alarmed her now. "Are you okay?"

He met her eyes and a soft smile crossed his lips. He gazed at her with a tenderness she'd grown to see more often recently but that she'd never felt more than in this moment.

"I've never been better. Payal, you aren't wrong. The journey hasn't even begun. And already, it's surprised me. *You've* surprised me. You've taken my entire life by storm and shown me what a rebuild looks like...how someone can reinvent themselves and create beautiful things out of what was and how people can reach for impossible stars if they try hard enough.

"I love you," he said. "I know maybe that's soon given we've officially been dating for about three seconds—"

She couldn't help but laugh, tears pricking at her eyes at the gravity of all he was saying.

"But I'm in love with all you are and all you give to me. The sass. The strength. The immensity of you. I don't want to live without it. And tonight, for the first time in years, England...our families. Our friends. I was home. You are home. You bring comfort and joy and love to places you are, and I want to build a home with you for the rest of my life."

Payal stopped breathing as Ayaan dropped down on his right knee, never letting go of her hand...never letting go of her. He reached into his pocket and pulled out a small black box with golden filigree and opened it.

A two-carat princess-cut emerald glowed in the light, with a thin halo of sparking pavé diamonds surrounding it and extending along the band. As she stared closer, the diamonds on the band ended with two opals—October, she knew instantly, was Ayaan's birth month. The opals would be hidden by her fingers.

"I wanted you to know I'll always be a part of you too and that I don't have to be seen. You just have to shine."

His sweet touch on her dream ring brought tears to her eyes. *How did he know?* Payal couldn't recall mentioning the emerald bauble she'd envisioned since she was a teenager, but she didn't have a moment to think as Ayaan kept speaking.

"I never saw you coming. I know we've only dated a short time, but I think I've always known you would be the lighthouse to guide me back to all the good things I didn't think I deserved. Marry me, Payal. Let's begin this journey for real."

The question hung in the air.

But it didn't take an extra thought or a moment's hesitation before she gave her answer.

"Yes," she said simply. "Yes, Ayaan Malhotra, I'll marry you. I love you. And timing doesn't matter because it brought us here… and home with you is where I want to be."

He slid the perfectly sized ring onto her left hand, and she held her hand up in front of her, in awe of the way it sparkled. Of the many pieces of fine jewelry she'd bought for herself—when she got her first promotion, when she rented a new apartment, and even when the line was selected for the show—she was certain nothing would ever hold a candle to the one Ayaan had put on her finger.

Ayaan stood and swept her into his arms, hugging her with ferocity and kissing the sides of her face and her neck with equal vigor.

"I love you," he kept saying as though the words would never stop being magical.

Payal knew they never would.

As they reached the door to her suite, sneaking in kisses when stragglers from the party weren't around, Payal nearly invited him in.

"Payal! Isn't your makeup artist coming at the ass crack of dawn?"

Sonam charged down the hall, a cup of coffee in one hand and a book in the other, a pencil behind her ear, and her Coke-bottle glasses atop her nose.

Payal read Ayaan's smiling eyes and nearly inaudible sigh: *What. A. Cockblock.*

Fighting the urge to laugh, she answered her best friend, who was trailed by Akash and Kiran, both in pajamas.

"We were a little busy," Payal said.

"What, you did it in the garden?" Sonam said, raising an eyebrow and evidently unimpressed and unsurprised by the potential of Payal getting it on in the middle of an English landscape.

Payal glanced at Ayaan, who grinned at her and nodded, before flashing her ring. "In a manner of speaking."

"OH MY GOD!" Kiran and Sonam cried out, and they both rushed forward to examine the bauble.

"You nailed it, Ayaan! I'm so glad it worked out in time," Kiran exclaimed, and she gave him a hug.

"What do you mean?" Payal frowned.

"Ayaan called me to find out what your dream ring design was. He knew you loved emeralds and thought diamonds were too common on engagement rings, but he wanted to get it right."

"Is that true?" Payal asked Ayaan in wonder.

"Why didn't you say something?" Akash, who had hung back to watch the scene unfold, turned to Kiran.

"I didn't want to ruin the surprise! Oh, don't look at me like that, Akash. We all keep our secrets sometimes, don't we? Even from each other."

At that, Akash and Payal exchanged glances before hurriedly looking away.

"Well, I'm happy for you," Akash said. "Congratulations! It's a really beautiful ring."

Ayaan smiled in thanks. "Unfortunately, I have to take it back with me because we have to exchange them tomorrow at the pooja."

"What, you're going to propose and then take it away?" Payal pouted.

"Only for a few hours. I promise it'll be right back where it belongs by the evening." He brushed a stray hair from her face, and her skin tingled where he'd touched it.

"Fiiinne," she said, rolling her eyes. "But there is something pretty wonderful about this, you know."

"What's that?"

"The ring was witness to a beautiful secret tonight. Our parents don't know. It's just us and, I'm assuming, your boys."

Ayaan laughed. "I told them, yes."

"So it's our found families and us...that's it. We're the only ones who know there was a proposal."

"Nothing like keeping secrets, right?" Akash said, and if Payal hadn't known him so well, she wouldn't have heard the pointed edge to his words.

The clandestine, appealing nature of tonight's events evaporated.

Ayaan didn't seem to notice.

"Always looking at the bright side," he murmured. "I'll see you tomorrow?"

"Like that's even a question, fiancé."

Fiancé. She loved the way it tasted on her tongue, knowing Ayaan was attached to the word.

He grinned, and she knew in a heartbeat that he was thinking of the same.

As they all split up for the night and Payal closed the door to Ayaan's receding body, she was certain she had, indeed, gotten everything.

Midafternoon the next day, she stared at the mirror and was struck by what she saw.

Payal had always envisioned a dark lehenga for her engagement: dramatic, elegant, and formal. The pastel-purple, sparkling confection in front of her was about as far from what she'd pictured as she could get. But she loved it anyway. It seemed to fit, all of a sudden, the idea of a happily-ever-after and a man who fit into her family.

She'd never anticipated that she'd feel so whole after years of being convinced she was never incomplete.

Ayaan genuinely thrilled her. And now she'd get to call him hers...forever.

She tried not to smile to herself, even pursing her lips together to fight the urge, but she couldn't help but let a little squeal out.

"Wow," she heard her grandmother's voice from behind her.

Ma and Nani had let themselves into her suite—all the more affirmation Payal needed that it was a good idea Ayaan hadn't spent the night—and they were standing in a row, marveling at her.

"Do you like it?"

"My girl..." Nani said with a small shake of her head. "You are a goddess." She cracked her knuckles against the sides of her head to ward off any nazar.

"You're breathtaking," her mother said with tears in her eyes.

Payal wasn't sure what she'd expected from her parents on a day like today...at worst, no reaction—which wouldn't be that different from daily life anyway—and at best, a compulsory "You look nice," but the tender way Ma was looking at her now, with tears in her eyes and pride on her face, was surprisingly heavy.

Wow, maybe you do love me.

"Of course we love you," Ma said vehemently. "Why wouldn't we?"

Payal hadn't realized she'd murmured her insecurity out loud.

"I mean...you just... We don't talk. You haven't said it often, Ma," Payal stuttered. "I didn't think—"

"Payal," Ma said quietly. "We didn't think we had to."

The gap between them was miles wide and tantalizingly close. Their emotions were already heightened, and now, Payal could feel the air shifting as though the years of simmering words and almost explanations were about to boil to the surface.

"Providing for me and being my parents are two different things."

She was about to speak again, to elaborate and to force the geyser to explode, when her mother's voice quietly, like cool water, washed over the room.

"You have always been a spirited one," she started. "Even when you were little and I'd ask you if you needed help or wanted a hand, you would push it away and do it on your own. I was so proud of that independence—a little heartbroken because perhaps I wasn't needed. But you never needed me. You have always been out the door before I got a word in. That's what I wanted to raise you as. That's what I got. Perhaps"—she mused out loud now—"I could have tried harder...but I didn't have an example to turn to. And you never seemed to need it."

"This worked out and I love Ayaan, Ma, but I needed you to speak up for me then. Why didn't you say anything like this when you saw I was being pushed toward marrying someone who, at the time, I didn't know?"

"Because we knew you'd show up," her mom said simply. "Call it pretention or taking you for granted...but you have always fought first, excelled, and then made yourself indispensable. We knew you'd be there for us again. You would fight. You would think on it. You would rise to the occasion. It's who you are."

"You made it sound like I'd be disowned if I disobeyed, Ma. That's not me rising to the occasion as much as you forcing a hand."

"Beta, we'd never disown you. Your friend Kiran...we aren't her parents. We never would have let you go for disobeying us."

"But you said... Wait, how do you know about Kiran?" Payal asked.

In all the years of CMC friendship, her mother had rarely, if ever, asked how they were beyond the compulsory "How are your Duke friends?"

"They've always kept an eye on you through me." Nani spoke up. "I've kept my fair share of secrets for you—after all, you are entitled to your choices—but they've always asked behind the scenes, my dear."

"I didn't know you wanted to reach me," Payal said in a hushed tone.

"And I didn't know *how* to," her mother replied.

The lid was off Pandora's box. Except the monsters that flew out slowly began crumbling—still in existence but in smaller pieces—as her mother countered each of Payal's misconceptions with reasoning of her own. It was hardly the right time, at her engagement of all places, to be discussing years of distance between them...but in a twisted way, the seemingly disparate pieces of her life seemed to be coming together this weekend, and this was perhaps the most important one of all.

Maybe there was no better time.

"For the record, you are beautiful. We love you. We're proud of you. And I am very happy that you and Ayaan seem to have built a real bond over the last months," Ma said.

The only sign of her mother's nerves was the way she wrung her hands together subtly in front of her. Ever poised, she betrayed no other signal that she had opened up.

"Thank you, Ma," Payal said. "I didn't think... I didn't know. And I'm happy you brought Ayaan to me."

"Let's go get you engaged," Ma said.

. . . .

AYAAN

"Rokas and sagais used to be small affairs, you know," Dharm said as he buttoned Ayaan's sherwani in his room before the ceremony started.

"According to my family, one hundred of our closest family and friends is small," Ayaan said.

The Long Gallery at Fanhams Hall had been transformed into an indoor garden. The wood paneling, reminiscent of an old library, and the large windows lining the left side and back side of the room had been draped with flower arrangements that gave the illusion that magenta roses and white lilies had simply grown from the old woodwork and wrapped themselves around the room. The ceiling, an old molded design in a cream color, appeared brighter, lightening up the room and making everyone look as though they were glowing.

At the front of the room was a stage set two feet off the ground, with a backdrop of white, orange, and dark-pink draperies forming a neatly pleated, wavy pattern behind where Payal and Ayaan would sit on two throne-like chairs in the center of the stage. Four pillars with vines curling around them and the same roses and white lilies hanging from the bars joining them together made a mandate that wasn't quite as grand as a wedding but had still added a garden-like feel to the room.

As he sat on the chair with his immediate family surrounding him and Kai, Dharm, the CMC, and the faces of so many other acquaintances—and some strangers—in the audience, Ayaan felt like a circus animal.

A drop of sweat trickled down the side of his forehead. His heart beat against his chest.

Payal and her family entered the room.

Ayaan had to blink his eyes to see clearly, and his mouth dropped open as his fiancée stepped into the aisle.

Payal was wearing a purple—lavender?—lehenga that sparkled in the light.

Her abs were taut in the short-sleeved cropped blouse, and her exposed skin reminded Ayaan of what it felt like underneath his fingertips as he ran his fingers up her sides. He unconsciously rubbed his thumb against each of his fingers.

She was radiant. Watching her enter was like witnessing the most beautiful sunrise he'd ever seen.

As she approached with her family, the skirt billowing around her and swaying with her steps, Ayaan watched her and swelled with everything from want to love to hope. Her eyes were dramatically lined and her eyeshadow, a glimmering metallic lilac, made them a more pronounced brown than he'd ever seen, nearly hazel.

She was in front of him now, only feet away.

As she stepped onto the stage, Ayaan drew a sharp breath. She lifted her chin and met his gaze. For a moment, the world stopped.

"You're stunning," he whispered.

Her resplendent smile in response was the most beautiful thing he'd seen.

"Hi, fiancé," she said cheerfully.

Sonam, who had overheard her from the front row, cheered, and the audience laughed and clapped alongside her.

As Payal moved next to him, her hand brushed past and he

was tempted to reach out, grab it, turn her around, cup her face in his hands, and kiss her.

"If we weren't in front of a priest and our family..." he muttered to her as she sat next to him.

"What about our friends?" she whispered back with a mischievous tone, her lips imperceptibly moving.

"They can watch. Looking the way you do, it'd be their privilege."

She laughed unabashedly, throwing her head back. "You know, you're quite handsome yourself. The sherwani is doing it for me."

"I'll do something to you," he murmured.

Mum, dressed in a resplendent maroon sari, and Dad, dapper in a gray suit, presented a silver tray with an envelope full of cash to begin their lives together as well as a diamond necklace set for Payal.

"Oh, my gosh! This is beautiful," Payal murmured, gently touching the stones set in yellow gold. "Thank you so much. This is too much."

"It's far less than what you deserve, Payal," Mum said quietly. "You deserve everything."

"Beta, we are so happy to have you," Dad said.

On the direction of the priest, they offered a red dupatta to Payal, a sign that she would be accepted into their family and that they had chosen her as the beloved daughter-in-law.

Ayaan sat straighter, remembering how Sarika had worn the biggest smile on her face when she'd been presented with hers and how Arun had joked the entire way through their engagement about the fact that her family would never be given enough to thank them for lending their daughter to the Malhotras.

Payal wore the same proud expression as his sister-in-law

that day, and she lit up at the notion of being a Malhotra. Ayaan couldn't help but think that Arun had been right about exceptional women joining their family.

"We're so excited for you to be our son-in-law," Payal's mother said to him. She reached onto a tray and fed him a laddoo. Her golden bangles caught the light and shimmered.

"I can't wait to marry your daughter," he said.

As the priest offered fruit, flowers, and offerings to the Ganesha idol he placed on the stage, serving as a physical stand-in for an invisible god, Ayaan found himself praying to the round-bellied deity that they'd find their way, continue to shine, and never stop being as happy as they were now. The mantras being chanted slowly lulled Ayaan into a stupor, allowing him to settle into a calm.

"Rings," the priest commanded.

Arun handed Ayaan the box that he had presented to Payal last night. He and Payal's eyes met in conspiratorial glee. Flashes of Payal's surprise as he'd gotten down on one knee, the tears in her eyes, and the joy on her face all played through Ayaan's mind again.

My God. I get to feel this forever.

"Second time's the charm," Payal whispered with a wink. "You're not allowed to take it away this time."

"It's not going anywhere," he whispered back.

"Promise?"

"Forever."

Slowly, Payal put her hand out for him to slide the ring on. He grasped her fingertips with his left hand and slid the emerald engagement ring onto her finger.

"Payal," the priest commanded.

She pulled away her hand reluctantly, audibly sighing and

eliciting a laugh from the family, before reaching for her mother, who held a tray with an open jewelry box on it. Aunty handed her a gold band that they'd chosen on their last trip to London, a thick gold ring with a domed edge.

Ayaan stuck his left hand out, refusing to take his gaze off her face as Payal slid the symbolic band over his finger.

The audience clapped and both of them startled.

Both sets of parents and Nani fed each of them half a laddoo, celebrating the union. Ayaan felt the sugary jitters building as he swallowed the fifth morsel of sweet goodness.

"Oh my God, this is so good," Payal said through a mouthful of sweet.

The shuffle of guests and chairs moving back on wooden floors echoed through the Long Gallery.

"You both are perfect. May God bless and protect you both," a kindhearted aunty said to them, cracking her knuckles against her head to remove the evil eye for them both and pushing their heads together as an age-old blessing.

Payal's perfume, a seductive floral scent, overtook Ayaan and he closed his eyes, breathing it in, taking in all he could of the day he knew his life had changed.

Guest after guest came to congratulate the parents, who shook hands, gave hugs, fed sweets, and exploded in cheers with friends who had been long overdue for a reunion. They pushed the couple's heads together, and Payal and Ayaan remained with their hands held together at their chests in greeting for well over an hour before the crowd made its way to the banquet.

A sit-down family-style dinner followed where a restaurant, one that Mum had insisted on, catered a full three-course Indian meal. Plates of samosas, pakoras, gobi manchurian, chaat, and tandoori chicken filled the tables before being whisked away, only to be replaced with rice, breads, chicken and lamb curries, paneer kofta, methi malai, and so many more.

Classical music, intended for dinner, was replaced with pop tunes from the early 2000s and eventually with today's music as all their loved ones went to the dance floor in a repeat of the night before. Flashing lights and colorful uplighting turned the historic site into a space reminiscent of a nightclub, and multiple uncles were escorted out of the ballroom, supported by their wives and walking in lines too wobbly to consider them sober.

An entire roomful of people had gathered for Ayaan and Payal. Only months back, he'd insisted on a smaller gathering so that he could avoid the fallout when they inevitably broke up, and now he wished he'd invited everyone he knew to witness the woman he was in love with…someone who was an art form in the way she gracefully handled the compliments about her appearance, questions about her line, and introductions to new faces.

When the night had wrapped, Ayaan only wanted Payal.

"I think the others wanted to gather in the common area for a little after-party," Payal said.

"Let's go change. Kai mentioned comfortable clothes," Ayaan answered.

"I say we wear no clothes and stay here," Payal murmured.

That was all it took for him to push her up against the wall near the door of her hotel suite. His lips hungrily sought hers out, and he felt her legs rise as though she wanted to wrap them around him, only stopped by the limitation in her skirt.

"Maybe we can be late," Ayaan growled.

Payal laughed, her hands still on his neck, pulling him close as her words said otherwise. "My mother and grandmother barged in this morning and they're still in the hall. I don't know that I'll ever want to leave if we start."

"Ugh, you're mean," groaned Ayaan. "I have to walk this off."

"Some cool air might do the trick," Payal teased. "But maybe you can sneak in like we're teenagers later tonight when everyone is asleep."

"Promise?"

"As sure as this ring on my finger," Payal said, and she gave him a lingering kiss.

"Okay...now I really need to walk it off," he said, looking down at the growing bulge under his pants.

"I'll see you soon," she whispered and kissed him one more time for good measure.

Ayaan chuckled as Payal closed the door behind her, resting his head against the cool frame and trying to shake out the desperate need for her.

He did love the grounds. Maybe a late-night stroll wouldn't be so bad.

A short distance away from the main house sat a Japanese teahouse called the House of the Pure Heart.

He'd proposed just in front of it last night and he couldn't help but marvel at the name. He may not have gone into this with the purest of intentions, but he had ended up with the most beautiful love of all.

Ayaan was fascinated by the two-story house with the wrapping veranda and the crisscrossing railing and sloping rooftop. A stone path wound its way elegantly through the garden, around a pond dotted with lily pads. A red bridge crossed the water.

The serenity unlocked such peace in him.

He hadn't anticipated he'd be excited to get engaged to Payal. Nine short months ago, he was terrified, but now he felt pride at how both intentionally and inadvertently they had made space for each other to grow and filled the gaps between them with kindness and understanding. He was a different person than he had been when he told his parents he wanted the CMO job and plotted to get it through this girl.

Now he couldn't live without her.

"Ayaan?" a female voice called out.

No. Fucking. Way.

He turned, and his eyes nearly bugged out of his head. They had to be playing tricks on him.

"*Neha?*" he asked in shock.

"Hi."

"What are you doing here?"

She fidgeted, toying with the oversize sweater she was wearing. "I just... I know this sounds so stupid, but I couldn't let you go without at least pleading my case for one more shot at us."

"And you flew all the way to England? For me? How did you even know?"

"I saw Arun's Instagram. We started following each other after the show, you know. And seeing the posts about all the preparations going on for this weekend drove home the fact that I was losing you, and if I wanted you, then I had to act. This is just... It's my big..." Neha was clearly uncomfortable. "It's my big gesture. Ayaan, I'm really sorry."

He did a double take. "I'm sorry?"

He couldn't even laugh at the fact that he'd echoed her words right back to her when he was, in fact, befuddled at where they'd come from.

"Our timing was off. We weren't healthy for one another. I get that. I focused so much on my career and I was angry at you about all the wrong things. You weren't there in heart. But we had so many good times too, and those make it hard to let you go."

Ayaan shook his head but whether in disbelief that this conversation was happening or in disagreement, he wasn't sure.

"Timing could be on our side now. You've changed so much this year. I can see it. Your success with your parents' company. The way you've thrown yourself into Besharmi. Even the way you stand is taller somehow."

When he didn't say anything, she continued.

"I know this isn't the best way to do this, flying here on a whim and proclaiming this, but I miss you. I know we weren't right for each other then, but maybe we can be now."

"Neha, I'm engaged."

"Yes, but it's an engagement... It's not a marriage. You haven't been together as long as we were, and it's business, not love, driving this thing, isn't it?"

His silence seemed to give her misplaced affirmation on what she was saying and encouragement to continue.

"I know I came down on you because you couldn't commit... but you are so different now. I've seen it. I want to understand you better and try to make sense of us. And if you can commit now, then maybe the timing is finally right for us. Maybe it lined up perfectly after all."

"Neha...what prompted this?" Ayaan asked. "I am terribly blindsided here."

"Your social media post with Payal," she said quietly. "It was one thing seeing you at Penrose with her, Dharm, and Kai. At the time, there was enough awkwardness in the air to know that maybe it was just business. It couldn't be taken seriously. But the photo..." She very nearly seemed to shudder. "It was like watching something amazing be taken away from me...or to know I gave it up. It really hurt to see it."

He hadn't even thought about who would see the photo when

he posted it. He was so thrilled to have Payal on his arm, glowing the way she did that night, that he'd simply shared his happiness with the world.

"This is my big gesture to show you I can be ready for this. We can push each other."

She took a step toward him and he could see his reflection in her eyes.

"Tell me you don't miss me, and I'll leave you alone," she whispered.

His heart was pounding through his chest, a visceral response to someone being near him who he used to want, used to crave, when he was lonely.

He looked around for an escape, and movement captured his attention on his right.

Standing there was Akash in sweatpants and a hoodie, with a look of total contempt on his face.

But before Ayaan could say a single word or give him a wave, Neha had closed the distance between them and her lips were a centimeter away.

With the smell of her fruity perfume came the realization, like a wave: he didn't want someone who missed his presence when they saw a social media post of him with someone else. He wanted someone who craved his presence even when she knew he was hers to keep.

He wanted Payal.

Stepping back just as her lips brushed his, Ayaan put his hands up.

"I'm in love with her," he said. "I'm in love with Payal. I'm marrying her. I'm sorry, Neha. I can't do this."

The door had well and truly slammed shut, and the relief on his shoulders from all the weight being lifted made him laugh out loud at his own idiocy for thinking he was meant for anything else.

But in the height of his proclamation, he hadn't noticed that Akash had slipped away into the night.

Chapter Twenty-Nine

PAYAL

As she slipped the outfit off her body, Payal's skin was on fire. She should have told Ayaan to join her, parents be damned. She'd never loved him so much and the emotion of the day needed a release.

Her phone buzzed. Come downstairs. Courtyard, a text from Akash read.

Her elation dissipated as concern took its place. Even for the normally abbreviated texter, Akash never used punctuation. Somehow, the message sounded far more curt and demanding than anything she could remember.

She yanked the pins out of her hair, tied it into a loose bun at the top of her head, threw on a pair of sweatpants and a T-shirt, slipped on some flats, and swiped her key off the entrance table before closing the door behind her.

Greeted by everyone from hotel staff, who seemed to know she was the center of attention for the weekend, to family members who wanted to say hello, it took her a few minutes extra before she was able to finagle her way to the empty courtyard in the middle of the estate.

"Hi," she said breathlessly to Akash, who was sitting by a fountain, staring into the distance.

He startled and then stood when he saw her. "Hey."

"I'm so sorry it took me a few minutes. Everyone wants to talk and there's so much chaos going on. Hey, what's wrong?" She'd noticed Akash's face.

Akash's jaw was clenched, his square face appearing more chiseled than ever.

His hands were in his pockets, and Payal could tell they had balled into fists.

"Akash," she coaxed.

"Are you happy?" he asked abruptly.

"What?" She tried to laugh, as though the question was so facetious that it had to be a joke, but his tone was unsettling and her attempt at a scoff sounded much more like a croak.

"Are. You. Happy?"

"Yes...Akash, I'm happy. Ayaan is wonderful. Why?"

His eyes darted around, growing more frantic underneath the ever-deepening frown that had creased his forehead. His weight shifted back and forth on his feet, and Payal sensed his energy from his unstoppable movement.

"Nothing."

"Tell me."

He gazed at her, concern flooding his eyes. "I just worry about you, you know?"

"Tell me what's on your mind. You're freaking me out. And I don't like it when we fight."

Payal sat on the wall of the fountain, feeling the spray from the gently bubbling water and the cool of the stone underneath her jeans.

When Akash didn't make a move, she gestured at the empty space in front of her, nodding at it so he'd finally sit and tell her what was on his mind.

After a moment, one that felt infinitely long and Payal was

certain had aged her twelve years, he sat, bending his leg underneath him.

"I still don't know if I like the guy," he confessed.

"Can you tell me why?"

He paused again. "He rubs me the wrong way...but mostly, I worry about you."

"Why?"

"Because I want, more than anything, for you to be happy."

He took Payal's hand and, by doing so, took her by surprise. His skin was warm and Payal couldn't help but close her fingers around his palm.

"Payal, you are one of my best friends. I might have joked about how you'd never find anyone...but the truth is that I don't ever think anyone will be good enough for what I hope for you. When I think of the type of person who should be with you, I hope he's someone who sees the magic in your eyes when something lights the spark of inspiration and you begin scheming. He has to be aware that you take what are, arguably, the longest showers on the face of the planet and the most probable reason the polar ice caps are melting. And he has to know that there is not a more elegant, beautiful, or sassy person in the room when he's standing next to you."

Payal's eyes burned.

Akash's appeared wet in the dimly lit night as he stared at her, imploring her to answer.

"I don't know what to say," she sniffled. "But thank you. You are the best friend I could ever ask for, and I know you're looking out for me. But, Akash, I know Ayaan is that person. At first, I think I feared that he would drown out my light...but it turns out we burn brightly together. And I have to trust that he sees the same joy. I know he does."

Akash nodded and squeezed her hand. "Then I'll support you.

I know I told you, many times, that I didn't like the guy…but you know him and I trust you, so by extension, I have to put some faith in him. I'll be happy for you, because you deserve nothing but joy. I love you, you know."

His eyes searched her face, and she knew, in that moment, they'd be friends longer than forever. Akash was the brother she had never been given and one of three best friends who had made up for the space in her family.

The weight of the engagement sat firmly on her shoulders as she let the words wash over her. Soon, Ayaan would join this group, and the dynamic, for better and not worse, would shift, the same way it moved when Nash had appeared in their lives. As each of them found partners, their circle would morph, expand to include new members, and transform the chemistry.

The future was so full of potential that the prospect thrilled her…but the change was so real that this moment, with her and her best friend, alone by a fountain and sharing a heart-to-heart under the stars, had become priceless.

Tears escaped her eyes as she tried to rein them in.

"I love you too, Akash."

"All right, enough of this," he murmured, and he cupped her chin in his hands, wiping away her tears with his thumb.

She pulled him close for one last hug, breathing in his fresh cologne and thanking the gods above for friends as caring as these.

Neither of them heard the footsteps approaching from the colonnade.

· · · · · · · · · ·

AYAAN

It was as though someone had punched Ayaan in the gut when

he wasn't expecting it. The air swooshed out of his lungs and a pounding ache replaced the space where his heart used to beat.

He'd been hoping to find Kai and Dharm to tell them about the craziness that had just happened.

Instead, he found Payal and Akash in the courtyard, their arms wrapped around each other as though they'd never get to do it again. It stopped him in his tracks.

He *knew* something was going on between the two of them. They'd always been so *close*. Payal had sworn up and down that Akash had gotten around plenty, and as he grew closer with each slow step toward them and watched Akash hold Payal's hand as they pulled away, wipe her tears, and draw her in again for a hug, Ayaan couldn't help but wonder if this was the beginning of a follow-up to their one-time hookup.

Jealous fury bubbled in his veins. He wanted to snap Akash in half.

"What's going on here?" He forced his voice to sound level and rational, but it bellowed across the courtyard with the volume of a cannon in the night.

Payal jumped. She wiped her face against her sleeve. Her eyes were red-rimmed, and she appeared irritated at the interruption.

Ayaan stared at Akash, who defiantly refused to turn away. In his detesting eyes, Ayaan saw that he knew about Neha, and he was certain, given their proximity and Payal's teary eyes, that he had spilled the beans about it. He knew that Akash had warned Payal against him.

"We were just having a conversation," Akash said quietly, shooting him a dirty look.

"It must have been some discussion."

"We were talking about her happiness and how she deserves the best," Akash replied unabashedly.

Payal glanced at him gratefully, and it was this soft, fixed stare that pushed Ayaan over the edge.

"What, like you?" Ayaan snapped. "I knew there was something happening between the two of you."

"What are you talking about, man?" Akash asked.

"Stop with the pretend outrage, mate. You think I don't know about your history?"

"Ayaan!" Payal exclaimed.

Akash turned to Payal with his mouth slightly ajar before seemingly thinking better of changing his focus to her. Instead, he faced Ayaan again. "We're best friends. Nothing more."

"You want me to believe that? You were wrapped up in each other's arms just now."

"You're being unreasonable, Ayaan," Payal said. "Akash was supporting me."

"We were literally talking about how happy she is with you," Akash said. "But even being friends, at least I believe the best in her. Apparently that's more than we can say about you, the guy she's supposed to be with."

"Well, at least I wouldn't make a move on someone I can't have," Ayaan said obstinately.

"That's rich coming from you," muttered Akash.

"Oh, stop it. The least you could have done is allowed me to tell Payal about the kiss myself."

Payal whipped toward him at the mention of the kiss. "What kiss?"

Ayaan stared at Akash, expecting him to fight back.

But instead, he raised his hands up, just a bit, as if to say, "I didn't say a thing." Then, to Ayaan's horror, Akash shook his head infinitesimally, looking disgusted.

Ayaan's blood turned to ice.

But it was Payal's expression that broke him. Her lips quivered and anger flashed across her big eyes. She'd frozen as though she'd been hit and was reeling from shock.

"What. Kiss. Ayaan?"

Ayaan closed his eyes, bracing himself for the inevitable damage that would come with confessing what had just come to pass with Neha.

He wanted to tell Payal it meant nothing. He liked her—no, even he was sure now, when faced with the threat of losing her, that he was, in fact, deeply in love with her. But she wouldn't believe it coming from him. Not with their history.

Not with his mistakes.

"Neha flew here."

Her eyes narrowed. "Why?"

"She saw a post on Instagram and she...she wanted to get back together."

"Did you kiss her?" Payal's voice cracked.

"No," Ayaan said. But before Payal could show relief on her face, he corrected himself, "But she kissed me...or at least, she tried to."

Payal inhaled through her teeth. Akash reached for her arm, but she shrugged it off.

"You invited her to our engagement?" She hissed.

"Payal, I promise, I didn't. I had no idea. She saw Arun's posts on Instagram and acted of her own accord. I didn't give her any signals that it was okay. I pulled away, I swear to God. I didn't want to lie to you about it," Ayaan pleaded.

She had to believe him.

"How could you let her come close to you?" Payal shouted.

"It was unexpected. She wanted to talk, and I thought it would be a conversation closing the chapter—"

Payal laughed humorlessly.

"I promise, Payal, I didn't know she wanted me back."

"Have you been talking to her all this time?"

The question, the doubt in her eyes, and the tone she took reminded him of the morning after they'd hooked up. He had been so hotheaded as he left, unclear in his explanation and too full of pride to be honest then.

With a sinking feeling, he remembered the second time. He'd done the right thing then, and still he'd hidden it and hoped that his budding relationship with Payal would sort itself out.

He'd taken away her voice, and he knew she'd never forgive him for doing it again.

He wasn't that guy anymore. He wanted to be the best for her.

"No, I promise. It never went anywhere. It was never meant to be her—"

"Then why would you let it go this far?" Payal cried.

Akash took her hand and Ayaan's heart writhed, knotting itself in jealousy and heartbreak. He wanted to wrench their hands apart. She was his.

"Shh, Payal, your voice is going to carry. Let's take this inside," Akash said, trying to soothe her.

It should have been him comforting her. He should have been able to convince her that Neha no longer meant anything and that it was Payal who made his world turn…but words escaped him and nothing he would have said could fix what had broken here.

"What's going on? Ayaan? Payal?" Arun's voice joined the fray.

Chapter Thirty

PAYAL

Payal couldn't breathe.

Every insecurity she had about Neha rose to the surface as she pictured her and Ayaan sharing a deep, passionate, meaningful kiss…just like the one she'd shared with him. One where she experienced the rush of love, care, and forever. She wanted to scream at the wave of pain it elicited.

He was supposed to be hers.

To make matters worse, Nani, the four parents, and Sarika had followed Arun into the courtyard, making the scene of her heartbreak the setting of a family reunion.

"What's going on?" Arun asked again. "We can hear your voices from inside. Is everything okay?"

She had to get out of here and catch her breath.

"We're fine," she managed. "Ayaan just admitted to something that didn't make me too happy, but I'm sure we'll get past it. You know…engagement party problems." She tried to laugh.

We'll never get past this, her inner voice said.

"Did he finally tell you the truth about how he agreed to the engagement?" Arun chuckled, oblivious to the direction Payal was pointing the conversation. "I'm glad it worked out though, Payal. Otherwise Ayaan would never have found the guts to chase after the CMO job."

"Oh no, it was just a…" Payal waved him off. Then what Arun had implied sank in. "Wait. What?"

Color had drained from Ayaan's face and his eyes had widened. His chest rose and fell at a faster pace, and he appeared to be shaking his head to get Arun to stop.

Arun hadn't noticed. He had evidently had a few drinks, and he was carrying a whiskey glass with a suspiciously low amount of brown liquid in it. "I mean, I guess it doesn't matter because you both agreed to this and you're happy now—but you should have seen my face when he used your engagement to negotiate getting named CMO. I wasn't sure he had it in him! You'd settle him down, you know? Good thing too, because otherwise, he would keep on screwing up his life, amiright?" He chortled but no one laughed.

The parents had turned to Ayaan, frowns on their faces.

Payal recoiled like she'd been slapped. Anger swirled inside her like a hurricane, and she churned inside.

You'd settle him down, you know? She had been a pawn in a game being played by everyone she loved when she had believed, deep down, that she was running the game.

Tears pricked at her eyes again.

"That's okay," Nani said now. "It's not like Payal wasn't doing the same thing."

Nani didn't drink, so Payal had no idea what mind-altering substance had made her grandmother speak, but she had unleashed a mushroom cloud that was about to level all of England.

"Nani!" Payal hissed, her heartbreak forgotten for a split second as she tried to control the rapidly escalating situation.

Ayaan stared at Payal with shock and hurt on his face. Questions swirled in his eyes and Payal couldn't answer them in front of everyone, but she knew this storm was only beginning to brew.

"What is she talking about?" Papa asked, turning to Payal, but Nani spoke again.

"Stop it, beta. You act so surprised that Payal would look out for her own interests. I'm glad the children had enough intelligence to see what benefit they could also take from this situation. God knows they are doing it for our families anyway. Payal was going to call off this engagement once her fashion line found success, but now the Malhotras have found benefit and she has found rave reviews for her line...and most importantly, she's really happy. We should be thrilled that this has been mutually beneficial and that this engagement will go through as planned."

"Ma!" Papa snapped at Nani. "What are you even saying? How could you encourage this type of deception? What about integrity?"

"It's all deception, isn't it?" Nani countered. "And integrity? Ha! Beta, you showed Payal she didn't need integrity when you sold her for the sake of a merger. You should have held her to greater heights and believed in her dream. She did what she had to—and she learned that from you."

Papa's face burned bright red.

"Neeraj, bhai, is this true?" Kuljeet Uncle asked Papa in disbelief. "Payal did not want this marriage? You talked her into it?"

"We didn't talk her into it," Ma said. "She knew what the family needed."

"Roopa, that's a lie," Nani admonished. "Stop rewriting a woman's lack of choice as a sense of duty."

"Payal, I thought you were happy," Bhoomi Aunty said softly.

I was, Payal wanted to cry out, but she couldn't find the words buried underneath all the lies.

Ayaan was still watching his family, his eyes taking on an emptiness that Payal could sense in her own chest.

It was all a lie.

"Well, if that is the case, Neeraj," Kuljeet Uncle said, "Payal's happiness should have come first. It isn't honorable to insist a child follow through on your wishes when they aren't willing to make the same decision. Forcing someone into a path they are not meant to be on is cruel."

"Well, then, you're one to talk, aren't you, Dad?" Arun asked. "You forced Ayaan into this to begin with, and you've been giving in to his tantrums for years. Forcing someone onto a path they aren't meant to be on? Ayaan is a royal screwup. He didn't earn CMO—he got it because you struck a deal."

"Arun! Stop." Sarika spoke, silencing everyone who had been bickering in the background. "I don't know what has gotten into you, but you've been so negative about Ayaan's work. He has brought the family so much success in the last few months, and Payal has been raved about...and rather than focusing on the positive changes, you've been fixated on the fact that he made mistakes a few years ago, and you've held it over his head for all this time because he disappointed *you* and you won't let it go. Stop it. It's a terrible look for all of you."

Arun avoided his wife's eyes, taking a swig of his drink instead.

Payal jumped when a hand clasped hers.

Sonam.

Behind her were Kiran, Nash, and Akash, who had joined them.

"Uncles, aunties, might I suggest that we take this inside?" Sonam asked with the authority of a doctor who had been triaging an emergency room in crisis. "Voices carry and you currently have an audience."

Sure enough, as Payal looked up to the building rising behind them, other guests of the engagement and the hotel could be seen at the window and even standing on the landing leading down to the courtyard.

"I think we're done here," Ayaan said quietly, his voice cutting through the darkness. "I'll be in my room."

Payal wanted desperately to run behind him, to grab his hand and explain herself and hear his reasoning too, but the hurt, betrayal, and anger cemented her in place. Instead, she watched him turn, shoulders hunched, and make his way toward the west entrance to the building.

"I'm going to mine too," she said.

"Payal," Papa said.

"Not now, Papa. I'm fine."

But after all the revelations the night had brought, she was anything but.

. . . .

AYAAN

Ayaan had never experienced heartbreak...until now.

It had seemed awful enough, irreparable even, when Payal had thought he'd betrayed her. Though he hadn't kissed Neha back and he'd stepped away, the hurt in Payal's eyes and the tears that had begun to form were enough to make him do anything to fix it.

But it was he who was betrayed.

After all this time carrying the guilt that he was the one who had constantly fucked up and been playing a game with his family, he had been the pawn in a greater chess game. He'd been outsmarted, outgunned, and outmaneuvered by every single person in his life.

He'd never been so alone.

Brokenhearted sadness turned to fury as the memories of kissing her, of laughing with his family, and of the success began to flood him. He raged at himself, at them, and at her for making a fool of him...for making family, love, and triumph draw near before ripping them away.

For the first time since he was sixteen, he had been whole again. And now he was in pieces, and he couldn't find a place to repair the brokenness.

Someone rapped at the door.

Wiping his eyes on the back of his hand, he opened it, revealing Arun.

"You are the last person I want to see right now," he said firmly, pushing it shut again.

"Wait, Ayaan—" Arun pushed back against the door. "I'm sorry."

"What the hell were you playing at, even bringing up all this baggage tonight? Or ever? What kind of person are you?"

"The alcohol made me do it?" Arun offered, along with a reconciliatory half smile, but Ayaan was in no mood.

"Funny how it's an excuse for me but sound reasoning for you to make mistakes, isn't it?"

His brother's face fell. "I deserved that."

Ayaan rolled his eyes, shook his head, and turned away. Arun followed him, closing the door behind them both.

"You deserve a hell of a lot more shit from me," Ayaan said, facing him again. "You have been on my case for the last fifteen years, Arun. Fifteen years! Don't you think that I carry enough guilt after the accident? Did you not think that I pushed myself to start a new life, get my degrees, and try to move forward? You have done every fucking thing in your power to keep me exactly where I was, and you played games with every single thing that mattered to me in your quest to be the best."

Years of animosity, of being second best and of being reminded of it, had built up in Ayaan like a pressure cooker. Losing Payal was like lifting the release valve off, and the fury increased and exploded in cataclysmic flames.

"We should have stuck together all along," Arun said quietly.

"We used to," Ayaan fired back. "But you bailed. The moment you saw conflict...the moment you had doubt in me, you chose to see the worst rather than believe the best, and that baggage of yours is the weight I have to carry every day."

Arun nodded, shamefaced.

"I was a kid, Arun. A kid! You all were so fixated on the fact that I could have gotten thrown out for the accident—never mind that I wasn't driving and that I was sixteen and scared—and how it would reflect on the Malhotra legacy that you distanced yourself from me when I needed you the most." Ayaan's voice cracked.

Arun's mouth had fallen at the corners.

"I needed you. And I finally got to have the experience of someone who heard about all of it, who saw hope in me, and your fat mouth blew it."

Arun nodded.

His silence only inflamed Ayaan further, burning away at any remaining restraint.

"You got to have Sarika!" Ayaan shouted and his voice dripped with fury. "You wanted her. And we all made it happen. We welcomed her, boosted you, and made sure you were happy. Mum and Dad stretched themselves so thin to ensure you got all you deserved. Was it *so hard* for you to see me happy that you had to ruin the one chance I had to have the same thing? Are you the only one who gets to be content?"

Arun recoiled as though he'd been slapped. "I... No. Never."

"And seriously, did it not occur to you to maybe *not* follow my ex on social media?"

"It seemed like the polite thing to do since we'd worked together. I didn't think—"

"You couldn't hide your stories from her? Keep some separation between business and family? Don't look at me like that, Arun. You're always acting like you're the grown-up. You should have had a backbone and you should have seen this drama coming!"

Ayaan knew that his brother, who didn't care much for social media unless it worked in his favor, had never considered what its impact could be outside of business. But his life had shattered so violently tonight that he had no method, no logic, no cohesive pattern to airing his grievances. Instead, he lobbed each of the pieces of his jagged, broken heart at his brother, wishing Arun could see how many different ways he'd been damaged and hoping he could cause the same.

Arun winced now. He seemed resolved not to retort and rock the boat further. "I'm sorry," he whispered, nearly inaudible.

But for Ayaan, it was too late.

"I loved her," he said, and his voice cracked. "I thought we'd have a new, fresh start as a couple and that no one would have to know about this awful thing I did because maybe I could make up for it...and you blew it. I blew it. And I'm so sorry."

Ayaan's eyes burned and he closed them, willing the tears back, but they escaped anyway. Heat rushed his cheeks, and hopelessness washed over him like a tsunami, drowning him in his mistakes. His knees finally buckled under the pressure, and he sat, exhausted, on the end of the bed, covering his face with his hands.

He hardly felt the arms around him as Arun enveloped him in a hug.

"I'm sorry," Arun was murmuring against his younger brother's head. "I'm so sorry. I promise, we'll make this right. We'll fix this."

But despite the comfort from the person he'd always hoped would protect him, Ayaan was certain that nothing would ever feel right again.

Chapter Thirty-One

PAYAL

Payal's hotel suite was full of protestations, angry shouts, and passionate proclamations of revenge and hatred.

"Payal, maybe he didn't—"

"For God's sake, Akash. Don't," Payal snapped. "You don't get to defend someone who is willing to cheat on his fiancée."

"Payal, I didn't say I liked the guy—" Akash started.

"No, actually, you said, and I quote, 'I hate him.' And you know what? I should have listened because he was a cheating bastard who played a game with my head. I'm not insecure enough to say seeing an ex is weird if he'd let me know about it or if it was on the street in passing. But she shows up at our engagement—how the hell did she even know—and then he kissed her and then told me I was a piece of his corporate chess-game strategy to earn himself some power."

"We know, honey. We were there," Sonam said with uncharacteristic gentleness.

"And the worst part—the *worst* part—is the doubt this has sown among all of us. What the hell else don't I know?" Payal slammed her cup down with so much force, hot tea spilled on her hand, and she hissed as it turned her skin raw and red.

"Are you okay? Here." Akash sprang out of his seat, pulled the champagne bottle out of the ice bucket, and put her hand in it.

Payal sighed, the cold soothing her irritated skin. "I hope he gets a fork jammed into his backside."

The others, to their credit, didn't laugh.

It was Kiran whose eyes drooped and who gave her a sympathetic glance. "You say that...but you're hurting."

Payal turned her head so that her reddening eyes were out of sight. "Why should I be? I did the same thing to him. He was a means to an end. I needed money to start the line. I wanted contacts to encourage investment in the line. I aimed for growth. I got all those things. I was going to walk away from the start."

"But then you wanted him."

I got him too, she wanted to scream.

She could have sworn it was real—the way he gazed at her face, like it was the only time he'd ever seen anything so enrapturing, before he slid inside her. The laughter they had shared as they'd grown familiar with each other. The comfort he had brought to her when he put his arm around her and she fit into the crook of his arm like she was meant to be there all along.

The way he'd gotten down on one knee and told her she was a lighthouse in the night.

The way their star had illuminated the sky for a brief moment... and the way it had changed her for good.

"Fuck him if he doesn't want to be with me. I am a catch!"

She knew how pathetic it looked—her declaration that she was worthy when she felt anything but, standing there in white pajamas like a bride who was in love and getting engaged to the man she hoped would cherish and honor her.

It only reminded her of the very same thought she'd had the first night they'd hooked up...before they'd shared so many secrets. Before all the kisses and the sweet nothings.

Before she'd fallen in love with him.

A dry sob heaved through her body.

Akash was by her side instantly, wrapping a protective arm around her and pulling her close, so tightly that it nearly held her broken parts together. Almost.

Tears flowed freely when she realized he wore the same cologne Ayaan did and that the musky scent was drowning her so she couldn't come up for air.

Kiran joined in a moment later, rubbing Payal's back the way she did in college when Payal couldn't sleep.

Three seconds later, Sonam put her arms around all of them, the steady weight of her head on Payal's shoulder anchoring her in place.

When no more tears would come and the quiet was punctuated only by Payal's occasional gasp, they broke apart.

"You guys should probably go get some sleep," Payal croaked.

"We can stay here," Kiran offered.

Payal shook her head. She desperately wanted to say yes, to tell her best friends to stay with her the way they did in college, or better yet, to rewind the clock so they could go back to the days of innocence before engagements, companies, jobs, and commitments locked them down.

"I should talk to him," she said.

"Do you want us to come?" Akash asked.

Payal simply shook her head again. "Thank you."

"You don't have to do this, Payal. If you want to walk away, you can. The money, this company, all of it—nothing comes ahead of your happiness," Sonam said. "I don't think anyone would argue if you walked away now."

Payal nodded.

But as they left her room, after squeezing her shoulder one more time, she wondered if that was true. She collapsed onto the end of her bed, her legs finally unable to hold her any longer. The pressure of the world pushed down on her.

She didn't know how long she sat, as the clock on the mantel ticked away and hours seemingly passed.

A knock sounded at the door, ringing like gunshots across the quiet room.

She jumped, her heart leaping out of her throat. When she went to the door and opened it, she knew exactly who to expect and a hollow ache settled in the place where her stomach used to be.

Ayaan stood there, shoulders hunched.

For some reason, she flashed back to the moment she opened the door to him the night of their one-night stand. She hadn't known the turmoil that was coming. She hadn't known she'd fall in love with the arrogant boy with the cocky grin.

She didn't know she'd be broken by him.

"Can I come in?" He sounded hoarse.

She bit her lip and slowly opened the door wider, allowing him to pass.

"We have to talk," he said, turning toward her as soon as she'd shut the door.

Ayaan was disheveled. His shirt hadn't been changed; it was unbuttoned halfway down his chest, exposing his undershirt, and it was lopsided, as though he'd clawed at it to pull it away from his neck. His hair, usually groomed to an inch of its life and spiked to perfection, was a torrent of haphazard chunks as though he'd run his fingers through it so many times that it had forgotten where it was supposed to be held in place.

"Is there anything left to say?" Payal laughed bitterly. "We were in this for our own reasons. We got what we wanted. We played with each other and the jig is up."

Ayaan jerked as though she'd hit him. "Please, Payal, that isn't true."

Anger and defeat rose in her. "So Arun was lying?"

"Was your grandmother?" he fired back. "How long were you going to keep that from me?"

"Because your history of truth telling is so great?" Payal snapped, the hurt quickly turning to white-hot rage. "Let me recap for you. You didn't tell me Neha broke up with you the morning of our one-night stand. Then you failed to inform me you'd continued talking to her after we'd agreed to this arrangement. Followed by the grand omission that you were using our arrangement to gain a higher rank in your family's business. Now topped off with the kiss tonight, really, Ayaan, you're one to talk about hiding things."

"Payal, I promised you that I wouldn't talk to Neha again and I upheld that! The near kiss wasn't my fault! Nothing happened. Why are you so irked?"

"Because we were building something!" she yelled, furious that he was focusing on one element of a much bigger problem. "Why do you keep pushing me away? If you didn't want me, you had to say so. If you wanted to focus on business only, you had to say so. How is it that you manage to break my heart time and again?"

On that final question, Payal lost her composure. Her eyes stung and tears spilled over again as the angry fire that had burned white-hot inside her, searing toward Ayaan, burned her instead.

· · · · · · · · · · ·

AYAAN

He'd done it again. He'd spoken out of frustration and anger and gone on the defensive before his mind could catch up and slow his tongue.

And now, Payal, the girl he loved, was in tears in front of him. She pushed her fist against her mouth, taking great, gasping breaths, but her wet eyes continued to spill despite her free hand frantically wiping at her cheeks.

"I–I don't. Payal, I hate hurting you. I'm sorry. I'm so sorry." He took a step toward her.

She backed away, and the strange look on her face took Ayaan a moment to register.

It was fear.

She was scared he'd hurt her again. The carelessness with which he'd conducted himself sank in further, and his heart shattered as he realized that the girl who saw a world of potential in him now had the same look of dread in her beautiful brown eyes that his family took on in the years after the accident.

The realization stopped him in his tracks.

"Payal, please—what can I do to make this right?" he asked, desperate.

"You can't," she sobbed. "It was never right to begin with. We lied to each other, Ayaan, from the start. What kind of beginning is that? What kind of partnership is that?"

"Don't say that. We are the perfect team," he begged.

"How can you say that? We lied to each other. You lied to me," she said again. "You jumped into this for a place of power at your parents' company. We're the perfect team because we make money. You had no intention of loving me."

"You did the same thing!" he shouted back. "You had no intention of falling for me either—"

"But I did!" Payal raised her voice. "I fell in love with you, you bloody idiot!"

His chest thumped as though his heart had leapt to the sky and then plummeted beyond the ground.

Her head dropped and she shook it, wiping tears away again. "I was so sure about you. I was so certain you'd changed. That I'd changed."

He took one step closer to her, his hands in the air as if to tell her that he would never hurt her. She stood rooted to her spot, her arms crossed tightly against her, and he took it as a sign to speak.

"Payal, this whole thing started because I was so furious at Arun and my family. But when they mentioned it was you that they wanted me to get engaged to, I felt relief because the truth was that I loved our time together that night. Everything about you was electric. And I know I screwed that up and I didn't deserve another chance. But the universe gave me one and I took it. I didn't know I'd fall in love with you. And I wanted to come clean about my original intent, but I hoped it wouldn't matter because we'd felt something, and I was so sure we could go all the way on this...on us. And I want to... I promise you I'm in this engagement for real. I'm so sorry about Neha. I didn't know she'd be here, and I promise you I have no feelings for her. It's only you. It'll only ever be you." Ayaan was desperate, and his own tears threatened to spill over. "I am so in love with you. Please. We can fix this."

He'd never envisioned saying those words to anyone, let alone spouting them in a setting filled with so much heartbreak.

"We can't... I lied to you too." She hiccupped. "I wanted to get back at my parents for never loving me the way I needed. I wanted my line to succeed. You had connections and your family had money. It was a business transaction. We were part of a deal."

"No," Ayaan snapped. "I refuse to believe that. We were more than that and you know it."

He knew when he met her eyes that she felt the same. It was

impossible to deny that they were meant to be together. She was willing herself to stay away from him.

"I'm sorry," she whispered. "For playing the same game."

"Payal, it doesn't matter."

"It's the only thing that matters."

"What are we going to do?" he whispered. "Do you want to break up?"

They'd just gotten together. They were supposed to be forever.

Payal stared at him, speechless and still at the weight that his words carried. "Break up?"

"I don't want to. I love you," he said again, as though the more he repeated it, the greater impact it would have on her coming back.

She parted her lips, but no sound came out. The absence of the three words in return tore at him, and he inhaled sharply at the physical pain the rejection caused.

"We can do this," he said. "I know this is a tough start but now it's all in the open. There are no secrets. And every moment we shared, all the times we felt something more, those were real. I refuse to believe they weren't."

Her eyes softened, reddened as they were. But she shook her head again, and Ayaan felt the ground open underneath him.

"The contracts are signed. Luxuriant belongs to Veer. We can end this in a few months, once the acquisition has been established. You'll have CMO. My show will be done, and hopefully, I'll be on my feet. We'll win all around."

Her voice, which Ayaan had always loved for its smooth delivery, was hoarse and hollow.

He did that.

And how could she say they were winning when this was their greatest loss? They had given up the most magical piece of the last year, torched it, and watched it go up in flames, all before their eyes.

"What are we becoming?" he whispered.

She turned away, and Ayaan knew that there would be nothing more to be said between them tonight. As she turned her back on the possibility of the two of them becoming anything real, he could have sworn he heard her answer his hushed question.

"Our parents."

Chapter Thirty-Two

PAYAL

She tried to sleep but fits of rolling and tossing overcame her until she tangled herself up in the sheets. Her emptiness was a void inside her, but it didn't settle like a hollowed-out cave that set up a home in her chest. Instead it was heavy. A rock.

Like dust settled on forgotten photo frames or corners of desks that remained unused, sadness coated Payal. The aura around her was a blanket of brokenness, and she couldn't shake it off.

She didn't want to.

Her dry heaves broke the silence every few minutes. There were no more tears to cry, or so she thought, before she'd think of her isolation and fresh tears would appear again.

Nearly delirious with a lack of sleep over the last few days from preparations for a ceremony that she'd now have to endure rather than enjoy and the pain of her loss, Payal curled into a fetal position, willing her insides not to disappear into wisps of smoke. Her soul was hardly hers anymore. The girl who had a backbone had crumbled into nothing, and with every blow, she disappeared into the air, unable to capture the same spirit that filled her before.

She was alone. And all she wanted was comfort.

She gazed at her phone, hoping it would light up in the dark and that even from the room down the hall, perhaps Ayaan would reach out and he'd say something to her—words of apology, words of comfort, reassurance that she wasn't, in fact, completely alone in the world. But the pitch black surrounding her stayed as dark as the sky, and the rock in her belly began to force itself up to her throat, a wail that just wouldn't release itself.

Her heart pounded, blood rushing to her head as she gagged on the reflex to scream and shout and let the gravity of the world she was carrying bleed out of her. But tears stung her eyes and didn't fall. The pressure pushed on the inside of her head, against her eyeballs and throat, but she couldn't cry.

She stared at the phone again.

Frustrated with herself, she rolled over onto her other side and clasped her hands together between her knees. The heat of her own fingers in between the spaces was as though someone was holding her hand, but Ayaan's memory flashed through her mind as he made love to her.

He'd gently pushed into her, thrusts she matched with her bucking hips.

Their hands were entwined against the bedsheets as she moved underneath him.

As they slept after hours of being one, she'd rolled over in the middle of the night and their hands had found their way to each other. His fingers crept through hers and found their home among the gaps in hers.

She tore her hands apart and stuck one arm under a pillow instead, crooked at the elbow for support. She was in a full fetal position now. Her arms involuntarily moved to wrap themselves around her, holding all her broken pieces inside before they slipped out and shattered against her floor into pieces as small as sand. She didn't trust that her heart, a pile of rubble, and her mind, a mountain of ash, wouldn't betray her and slip away in her sleep.

All she had was herself, and now she needed to keep her wits.

But she was so tired. Her muscles cried out in protest as she moved even an inch under the covers, aching to the very bone with the expectations that had been set upon her and the pride that had been taken away in return.

She had never agreed to this bargain—the one where she lost herself to save everyone else and where she had nothing of her own left to her name.

Her broken heart thudded against her chest, and she listened to the steady beat, feeling the thump against the side of her head. She lost herself in the rhythm for a minute or two, breathing in for every four counts and breathing out. The anxiety inside her weakened, but only enough to let her close her eyes.

And there she fell asleep, coiled up in her demons and caught up with her nightmares of screaming in a room alone as the world chewed at her skin, her muscle, and her bone until there was nothing left but black.

· · · · · · · · · · ·

AYAAN

Ayaan tossed and turned for another hour before he had to get up. He thought about stopping by Payal's room again...but what would he even say? Instead, he rolled out of bed, did some push-ups to wake himself up fully, and made some coffee in the coffee maker.

Meet us in our suite, Dad's text message summoned him. Eight in the morning was far too early for a family meeting, but Ayaan made his way down the hall and knocked.

He was met with Payal, her parents, Arun, Sarika, Mum, and Dad, gathered around a coffee table in silence, and all of them turned in unison upon his entrance into the room.

"Come in," Dad said.

Ayaan couldn't help but feel as though he was being invited into his own family gathering. He entered and sat down on the free chair at the desk before shooting a glance at Payal.

She was in a blue Duke hoodie and gray sweatpants, barefoot, barefaced, and barely present. Her red-rimmed eyes were swollen, and it appeared she hadn't napped since their confrontation just a few hours ago.

Ayaan wanted to reach out. He needed to touch her cheek and kiss her forehead and tell her everything would be okay.

But she wouldn't meet his eye.

"I don't know what yesterday's fight was about," Ayaan's dad said now. "I understand that we've had some miscommunications about what this engagement would mean."

"We have to put on a united front," Payal's mother said. "Whatever our drama behind the scenes, we cannot let it escape this room."

Ayaan's heart broke for Payal as she nodded, her spirit seemingly vanquished.

"It was a misunderstanding," she said. Her voice came out stronger than he'd expected.

"Payal, do you still want to go through with this?" her mom asked her, frowning.

"What do you mean? They have to, Roopa," Dad said incredulously.

"Dad, give it a rest, will you?" Arun spoke. "Ayaan and Payal should decide for themselves and make the right decision rather than being pressured. Give them the space to do it."

Astonished, Ayaan turned to Arun.

His older brother gazed at him, bobbing his head once as if to tell him he had his back, and said, "Ayaan, you let us know how you want to proceed."

Gratitude filled him.

"Payal and I have some issues to figure out, and we may or may not decide to be together in a few months."

He couldn't bring himself to say that they wouldn't. A sliver of hope still shone in his heart and he couldn't dim it...not yet.

At the sight of the parents' worried faces, he put his hand up and added, "We can wait until the dust settles before we make any announcements, for the sake of optics. We know family and business come first...but that's what brought us here in the first place. I'm going to need you all to let us handle this, or the entire merger will go up in flames."

At the implication of further damage, the parents held their tongues.

"Well, that's settled," Sarika said lightly.

"No, it's not settled—" Payal's dad said, but her mom cut him off gently.

"Payal, you may be able to get a few hours of sleep before brunch. Why don't you go do that? It's been a long night for everyone," Roopa Aunty said.

A grateful look crossed Payal's haggard face and she murmured a thank-you as she left.

Ayaan watched her, wishing he could speak with her.

A few hours later, Payal sat next to him with a porcelain smile on her face, one that didn't reach her eyes. She hadn't looked at him to affirm how she felt about any of the guest greetings or the commentary on what a party they had thrown. It was as though their bond had not only been bent but utterly shattered by the events of the night before. He'd envisioned them laughing together and thanking well-wishers with knowing glances at the other about all that was to come with the blessings being showered upon them.

Payal was a master class in holding it together, lifting her head high, offering a tentative smile, and always turning the conversation back to the person offering the blessings, as though she wanted to shift the focus off their mismatch and onto anything more pleasant.

"You look like you got hit by a bus," Kai said when Ayaan excused himself for a drink.

"I kind of wish I had," Ayaan said.

"How's Payal doing after your fight?" Dharm murmured. "How are you?"

Ayaan had filled them in on the drama after brunch.

"I'm a wreck," Ayaan admitted. "It's like...I had it all. I had her. We had everything we'd been working for. I should have told her. I know that now, but I thought maybe where we'd arrived mattered more than how we got there. She'll never forgive me for this."

"I'm sorry we told you to keep it to yourself," Kai said, silent until now. "We thought the same thing."

"You both always give me good advice," Ayaan said. "Don't worry about it. This is on me."

"You have time to make this right," Dharm said. "This ceremony feels like the end of a weird journey. Payal still has her show that she needs you to do your best on. Keep your head on straight. There is still a chance to revive this."

"It doesn't feel like it," Ayaan said quietly. "But I guess we have no choice but to carry forward."

He glanced at Payal, who was surrounded by Kiran, Sonam, and Akash. They listened intently to Akash, who ended his remark with a grin and caused the others to erupt into giggles.

Ayaan would have done anything to be the reason behind Payal's laugh.

Surrounded by flower garlands and market lights hanging from the beamed ceiling in arches, she was breathtaking. Loneliness washed over him.

He wrenched his eyes away from the painful sight.

They actively avoided each other as they ate, taking their plates from table to table to mingle with guests and say hello. Occasionally, someone would want a picture with them both and they dutifully smiled and thanked them, with an odd joke here or a fake laugh there to maintain the facade that all was well.

As the valets packed their belongings into the cars, Ayaan tried one more time.

"Are we going to talk?" He leaned over and whispered out of the side of his mouth.

"There's nothing left to say, Ayaan," Payal said, determinedly staring into the distance.

"I love you," he whispered. "Please. That has to mean something."

Payal said nothing, biting her lip. Her fists had balled themselves in her lap.

A moment later, the photographer gathered the two families to take a final picture together.

Ayaan knew that the photograph had only captured all of them looking miserable.

Chapter Thirty-Three

PAYAL

A month had passed, the fashion show was only hours away, and Payal still ached inside when she thought about the smile she'd plastered on her face, determined not to show any cracks in the facade, after the highest point in her life and the biggest fall she'd ever taken.

She had no idea where she had found the diamond-strong will-power to move forward and handle the scrutiny that had come not only at the engagement but across public platforms afterward.

Are you and Ayaan Malhotra still together? someone had commented on her latest Instagram photo, a behind-the-scenes of the fashion show where she stood next to her tailor, laughing—though the audience didn't know how hollow it sounded in real life—with the model in front of them who had tried on a dress and exclaimed, "If this doesn't get me laid, nothing will."

She ignored the comment and scrolled through the others.

She and Ayaan are so cute, another said.

Two weeks ago, she'd been the subject of an Instagram post on an anonymous South Asian gossip site.

Have an up-and-coming designer and prominent social media influencer broken up, just after their engagement? Sources say they haven't been spotted together in public in a month, and everyone is wondering whether fashion, finance, and fiancées were a disastrous combination for this former couple.

The comments below the post, a text paragraph overlaid on a photo Payal could keenly observe had been taken backstage at her show, speculated on a few different potential couples that the post could be about.

If she was honest, the speculation gave her a mild prick of annoyance, but she knew the vague statements about not being seen for a month could have been pulled from anywhere. After all, they hadn't had major events to go to together. Just a dinner here with clients. A brunch there with companies courting Ayaan for brand sponsorships. It wasn't as though they had paparazzi. South Asians were notorious for gossip about anyone mildly reeking of celebrity, and Payal knew that any mention of her would be immediately washed away by the next wave of gossip that came in. It must have been a slow news day.

But the photo on this particular post had launched an emotional grenade, despite its relatively innocuous caption. The look of sheer happiness on her face and the pride on his as they clasped each other were so full of joy, so different from what they felt now. And the memory of the next night, which had prompted the cascade of emotional confessions and sex, burned her.

Her heart wasn't equipped for this part of public life...and she exited the app, closing her eyes and reminding herself that this would pass someday.

She and Ayaan had stuck to business-only contact since the

engagement. They texted nearly every day, but Payal couldn't bring herself to extend her boundaries past professionalism. Her protective gates had come crashing down at the engagement party, and no amount of cajoling, brute force, or willpower would raise them.

And the truth was that she was afraid of what would be said if their communication expanded beyond perfunctory greetings and business. She was terrified that she wouldn't be ready for the day he said he was happy or, worse, that he was on the market again. She worried that if he said he wasn't happy, she'd endeavor to make him so and leave herself vulnerable. She couldn't afford to do that.

Her heart gave an aching thump as if to reaffirm that she made the right choice.

The terror alternated with anger at his ability to make her a fool. If she felt that way about him after a month of replaying their fake romance—except it wasn't fake to her—then he *had* to feel the same level of hatred when he thought about how he'd been a pawn in her game too. She didn't want to hear that he had gone from "I love you" to "I hate you" after giving it more thought.

Equally strong came anger toward herself. While she hadn't reunited with her family in a scene worthy of a Bollywood movie or forgiven them for what choices they'd given her, she knew that she alone had made the decision to capitalize on Ayaan's connections for her brand.

She'd decided to sacrifice him to get what she needed.

And she had contributed equally in throwing it away.

Instead of taking the risk to find out what he thought, she said nothing.

Did you speak with so-and-so magazine about NYFW? Have you had a hamper sent to some of the press outlets as thanks? I'll email you the most recent sales numbers. Their exchanges had been devoid of anything that signaled the last few months had mattered.

How are you? read one message from Ayaan. *Could we talk?*

But she ignored that one.

The phone rang.

"Just doing a check on your headspace," Sonam said. "It's a big day today!"

"I'm...excited for today."

"Are you?"

"And terrified. And ready. And heartbroken. You name it, I'm probably feeling it," Payal said.

"Think. You'll have an after-party when this is over and you can let loose!"

"You mean the one Ayaan's family is throwing me?" Payal gave a humorless laugh. "I'll try."

"Have you seen him since we talked last week?"

"No...I haven't seen him since the party."

"So tonight..."

"I'll do my best not to lose my mind in public, yeah."

"Your families will be there to distract you, though. Nani will too."

Payal smiled. "I know. I'm excited to see her, if not all of them. They've been quite persistent that the families have to put on a united front. I think they want to avoid the public perception of drama, even if we're falling apart at the seams, so that if this engagement does formally break soon, we can avoid the nuclear fallout and resist any damage to the brands."

"I'm sorry love has been so entrenched in business," Sonam said quietly. "That can't be easy. It sounds like a fucking nightmare, to be honest."

"Well...putting on a show with my family isn't new, even if it comes with a new dimension of pain," Payal said.

"You'll be great. I have no doubt. I wanted to say good luck before you head over to the venue. You were born for this."

"I appreciate you calling at"—Payal checked her phone—"six in the morning, and that you trusted me to be awake."

"Hustle never sleeps, right?" Sonam laughed. "I'll see you tonight. I love you."

"Love you too."

Payal double-checked her list, made sure she had the Asian EnPointe run-of-show in her bag, and packed her outfit, shoes, and makeup for the show and after-party and chargers for her phone and iPad.

Before she left, she pulled the jewelry box from her dresser and slid the emerald engagement ring onto her finger with a pang. *Got to give them a show.*

Then she left for the venue, a rooftop in SoHo that overlooked the city.

When she arrived, the chaotic rush gave her an adrenaline spike. Runners and designers were examining tall models, who they'd selected from look books handed over by agencies, and pinning outfits where they needed to be further fitted. Makeup artists and hair stylists lined a room with styling stations for each designer. Models went in, got their makeup done, moved to hair, and got dressed, like an assembly line.

The runway was a white one set in the middle of a sea of chairs. Press lined the short end, where they sat on risers to capture the most flattering shots, while the audience surrounded the stage on the two others. An aisle opened up for models to move from the inside of the building and up a few stairs to the catwalk, where they would strut down, make a turn, and come back toward the studio.

Payal's eight models had been painstakingly selected by her, Niyathi, and Saachi from images provided by an agency that focused on nontraditional beauty types. They'd done their best to be representative of the diaspora. After all, the monolith of fair-skinned, thin models did nothing for bringing cognizance forward about what South Asia looked like. Instead, they'd chosen their representatives from inspiration gleaned on their trips home and the mixed communities in the West, and their lived experiences factored into the show. One model was Nepali and appeared more characteristically East Asian than stereotypically South. Another was a six-foot-tall, long-haired trans woman from Bangladesh who had moved to the United States to escape persecution. Yet another was a Telugu girl who had grown up just across the river in Queens and had heard her long name mispronounced and made fun of for her whole life.

Payal examined the eight pieces on the rack, the culmination of her career so far and the result of investments from people like Misha, who had believed in her talent. She thought about the conversations she'd had with the CMC only two years ago about wanting to quit her job and start a line. It had been on her bucket list. She remembered that, for all his faults, Papa had seen it as a diversification opportunity for the business.

For all that was happening, she couldn't forget Ayaan's aid to get all eyes on her.

This was the start of everything for her...and happiness replaced her nerves. Ambition flooded her veins. The sound of the bustle around her acted as armor against the pain she'd been fighting.

A few hours later, as eight fully dressed, made-up models stood in front of her with various hairstyles from traditional South Asian historical periods, accentuated with fresh jasmine flowers and roses, in a sari, two suits, a dress, a blazer and crop top, a salwar kurta, a gown, and a T-shirt and sweats inspired by the streets of Mumbai...she was certain that this was her moment.

"Let's go," she said.

. . . .

AYAAN

This was leagues worse than the first show they'd conducted together...a roller coaster of highs and lows that Ayaan couldn't understand.

Their last one had been indoors, soaked in bright lights and loud music, and closed off from the rest of the city. This show was on the rooftop of a building overlooking the towering skyscrapers above and short brownstones beneath them. The late-afternoon sun had eased on an uncharacteristically warm fall day, and the break from the heat had made the weather breezy and perfect.

But at the last show, they'd worked together, and he'd been at the venue ahead of time with her to handle some of the heat and delegate tasks to manage the flow. This time, he'd managed so much of the communication and marketing ahead of the launch, but now, at the event, he'd only taken calls and spoken to some of his contacts in the audience and in the building.

He hadn't even seen her properly, just a whizzing blur in a crowded room.

Payal had been provided fifty tickets for the show. Mostly, they'd been used on industry connections and other South Asian representatives who had begun to wear and love Payal's designs. But Ayaan, his parents, Arun, Sarika, Payal's parents, and Nani had also been settled into the second row.

"Ayaan, will you be staying after this to help Payal wrap up, or will you be at the setup for the after-party?" Arun asked.

"I'll come with you to Brooklyn," Ayaan said. "Payal will handle the press interviews. She deserves to shine."

He didn't want to admit that perhaps she didn't want him there at all.

The gaps in their communication had been her choice. He hadn't wanted to pry in, to force his way into the walls she'd built up against him again, but he desperately wanted to speak with her and clear the air.

Occasionally, he was hit by a tsunami of destructive emotion, the kind that used to send him to the bar or to the arms of someone who could make him forget for a night. Fury at her for toying with his emotions so she could be here, shining in her glory, at this fashion show. Rage at himself for not seeing it coming and for letting it get to this place. Heartbreak at the fact that he was so certain they loved each other deeply and that they had both set flame to what they'd built.

And hope, that sneaky, reality-defying emotion, that they could work through these secrets.

Sarika gave him a sympathetic smile and put her hand on his. "No improvement?"

"Let's just focus on the show, Sarika. A 'united front,' as it were."

She squeezed his hand in response.

A DJ, located in the corner of the rooftop, began turning up his music, the beat changing from house music to a loud mix of bass and cultural tunes from various parts of Asia.

Payal was the third designer in the lineup, and Ayaan waited in anticipation, bouncing his leg up and down, as eight models per designer wore clothing inspired by different parts of Asia. At the end, the designer would also walk on the runway—typically shyly waving—with the final walk presenting all the pieces they'd worked on.

Two minutes later, the next would start.

About a half hour later, after waiting on tenterhooks, the music slowly transitioned to a rousing Bollywood beat.

Sarika tapped her foot in time with the song. Ayaan held his breath.

The first model, lithe and tall, swayed down the runway, her head held defiantly high as though she challenged the world to take her on. Her hair was in a high bun with a garland of jasmine wrapped around the base. She wore a black minidress with elbow-length sleeves created out of embroidered silk that Ayaan knew Payal and Saachi had sourced directly from artisans in India. Her legs were exposed, as though the dress was a mini, but a long black train began at her waist and billowed behind her.

The audience gasped as they saw the details.

The train, black on the outer side, resembled a stylish ball gown, while the underside, only viewable to an audience or some-one facing the model, had stripes of bright silk sari pieces with gold and embroidered sequins—Ayaan realized they matched the sleeves—along the entirety. Like a cape or a trail of glitter, it moved in the wind lightly though the material was thick.

"Wow," he heard someone whisper behind him.

He'd never been so proud of Payal. He didn't even realize he could exceed the pride he'd felt at each milestone she'd achieved in the last ten months.

As the model walked to the end of the catwalk, doing a dra-matic spin as she held the sides of the train and allowed it to swoop along the end of the runway, the next model took the stage.

She wore a sari, stitched strategically into a dhoti on the bottom. The sari, a navy blue, had spirals of gold that looped up her legs and spaced themselves out as they climbed her body, as though she were on fire. The pallu, which would usually go over her left shoulder only, had been thinly split, forming a V, and draped over both her shoulders, creating the effect of both a sari and a dupatta at the same time.

People actually clapped.

Design after design, model after model, each a piece of Payal's soul, strode the catwalk, and with each one, Ayaan grew more aware of exactly how talented she was. Seeing a runway, lights, music, and people wearing her designs and showcasing their culture on a platform that would, no doubt, garner attention was a different spin on all they'd worked for over the last ten months and what Payal had worked for longer than that.

As the final line of eight models walked down, the entire collection in its full glory, Payal walked along the end.

She could have been one of them.

Countering their glamour and glitz, she wore black leather pants and a black cap-sleeved crop top with a black and gold-patterned bomber jacket over her shoulders. Simple flats, contrary to her typical style of towering heels, adorned her feet. Her hair was in a high ponytail and curled to add volume.

"She looks breathtaking!" Sarika cried.

"Payal is always breathtaking," he replied.

The audience stood and clapped, an ovation Ayaan had never seen. Decorum be damned, some people even cheered and Ayaan was certain it came from the direction of some of the influencers they'd invited to sit in the front row.

There were rare times in life when one knew the tides had turned and that a particular moment would define their path forever.

Ayaan was certain that this was one of Payal's.

And though tears burned his eyes at the pride he had in watching it, his heart broke all over again at the fact that he couldn't be a part.

Chapter Thirty-Four

PAYAL

Ten months of living, breathing, and devouring Besharmi, and the show was finished.

As Payal waved out at the audience, bringing her hands together in both a namaste and a gesture of thanks, she breathed in the rare air of success and feeling as though she'd made it.

For a moment, she forgot the pain.

Instead, she was surrounded by the now-glowing city lights in the New York City dusk, showcasing models wearing her line for the world to see the beauty of the culture she came from and receiving rapturous applause from those in the industry whose opinions mattered most.

And those who weren't in the industry at all but who mattered nonetheless.

From the corner of her eye, Payal spotted her parents clapping with beaming faces that she hadn't ever witnessed after her early years in school. The CMC was somewhere here, and as she heard a loud sound, she was sure it came from Sonam's legendary two-fingered whistle. Nani stood as tall as ever, applauding, with tears in her eyes and exclamations that Payal was unable to hear but knew were filled with pride. Ayaan's family demonstrated equal enthusiasm, his parents, Arun, and Sarika dressed impeccably, as though they had no more important place to be but right here in Manhattan.

She let the love wash over her before her sight turned to the one person she'd avoided until now.

Ayaan...whose work had amplified that she had gotten here. Who had broken her heart, but who she couldn't imagine being here without.

She turned away.

The next few hours were a blur of gathering the outfits, having Niyathi and Saachi aid in unpinning the clothes, thanking the models, giving each of them the gift baskets that Ayaan had ordered for them, hanging the clothes up and sending them back with the courier, and lining up for interviews.

The Asian EnPointe team had arranged for a red carpet where designers could line up and speak to the media about what their lines entailed. The question, "What do your designs represent with regard to your South Asian identity?" had never meant so much.

As the clock raced toward 9:00 p.m. and the buzz began to die out as people headed to their parties, other shows, and nights out, Payal took inventory of the tasks that needed to be done.

Her phone buzzed as she wrapped up, and though she'd ignored it all day unless it was a mission-critical message, she finally opened the slew of texts from friends and family, congratulating her.

Sonam: YAAAAAAAS.

Kiran: Payal, you were incredible! The models were so
   beautifully dressed and their hair and makeup reminded
   me so much of home.

Akash: DRANKS!

Sonam: Really?

Akash: Congratulations, Payal! It was epic and you are a
legend.

Kiran: That's better. You should have opened with that.

Akash: She knows I think she's a visionary.

Sonam: We all do. We're so proud of you, badass!

Payal: Love you—and see you soon for DRANKS!

Giggling to herself, she put her phone in her back pocket.

"Payal," she heard.

Papa stood in front of her.

"Hi, Papa, what are you doing here? Did everyone else go to
get ready for the after-party?"

"They went to a late dinner before the party. Ayaan suggested
Baar Baar. He said he had a great night there with you."

Payal swallowed. "Why didn't you go?"

"I wanted to talk to you. I took a walk for a bit to clear my
head and then came back."

"Is everything okay?"

He took a deep breath. His hands were in the pockets of his
suit jacket, and Papa, to Payal's knowledge, had never looked so
contrite. "I'm sorry."

She tried not to look surprised. "For?"

"I never should have made you do this when you weren't
ready. I hope you know I thought of every possible alternative
beforehand...and I never would have given you away or even proposed it had I found one that worked to everyone's benefit."

"It's fine. I was in over my head, Papa. I thought—" Her voice
cracked and she went silent, determined not to say anything else, on
this very best of days, about all she'd hoped for and all she'd lost.

"Payal, your mother and I are very different people. Our marriage may not have been the best example of cohesiveness. But we love you. We have you, and that is our greatest legacy as a couple and as people. I know we aren't close—but at the engagement, when I wasn't the one you went to for consolation... When I realized Nani was always the one you turned to, who you confide your fears in, who you conspired with when you needed to get your way...something snapped. It became glaringly obvious that I had failed as a father to earn your trust, which was my one job."

Payal didn't say anything. Ten months ago, she would have agreed. Now...after falling for Ayaan, she didn't know which way was up.

"You've loved fashion since you were little. I remember when you were six and you pranced around in a lehenga that your masi had sent from India, and you kept saying you were a princess. At the time, the company hadn't grown to what it became, and I saw Ma dance with you in the living room in a sari, and I thought, 'This is what dreams are made of.' And somewhere along the line, after we couldn't have any more children, after the company grew and I became busier, after your mother found her own social groups and interests...it became less about the dream and more about the chase for the next achievement, the next benchmark, the next million made. I don't know how we became like this."

He sighed and took a deep breath, as though to steady himself. "It's impossible to make up for, and I'm not a man who relishes looking back. But looking forward, though I may not have the right, I hope I can leave you with one thing."

Payal watched his face, tight with emotion, and nodded to allow him to continue.

"I let go of what dreams were made of. I urge you not to do the same. You are bright and beautiful. I am so proud. And if you are in love with Ayaan, you shouldn't let him go. But if you aren't, Payal, and I mean this: do not go through with this engagement. I understand now that there was a cruel lack of choice for you to act on. The dignity you've shown despite the pain you've been in, silently suffering, has been both astounding and heartbreaking. It never should have been necessary."

His words had come faster and faster, as though he couldn't contain the many thoughts that he'd had about the situation in the last month and that if he didn't race to get it all out now, he never would.

Payal hadn't realized there were tears streaming down her face. Years of resentment, questions, heartbreak, and her own doubts poured out of her eyes and down her cheeks. The damage had been done. But this was one small step that lessened the burn.

"Thank you, Papa," Payal whispered.

He came over to her now, closing the space between them, as though he'd give her a giant hug. But instead, he put his hand on her shoulder and gave it a tight squeeze.

"You're free to do as you please. You deserve it. And for the record, I'm very proud of you."

· · · · · · · · · · ·

AYAAN

The bar had never been so welcome.

"An old-fashioned, please," Ayaan requested from the bartender.

He settled in on a barstool in the farthest corner of the long bar, away from the action, where he could observe the party and all its splendor.

The old brick foundry in Williamsburg had been transformed

into an event space worthy of a Hollywood production. The two-story hall was teeming with people—friends, family, and associates, all of whom were ravenously diving into the tables full of hot samosas, chaat, kebabs, finger sandwiches, and cross-cultural mixes like Indian-inspired quesadillas and pasta infused with spices. Two bars, one upstairs and one downstairs, had been set up with long counters and high-top tables nearby.

The brick walls had enormous hanging tapestries of the models from the charity fashion show, each wearing Payal's designs and walking down the runway. The two stories of the building, joined by an iron staircase and a loft, were an explosion of color with uplighting that cast rainbows across the room. A DJ on a stage in the center of the back wall played a deafening cultural fusion of East and West, and people bobbed their heads in time to the bass as they socialized and laughed.

The branding and marketing efforts of the last ten months had come together in an explosion of fusion tastes and sights, amplifying the show further and making sure every attendee remembered Besharmi's mission.

Ayaan's parents had spared no expense in this endeavor. Yet as loud as it was, Ayaan was in a contemplative mood. Though people approached him, congratulating him on the engagement and shaking his hand on the acquisition—"You must be so proud of Veer and of Payal!"—he didn't seek anyone out for a change.

"Whiskey is your poison of choice too, huh?" a tenor voice said next to him.

Ayaan turned. Akash had leaned against the bar beside him, gotten the bartender's attention, pointed at Ayaan's drink, and gestured to himself. In a silent interaction, he received his drink.

"Yeah. I like the simplicity of it."

He'd fully expected Akash to respond with a cutting remark

about how Ayaan had complicated everything, but to his credit, he gave a swift nod and took a sip of his own.

"How are you?" Akash asked finally.

"You know. Good," Ayaan said, not mustering up any energy for a believable lie.

"You should tell your face that."

The words reminded him of Payal and the interactions they'd had with that very same dialogue.

"I...am an idiot," he said.

"Did you care about her? For real?" Akash asked.

Contrary to all indications over the last few months of acquaintance, Akash's face betrayed no sign of malice or judgment. Instead, a steady, inquiring expression remained on his face and he gazed intently at Ayaan, waiting for an answer and patient to receive one.

"More than anything," Ayaan said quietly. "I don't think people realize sometimes what's good for them and how people change them until the void sets in...and the light goes out."

"Trust me, I know more than you probably think I do," Akash said, and Ayaan remembered Payal mentioning his bad breakup after college.

There was a pause where Akash seemed to acknowledge that Ayaan didn't have any energy in him to talk unless needed. He took a sip and spoke again.

"Payal is certainly a light," Akash said. "The first time we met was in college. The girls will say I was nonchalant and dismissive, but I noticed her the second she walked into the room. Confident. Proud. A handful, which you know."

Ayaan gave a small chuckle.

On cue, Payal appeared at the entrance and the crowd erupted in cheers.

She had changed into a simple black dress and gold, glittering pumps. Her long hair was pulled elegantly into an updo at the top of her head, with a stray curl or two escaping the confines of her bun.

Her parents and Nani—God bless her, the woman was waving her arms in time with the music—greeted her at the door and gave her a hug. Hordes of guests conglomerated around her, and she was lost in the crowd to both of them in seconds.

"She was always a force," Akash said now, still watching her. "Whatever she wanted, anything she put her mind to, she'd figure out a way to get."

"Did you have feelings for her?"

"No," Akash said. "We have—had—an interesting relationship. It's flirtatious at times, but not because there's anything there. It's because inherently, Payal and I are similar. We're kindred spirits who love to play with life. You don't find that often in the world."

Ayaan let that sink in. Shame overtook him for jumping to all the wrong conclusions instead of asking the question at the right time.

"Ayaan! Your fiancée is here! You should say hi!" a well-meaning uncle said, quite clearly three sheets to the wind already.

"I want to let her enjoy the attention!" Ayaan declared with false enthusiasm.

The moment the uncle turned away, he let his smile fade. For the sake of a distraction, he asked, "How about the others? They're a fun group."

Kiran, Nash, and Sonam were on the periphery of the horde, lurking in case Payal appeared to need assistance but waiting their turn. Sonam, dressed in a smart Besharmi power suit, made a comment, her eyes enormous, and Kiran and Nash threw their heads back in laughter.

Akash laughed as he watched them too. "It's never boring. But no. All platonic. Contrary to what society tells you, it is possible. Besides, if I ever thought about making a move on any of them, Sonam would slap the teeth out of my head and tell me I'd ruin the dynamic."

"I thought you were trying to make a move on Payal the night of the party. Jealousy took over. I'm sorry."

Akash acknowledged Ayaan's apology with a bob of his head. "Me too. I think it was always meant to be you. That sounds awfully fatalistic. I'm not one for believing in destiny or soul mates. But I believe in love. I know Payal loves you. Whatever complications you've both put in your path can always be moved. This isn't a race to the finish line where you cross immovable hurdles. It's a marathon where you have to adjust the obstacles."

"Why are you on my side?" Ayaan asked curiously. "You hate me."

Akash smiled to himself, spinning his glass. "I don't hate you. As the girls love pointing out, I might be similar to Payal, but I also see myself in you—and some of that isn't pretty. The belief in love but the fear of commitment. The obsession with freedom. The terror that someone can have a hold on you that feels unbreakable and the constraint it can feel like because you haven't placed trust in it yet. And I'm protective over her. I want her to have the best. We have ten years of history, stupid decisions, drunken mistakes, and life-changing conversations between us.

"But because I wanted the best for her, I was jaded. I thought she wouldn't be able to find it, which was an ass move on my part. Because that said I didn't trust her judgment. When she broke down the night of your engagement—the hurt in her eyes—I realized I had to trust her. She was so broken, and she wouldn't be if this wasn't real. She was so invested in you. And you can't be all bad if Payal Mehra sees something in you. I know that firsthand."

"I want that with her too…but I really fucked this up."

"Yes," Akash said simply. "But I know Payal. She knows you. And I refuse to believe this is a broken situation."

"Mmm."

"I will say once, to your face, that you were a dick. You can't trade someone's life in for a position at a company, no matter how badly you want to succeed."

Ayaan took a deep breath. "I gave the job up."

Akash's stunned reaction gave Ayaan a little satisfaction. "What?"

"I told Arun I wanted to step back. I couldn't go on in good faith knowing that I had sacrificed what really mattered. I fully expected him to think I was flaky and for my parents to believe that too, but to their credit, they understood. They love Payal. And it was a reckoning for them that our interactions over fifteen years had forced us to this place."

"You gave it up for her?"

He shrugged. "She's really important to me. If I took it, it wouldn't be right because of the cost it took to get there. I don't want it without her. I don't want any of this without her."

Akash studied him and he felt the scrutinizing stare. "What are you going to do?"

"I'll open my own firm. Boutique. Social media management and marketing. I'll do whatever it takes with Besharmi that Payal needs me to do. I owe her that much."

"Does she know?" Akash asked.

"No."

"Why didn't you tell her?"

"Because it wasn't a performative power move. Akash, I am

deeply in love with her. Payal is the love of my life. If I ever take over Veer in any capacity, it'll be because I earned it and because she's by my side and because she wants to be there with her whole heart. Anything less is a disservice to us both."

Akash appraised him.

Ayaan refused to look away.

"Maybe you're better than I thought," Akash said finally.

"If only Payal thought the same."

Chapter Thirty-Five

PAYAL

"There's the girl of the hour!" Kiran was holding a martini in one hand and clutching Nash's with the other.

"Payal, congratulations!" Nash exclaimed with a one-armed hug to go along with his praise. "I'd have found you sooner, but Kiran kept insisting we needed to give you some space."

"You all are my favorite faces to see, whenever that chance comes," Payal reassured them.

Sonam joined them and simply shrieked, throwing her arms around Payal as a greeting.

"I cannot believe we still have to tell you to use an indoor voice," Akash said, shaking his head at Sonam. He turned to Payal. "You were exceptional. How do you feel?"

Payal raised her eyebrows. The adulation and the enthusiasm were both contagious and energizing and effortful and exhausting. She simultaneously wanted to dance the night away in celebration and take a nap for the next three years.

"Remember how we used to double-fist drinks in clubs and then come home at four in the morning and then get up, shower, and go to class at eight?" she asked.

"Yes..." He frowned.

"How the hell did we do it?"

He laughed. "I take it you're feeling the age-related introversion then."

"Like a bus," she replied with a smile. "But in all honesty, I am so grateful. For all of you. For the Malhotras. Even for my own family. Today is a love fest, and I wish I could take this feeling with me for the rest of my life to remind me how hard work looks and happiness tastes."

"Well, we appreciate it. But I think one person deserves a lot more thanks than we do," Sonam said, ever the honest one.

"I agree," Payal said but didn't add any more.

"Even if he was an ass."

"I know."

"Your parents and Nani were ecstatic, Payal," Kiran jumped in. "You should have seen them rocking out to the music and cheering you on."

"They were so proud!" Nash said.

"My dad said he was proud of me," Payal said. "He said I was free to do what I wanted and that I deserved a choice."

"To be honest, it's about time. You and Kiran...this loyalty thing is beaten into us sometimes. You've always had your freedom and you shouldn't have had to earn it, but I'm glad they finally came around to this," Sonam said with flourish.

Payal exchanged a grin with Kiran at the inevitable philosophy Sonam injected into conversations even when tipsy. Nash seemed amused, his blue eyes sparkling under the lights at Kiran and the fact that she'd chosen him.

"So...are any of the models single?" Akash asked.

"Behave," Payal commanded.

Akash rolled his eyes.

Sonam pointed a finger at one of the hanging tapestries and said something Payal couldn't make out. Kiran and Nash had turned toward her, and before Payal leaned in, Akash spoke.

"Hey...you didn't talk to Ayaan yet, did you?" he murmured out of earshot of the others.

"No. I'm kind of ashamed to," Payal admitted as quietly as she could, given the deafening music.

"You should."

Payal frowned at him, raising her hands in question. "You hate him."

Akash met her eye and didn't turn away. "You should talk to him."

It was this prompt that made Payal do a double take. Akash was serious, his jaw clenched and his gaze intense. He wasn't playing around.

"Okay," she agreed. "I'll talk to him tonight."

"I think they want you to make a speech," Akash said.

He gestured to Ayaan's parents, who were waiting by the stage with bright smiles on their faces and pride in their eyes. They waved her over and pointed at the stage.

She gave them a wave and squeezed Akash's arm before making her way over.

"Payal, beta, I'm so proud of you!" Aunty exclaimed, singing her praise for what felt like the millionth time.

"Let's say a few words, shall we? We should thank people for coming out and I want a chance to show off how talented you are," Uncle said.

He took the steps up and the DJ slowly decrescendoed the music. A few guests near the food tapped their utensils against their glasses, the silence growing amid the tinkling. Uncle took the mic from the DJ and held it in front of him.

"Welcome, everyone. On behalf of Veer and both the Mehra and Malhotra families, I wanted to welcome all of you to this celebration of our soon-to-be daughter-in-law Payal's line, Besharmi!"

The crowd cheered.

Payal's cheeks grew hot and she hoped her smile was steady.

"We could not be prouder of all she's accomplished. Her designs were impeccable today, weren't they?"

They cheered again.

"And now, the woman of the night, Payal Mehra."

The applause was rapturous and Payal wanted to bottle it each time it resounded in her ears.

She took the mic from Uncle, giving him a tight hug as he walked to the side of the stage and allowed her to have her spotlight.

"What. A. Day!" she exclaimed to laughter and hoots. "Firstly, I have to thank all of you for being here. The immensity of emotions that I have felt today for all the gestures of kindness—the love of the line, the expressions of support, people asking me if I've eaten, text messages wishing me good luck, a joke out of the blue to lessen the stress—have filled me with such gratitude.

"My father told me today that he has a memory of me when I was six, wearing a lehenga that my aunt had sent to us in the UK and dancing with my mother, who wore a sari. At the time, for him, he said he thought to himself this was what dreams were made of."

Payal saw Ma look at Papa in surprise, the memory dawning on her face.

"What he doesn't know is that very night, as I danced with my mom, I was admiring her sari. She always wore the best ones, you see, when she went to the Indians in Business dinners, and they glittered like stars in the night. At six, I was quite convinced I was royalty since I'd been born of a woman who got to wear the stars on her body."

"You still think you're royalty," Akash shouted up at her.

The audience laughed.

"Okay, that's not untrue," Payal said, pointing at him. "It was those moments of happiness and tiny inspiration that led us here tonight. Nights where I watched my mom. Parties where I saw aunties go from women who upheld their homes to goddesses who could take on the world. And the way their body language shifted as they wore remnants of home. It inspired fashion. It fired up my drive. It solidified the knowledge that what you wear can often shape what you believe in yourself.

"I'd be remiss not to thank Bhoomi Aunty, Kuljeet Uncle, Arun, and Sarika, the UK-based group at Veer. Your support, check-ins, investment in the company beyond monetary means, and right down to the weekly phone calls are what make me believe in this merger. You've taken such care of Luxuriant, of my family, of me, and of my line.

"I'd also like to thank Saachi and Niyathi, my runner and manager, the two most important people in Besharmi, who worked tirelessly to make sure every detail was impeccably thought out."

Saachi shook her head, as though she was saying "It's nothing." Niyathi, a quieter girl, leaned against the bar, uncomfortable with the attention already.

Payal continued speaking to draw it away.

"The entire team behind Asian EnPointe deserves kudos for their extraordinary efforts at providing makeup, hair, vision consultations, venue, media exposure... The list goes on and so does my thanks. And of course, my CMC, the light of my life and the best friends there are."

The three of them cheered and Nash put his glass in the air.

Here it was…the moment of truth.

"And my final thank-you goes to Ayaan Malhotra, the CMO of Veer," she said softly.

Ayaan's head popped up at the bar. It was the first genuine eye contact they'd made in a month. And when she said his name, the syllables leaving her lips like they'd belonged there her whole life and they always would, she didn't know how to continue.

He grew very still, waiting.

"Ayaan," she said again before swallowing. "Besharmi was doing well before you came along. But you lit a fire underneath it, and it ignited so spectacularly. And you warmed the passion for it in me. The long nights became whirlwinds of conversation and the happiness made them feel like short hours. We've had difficulties and we've had losses, but each one has come out with a victory. I hope that's always the case," she finished.

Her voice cracked on the last syllable, and she took a deep breath to steady herself. As she did, she realized Ayaan was moving toward the stage. Toward her. And the world seemed to fade away.

As the energy from the crowd emanated to her onstage and the rush of the day found spaces inside her to settle into, a giant wave of realization crashed over her. She gazed at him gently coaxing people out of his way and excusing himself as he pushed through the crowd.

It didn't matter what had got them to this place. They were better together.

And she missed him immensely.

Feeling the eyes on her, she flashed on what she'd just said: They'd had difficulties. Their lies had felt like losses. But perhaps they would grow from this. This too could be a victory.

From her lips to God's ears.

. . . .

AYAAN

It was when Payal spoke that Ayaan knew she forgave him…and if he hadn't misunderstood the subtle message in her words, he knew he could earn her trust again.

This was the opening he needed.

This could be a victory for them both.

"Excuse me," he murmured to the couple so closely bonded near the foot of the stage that he was certain a crowbar would be needed to pry them apart. The girl shot him a dirty look as he pushed past, as though he'd interrupted a significant moment in their lives, but nothing anyone else was going through mattered as much as this chance did for him.

He just had to talk to Payal.

"Hi," he said as she stepped down from the stairs and the audience's claps faded as the buzz began to grow again.

"Hi," she said breathlessly.

Despite her kind words, the apprehension Payal wore on her face was evident. Her eyes were searching his face, and Ayaan hoped fervently his face showed that she could have faith in him and in them again.

Questions hung in front of them. Ayaan wasn't sure what to say first—how sorry he was, that he had fucked this up entirely on his own, that he'd led her to making these decisions to begin with by being such a jackass—or whether to just kiss her, here, in front of everyone who knew them, because by God, she was beautiful and he loved her.

He opened his mouth, but another voice overtook the room, and he turned toward it, confused.

Dad, who in all his years networking had evidently never learned to read the room, was summoning Ayaan to the stage too.

"Well, after that speech, the man Payal has mentioned as her force, Ayaan, should come up, don't you think?" he said into the mic and then gazed at Ayaan expectantly.

"Could we just... Could you just hold that thought?" Ayaan asked Payal frantically.

After a month of unbearable silence, he was anxious that this chance to finally speak about their relationship would evaporate.

Reading his panicked expression, Payal gave a small smile and nodded. "I'll be here."

Ayaan nearly bounded up the stairs, appearing enthusiastic to the crowd but selfishly wanting to wrap this up.

But as he stood in front of his colleagues, his peers, his friends, and his family, an odd peace settled over him like a haze.

Payal had built so much of this on her own. But defying his parents' and Arun's expectations of him, he'd contributed in some way, and though he wasn't self-centered enough to take too much credit, he could take some.

They'd created so much together. And they had changed so much in the process.

"Like my dad and Payal have said, tonight wouldn't have happened without you, so please give yourselves a hand."

Ayaan laughed as Kai and Dharm patted each other on the back as though they had any hand in Besharmi's success.

"Tonight isn't a celebration of me, so truthfully, I'm not sure what I'm doing up here. All I did was aid in the growth of an already designed, established, and growing line...and the truth is that Payal did that. From taking the inspiration of nights when she was six years old to channeling her cultures in the most powerful way she could, she is the one who spent long nights thinking about this. Every time I speak to her, the wheels are turning on how to move Besharmi forward. It's a passion I've rarely ever seen in my life.

"One of the greatest privileges I've gotten to witness is, in fact, what we don't see on a runway. It's how she's dealt with specula-tion and commentary, particularly about us. There were some low points in the last few months, particularly in the public eye.

"And in those low points, I kept glancing over all the big moments of my life, trying to find a flicker of light to illuminate the gaping void. I clutched at funny memories and grasped for dear life at the times I felt the most alive. And I always came back to one night in London, not too long ago, when I watched barges float by and shared secrets with the only person who has ever managed to not only shine herself but to make other people glow with her effervescence."

Payal, who had dropped her gaze to her hands at the mention of that beautiful night, toyed with her engagement ring before she looked up again.

"I have often felt like those barges—unmoored, floating away in the tides, with little to no direction. When I have looked for guidance, for comfort, for an anchor in life, I come back to the same person every time." He cleared his throat, overcome by the emotions of the last few months and the desperation that overtook him now. "Payal Mehra, you are the lighthouse in the pitch black, guiding me to the shore...bringing me home. You are the love of my life. I am so proud of all you've accomplished, and I am in awe of the grace you exhibit under fire from the entire world."

He handed the mic back to the DJ, and to rapturous cheers,

sounds of "aww," and claps, he descended the stairs back to the woman who stuck to her word and stayed right there, holding her thoughts.

"That was…sweet."

He couldn't read her face. Was she impressed or disgusted by his display?

Up close, she looked exhausted. Though he knew she'd gotten her makeup skillfully applied by a makeup artist, bluish bags puffed underneath her eyes. She was already slender, yet she'd lost some of the healthy glow and fullness in her cheeks over the last weeks.

Anyone outside her circle would think Payal was a stunner—and Ayaan knew that while she was the most beautiful girl in the room to him, she'd lost a little life in her eyes.

He was the reason why. And he'd never been so sorry.

"I meant every word," he said.

"I know you did," she said.

"Payal—" he began.

"Ayaan—" she started.

They gave an awkward laugh and she gestured to him to speak.

"You were exceptional today. Actually, you're exceptional every day. You leave good things in your wake, Payal. It took me longer to realize that than it should have…but you leave everything better than you found it, and that includes me."

Once he started talking, it was as though he couldn't stop. The secrets and deception of the last ten months had finally caught up and Ayaan was tired of keeping up a farce. Transparency was a way of life, the only means of communicating he had the energy for tonight.

"I always wanted my brother's approval and my parents' trust. When they were willing to give me the CMO job for the family company, it felt like I'd finally earned their respect. I did a callous thing to get it. I led someone on who I love deeply. Which proves that I didn't deserve it at all...and worse, with the way that my family has begun to come together in the last month, perhaps I had a misguided notion of trust and love to begin with. At the risk of sounding terribly cliché, I had to love myself, forgive myself, and trust myself first. By the time I realized that, it was too late. And you found out in the worst way, and for that, I'm sincerely sorry.

"But I need you to know...I love you. I have never loved anyone like I love you. You are the reason I came to this place of peace. The only thing missing is you. And I understand that it doesn't mean much because there has been so much hurt between us. And...I understand if you want to walk away—"

Payal shook her head.

"But please, please give us another chance. We're perfect together. And I don't want any of this without you."

"Akash told me to talk to you," Payal said. "Did you have a conversation?"

For the first time, Ayaan gave a silent prayer of thanks for Akash's nosiness, and for once, rather than wishing he'd sit on a cactus, he wished him a long and happy life.

"We had a chat," he said.

"About?"

He hesitated. "The fact that I gave up the job...and I'm going to start my own firm."

Payal's mouth dropped open before her face lit up. "Ayaan! That's amazing. You're going to do wonderful things!"

"I owe that to you," he said.

He looked down at her, and the ice between them seemingly thawed.

"Payal, I don't want this without you. All that I did was for all the most misguided reasons. The only right decision I ever made was giving us a chance."

Payal swallowed. "I missed you."

The words were music to his ears.

"And I was mad at myself. I did exactly the same thing. I looked out for myself—"

"You wouldn't have had to worry or feel trapped had I been honest with you our very first night—"

"Well, yes, but I could have worked harder or believed I'd succeed without the games. I owe you an apology too. I'm sorry I didn't live up to what I asked of you—"

"I love you."

"I love you too."

They gazed at each other, the weight of the last month breaking away from their skin, and instead, Ayaan was alight. He stepped toward her, his hands on either side of her face, and pulled her in.

Their lips met softly at first, still hesitant, but the sensation of Payal's tongue gently running across his bottom lip was like recognizing a part of himself that he'd simply been missing all along. His body cried out, "There you are!" at her touch.

When she pulled away, her radiant smile was all he'd ever needed.

"Payal!" Her mother looked shocked at the overt display of affection.

"Oh, please, Roopa," Nani said, waving her off. "They're young and horny. Let them have their fun. Life is too short to be coy about love."

"Indeed," Payal whispered to Ayaan, pushing in close to him and laughing.

He leaned over and kissed her again, and he didn't care who saw.

Epilogue

It was just before the Christmas holiday, and in tune with the changes that Payal and Ayaan had brought to their families, even the location of the celebrations had changed. This year—tonight, in fact—Ma, Papa, Nani, Mum, Dad, Arun, Sarika, and Sarika's baby bump would be landing in New York for a week of festivities.

Payal and Ayaan, in their new two-bedroom apartment in Williamsburg, would be playing host for the first time in their lives.

"Nash and Kiran are having a New Year's Party. Want to go?" Payal asked as they lay in their shared bed, cuddling in the still-dark hours of the early morning.

"Is Akash coming?" Ayaan asked.

Payal glanced at him warily. "You like him now?"

"He's growing on me!"

She rolled her eyes in response.

"Besides," Ayaan continued, giving her a side gaze and a wink. "You're mine now."

"Oh, am I? I belong to no man."

"Yeah, you do. And I'm yours—so even if Akash wanted you, he'd get both of us."

"Ah, a package deal, huh?"

"I've got a package for you," he said with a grin. He wrapped his arms around her, pulling her into the crooks of his elbows on top of him.

"Don't I know it? Besharam," she exclaimed, using the male equivalent of the very word that inspired her line. *Shameless.*

"Damn right," he said.

She leaned down and kissed him. "I have a surprise for you."

"What's that?" Ayaan asked.

"Come with me."

She popped out of bed with far too much energy for this early on a Saturday and hauled Ayaan with her.

"Brrr, it's freezing," he said, rubbing his arms and looking for a T-shirt.

"We'll turn on the fire. Come on." She bounced from one foot to another. "And close your eyes."

"You're so bossy," he said but complied.

Slowly and steadily, she led him to the living room, covering his eyes with her own hands before they reached the threshold.

"Surprise," she whispered into his ear and let go.

Ayaan opened his eyes and gasped.

The eight-foot Christmas tree, bought two days ago under the pretense of decorating with family—"Something simple!" Payal had claimed—stood in the corner by the fireplace. It towered over the ledge of the mantel, and the lights twinkled from bottom to top. Garlands of metallic red, gold, and white draped themselves around in scalloped patterns.

From top to bottom, Ayaan recognized the ornaments he'd collected since he was a child and had last seen in a storage nook at his parents' home. A handprint in a mold from pre-K. The Mickey Mouse ornament from his family's trip to Disney World when he was six. An Eiffel Tower from a trip to Paris for his own nani's eightieth birthday when he was twelve.

A few new ones glistened too. A round white bauble with NYU's logo hung from the top. A photo of Payal and Ayaan the day after the fashion show, once they'd finally gotten past all the issues, hung in a beautiful silver frame with embellished engagement and wedding rings on the top.

"I have a gift for you too. I was going to give it to you when everyone was here, but maybe now is better," Ayaan said.

"I love presents!"

"I know!" Ayaan said, laughing.

He ran back to the bedroom, coming back with an envelope.

Payal ripped the top off the packet.

"I worked so hard on wrapping that," Ayaan deadpanned.

She ignored him, pulling out two tickets to Disney World. She read them and looked up to Ayaan with playful disbelief in her eyes.

"No way."

"You mentioned once that you didn't have many family vacations growing up. Now you're part of mine—and you will. You bring so much magic to me, Payal. Besides, you're the only one of us who hasn't been to Disney World."

"I love you!" she cried out and wrapped her arms around him for a deep kiss.

When they pulled apart, he looked into the same big brown eyes that he never thought he'd have the chance to look into again.

"To our greatest adventures."

Acknowledgments

Writing the acknowledgements for this book is different…this book was the pandemic book. The one I wrote huddled away as the world shut down and we were all quietly coping in whatever way we could. Payal and Ayaan's love story was a break in the monotony. I am so thankful for their dysfunction, their loud fights, their silliness and their bougie attitudes for providing entertainment at a dark time!

On a less fictional level, my thanks goes to God and my parents first every time. It is my privilege to call you my Amma and Nanna, and my best friends. Sanjeev, there are simply no words for the peace you bring to my life - the gut busting laughter every day, the innumerable hugs, the way you slide a bowl of food in front of me when I forget to eat, and the titanium spine you've shown when we've had to face the world's difficulties. You are my happy place. Sridhar and Bhargavi, my brother and sister-in-heart, you both are the lights in our lives. You ignite excitement and push me every day. To the Sridhara, Pisupati, Golluru, and Reddy family members worldwide…a thank you for your belief and encouragement. And to the many loved ones who have been a part of my journey as I've transitioned in the last few years from daughter, to girlfriend, to wife, to mother, and changed jobs and cities, I could not have done it without you.

A resounding thanks to Sindoora Satyavada and Bijal Vohra for their insights into the BTS of a fashion brand. Writing about a South Asian brand was special—through the work with *That Desi Spark* and my co-host (and more importantly, friend for life, Nehal Tenany), I've had the luck and the privilege of being invited into South Asian spaces I never dreamed about growing up in my little hometown. To experience those moments that have shaped my identity and writing each day is remarkable, and to learn more every day is something I hold so close. Thank you to those who have made it possible.

A special thank you to my agent, Stacey Donaghy, for believing in me from day one and serving as part counselor, part business woman, and all friend since 2014. To my editor, Christa Desir, you are an angel in every sense. I'm convinced we're two souls meant to work together—your heart, understanding, support, and passion light up the world. To the amazing team at Sourcebooks, your work is extraordinary, your dedication unparalleled, and your efforts unmatched. Thank you for investing your precious time in me and my work.

And to all the readers who have encouraged me, uplifted me, referred my books, taught me, shouted my name in a room full of opportunity, cried alongside me, and gotten up to fight another day with me...Thank you. Between the writing, publication, and release of Love, Chai and now, Sugar, Spice, have come part of a pandemic, many life changes, monster wins, and some devastating times. I could not have gotten it through it without your push, your support, your purchases of my books, and your unending love.

About the Author

Annika's debut novel, *Love, Chai, and Other Four-Letter Words*, the first in the Chai Masala Club series, earned starred reviews from the *Library Journal* and *BookList*, and was described as a "love letter to both Indian culture and the streets of New York City," by *Publishers Weekly*.

She is a co-founder and co-host of *That Desi Spark* podcast, one of the largest independently run South Asian podcasts in the world, which has led to appearances on the BBC, *Forbes*, and on a Spotify billboard campaign. She currently lives in the New York City area, and is a lover of long conversations, superhero movies, reading, and travel. Annika can be found @annikasharma on Instagram, Twitter and Facebook.